"A rich, concept-drive
Trilogy
LEE HUNT
THE WORLD OF DYNAMICIST
LAST
WORST HOPES

BOOKS BY LEE HUNT

The Dynamicist Trilogy

Dynamicist

Herald

Knight in Retrograde

In the world of Dynamicist

Last Worst Hope

In the world of The Dead Gods

Bed of Rose and Thorns

TESTIMONIALS FOR LEE HUNT'S WORKS

For Knight in Retrograde

"Strong characters face a maelstrom in this intense, intellectually rigorous fantasy series finale. This final volume of Hunt's fantasy trilogy bursts at the seams with notions of science, spirituality, and politics pertaining to the 21st-century political climate. The unique pulse of this series remains the author's dedication to thematic sprawl and a hard-science magic system." —*Kirkus Reviews*

"This is a sterling end to a rich, concept-driven series. This trilogy finale will thrill readers who want thoughtful, inventive fantasy powered by ideas." —*Booklife Reviews Editor's Choice Winner*

"I highly recommend the Dynamicist trilogy, and Knight in Retrograde in particular – Hunt has crafted something truly special here." —*J. Scott Coatsworth, Liminal Fiction*

For Herald

"Surrender yourself to Lee's fantastic world of magical physics to rediscover what you thought you knew about reason, morality and the unbreakable bonds of friendship and love. As an innovator and physicist, I found myself reflected in the characters of The Dynamicist Trilogy. I felt chilling empathy for their challenges when fear shot up my spine and a strong sense of tribalism with their desire to invent and change the world. Wisdom grabs at the reader from every page." —*Amanda Hall, CEO of Summit Nanotech*

"A bold fantasy sequel that delivers on the first volume's call to action. This has deep relevance to life in the early 21st century." —*Kirkus Reviews*

"This is an exciting, expansive, and ultimately satisfying exploration of the meaning of heroism, the economics of magic, and the role of innovation in society. Readers looking for a thoughtful take on the wizard-school story will enjoy this mix of philosophy, mathematics, and action." —*Booklife Reviews*

"*Herald's* quite a ride, one I'd recommend taking if you love fantasy and want something that's not like everything else already on your SFF shelf. And that's one of the highest compliments I can give to a well-written, page turning book like this one." —*J. Scott Coatsworth, Liminal Fiction*

For Dynamicist

"I highly recommend Dynamicist – it's a well-thought-out, high-minded fantasy with a very satisfying set of twists and turns that's not quite like anything else I have read in high fantasy. And to me, that's a great accomplishment indeed." —*J. Scott Coatsworth, Liminal Fiction*

"This is a compelling story for readers who crave complex world-building. This intricate, philosophical update to the wizard school story will appeal to fans of cerebral fantasy." —*Booklife Reviews*

"A philosophically minded series opener that deftly merges science, fantasy, and college life." —*Kirkus Reviews*

FIRST EDITION

Cover art by Greg Arkos

Interior design & typesetting by Other Worlds Ink.

Distributed by Ingram Spark

Printed in Canada by Blitz Print

Library and Archives Canada Cataloguing in Publication

Title: Last Worst Hopes / Lee Hunt.

Names: Hunt, Lee, 1968- author.

Description: First Edition. 2022 ISBN 978-1-7779734-0-7 (soft cover); 978-1-7779734-1-4 (Ebook/PDF); 978-1-7779734-2-1 (Audiobook)

Edited by: John McAllister (mcallister@gmx.ca)

Created with Vellum

For the dead poets.

CONTENTS

ENGEVELEN

Map of Engevelen near the end of the Methueyn War

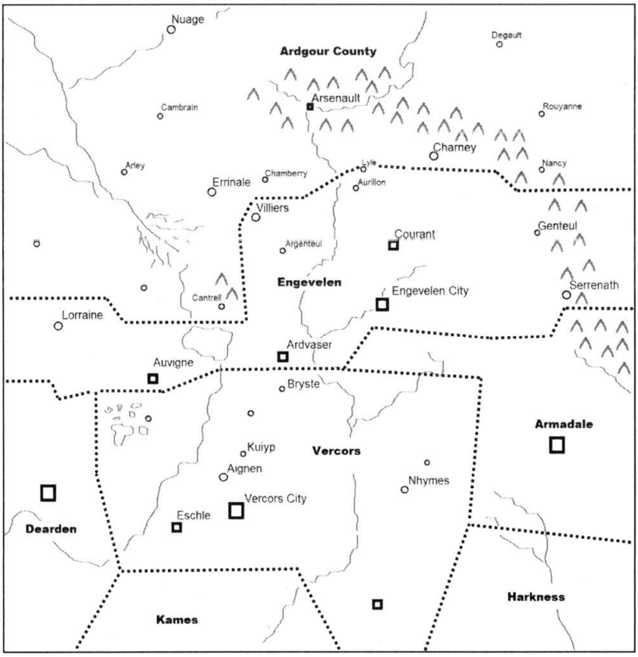

SELECTED PEOPLE AND PLACES

In the city of Villiers

Old Man, or Mick, real name unremembered
Brigitte Landry, manager of the house on the hill
Roland, head orderly
Lady Aurorette, an old lady with a wheeled chair
Carol, an old lady who acts as attendant to Lady Aurorette
Dougray, or Doog, an old man with a froggy voice
Louis, an old man with two teeth somewhere in his mouth
Warley, an old man with poor hearing
Sir Valence, a philosophical old man and former Knight of Engevelen

In Engevelen City

Lady Christine Cressy, Princess of Engevelen
Lady Severine, principal advisor to the princess
Lord Liam Laval, advisor to the princess
Peridot, a Major in the Renet

Katherine Valcourt, or Val, Acutist wizard. Member of the Elysians
Rebecca Laurie, Statician wizard. Member of the Elysians
Halwyn Glace, or Green, Statician wizard. Member of the Elysians
Calvaine Chesshyre, Statician wizard. Member of the Elysians
Samantha Westerberg, Statician wizard. Member of the Elysians
Christopher Carlyll, Statician wizard. Member of the Elysians

In the city of Courant

Farrah Harbinger, Harbinger Wizard of Engevelen
Lieutenant Davignon Delatam, or Dav, an attendant to Farrah
Lady Sylvie, chief attendant to Farrah
Alain Overbree, Acutist wizard, liaison to Farrah and the crown
Captain Barbara Bysshe, chief of arms to Farrah
Sergeant Patrick Proulx, a soldier, leader of an eight
Private Darcelle, a soldier
Private Harcourt, a soldier
Private Tayleur, a soldier
Private Raydell, a soldier
Private Marianne, a soldier

Soldiers of Leaders of Vercors

Veronica Brice, Duchess of Vercors
The Shining Knight, a wizard and knight of immense power. Thought to be dead.
Captain Lowri, or Captain leftover, commander of a company within the Elysian force
Sergeant Reyn, leader of an eight
Corporal Alwena, a soldier and a name caller
Private Tudor, or Turd, a soldier
Private Aron, or Error, a soldier
Private Dafydd, or one-half of Dafydd-Dill, a soldier

Private Dylan, or the other half of Dafydd-Dill, a soldier
Private Eurion, or Urinate, a soldier

From Novgoreyl

Count Nehring Ardgour, a powerful wizard
Lady Marias Garragorah, an ambassador
Varvara, a Vymyty wizard
Vsevold, a Vymyty wizard
Taratoraff, a refugee

Deladieyr Knights, junior order to the Methueyn Knights

Sir Revenberge
Escuyer Aveline Vanier, or Ave, a candidate
Escuyer Byron Breaux, or Bro, a candidate
Escuyer Acklyn, a candidate
Escuyer Woofter, a candidate, dead.
Escuyer Catherine Kattar, a candidate
Escuyer Soukhmanthath, a candidate

Methueyn Knights, knights joined by the Methueyn Bridge with angels of their name

Urieyn, Angel of Music. Symbol, a blazing sun.
Sendeyl, Angel of Endurance. Symbol, a broken sandal.
Michael, Angel of War, usually male. Symbol, a great sword.
Heydron, Angel of Protection, usually female. Symbol, a shield.
Darday'l, Angel of Knowledge. Symbol, a scroll hung on a maul.
Volsang, Angel of Righteous Vengeance. Symbol, an axe.
Hervor, Angel of Warning. Symbol, a bursting horn.
Leylah, Angel of Night, usually female. Symbol, a crescent moon.

Transcendental beings

Nimrheal, a demon who punishes creativity
Skoll, a demon, bridged by Nehring Ardgour
Hati, a demon, bridged by Nehring Ardgour
The One True Devil, an unknown adversary

PART ONE
LAST WORST

PROLOGUE

Prologue. From the Library of Lady Koria Valcourt

Few events have garnered more historical attention than those of the Methueyn War. And fewer still are less understood.

Most scholars have focused on the life of Nehring Ardgour, undoubtedly the principal player in these events. He was the most powerful wizard in history, but perhaps the least *human* human being there has ever been. As a child, he nearly succeeded in stealing the Methueyn Bridge, that unfathomable device that allows the Methueyn Knights to share heavenly communion and power with the eight Methueyn Angels in Elysium. While still only a young man, he invaded the northern half of Engevelen and held it for a generation, mining it for the secret elements he needed to build a doorway into another, better world. Entire wings of libraries have been devoted to speculating on why he used his hard-fought power to open a door to hell instead, and bring forth the demons Skoll and Hati, and the hordes of skolves that served them. Ultimately, the why of it does not matter.

Other historians have focused on the Methueyn Order, the holy knights connected to heaven, and the reasons that they alone, at first, went to war with Ardgour. And why, acting alone, they spent the lives of their lesser order, the Deladieyr Knights, and the squires to those knights. But for all their power, the Methueyn Knights are an uninteresting subject, for they lacked the ability to change or grow. Theirs was the curse of too much confidence and too singular a focus.

As the war ground on, all these great heroes fell, and in the end, it was a group of misfits and castoffs—my arrogant and literal-minded ancestor among them—who made the difference. None of them seemed adequate to the challenge, but when everyone else was gone or had failed, these last hopes found their purpose.

Only now, two hundred and fifty years after their struggle, have we finished what they started and reclaimed the wilderness and the Bridge that were lost at the end of their war. So many of us died getting here. Thinking of my lost friends, I finally understand how those last worst hopes must have felt, retreating victorious from the rubble of all they knew.

CHAPTER 1
SLEEP

Hoping to find sleep, I count my crimes against humanity. Yes, most people count innocuous things like sheep, but I want to tally my crimes and tell myself that I am still human. Many would think that counting the harrowing acts that led to so much misery and death would do the opposite of putting me to sleep, but my strategy works because I did not actually *commit* the crimes. I am a politician, a diplomat; I do not *do* the deeds, I *enable* them, apologize for them if necessary, deny them when I can. In trying to find both my own last best vestiges of humanity and any sleep that might be available, a narrative of honesty surely could not hurt.

What also helps is that I have not been personally involved in any of it. I had not been responsible for talking the Methueyn Knights out of hunting down and killing Nehring when he attempted to steal the Methueyn Bridge as a child. My predecessor had successfully argued for mercy for the folly of the young. That had been a great victory of diplomacy, especially given that hindsight proved the event to have been but a small taste of things to come.

The invasion of Engevelen by a now adult Nehring Ardgour was also before my time. That awful crime stole half of the greatest and most respected country in the world, and at the price of only a little slaughter, though a lot of slavery. Keeping that malfeasance from turning into an uncontrollable war had been a major feat of diplomacy by my predecessor. Promises to never do it again had deescalated the conflict and enabled everyone to sleep better.

Yes, this counting *is* good for sleep.

But on my side of the ledger are the colossal issues of the present day. The widespread slavery of Ardgour's people for his ... public works projects. An entire generation has been eroded digging in the earth for those inscrutable purposes. Misinformation proved to be the best tool to shovel over that ongoing and arcane awfulness. The summoning of the demons Skoll and Hati was, of course, a far worse problem to deal with. Every wizard across the planet felt the horror of it, but I assured everyone that the two demons would go straight back to hell. I *guaranteed* it.

But they did not go back.

Instead, Nehring only compounded the horror, bringing across, in their tens of thousands, those devil-like beings we call skolves. Not as bad as Skoll and Hati, but unequivocally bad nonetheless, indubitably an assault on all of mankind. I stood in front of each nation and called it an "accident." It might even have been one. As previously noted, I do not *know* these things. I do not do the deed, I obfuscate it.

I may have failed to talk the Methueyn Knights out of declaring war on Ardgour, starting the so-called Methueyn War, but I *did* succeed in discouraging the other nations from immediately joining in. Now, a few short years later, the war has grown larger. The remains of Engevelen have joined the Methueyn Knights in fighting Nehring Ardgour and his demons. Engevelen by itself proved too weak. Matters had become so bad that the Methueyn Treaty was invoked, and certain forces from each member state joined the war. *That* was a diplomatic loss for me.

Those were my contributions to the current state of the world. The major ones, anyway. Now I could sleep. It used to be, when I was a little girl, that I dreamt of being a hero. Perhaps, having recounted my crimes, I could now have that dream again.

I may not deserve it, but even a ruined and compromised politician can dream of a better world, one of beauty, joy, hope, and happiness, of the implausible possibility of virtue recovered and heroism rediscovered. However much I had let myself—well, the world—down in waking life, there was always the slim possibility of finding the ephemeral buried treasure of blessed delusion in the world of dreams. Such a fantasy almost never happened. And I deserved the nightmares, after all. Yet, as I descended deeper into unconsciousness tonight, it seemed that this childhood dream would be my unearned reward. I could almost see the little girl of my youth once more speaking truth in the face of lies and entrenched power. There she was. The hero!

But then, like a fickle wind, something on the boundaries of my dream abruptly changed. The little girl disappeared.

Something came for me, for the adult me, the frightened, morally compromised woman of the world me. The criminal against truth, me. Something came for *that* me, the coward. Something that would require all the integrity that I had already dropped into the refuse heap of my adolescence.

Even if I had not so easily and so fully discarded them, dreams of heroism and a better world would have been no substitute at all for armor, no defense. These delusions meant nothing to what approached. The darkness did not protect me, nor did the veil of sleep, the solid barrier of three-foot-thick cold stone walls, or the alert guards in colder steel who patrolled the halls. Not one of those things mattered at all to what came. With a bare flicker of sound and a complete absence of light, a presence spilt reality and manifested itself at the foot of my bed. A cold intelligence bore down upon me, heavy, unsympathetic, intruding upon my mind as suddenly and unequivocally as it had appeared in my bedroom.

Eyes still closed, I shrieked.

An electric shock made me shudder and involuntarily open my eyes. A darkness flickered at the foot of my bed, somehow opaquer than the rest of the night. Being aware of it was a thing like proprioception, for there was no light at all in the windowless tower, no real difference in the darkness in so far as darkness has anything to do with light. There was a sound though ... like a flame might cause ... like angry grease burning in a too-hot fire. I had encountered Nimrheal twice now, flickering disturbingly like some murderous and unpredictable black flame, shrieking at painful volume, poorly bound to reality, a violent best representation of something undefinable and outside our world. This presence reminded me too much of the demon. Far too much. Perhaps twenty years spent evading Nimrheal had somehow transformed Nehring Ardgour into a being very like the demon itself.

Garragorah.

It is a horrible new thing, the sound of Ardgour's voice. It no longer sounds human. It reverberates—crisp but resonating—like something spoken in some great cathedral instead of my bedroom; loud, deep, and intimidating, as if it from a giant. I feel Madalise go stiff beside me.

She knows not to open her eyes and look for whatever mouth could shape such a sound. There is no mouth to be seen anyway. If his lips move, they are impossible to resolve among the layers of black, flickering shadows. I am not sure if the apparition before me is really Nehring Ardgour, or better put, fully Nehring Ardgour. My lord would have hated the smells of a bedroom, he would not have come here in the flesh. The very earthiness of the place would have offended him, the animal odors, the sweat, the bad breath of the mouth breather. He hated any reminder of our ungodly limitations such as the need for food, sleep, or the release of sex. Ardgour hated the animal nature of humankind, hated humans and their crude coarseness. And since the many battles with Nimrheal, the inexorable loss of the Vymyty—since both Volsang and the Shining Knight of Vercors began stalking him at each hidden fortress, mine, or laboratory—Nehring Ardgour had become a presence unfirmly rooted in time or space. Or in humanity. He seemed to have moved beyond all that now, but the question of what stood before me, specter, man, or something else, did nothing to put me at ease.

"My lord?" I say after licking my lips and reaching over to pull the thick, soft bedcovers up and over Madalise's head. The blanket is only a pretend protection, but I try to fool myself that it is worth something, and that under the too-thin cover of the thick duvet, she will not feel the sick pressure of Nehring Ardgour's mind upon hers.

You must go to Engevelen, to the Council of Knights who meet there to decide how best to kill me.

"What?" I ask, dumbfounded. It is an impossible, a ridiculous request, considering our war with Engevelen and the Knights.

Tell them they must take up their bridge to heaven, the thing they call the Bifrost, and bring it to me.

I speak before sense can hold me mute. "But my lord, you tried to steal the Bifrost." And that was just the start in a sleep-counting-long list of atrocities that Ardgour—we—have committed. In every meaningful way, we have utterly betrayed everyone. We have shown every nation on earth, Engevelen most of all, that we are not to be trusted.

Yes. You must obtain through words what have I failed to take by force.

The incongruity of his orders had me flummoxed, caught between mortal terror for myself and for Madalise, stiff and shaking under the duvet, in utter, unaccustomed confusion over this change in plans. I had thought we were almost ready to execute Nehring's great scheme, the work of a generation, his apparatus. That I did not know what it was supposed to do was not the point. I understood that he had a plan. This was not it.

"But, my lord," I say like someone stupid enough to volunteer for her own funeral, "this was not the plan."

The day had finally come round once more when I was so stunned that I actually gave utterance to what I thought. Since I had been a heroically dreaming child, no one had ever observed such a wonder. It is, after all, a poor ambassador who indulgences her own personal truths.

The other Lords of Novgoreyl have turned against us.

My stomach falls.

No one is with us. No human, anyway. At least we still have Skoll, Hati, and the skolves.

Not a preferable situation, but that infernal army might still be enough.

Skoll and Hati have broken their leash.

"When?"

Some time ago. That news, I suppressed here.

Knights in heaven. Lie on my face, Leylah.

A thought flashes like lightning. *The Renet! This is why they attacked.*

Fuck. Fuckity fuck fuck. Fuck.

Pull yourself together, woman! I stifle a hysterical, what could have been a fatal, laugh and tell myself this day has been coming ever since the demons arrived. In better, more human days, Nehring had explained how it could happen, but he had planned to start his apparatus before the demons realized the limitations of his power over them.

"So ... you have a new plan, then?"

There is no answer. Nehring Ardgour has a limited patience for stupid questions. I need to pull myself together and put my negotiator's face on.

"May I know your mind, Lord?"

How could you possibly know my mind? Has your consciousness travelled to other worlds, seen gods and monsters, looked through the fabric of reality to the modulii that constrain all possibility? Have you broken the inventive barrier and tripped Nimrheal's interdiction? I alone have done it and lived. Not once, but eights of times. You may not know my mind. You cannot.

And what on knights' earth or Nimrheal's hell do I say to that?

A moment of silence follows as I attempt to answer my own question. I wish it had been a rhetorical one, but I do need an answer. For a few short, long moments, his shadow burns the darkness, crackling disturbingly in the night.

"My lord," I begin again, filling the silence, forming a tremulous shield of words against his dark and menacing presence, "I only wish to be able to convince them to do what you say and come here." I risked a look into the dark shadows where Nehring Ardgour's eyes should have been. That was a mistake. Looking into a bottomless nullity only enhances the feeling of otherness. Looking at the flickering nightmare also encourages the hysteria to return. Insane, suicidal laughter attempts to jump ship from my mouth. I bite down on it, bite my own lip until I taste the copper of blood, before I dare continue speaking. "After all that's happened, we must gain their trust."

How would knowing the truth gain anyone's trust?

I close my eyes, looking for my center, trying to summon wisdom. "Perhaps we have come to the unlikely point where only truth will serve."

Who understands truth? Deep below this room, down there in the darkened gaol under your castle, a poisonous transformation is happening. It is the splitting of nature, an assault on what you know of fragile matter.

It was this fragile matter that had done in the Shining Knight, had driven off Volsang for a time. "The mine?" I say, thinking of the mirrored breastplate burning and the quiet voice screaming to the heavens.

One of the many mines.

One of the many crimes against humanity that I had facilitated. Many have been consumed by what we have mined. "I don't understand, my lord."

That is the problem. Your thinking is insufficient to grasp that one piece of knowledge. One of many pieces. If you cannot speak to this one small thing, how can you possibly understand the breadth of what is happening, let alone describe it accurately? You are an ambassador, a paper-thin politician, a mouthpiece skilled in eloquence, lacking in deep knowledge. How can you speak to necessity, describe its horror, entreat these others to aid in it?

Sure, let's just mangle the messenger, flagellate her with philosophy, injure her with her inadequacy!

That thought comes from the part of me that became unstuck from reason the instant Ardgour materialized in my bedroom. Insane though it might be, as reckless, poisonous, and dangerous as it is, it is the only truthful voice left in my mind. It is the part of me that wonders if my demon-summoning lord has become a demon himself, or is perhaps something even worse.

Fuck, I cannot listen to that voice. I need to lie. I need to listen to the part of me that wants to survive. I need to speak carefully, like an adult, not truthfully like a child.

But I also need something to work with. "And yet you ask me to do this."

I *tell* you to do it.

Such is the hell of my life. I make another attempt at reason. "If I am . . . limited, I am limited like them. They won't come unless they trust that it will be in their best interest. I will need some kind of story for them."

A yarn.

"Yes," I agreed. *Please give me something.* "A story. What can I tell them, Lord, that will persuade them to trust your request?"

My request? It is no request. Tell them *that*.

"My lord," I say, ransacking my cowardice for courage, "that will not be effective. The Methueyn Knights hate you for the skolves. They make war on you for Skoll and Hati." I swallow. "They will not take your orders."

Then think on what a generation of my people have done here. Let no ignorance or incapacity stand in your way. Spin your yarn.

Think on a lost generation, think on the Vymyty, all but spent. Think on your dead wife. But you *don't think of those things anymore, do you, my lord? Did you ever? Why would such a story matter to angels in heaven if it means nothing to you here?*

I want to scream my questions back at him. The mad part of me wants to shout to the broiling presence that it should go spin its own narrative, but I would like to live another night. I must treat this order seriously. Almost as if in preparation for his request, I had already been thinking on these things, counting them off to rationalize my entry to the unconscious. But even the most self-serving interpretation of events looked awful. Even if I spin better than I have ever spun before, speak with an eloquence and passion transcending all my other efforts, the Methueyns will not respond to any narrative involving our tragedies. "I need a story about something they care *personally* about."

They must bring the Bifrost to me now, or Skoll and Hati will take it from them later.

"Why would they believe that?"

Have you ever seen a cattle feeder? The cattle eat and food falls down the pan to be eaten, the removal of food freeing new food to fall. Until the device runs out of food. The Methueyns die and the Deladieyrs cross the Bridge to replace them. But the Methueyns have almost run out of Deladieyrs. Their religious feeder is all but used up. Skoll and Hati will have the Bifrost when that happens.

The image this metaphor conjures does not settle my nerves. The Methueyns are unlikely to be positively disposed to it. Not much of a guess there. No one likes to imagine their own failure. "I need more, my lord," I manage to say, because I certainly do. "I need an argument for legitimacy."

Their harbinger is about to make an assault on the locus. Ask them what she sees lying there between the threads of the severed knot.

Thank you for nothing. But I think about the conundrum of having no argument whatsoever while Nehring Ardgour's shadow boils demonically in darkness and my love tries to hold still as if dead under the duvet. She has to pretend that the blanket means something. I have to pretend I can accomplish this mission. He is not going to give me anything else. I am sure of that. The time for objections is over. That has not been made explicit, yet I know it. I have been at this for a very long time. In all the days since I dropped my childhood dreams down the outhouse shaft, I have always been able to sense when the time for talk was up. I have lived to count my crimes only because I have had perfect survival instincts.

Political life has strengthened me against the need for actual reason so long as I can conjure the simulacrum of rationality. The best negotiators push audacity to the furthest levels, ignore their own hypocrisy, and ask for the unreasonable in calm, cool, implacable voices. In fact, the best deals I have seen done, the real win-lose moments of history, have all been attended by an absence of empathy, remorse, or reciprocity. Looking back, it is often a wonder to me that such deals could have been accepted by the other side. Perhaps it is the bold-faced confidence of the negotiator, the pretence of reason, the sheer, brazen commitment to the specious argument, that does it. Perhaps all those things combine with a disbelief from the hoodwinked that anyone could ask for something so unreasonable. Surely there must be reason here somewhere? There must be! But there must be something else, too. Leverage. Did my lord just give me that?

Even as the smile starts to spread across my face, he disappears.

In a blink, the flickering nullity that was Nehring Ardgour evaporates. I don't think his teleportation made any sound at all despite the reports of some of the very few others with that talent. But it *felt* like a sound had been made. Nehring's presence had been attended by an appalling boiling or burning sound in the background, like a fire consuming his violently trembling shadow. The sudden absence of that unnerving accompaniment shouted as loudly as darkness when it transfixes daylight. With his evaporation, so went my confidence. The absence of such an awful presence should have made me feel better. And in some ways, it did. But his leaving was like his arrival, a show of power over which I had no influence. How was I supposed to have an effect on a world in which beings like Nehring Ardgour lived? When his slightest acts, such as leaving a room, weighed so much more heavily on reality than the sum of all my accomplishments, what could I dream of doing that would make any difference?

That realization will at least help me sleep better.

CHAPTER 2

THE ONE TRUE DEVIL

"You will never feel more isolated than when in single combat."

Major Peridot to Davignon, moments before the Battle of Charney

Materializing out of nowhere like a devil, the words manifested on the page through a hole in Dav's awareness. He did not remember writing them. The feather pen that must have spelled them out lay on the cobbles by his left foot, dropped somewhere between the act and the realization. Seeing the mangled, violent letters was deeply disturbing, though the young man tried not to show it, tried not to cry out, hoped his initial flinch had gone unnoticed. The vein standing out sharply from the right side of Dav's forehead was the only indication that what he saw horrified him. To look upon his notebook was to see his own doom. But he could not doubt it—it was his book and only he wrote in it. Dav understood its meaning; he had seen letters like them before.

He recognized what they spelled.

The fate the letters proclaimed had always been his doom. Nothing he could do was capable of changing it. No effort, no coaching, no therapy, no priest, no request for help, not switching hands, tying his left hand down and striking himself in the head with his right, wearing an eye patch, fasting, pleading to Elysium, getting more—or less—sleep ... nothing. There was no escaping. The letters only spelled what they did because there was something wrong with him, something in his nature, something wholly orthogonal to his upbringing and training. The defect could not be shed; it came from inside. The letters on the page foretold that his life would be described by the inexorable three hundred and sixty degrees of a circle. It was a reminder of the past, yet a prophesy of what *would* be. In a world incapable of change, carrying such an abomination made living a kind of hell, for there could be no hope of improvement. No hope at all. It was a herald of his fate. All tragic flaws guarantee a tragic end to the flawed.

As sure as my name, nothing makes this right.

Dav closed the notebook, blinked his eyes, and looked up, moving from microcosm to macrocosm, taking in his city. He sat, still in his field chain mail and Renet expedition vest, at a table outside the café. On the table beside his notebook sat a cold cup of tea, half drunk, the aging cream making a wrinkled skin across the top of what remained. A cream-colored cloth napkin lay on his lap. Over the polished cobble street people walked, some in a hurry, tight and scared, some to all appearance unaffected by the approaching peril, laughing, holding hands, looking up at the sky like trouble would never come.

As if not just Dav was doomed. They all were.

Dav could understand why. Cafés were still open. Food was not yet scarce despite the influx of refugees from Aurillon and the other evacuated cities. The ragged bands of evacuees had been escorted in orderly fashion to discreetly located emergency quarters. The streets were clear of debris and in the impeccable state of repair that all Engevelen's cities were so well known for; any litter from the evacuees was ruthlessly collected. Dav's feather pen was the only refuse in sight. There were very few soldiers on these immaculate streets, at least for the moment. Most of the available personnel were out patrolling the fields, trying to persuade reluctant farmers to evacuate, or manning the walls, watching the horizon. Most people were still unaware that much of Engevelen's armed force—the entire Renet, in fact—was missing in the field. Not every city in the country was as lucky as Courant had been so far. Most towns farther north had been rolled over by the creatures that Nehring Ardgour had bridged to earth from hell. But for this frozen instant in time, in this one place, there were few signs that Engevelen was in a profound state of crisis.

Perhaps the crisis was easier to deny because the people of Courant considered themselves special, enlightened, above it all. Courant was, after all, a staggeringly beautiful city, its elegant architecture the jewel in what remained of Engevelen. It was a place of tall, stately, stone buildings, twisting pozzolanic aqueducts and arched stone bridges, wide squares and magnificent libraries, museums and places of learning. Even the abundant refuse such a large, wealthy city produced was rigorously and beautifully managed. The raised composting mounds of the enormous and plentiful hugel gardens concealed and recycled waste like nowhere else in the known world. Population pressure had forced most of the gardens to be planted outside the city walls, spreading to the west. In their season, the hugel gardens grew enough produce to feed more than half the city. Indeed, Engevelen as a whole was a country that—until the current crisis—had resolutely made use of the vanishingly few innovations that still occurred while respecting their awful cost in lives.

Courant was also the home of Harbinger Hall, which sat across the street from Dav's café, a gorgeously crafted dolostone edifice that showed how much the confident, upright citizens of Engevelen preferred to look forward rather than backward. Like Dav's notebook and the twisted letters written there, Engevelen's past told of a darker, less orderly trajectory than anyone wished to admit. Better to look among the multiple pathways of the future for a better possibility than dwell upon the cold, bleak landscape of history.

A sharp, painful flash of light from the back of his eyes and Dav saw it all again, but differently now. Nothing fit as it should. The city at once became a puzzle whose pieces had been jumbled and scattered by a cruel, jesting god. He saw only a mass of ruins, buildings mixed up, out of position, fallen, broken. Aqueducts lay twisted and ruined, their water spent. Garbage was strewn everywhere, and the hugel mounds were smashed open, their hearts of compost and wood scattered and desiccated. Bodies lay everywhere, ruined, broken, limbs torn off as if misplaced, heads crushed under stones or the massive, elongate paws of Ardgour's devils—the skolves. One man lay sprawled on the street with his crudely hacked legs placed where his arms should have been in a mocking amalgam of misplaced body parts. A child's head was stacked on an old man's body, a scarecrow lay on the rubble, its hay arms crossed as if in repose while naked men and women were staked to posts encircling it. Words had been scrawled everywhere in blood and feces, spelling out the same parody of language Dav had unconsciously written in his notebook moments earlier. Street signs had been defaced to tell the same unnerving tale.

No. This isn't right.

Another blinding flash made Dav blink again, and the buildings were instantly whole once more, the limbs of people, now upright and walking on the cobbled street again, back in their correct places. The heaps of garbage were gone and, Dav imagined, the great composting mounds of the hugel gardens pristine again, covered by the green of cabbage, peas and other flourishing crops. He drew in a deep breath, slowing it down from the gulp it wanted to be, and widened his focus. He needed to see more than one narrow, myopic slice of the world.

I need it all to be correct.

"That is the wrong way, Lieutenant Delatam."

The carefully enunciated, coolly—possibly cruelly—chosen words startled Dav. He managed to keep from whirling about in a panic, but did start and look around. *When did I spill my tea?* The wrinkled skin of cream was a blotch on the table sliding toward the edge and his lap, carrying along the less viscous contents from his cup. Dav quickly brought his napkin to bear and caught the mess before it could ruin his clean, carefully creased trousers or splotch onto his vest or mail. He felt a little wetness on his face, but it was too late to use the napkin there.

With deliberate care, Dav placed the wet napkin on the table, pushed his chair back, stood, and saluted the striking, dark-skinned woman who had interrupted his reveries.

"Captain Bysshe."

Barbara Bysshe was of average height, with dark hair and surprisingly blue eyes. Those bright orbs often seemed to settle upon Dav, though the thought and intent behind them was always hidden. She wore a dress uniform of dark blue and red rather that the field gear Dav had chosen.

"I could be called back to the Renet at any moment, Captain."

"I sincerely hope that will not be the case, Davignon." Perhaps the captain's first words had not been sarcastic after all. She did not point out that word from the Renet was long overdue or offer any conjecture on the probable cause. "You have already saved your Major Peridot. Now you serve another: the Lady Harbinger." She looked pointedly at the mail that showed through Dav's open vest, her blue eyes shining like sharp lanterns from her dark face. "And she does not need to endure the smell of mail while she works."

Dav was not tempted to change out of his mail. He would never attempt to compete with Bysshe over who was in the best trim. He had seen all too vividly that a neat uniform did little to protect soft skin.

"It does bring to mind the question," Dav replied, taking his sword, belt, and scabbard off the back of his chair and buckling the whole cumbersome apparatus around his waist, the longsword and scabbard hanging over his left hip, "of why I am here at all."

"Many have asked," she replied, a hint of wryness in her tone.

"Out loud?" *Of the Harbinger?* Dav observed that aside from her flashing eyes, Barbara Bysshe did have a cool way about her. *Cold* was the more popular way of describing the true heirs of Engevelen, the few that remained, connected by blood, recognizable by color. Cold, proper, and professional. Atavisms of a great, ancient, dying culture. Naturally and effortlessly aloof as only the truly superior can pull off.

Whether Captain Bysshe was simply a cool, calm professional or a cold, aloof aristocrat remained to be seen. Dav had only met her two weeks ago.

"Not so much out loud. That, Lieutenant, may be why your presence here remains a mystery."

"Perhaps I should ask." Was it guilt that prodded at him?

Barbara's hands went to her hips and her gold-weaved belt. She had a sword of her own, though it was short and on her right hip and its steel not comparable to the blade he had been awarded after Charney. "Why? Do you want permission to go after the Renet or permission to feel better about leaving them?"

Yes and no. He felt a need. And a fear. "I should be helping them."

Irritation crossed her face, the first clear sign of emotion that Dav had seen on her since she had appeared at his elbow. "No, you should not. They were about to discharge you, Davignon. Your written test, it ..." She stopped and pursed her lips. "Hero or not, field commission or not, no one holds a position as officer without passing the written test, and what you wrote—"

"You saw my test?" he interrupted. *You saw the words my* hand *committed to paper?* Dav had clung to the hope that the papers had been handled discreetly. A false hope, evidently.

"They could have demoted me back down to sergeant. Given me back my eight."

Now Barbara smiled—patronizingly, Dav thought. "You don't know how the upper hierarchy of the Renet works, do you? You were promoted to officer because of your actions at Charney. And once an officer, always one. There is no demoting to the ranks, Davignon. Too embarrassing. Not to the officer but to the officer class. And to the Renet. You were done."

"Then I was lucky that you came along."

Dav could not disguise the bitterness in his tone. *Peridot must have lost the argument.* Even the best of friends could not guarantee every outcome. He still remembered the major assuring him that his record and the results of the field test would be enough, but then he remembered some of what the written test had revealed. *"I cannot reliably tell east from west, up from down, or left from right. Not on paper, anyway." How could anyone see that and not think I am either an idiot or insane.* Perhaps Peridot had turned out to be as naive as Dav had just realized he himself was.

"No such thing as luck, Lieutenant." The captain's expression was more than a little superior. "The Harbinger does not operate by luck. She said that *we* must have you." Her blue eyes bored into him. "Though I am not sure why."

The words could have been read as an insult, but from his own experience, Dav was leery of trusting the shape of words just now, and with Captain Bysshe it was always difficult to know. The woman was opaque; even expressions that seemed clear as day might mean something other than what he thought. *I'm always getting it backward.*

"That makes two of us," Dav replied. If Captain Barbara Bysshe was puzzling, Farrah Harbinger, Engevelen's greatest wizard, was inexplicable. Her interest in him was a remarkable enigma even by her usual standards.

"Hmm," she said, shifting her head back in a gesture that could have been wry acknowledgement. "Well, stand straight and tall, and you will get through it."

She seemed to be staring at Dav again. He wondered how much she believed what she had just said. This was the oratory of Engevelen, the trite phrases that reinforced a prim and proper sense of tradition and decorum. Such statements were not meant to be acted on; they were the rhetoric of an ancient, failing country. Apparently satisfied that her hollow cliché had been properly internalized, Barbara continued.

"We are summoned."

Dav straightened up. This was concrete news, not mere rhetoric. It could augur a chance to justify his presence in Courant, perhaps even redeem him for leaving the Renet.

"Yes, sir," he said with a precision that momentarily approached Barbara's.

The captain frowned. "You left something under your chair."

It was his enemy. His feather pen. He moved the chair and maneuvered under the table despite the sword on his hip. Retrieving the damned—or damning—pen, Dav returned to his feet and asked, "Are they coming back, do you think?"

"That is what we are going to find out presently, Davignon."

~

It was said that the great Harbinger Wizard never attempted a far Heraldry from the same location twice. "The window gets dirty," she had been heard to say. Dav did not know what that meant, but he knew that Farrah Harbinger was said to be the greatest wizard of Engevelen. She was also the first wizard that Dav had ever spoken to. After he had been admitted to her circle, assigned as a staff officer serving her—and apparently saved thereby from an ignominious discharge for what he had written on his test—Dav had met several other wizards. These rare creatures were only ever seen, or so it was said, at the highest levels of government or during periods of the greatest upheaval. In the popular mind, wizards were even more destructive than they were rare. Where wizards went, destruction followed. *Look at Nehring Ardgour, he's a wizard and he's destroying the world.* And now Farrah Harbinger was going to attempt a far Heraldry to stop him. Whatever that meant. Dav knew there was much that he remained ignorant of. Despite his new role, he suspected that he might in fact be the idiot his written test had suggested he was. He had no idea where in Harbinger Hall he and Captain Barbara Bysshe might now be going.

Whatever else Dav might be—whether there was a devil in his left hand or if he was simply not in his right mind—he was careful. A lifetime of wrong-handedness had taught him that care was required. The world was not made for him, but he still had to live in it, and not only would he pay for his mistakes, others might also. And so it was that within hours of arriving in Courant and being given access to

Harbinger Hall, Dav had explored the enormous stone edifice from top to bottom. He had even found the deep underground cistern and its circular pool. *Had to be an oracular aid of some kind.* He had thought he knew the whole immensely complex structure. But this curious and lonely room was far from the only enigma in the building. He could find no one who knew of any upcoming work, but there were numerous floor-to-ceiling stacks of bricks and barrels of fine-grained sand stored in an anteroom of the basement wine cellar. There was a tiny, windowless library hidden behind a dusty bookshelf, and a false door on the third floor of the library, a floor only accessible by a wrought iron circular stairwell of dubious strength. But a lamp full of leviathan oil waited on the chairside table there, and a vent had been crafted to draw the smoke away.

Other potential heralding locations were less hidden. Everyone allowed into Harbinger Hall immediately found the eight-apsed main hall, designed in the classic shape of the Steel Castle, though without the finely carved images and dioramas of the Methueyn Knights that would be expected in a church. Each apse had but a single chair within. Dav had crawled across the camouflaged floating bridge and found that its terminus would make a perfect shooting position into any of the apses for someone with a crossbow. There were uncountable other private libraries, meeting rooms, and narrow passages that Dav had reconnoitered, but Barbara Bysshe led him past the main hall and ignored all these other locations, working her way steadily upward.

The observatory.

In Engevelen, an ancient sense of bad luck clung to the idea of observatories, most notably after the loss of the Auvignes, but it was a country with a stubborn reluctance to abandon anything its people felt made them superior. Past catastrophes were irrelevant, it was said, for the price had been paid. The attitude paradoxically led Engevelen to accept new inventions, rare as these had become, and as sure to be punished by Nimrheal as they were, while stubbornly hanging on to old inventions even if their time and usefulness had long passed. The great, but aging, underground cisterns were still maintained even while the better, above-ground aqueducts were heavily invested in. Either method made sense, but not both. And observatories? Dev had never heard of anyone discovering anything through the lens of a telescope. Not in his lifetime or for generations before as far as he knew.

Harbinger Hall's observatory was at the top of a slender stone tower accessible only from the steepled roof of the main building. It housed a signal mirror, an enormous telescope, and a single, very comfortable chair. Like a throne for a queen who valued the comfort of a padded seat and wide armrests, Dav thought. And when Dav and Bysshe climbed the final set of polished, tight, claustrophobic stairs onto the landing and ducked under the long arm of the telescope, they found the queen of wizards waiting there, cool and austere on her throne.

"Davignon, you look as if you have had a vision of your own," Farrah Harbinger said, speaking past the huddle of attendants crowding and jockeying for position in the small space. "Perhaps we can begin our meeting now." Her loudly spoken words cut sharply across whatever conversations had been happening, whatever desperate or fanciful schemes were being mooted, abruptly diverting the intense attentions of everyone onto a very perplexed and nervous Dav. Farrah Harbinger was aging, though not old, not quite, yet. She was perhaps about forty years of age. Her dark skin and hair made her sharp green eyes seem to shine from her face. She was a classic lady of Engevelen in every sense, poised and straight-backed on her throne, an urbane, collected expression sitting as naturally on her face as the rich, fresh-pressed clothing draping her body.

Closest to her, but not smiling, was Lady Sylvie, her chief attendant. Sylvie was of an age with the Harbinger, but with hair gone strikingly white against her ebony skin and dark red dress. Sylvie frowned as if Farrah Harbinger's comment was an admonishment. "A little faster, sir, when the lady calls," she said in clipped intonations. *Definitely an admonishment.*

Next closest was Alain Overbree, whom Dav knew was some sort of wizard—perhaps a senior one, though junior to Farrah. He was also in good trim, wearing a crisply pressed gold tunic, matching pants, and gleaming black boots. Alain's skin was the washed-out olive of most Engeveleners in these latter days, the same tone as Dav's, but his expression was more curious than Sylvie's. Dav had already observed that Alain carried himself like some sort of intellectual, and the man's forehead always showed convolutions as if he was constantly on the edge of discovery or about to ask some deep question. He seemed to view the Harbinger's quip as a riddle.

A step away, crowded by the eyepiece of the telescope, was Sergeant Patrick Proulx, leader of one of the eights that attended on the Harbinger, a strongly built, clean-cut young man. He also had the brown eyes and lighter skin that centuries of failure had brought to Engevelen. Like Barbara Bysshe, he wore a dress uniform rather than armor. Proulx sported an affable expression and nodded amiably at both Dav and Barbara. He seemed to view Farrah's comment as a joke.

Dav was not sure if Farrah Harbinger had meant it literally when she wondered if he had had a vision. He hoped her legendary talent for knowing things did not include what he had written or worse, what in a nightmare glimpse, he had seen. "I apologize for being tardy, Lady Harbinger, Lady Sylvie," he said.

"Oh, it is not your fault, Davignon," the Harbinger said, still looking at him with the tiniest of smiles, "Our good captain was engaging you in conversation, attempting to unlock the mystery of why you are here."

Dav felt Bysshe shift beside him, trying to stand straighter, for once not looking at him.

"You must not blame her, though," Farrah continued. "Everyone here is asking the same question."

"Are they?" Dav asked, almost certain that he was being teased.

Farrah Harbinger nodded slowly and pursed her lips. "No. Though they should. What they are wondering is why I have chosen to attack the locus today. They know that such an action might kill me and do not understand why I would take the risk."

"I am wondering how to stop you," said Lady Sylvie with a visceral growl in her tone, her attention back on Farrah Harbinger. "If this lieutenant can help us do that, we shall all be satisfied."

Alain Overbree, who had been gazing speculatively at Dav and Captain Bysshe, abandoned whatever deep thoughts he may have been entertaining and looked upward, squinting into the sun. "I did not think a locus could be defeated, except by events." His eyelids fluttered, watering from the bright light. "It would be like trying to map the sun with your naked eyes." He lowered his gaze to the throne and the great lady seated upon it. "You cannot. It will blind you."

The Harbinger ignored him. "Have *any* of you seen Skoll or Hati?"

Dav stiffened, but only Alain answered. "I hear that they are like a very powerful Methueyn Knight."

"Is that so?"

"Yes," Alain affirmed, puffing himself up in a show of confidence. "Many of the survivors are reported to have said so." He raised his eyebrows and continued pedantically, "What a Methueyn is to a Deladieyr, Skoll and Hati are to a Methueyn."

Dav did not know what to make of this performance, but he observed the reactions of the others. Captain Bysshe's face was expressionless. Locked so, he thought. Perhaps she was out of her depth too but did not wish to show it. Lady Sylvie still looked annoyed, though with a hint of a lip-curl, a suggestion of superiority. Sergeant Proulx appeared to be on the verge of laughing, his smile was so wide.

Farrah Harbinger did laugh, though briefly. This ended further commentary from Alain. Farrah smiled, but when she spoke again it was with little humor. "Analogic reasoning requires a knowledge of all the subjects being compared. Which in almost every meaningful way, we lack. But returning to my question, you have never yourself seen one of the demons. Best not to make analogies in the blind, my dear Alain. Of all of us here today, only two have seen the Skoll or Hati and lived, and only one of those was truly there."

"Who?" asked Proulx, as if on cue.

"Me, through Heraldry," Farrah's bright green eyes momentarily closed before she finished her sentence, "and Lieutenant Davignon."

Her eyes opened upon Dav like two vast green windows coming unshuttered. "In the Battle of Charney."

It was not much of a battle.

Dav felt not just the Harbinger's emerald orbs on him but Barbara Bysshe's and everyone else's eyes too. He said nothing. The Harbinger had answered her own question. *And she intends to continue telling her story, whatever it is.*

"Most people enjoy attention, Davignon," Farrah continued, as Dav knew she would. "Not you, though. When I view the demons through Heraldry, I find them more than frightening enough, but you saw one of them live and in combat."

"Finally. Some sense from all this," said Lady Sylvie.

"Which one did you see?" Alain Overbree's eyes were bright. "Skoll or Hati? *Was* it like a Methueyn Knight?"

"I don't know which one," Dav replied. *Skoll?* He remembered its power, how the ground shook when it charged, how the skolves genuflected when it came near. How terrified he was. "And I don't know if it was like a Methueyn."

This seemed to frustrate Alain. His face took on a curious mixture of helpful exhortation and disgust. "Think, man! You've surely seen a Methueyn Knight." Actually, Dav had not. He did not travel in Alain's circles, not until recently anyway. "Surely you have some opinion," the wizard added.

"All my thought was on surviving," Dav replied.

Proulx nodded affably at this, but Alain Overbree was unimpressed. "You weren't even curious?"

Dav snorted. "There was no time for curiosity." He considered himself lucky to have saved Peridot. It was a measure of that day's helplessness that he had no idea what he would have done if there had been more time. Only a lucky wrong turn had enabled them to survive. Involuntarily, he looked down at his left hand.

Alain frowned. Dav's reply and his unwillingness to speculate further did not feed the pedant's interest. "Well, you have more time now. Think about it. What was the demon like?"

Dav looked around. He was the center of attention, which he abhorred. Farrah Harbinger did not look as if she was going to jump in and rescue him this time. He took a slow, deep breath, and suddenly remembered something. "I saw a falling star once," he said. "Close by. It fell, on fire, and obliterated the hill behind my farm. The pig fence was blown down from either the explosion or the ... shaking that came after. The demon I saw reminded me more of the falling star than anything else I've ever seen."

"Well," said Captain Bysshe, speaking into the silence that followed Dav's preposterous analogy, "that does sound awful, but I trust you were able to repair the fence at least and keep your animals."

"The pigs were all dead." The hair had been burned off their charred skin, and their hooves had melted. Dav remembered his sisters crying over the smoldering carcasses, his dad saying nothing but looking almost as bereft. Dav had also not said anything. He had certainly not admitted that for a little while the pigs had smelled mouth-wateringly good, though that did not last. Another image flashed into his mind—Courant destroyed again, bodies and body parts scattered everywhere. He closed his eyes, resisting the parallel between the memory of the pigs laid out dead from the falling star and the strange vision he had just endured of his own murdered countrymen.

Pigs and men, falling stars and demons . . .

"And thus we do learn something after all," pronounced Farrah Harbinger. "The demons Skoll and Hati are beyond the human realm. They are not comparable to some rogue Methueyn Knight such as Sir Seygis, but are something far, far worse. Look at Lieutenant Davignon here. His face tells it all." She nodded at Dav, eyes narrowing. "And Nimrheal is still worse. As far beyond Skoll and Hati as they are beyond a traitorous knight."

"Matters will be much worse for us if we lose our harbinger," Lady Sylvie replied. "We cannot replace you."

Dav did not think that Lady Sylvie's sole worry was the difficulty of finding a new harbinger wizard, despite the cool, blank expression she projected.

Farrah Harbinger laughed once more. "What use is a harbinger that does not do her job? We have had lame-duck harbingers before, you know. Ones who could barely predict the weather tomorrow, let alone far herald."

"But why attempt to break the locus? Everything we know tells us it cannot be done, that even the attempt may be fatal." Alain's face was not as cool as Sylvie's, but whatever he was feeling, Dav suspected, had more to do with pedantic curiosity and a feeling of superiority than genuine concern. "And even if you succeed—and live—the information you retrieve may change nothing."

"Enough," the Harbinger said flatly. "This conversation is in danger of becoming a hugel mound." Her lip curled. "And we all know what is at the heart of those."

"But—"

Harbinger spoke easily over Alain Overbree, "I am going to break the locus because I must. For two months, I have endured heraldic dreams that resemble seizures more than visions. And nothing of what I have seen—as disjointed and out of context as it may have been—was in our favor." She locked eyes with Lady Sylvie. "I have seen Courant surrounded by skolves and our walls thrown down by Skoll and Hati." She turned to Alain. "And I have seen your trainee, Katherine Valcourt, and her fellow Elysians destroyed by their own recklessness." Farrah smiled mirthlessly at Dav and added, "I could not tell if it was in the future or in the past, but I have seen the annihilation of your Renet."

And if it is in the future, will I have been responsible?

"You reached into hell and saved Major Peridot once, but you have not saved her from everything, Davignon."

The Harbinger turned and impaled Barbara with her pitiless stare. "Other cities of Engevelen will fall. They will fall until none are left. Until her soldiers, without exception, are scattered or slaughtered."

Farrah Harbinger scanned her court again, one anxious attendant at a time, before continuing in her unnervingly cool manner.

"In my . . . visions, nothing and no one remain, not even Nehring Ardgour or his people. Skoll and Hati stamp across the broken stones of our country, grinding the rock to dust." She paused before concluding the bleak picture. "And finally, I have seen Nimrheal flicker across the ruins of our country and find no one left to kill."

For a long moment, no one spoke. Then, in deadpan, Proulx said, "Well, that all sounds quite awful."

The Harbinger snorted. "Seeing is the pain of belief. When I break the locus, you will all have a chance to see what I have seen."

Dav flinched. He had never seen the Harbinger herald, but he had heard a great deal about the singularity of her gift. Her heralding was attended by a phenomenon that no other living herald enjoyed. Whatever the Harbinger far heralded showed in her eyes. It could be seen by an observer standing close enough to her while she heralded. The images, however, were said to be twisted. Backward, inverted, difficult to interpret. And inducing a severe, disorienting nausea.

"So if you have parsed all this, do we not already have warning enough to act?" asked Lady Sylvie. "We must either evacuate Courant or use your knowledge to convince the other nations it is in their interest to lend us more support. The Elysian movement could make a difference."

"Evacuation of a single city will not save Engevelen, and we are too late for slow-moving political shifts to make a difference," Farrah Harbinger said. "I have deduced, you see, that we have another enemy, the worst one of all. I do not doubt Lieutenant Davignon's account of Skoll and Hati being analogous to a falling star. They are indeed a terrifying, otherworldly peril. And we all know how intractable an enemy Nimrheal has been over the ages. But all these demons pale before a still worse enemy."

"Nehring Ardgour," proposed Alain.

"No, not Nehring," replied the Harbinger. A hint of a smile brightened Farrah's dark face, making her green eyes shine brighter. "I have seen his end. No, a far worse demon comes, a demon of entropy that waits for us at the end of Engevelen's time, an enemy we cannot hope to defeat, not as we are. This is why I *must* break the locus. If we only faced Skoll and Hati, their skolves, and even Nimrheal, we would be in horrifying, unprecedented, jeopardy, but we could still hope, still fight to some purpose. This new threat is one that we cannot fight as we currently are. It is an enemy that will turn all our might, and all our devices, to . . . nothing."

Lady Sylvie's lips were tight and bloodless. "What. New. Enemy?"

The Harbinger looked from Lady Sylvie to Dav. She stared at him as if directing her next words to him alone.

"It is a demon the like of which you have never seen before. It is the One True Devil."

CHAPTER 3
WHEELBARROW

"Something went wrong. No. I *did* something wrong," the old man confided to his elegiacally squeaking two-wheeled companion, "but I can't remember what it was."

Crrrk, crrrk, crrrk was the only reply. The handcart's bent wheels squeaked out a sad and pathetic cycle of remonstrances, warning with each revolution that it might not be up to carrying any new or substantial burdens. Its halcyon days of silent, uncomplaining labor were behind it, forgotten and discarded like the gray paint that had cracked and fallen off years in the past, left behind like the youth and memories of the creaky old man who pushed it. Discarded, as he had been.

His voice was as deep as the wheelbarrow's was not, but like the wheelbarrow, he swayed a little from side to side as he pushed the cracked and bent old cart forward through the rubble of his formerly glorious city. "What was it?" he asked more loudly as he lifted the sad-looking handcart over a jumble of rocks. Looking up, he saw that the street ahead was completely choked with rubble from the collapsed walls of the old Hall of Justice that had once commanded the elegant square at the city center. He wrapped his long, wiry, white-haired arms around the handcart and pulled it higher—protectively up to his chest

—and stumbled up over the chaotic mess that used to dispense Engevelen's famously impartial common law in the city of Villiers.

"That feels better," he observed when he finally reached smoother road. "Now, where is it?" The old man squinted up at the light blue sky, then to his left and to his right. He thought he could hear raised, troubled voices. Up a side street just ahead and to the right. He followed the sounds, forcing his arthritic legs to move faster, rocking back and forth as he pushed his wheelbarrow down the road. Houses crowded the cobble, and twenty-foot-long stone planter boxes separated the narrow walk from the road.

There was comparatively little debris on this street, though it was clear that at least the fringes of the battle had passed through here. A series of pyramidal rock piles dotted the street, and there were lines in the thin dust leading to the mounds, indicating that someone, and recently, had swept up the smaller detritus. On some of the front stoops of the remains of the houses, luggage, crates, artwork, and other possessions had been piled. Sometimes the items were piled on much larger carts than the one the old man pushed. A boy of maybe eight or nine strode purposefully by, carrying a loaf-sized rock and, with some solemnity, in complete silence placed the rock among the rest of the rubble on the street. The old man paused, leaning on his cart to watch the child. The boy marched back to one of the houses. Its front wall had been caved in, but the houses on either side were untouched. The boy rummaged around, pulling at the mess of rock in front of the house, finally finding another chunk of stone that he could carry to the street.

"Don't know how that happened," the old man called out in his deep voice, "but they might need that rock when they fix it." The boy ignored him. Then, as the shouting began again, the old man carried on down the road. He passed other silent men, women, and children, either cleaning the streets or piling things up on their stoops. The rock piles and pyramids of possessions combined in the man's mind for a moment. His hands, the veins bumping out, making gnarly hands gnarlier, tightened on the handles of the cart. He knew he had set out with the cart for a purpose, but what was the mission? The emotions that rose up within him—anger, frustration, grief—begged for release, but he was stuck. His tottering mind, his failing memory, and the lonely certainty—his only certainty—that he did not know how to help those he passed, locked his feelings in.

The sound of a vicious argument drew him on.

He dodged his wheelbarrow around a cracked planter box, the front wheel running through a narrow line of unswept dark soil that had escaped its confinement, and saw a woman facing off against three soldiers in the livery of the municipal guard. It was clear that this was the source of the noise that had drawn his attention. A pulse of anger pounded through the old man's blood. He pushed the handcart faster and ran, no longer swaying from side to side.

"Ma'am," said one of the young men, a corporal in chainmail and a clean uniform tunic, "I'm sorry but we will not be b—"

"This street is a disgrace," she interrupted in a strident and punishingly enunciated voice. "And it's been like this for a week. That is *not* how we do things here. You promised to help clear the refuse and it has *not* been done. Your performance is *unacceptable*."

What? Confusion instantly transformed the old man's athletic sprint into an oafish muddle and then, almost as quickly, to a sloppy halt. Uncertain of himself, he took up a station a few paces away from the agitated quartet. A neat-looking home stood behind the woman, but her front steps had been crushed by some heavy object. Whatever had done the damage was gone, leaving only wreckage behind.

"Are you the carpenter?" The lady said, sharp eyes suddenly upon him. She had the dark skin and light eyes of an indigenous citizen of Engevelen and seemed neither young nor old, but she was certainly straight-backed and severe of expression. Her hair was neat and shoulder-length, her clothes clean, and she wore a white apron with red carnations embroidered upon it. "You're *late*," she said as if she was a judge pronouncing a sentence. "Very late."

Perplexed, the old man struggled for a moment, at a loss for words. "I—I don't *think* I'm a carpenter." Events and time had a habit of getting away from him, he knew that. The present just slipped away. He sometimes forgot a story mid-tale. And he was aware of this, sometimes. That awareness, the knowledge of an incompetent, unreliable memory, made him hesitate. He *thought* he was not the carpenter. *But am I? Did I forget what I am?* He looked down at his rough, gnarled hands. Old scars covered them, dull, creamy white streaks through which no hairs grew. A carpenter might have hands like that. He looked at the corporal, who was eyeing him up and down, frowning, but also trying to smile. Uncomfortable, trying to be polite. He had a short sword on his hip and two men at his shoulders, but he was also hesitant.

The woman was not. "You look like you have been alive forever," she stated, as if that settled the matter. "You *must* be the man I asked for." When the old man did not reply, she added, "You have a wheelbarrow, don't you?" It was not really a question.

The old man looked down at his rickety cart. "It's empty."

She was not a big woman, but she produced an enormous sigh. "That isn't the only thing that's empty." She crossed her arms and slowly shook her head, eyes narrowed, lips pressed thin.

"Is this the best I can expect from the city now? Some confused old tradesman who doesn't even know to bring tools?"

"No," said the old man.

"No?" the woman sneered.

"No, I mean, I don't think I *am* a carpenter. I—I was on my way to get something," the old man said in as smooth a voice as he could manage. It made more sense as he said it, helped to put the sequence of events together in his mind. "I heard your voices and thought someone needed help."

The woman's eyes were hard and her response quick. "I do need help—with my front step—but apparently you and these soldiers are not interested in helping me."

The corporal tried to smile at the woman, but his face was too stiff with embarrassment. "There are no city carpenters being sent out to residents, ma'am," he said in a bureaucratic tone that belied his reddening face. "All non-essential personnel are under an evacuation order. An order, I must respectfully state, that includes you." He made another attempt at a smile and spared a glance at the old man. "This gentleman's cart is surely for luggage. He must be taking it to his residence."

"If you think I am going to leave my home, you are as confused as this . . . carpenter," she shot back, all her attention on the soldiers. "I am of Engevelen. We. Do. Not. Leave."

"Please ma'am," the young soldier said, hands up in a conciliatory gesture, "all of your neighbors have organized their evacuation luggage on the street. You must also do this so that your possessions can be tagged and collected."

"You will be tagging and collecting nothing of mine," declared the lady. She turned sharply on her right high heel, marched almost regally to her house, and carefully avoiding the broken steps, ascended and entered.

The corporal stared after the lady for a moment, then pulled off his helmet and wiped his brow. "There's one on every street," he muttered.

"Two or three on most," one of his soldiers said.

As the corporal put his helmet back on, he seemed to remember the old man. "Sir?" he said, "Do you need assistance, sir?"

The weapons that the young men carried reminded the old man of something. Sharp blades and leather. Each had a smell, a feeling, a connection to experience. Their chain mail had a smell, too ... the oil ... it brought back memories just out of reach, reminded him that he had his own purpose. In a stronger voice than he had used with the woman, he said, "No, I'm good to go, corporal," and continued down the road, pushing his cart.

I used to have a sword. It had been bigger than the ones the municipal guard carried. Much bigger. A two-hander, heavy, hard to stop in flight. He could not remember his name, but he knew where he was going. And why.

"I can't let you into the armory, sir." The soldier's chainmail swished as he crossed his arms below his broad chest. He was shorter than the old man, just shy of six feet and thickly built. Half of his left eyebrow had been replaced by a white scar that blazed on his ebony face.

"I need those swords," the old man repeated for the eighth time. "*We* need them."

"Why might that be?" The soldier was a sergeant, and his gentle, wry expression suggested patronization as much as his question. It was a familiar expression to the old man. Most people smiled like that when they told him no. He *knew* that. The sergeant was still smiling and still talking to him, explaining his refusal. "Civilians have been ordered to evacuate. The most vulnerable are being escorted out today. You should have been one of them." He paused and widened his smile. "And who exactly is 'we'?"

"Me and my friends," the old man replied, exasperated. The question was irrelevant under the circumstances. This was an emergency. He lifted the arms of his bent old wheelbarrow. "I can carry enough for everyone in this."

Now the soldier chuckled. "I don't think so, old fellow. You don't want to be running around town with a cart full of sharp objects." He shook his head with a rueful half-smile. "Someone might get hurt. I don't want that on my conscience."

The old man put down the wheelbarrow, dug in his heels, and straightened his back. The words came to him out of old memories, words engraved indelibly by some long-ago training. "I have a right—as a citizen of Engevelen—to a sword upon request to defend my person, my neighbors, and my country. This law is subject to the Methueyn Treaty to which Engevelen is a signatory."

The soldier's head sank back into his neck. "Wow. Really. You can be eloquent when you want to be, sir."

"First time anyone's called me that."

"What, sir?"

"No, eloquent."

"Well, look," the soldier said after more chuckling, "you're right, you *can* legally make that demand. Not many people know that anymore. Leave the ... uh ... cart out here and come on inside. I can't just hand over government property without a form. You'll have to sign something."

He led the old man to a desk in the anteroom of the armory, where a lantern cast a dim, wavering light on some papers, a manifest, a bottle of ink, and a quill, but he could not locate the form they needed. It had been a long time since there had been a citizen request for arms, but he drew up a brief letter. "Now, just write your name and sign here," he said under a horizontal line at the bottom.

"My name?" That was the question that vexed him. "I . . . cannot remember." *I used to hear it all the time.* He frowned. "Do you know?"

"*Very* funny. I just met you."

The silence that followed lasted long enough for the soldier to realize this was no joke. "Where did you say you came from, old fellow?"

"From the house on the hill."

The soldier's eyes widened, "The House of Fools?"

Time slipped. A crashing noise. A color, red. When time returned, the old man found himself pinning the sergeant against the heavy iron door, his white-haired arm hard across the man's bare throat. The table was on its side against the wall to his left, and the chairs, papers and ink were scattered.

"L—let me go," the soldier wheezed. He was on his toes, gasping for air.

"I can't let you call it the House of Fools." The old man's deep voice reverberated like a colossal bell off the stone walls of the anteroom.

"It—it's just a f—figure of speech. A nickname. Do you know w—what that is? A j—joke. I can't b—breathe."

"I know what it is," the old man stated firmly. "And I can't let you hurt the people there by talking like that."

The sergeant's eyes, which had been screwed half shut in pain, opened wider and swung up into the hardened face of the old man, who seemed bigger, taller and straighter, now than before. Almost a different person. "I'm s—sorry. I—I won't say it a—again."

The old man eased his grip and took a half step back. The soldier's face was tearstained from being choked, and once he regained his balance, he bent double, catching his breath. Recovered, back straightened, his eyes went to the hilt of his short sword.

"Don't draw that."

"I wouldn't," the soldier said, aghast. He breathed, swallowed, and vowed, "Heaven strike me down if I draw on *you*, old man." He began to wipe his eyes with his mailed arm, but quickly stopped and squinted. Hard metal rings and tears do not mix. "I'm sorry. Everyone calls the home that name, but it never occurred to me how it might make the folks there feel."

"I don't like seeing people hurt," the old man said.

"Sir, that is why we are evacuating the city, you know," the soldier replied, eyes searching the old man's lined face. "To keep them from being hurt. Skoll and Hati might—probably will, according to the commander—come back. It would be better if you helped your friends pack up and escape rather than give them swords that—I don't mean to be cruel—they probably can't use."

"Sometimes it's better not to be saved," the old man replied. His voice seemed to harmonize with some natural frequency in the room.

The sergeant blinked and said nothing for a moment. When he did speak, he sounded resigned, but there was also something more in his tone. "My name is Havard. Do you really not know yours?"

"I do." The old man frowned. "But it isn't my true name. They call me Mick."

"Well, listen, Mick," Havard said, "I'll sign out the swords in your care—as long as I can find the ink bottle and there's anything left in it —but I'm worried you don't understand what we are up against. This isn't like another probe from Armadale or southward pressure from Ardgour like we had five, no wait, seven years ago. These demons, Skoll and Hati, they are a knights-damned disaster. And we don't even know what they want, why they come, or why they leave. We sure as hell can't seem to show them the door. And those skolve things they have with them are an even bigger problem in a lot of ways. They kill more people, that's for sure. A lot more."

Mick was fairly sure he had not seen any of the skolves everyone was talking about, and he was certain that he had not seen Skoll or Hati, whoever they were. And what this soldier was saying was not exactly what he remembered hearing back in the house on the hill. The word there was "temporary evacuation," as if some more palatable solution would later be forthcoming. "Why are you telling me this, Sergeant?" he asked after some thought.

"I don't want you and your friends back at the home thinking that staying is anything except suicide. This is *bad*, Mick. You and your friends really need to evacuate while you still can."

"Can't do that, Havard."

The soldier's patient expression collapsed. His face turned red, but Mick did not think it was in anger. "Why not?" Havard pleaded.

Mick thought about his days in the house on the hill. He could not remember many of them, or when he had first been brought there. It had been after he lost his name, though. Even if too many of the days in the house were a gray pastel smudge in his mind, he knew that a lot more folks had arrived over the years. They had come in all shapes and sizes. In variations that strained description, that were beyond the expectation of anyone not of the house. They were all so surprisingly unique, except that all were old. And only left the house one way. But how they were removed, how they disappeared between one meal and the next, was not spoken of by anyone. It was studiously avoided, ignored, disbelieved. A wound not picked at except silently. Alone.

"Because some of my friends already left," he said at last, treading close to the ineffable line.

"Already evacuated? Well, that's goo—"

Mick interrupted, saying "No one has ever left the home by evacuation."

"I don't understand what you mean," Havard said, eyes red, "or what this has to do with swords."

"No one should go quietly." *Unremembered and unmourned. No matter what we have done wrong.*

THE WHEELBARROW SQUEAKED louder under its new load, but Mick seemed to push it along more easily. It had been piled high with weapons. The load could have been tidy and symmetrical, but Mick had requested that the sizes be mixed. It was mostly short swords. Havard had been right; most of the folks at the house on the hill would have trouble wielding a heavy weapon. But for himself, Mick had chosen a mighty, two-handed claymore. The load, though mixed, had seemed to fit together well enough when Mick started toward home, but every bump from the rubble made the heavily laden wheelbarrow less manageable. The farther he pushed, the worse the load became as the metal shifted around, tossing sharp edges everywhere, threatening to pitch some off onto the road. The worst moments came when the whole wheelbarrow seemed to turn suicidal and rotate out of balance, a movement that started gently enough but quickly approached a tipping point beyond which the whole load would have violently rolled over, with potentially deadly consequences for the old man pushing it.

In between battling to keep the wheelbarrow of death on the straight and narrow, a song went through Mick's head. It was often there, it seemed. He hummed and muttered it, though he could only recall some of the words.

> Raise up my shield, sun's light will warm!
> Raise up my maul, my scroll and pen!
> Raise up my horn, to heavens warn!
> Blah, blah blah-blah, blah-blah blah, blen.

"What's that?" Mick said aloud, interrupting his own singing. Dusk was coming on, and the street he was pushing his noisy, insecure burden through was desolate and ruined. There were no piles of luggage here, no citizens cleaning the street or tidying up the damage, only abandoned ruins. He heard it again, a whining sound coming from up ahead somewhere. He pushed harder, almost jogging, then hit a rock that bent his trajectory sharply left and pitched the whole cart sideways onto the cobbles. Assorted swords and other weapons went flying, landing on the street with a discordant clatter.

"Knights damn it." Mick scrambled, trying to gather up the sharp metal quickly, listening for the whimpering sound at the same time as he juggled swords, bungling the job when one short sword slid across the jumble of blades and fell off the other side. The wheelbarrow and its chaotic, pointy contents now looked like some deadly, gargantuan version of that pick-up-sticks game that some of the folks back at the house played.

The whine cut across his hearing once more. He whirled, but there were piles of debris everywhere and collapsed houses up and down the street. It was an orgy of destruction far out of proportion to the reported body count. Whoever had come through the town—Skoll, Hati or whatever they called them—had apparently enjoyed knocking the old stone buildings down.

"Do you need help?" he called out desperately. "Where are you?" Nothing. "My ears aren't what they were."

He heard the cry again, faint but just ahead. There! At a half-collapsed house that was little more than a pile of odd, angled stones under a broken roof.

"I'm coming!" he called out to whoever was inside, then circled the ruin, still pushing his wheelbarrow of weaponry. On the far side he found an opening, a sort of a cave, with a precarious-looking roof barely higher than his hip. He dropped his squeaking cart and crawled in, meeting pitch darkness almost at once. "Ow!" He banged his head on a jutting piece of stone. The space became more confined as it went on, and he had to flatten out on his hairy belly. Dirt and little rocks got under his shirt, rolling around as he pushed forward.

"Whewmm," came the sound from just ahead.

"Hello?" Mick said, skootching forward a little farther, reaching with his hands. His right hand felt rough stone, but his left found something wet. He squinted and could just make out two eyes reflecting the tiny amount of light that made it past him. It was a dog. "Who left you here?" Mick asked, but some undulled part of him remembered that disasters always left someone, or something, behind. That knowledge checked the anger that had suddenly arisen in him. He did not know what had happened, who had been home, or how they had left their dog behind. Or if they had been alive to wonder and worry.

Please, Elysium, may there be no people under there.

"Is it just you? Just you, puppy?" he whispered to himself. Sliding forward a little farther by rocking his whole body from side to side, Mick got both hands around the neck of the animal. "I'm just going to pull you out, puppy. Okay?" He pulled.

The dog screamed and bit his left wrist. "Stuck." He relaxed the pressure he had applied, and the dog stopped biting, but kept a gentle pressure on his wrist. There was very little wetness from the bite. "Ok, let go now." He got his wrist back. The dog whimpered once more. It was a sound all mammals made when desperate enough, when their need for help exceeded the risk of vulnerability that told them not to advertise their plight. It was a plea for safety that transcended species, went straight to the soul. Mick could not ignore it, did not want to.

"I-I'll just have to lift this up for you, puppy." Mick didn't know what he was lifting. Was it one rock or the whole house? He could not find leverage all stretched out as he was. "Damn," he muttered. *How long has this poor thing been here?* He guessed it must have been days. The dog had almost no saliva in its mouth. Filled with angst, Mick tried once more to life the rock off the dog. He pushed, then pushed again, and moved nothing.

"I-I don't know if I'm strong enough, puppy," Mick whispered. The dog whimpered back, but softly. "Time is running out for us both, isn't it? I can't remember my own knights-damned name, and you're stuck under your own house." Mick's face was wet. "We're both in the dark, with the end creeping up on us." He reached back again for the furry neck and stroked the dog gently with his fingers. "I'm sorry. Time seems to have too much leverage on us." *Oh. Leverage. I really am slow.*

"Hold on, puppy, I have an idea." he said and scootched backward until he could turn around and crawl out to his wheelbarrow. He tipped it over—which seemed to be its new favorite position anyway—sending the pointy ball of swords clanging into the cobblestones again. He grabbed the big two-hander and crawled back into the ruin.

Jamming the sword into the stone without impaling the dog was nervous work. Figuring out how to use the great two-handed blade as a lever was counterintuitive. Mick ended up on his back in the confined space, pushing up on the long handle. Nothing. *It might be the whole house.* The dog whimpered again, sounding still weaker than before. Mick slid on his back until his head was almost touching the dog's nose and pushed on the sword handle as if it was all there was in the world. All that mattered. One thought, one hope, one reason for being. He felt complete in that moment, for nothing could be forgotten when there was only one thing to live for. With a grinding noise, the rock moved, though only a few inches. "Come on out now, puppy, come on," he instructed. The dog did not move. Mick left one hand on the sword, pushing twice as hard and violently shaking, and reached back with the other for the dog. When he felt furry neck, he pulled. The dog came free with a yelp, its head resting on top of Mick's chest.

It tried to lick him with a sandpaper tongue.

The dog was a half-grown shepherd, weighing maybe thirty pounds. Its fur was matted and crusted with old blood and dirt. Mick could not tell if the dog could walk. There was no room to put it on its feet. It had stopped whining, but its eyes labored to follow the old man's movements. "You're kind of done for, aren't you?" Mick said gently. He knew what those eyes meant. People always said, never base your understanding of animals on your understanding of men, but that was horse crap. What he saw in the dog's eyes, he had seen before in people. Often. He saw that resigned look virtually every day in the house on the hill, though it was not spoken of aloud. Never discussed, dignified with speech, or admitted to.

"I'll call you Fenris," he told the dog. "Fenris," he repeated to it. *You'll like that name.*

The sun was disappearing, and his options were disappearing just as quickly. He realized he would not be able to carry both Fenris and the wheelbarrow. He had no jacket to try to stuff a too big dog into. There was no chance of doing it with a shirt. A pile of swords did not mix with a dog in the cart.

"What are we going to do, Fenris?"

CHAPTER 4

ELYSIAN DREAMS

"Wizards are blind to their blindness."

The Shining Knight

"That looks perfect," Val said, observing the troop disposition. It was just as she had heralded, just as she had imagined.

Even if I have never done this before.

Lady Katherine Valcourt, commander of the Elysian mobile force, had never been in a real battle before, held no military rank, had undergone no training on how to work with armed soldiers, and understood nothing of the tactics required to use wizards and soldiers efficiently in battle. She only had analogies drawn from games and books.

Like minerals in a brick, like bricks in a wall, like pieces on a game board, they are laid out. Like is to like is to like, and thus we go from what we know to what we thought we didn't know.

. . .

Of soldiers she had plenty. There were three groups of eight Knights of Armadale lined up thirty feet behind her, ready to take cover, and Sergeant Reyn's group of eight soldiers from Vercors—some kind of rangers, apparently—taking positions about ten yards in front of her. She had followed some of the advice of Captain Lowri in the disposition, but the captain was momentarily out of sight. Val wanted to ask her if there was a reason other than liking the number eight that soldiers were grouped that way. Val had quite a lot of questions she wanted to ask.

Like must be like. This needs to work.

If it did not, it would likely be the end of her hastily formed multinational force. They might all be dead too, but Val did not care about that, not as such. She desperately needed the fragile alliance to hold. *That* was what required survival. And victory.

"I'm ready to drop the doll," announced Christopher, eyes bright, bouncing on his toes, holding the figurine to his chest.

Val tried not to flinch, but she did.

Every plan is good until the first mistake by uncontrollable subordinates.

Wizards were the worst. They did not listen. They thought they were special, and so they tended to ruin what they touched. *This* Val knew about; she *was* one, though an Acutist, while Christopher belonged to the Statician school. Statician wizards were fond of saying they liked statics, not statistics. They hated math and science, believed in instinct, and claimed to already know, deep in their bones, what they needed to find out.

They were like drunk men or reckless, ignorant children.

"Let's wait for Green," Val said with all the coolness she could pretend to. "He is still ferrying all the eights on the other side of the village." Halwyn Glace, or Green as he was nicknamed, was the only wizard they had who could teleport. Val might lack all experience in the military, but she knew a vital resource when she saw one. Green was important.

"How much longer?" asked Rebecca Laurie. "I'm ready with my lines." Both she and Christopher were from Vercors, they both had the dark hair and pale skin of that country, and they were equally stoked to begin the engagement.

"Let's take up our positions," Val said by way of a reply. She had no idea what the correct arm signals were to indicate this, but she waved at Sergeant Reyn of the Vercors eight and then back to the knights. She saw Reyn's eight smoothly take to the ground, up against the small berm on their side of the road, and behind her she could hear the clatter of the knights as they did the same. *Where are the skolves?* Crouching on the other side of the road from Reyn's eight and behind her own berm with Rebecca and Christopher, Val realized how little she could actually see now. *No wonder everyone wanted to stay on their feet.* She had also failed to consider that the knights' armor was heavy. It would be difficult for them to get to their feet quickly.

"That is excellent," she said for no good reason other than that it was awkward lying there peering over dirt and grass, waiting. She could just make out the tree line in the distance and, more clearly, the squat grain bins in front of the line. But no skolves yet. This was worrisome. Analogic reasoning rested upon the assumption of functional relationships, the specific and unique rules binding one thing to another. But even her cursory Heraldry had shown her that there was more than one way for the battle to go.

Please, please be correct. Please let this be the version that works. If we come out of this victorious, I will have learned what I need to know, but let this not be the end. Val hated begging, even to herself—she was a Lady of Engevelen, a young woman of poise—but it was proving difficult not to hope and pray when push came to shove.

Still no skolves. Christopher shifted impatiently next to her. A blade of grass tickled Val's face. Time seemed to crawl.

Is this what I heralded?

As wizards went, Val's Heraldry was, she had to admit, mediocre. She was far from sure what would now transpire. When she had proposed the formation of this Elysian force in court, she had projected a confidence she did not feel. She knew that she could not really be sure her idea would work. *Needed*, yes. Engevelen needed help. But here, so far from court and reductive political boasting, she felt her uncertainty keenly. Val had tried to look through probability and see where the skolves would come from and how the battle would go. It had been a tangle, not a locus-sized knot, but a flashing, reverberating, superimposing set of outcomes that was all but impossible to follow. Val had only just prevented herself from vomiting. That would surely have destroyed whatever remaining confidence the knights and soldiers had in her. Quite a few of the overlapping images of *what might be* had shown a rout, with most of her soldiers killed, while in other, more difficult-to-parse scenarios, she had seen, yes, victory, but at great cost. In some scenarios, they had been attacked on both sides of the village simultaneously, and in others, the skolves had only attacked her side. Val had enlisted Captain Lowri in a hasty redistribution of her forces based on what she thought she had seen through time's kaleidoscope. She hoped that, like bricks in a wall or pieces on a gameboard, the knights would make the difference. She had also told Christopher and Rebecca to be ready. They had been far from the edge of combat in Val's original plan. The threat of defeat, death, and the disbanding of the fledgling Elysians had prompted Val to risk the wizards.

"There they are!" exclaimed Christopher, scrambling to his knees. He had a good eye. Val could just make out faint movement at the tree line.

She put a hand on his shoulder and whispered, "Wait."

The skolves moved closer. She could see them clearly now. Christopher twitched. Rebecca breathed in short gasps. Val silently cursed at both of them for their nervous excitement and overlooked her own impatient trembling.

The skolves were very close now, frighteningly close. Rebecca Laurie's blue eyes widened, and she smiled triumphantly from her position crouched on the dirt of the berm. "A stitch in time makes—"

"Don't you dare finish that rhyme!" Val hissed, then cursed herself for completing the dreaded sequence herself. "It's not yet time." She winced and cursed herself again. Rhyming was stupid. It was something that children did, not something wizards—or certain Statician wizards at least—should be known for. The rhyme was most decidedly *not* the reason, no matter what Rebecca liked to say. And this was definitively not the time for it. The fate of nations should not hang in the balance of ill-timed meter and assonance.

The skolves had not moved fully into position yet. This was the third potentially isolated group of skolves that Val had seen, though the first from so close and the first she planned to fight. They were tall, taller than all but the most exceptional human could hope to reach, covered in coarse hair, and carried a mismatched medley of weapons. They had the face of a wolf crossed with a horse, she decided, and a rawboned look, all skin, bone, sinew, and muscle. In many ways, the skolves appeared an out of place hodge-podge, not unlike the Elysian force she had with her, which contained at least a few soldiers from every country in the Methueyn Treaty. The mix of uniforms arrayed here behind the berms and on the other side of the village gave her some trepidation, but mostly about their theoretical effectiveness. The skolves frightened her too, but in a visceral rather than a political or theoretical way. The strange creatures were stronger than anyone not Elysium-touched, and faster too. In battle, they were said never to retreat. All fights were to the death—the last death.

The group—six, she counted—suddenly paused, giving Val the opportunity to realize something new about them. They looked pathetic. Ragged. Hungry. Out of place. Her Heraldry had not shown her this.

If the skolves truly came from some other world—hell, if the Bishop of Engevelen could be believed—then they really were cosmically out of place. But Val was not so sure. The skolves did not look like Skoll or Hati, so why would they have come across the barrier between worlds as the two demons had done? The idea was plausible superficially, but not a reasoned view. That Nehring Ardgour would reach a second time into hell, after pulling two horrible demons from there, seemed insane. Having once made such a catastrophic mistake, who in their right mind would open the same ghastly portal again?

Hardly matters where they came from, Val. Stay focused on where they are going.

"What's the holdup here?" asked Christopher. "I'm about ready to bust a doll."

Val could see that he held the porcelain doll in his hands even as he shifted next to her just below the top of the earthy berm. The ivory-colored, foot-long figurine wore a fine purple taffeta dress and had painted lips and long curled eyelashes. He held it like a man about to clutch it to his chest or twist its head off. The thing was creepy, almost human.

It looked like Christopher held murder in his hands.

"Yes, let's about it," agreed Rebecca, smiling just as evilly. She pointed to Reyn's eight crouching behind the next berm nearest the skolves. "They could be over the fence and on those grunts before we blink. Then what would happen?"

"They'd probably run away, fail to escape, and be eaten," replied Christopher. "Our knightly friends," he rolled his eyes toward the other berm behind him, where the groups of knights from Armadale crouched—against their better judgement, they had said—"would likely just watch it happen and then charge to the rescue after our peons were all eaten up." He shook his doll. "Let's crack the sky!"

Val almost rolled her eyes. "No. Not even skolves are that fast." She considered again her eclectic group of fighters. The Vercors contingent and the honor-bound Knights of Armadale were supposed to be on the same side, but they acted very differently. One group was cautious, fidgety, independent, the other honor-locked, armor-bound, rigid. As different as Val supposed she was from Christopher and Rebecca, as different as Statician from Acutist wizards. The groups of soldiers she had sent to the north side of the village were from Kames, the ones on the south side from Harkness. Who knew what they were doing or if they were managing to cooperate? *And what's in store for them? Is this one of the scenarios where they are attacked also?*

"We wait until we hear from Green," Val insisted, as much to herself as to her fellow wizards.

The skolves continued creeping forward, then paused beside one of the squat, round grain bins, sniffing the air. *Can they smell us?* The edge of the village was fifty yards behind Val's position, and thrice that distance for the skolves. The wolf-like creatures might only be pausing to take stock of the situation before venturing into the village, or they might be picking up the scents of their enemies and planning how they would devour them.

"Knights, they stink," whispered Rebecca, scrunching her nose on the other side of Val. The stench of rotten meat rolled over Val in a hot wave, but despite the overpowering reek, she retained enough acuity to realize that the skolves could not have smelled her team of Elysians. They were downwind of the beasts.

But why have they stopped?

It was unlike skolves.

"Let's just do it," Christopher said again. "They could be onto Leftover's troops before we blink. Then they'd be too close for Marianne here to take care of." He shook his creepy doll at Val as if it were affirming his point.

But the skolves had not been getting ready to charge the soldiers. They suddenly turned sideways in the azimuth of the grain bin, then trotted over to it. It was a feeder, about five feet high and fourteen across, with a heavy wooden roof and a trough a foot above the ground at its perimeter. Grain went into the top through a bolted hatch. Gravity and mass then pushed the grain down under an adjustable grate and filled the outer trough for cattle to feed from. The skolves seemed to stare at the grain feeder for a moment, then they suddenly fell upon the trough, shoveling paws full of grain messily into their long jaws.

I never saw this. Val's Heraldry had completely missed this possibility. Or she had been unable to parse it from the mess of images.

Pop.

The tiny explosion detonated at the same instant that Halwyn Glace appeared out of thin air, standing a pace or so away from Val with his knees bent and back straight, pushing both hands out from his body as if against some vast resistance. If the skolves had not been so greedily and loudly shoveling raw grain between their teeth, they would have seen and heard him too.

Val gestured frantically at him. "Get down, Green!" she hissed.

As Halwyn's dark blue eyes widened at Val's urgent command, Christopher sprang to his feet, porcelain doll held tight. Val could hear Rebecca moving on her other side, but before she could intervene with either of her colleagues, Christopher cried out, "Eat this, devils!"

Crrrk!

He snapped the doll's head off and aggressively threw the pieces away from himself, over the berm in the direction of Captain Lowri and her men. "Shit!" he said as the pieces flew through the air. "I didn't mean t—"

Before Halwyn Glace could react to Val's warning, before the doll's head or body could complete the hyperbolic journey toward the crouching soldiers, before Rebecca could utter whatever rhyme she had penned, and before the skolves had time to whirl round from the storage bin, a painful shock stabbed through Val's body—and simultaneously, a flash of hot white light bloomed around the skolves and the grain bin.

Whump-whump!

The skolves, the grass they stood upon, and the wooden roof of the grain bin instantly combusted. A secondary, smaller detonation sprang from the head and body of the porcelain doll that Christopher had thrown into the air. Val could barely see the nearly invisible waves that rolled out from the two pieces of doll in every direction, including down.

"Aaaaaghh!" several of the troopers screamed as the waves swept over them. Frost instantly coated them from head to toe. Even in Val's sheltered position behind the berm, she was hammered by the percussive waves of freezing air as they shot away from Christopher's manually decapitated doll.

BOOOOM!!

The grain bin fire had been burning only a moment, the skolves had barely begun their unforgettable high-pitched keening, and the soldiers' curses had barely left their mouths when the grain bin exploded, flinging the already burning skolves outward along with a deluge of flaming kernels of grain.

"Hell-ya!" cried Christopher exuberantly, despite the condensation slicking his face and blotching his tunic.

"Put out the fire!" shrieked Val, standing up and pointing at the smoldering skolves, the ring of flames surrounding them, and the scattered, burning debris of the grain bin. Clumps of red-hot grain carpeted the ground fifty yards in every direction from where the obliterated bin had stood.

"Why?" cried at least one of the frosted soldiers—though, Val suspected—not at her last command.

"Oh, my eight knights, it's stuck. My helmet's stuck to my head. Get it off, get it off, get it off!" This desperate plea came from a soldier who was rolling around on the frost-covered ground, clutching his helmet with both hands

Halwyn's dark, shoulder-length hair was dripping as he took in the pandemonium among the soldiers and the smoldering fires beyond them. "C-couldn't you h-have waited one d-damned minute?" he said, shivering from hypothermia and shaking his head at Christopher, who had put his hands on his hips and was nodding in vast satisfaction.

"I told you not to shave your head, Dafydd," came a calm female voice from among the soldiers. Corporate Alwena, Val remembered, though she was barely paying the rangers any attention. "This is half your fault."

"Half! How's this half my fault? It won't come off."

"That's what wizards *do*," declared Rebecca, turning around to look at Halwyn, Val, and Christopher. Her long, dark hair was soaked, but she was smiling euphorically and pointing at the spotty fires and the charred carcasses of the skolves. "*That* is what we do!"

"You should have waited," maintained Halwyn.

"Mmff, help me," rose a whisper, barely audible over the crackling flames and the crosstalk between various soldiers and the wizards. "I'm s-stuck."

This piteous appeal made Val look past Rebecca to another soldier, who was on his knees in a very odd posture. His right arm, encased in chain mail, was held at an odd angle, up and across his face. She realized that the iron rings were frozen to his face.

Eww. What a sticky problem!

But first, action was urgently required elsewhere. Val called over to the struggling soldiers. "Get that fire out before it spreads and burns down the village. Whoever isn't ... frosted to their equipment, go throw dirt on the flames. Now!"

For some reason, the soldiers seemed to be ignore her very reasonable instructions.

"Just stay there," said Alwena in a long-suffering tone to the unfortunate soldier with his face frozen to his chainmail. "I'll come warm it up."

The whispered response was fearful. "H-how?"

"I won't lie to you, Dill, I'm gonna have to piss on you a little bit."

"What about me?" cried Dafydd, still clutching his helmet. "Will you have enough left over for me?"

"You're right, we need another pisser," replied the corporal in a calm, even tone. "Urinate!" she called, switching to a loud, authoritative voice. "Go piss on Dafydd's head."

"If I do, are you going stop calling me that?" asked another soldier in chainmail, but whose limbs were fortunately free.

"Who would have thought a grain bin would blow up like that!" exclaimed Christopher, seemingly oblivious to the misery all around him. Val had not thought so, had not seen it in any of her Heraldry. It had ended the fight almost before it had started.

"Too bad there weren't more of them," lamented Rebecca.

Corporal Alwena never heard either wizard. She was busy with the soldiers. "What do you think, Eurion? I gotta go with what works. That's military protocol. Isn't that right, Sergeant?"

Sergeant Reyn, a quiet, serious-minded fellow from what Val had seen of him, turned from speaking to another soldier and answered Alwena. "Just get the pissing over with, Corporal, and let's move on." Reyn had short dark hair, a moustache, and a goatee, giving him a handsome, if rakish, appearance.

"Yessir," Corporal Alwena responded crisply. She began undoing her belt.

This can't be happening. Caught between the twin horrors of watching the fire or the imminent urination, Val found her voice. "You know I could probably thaw that out empyreally."

The unfortunate Dill rolled to the side so he could see Val. It was an awkward movement, with his arm frozen to his face and his body stretched out helplessly on the ground. His eyes were wide. "S-stay away," he said tremulously.

It hurt Val not to be trusted. "I can do it *carefully*," she said in the sort of voice normally used only when talking to babies or skittish dogs. "You won't be hurt."

"We've all seen the legendary subtlety of wizards," said Alwena. Her voice dripped with sarcasm. She thrust her head at the rising smoke. "Is that your legendary subtlety over there?"

But I'm not like them! Alwena's cynicism stung. Val prided herself on being different from the Statician wizards.

As Corporal Alwena straddled Dill and started dropping her pants, he whined, "Dear knights, how did it come to this?"

The fire was spreading. "Sergeant!" Val bellowed as loud as she could. The situation was getting out of hand. "The fire!"

Reyn's eyes were narrow slits when he turned to her, but his voice was calm and level. "Yes, Lady Valcourt. We are attending to it."

"Just be glad we don't need Turd's help," said Alwena, struggling to get her pant leg over her right boot. For all her tugging, it would not go. "Knights damn it," she cried as she lost her balance and almost toppled to the ground beside the still whimpering Dill.

Halwyn Glace stood speechless, shivering slightly—though Val could not say if it was from shock at the bizarre scene in front of him or a side-effect of teleporting—unable to take his eyes off the spectacle. Val shook her head in disgust and focused on the fire.

It would be better if she peed on the fire. *Dill can wait.*

She glared at Reyn.

Nobody listens! This could all have been avoided if people just listened to me.

Reyn was speaking quietly to one of the soldiers.

That is who she meant by Turd! Private Tudor. Of course.

Val vaguely remembered being introduced to the soldier with this deplorable nickname when Captain Lowri had selected their strike team. He was the one that Sergeant Reyn had been speaking with. Tudor had produced a shovel from somewhere and was now marching toward the burning wreckage of the grain bin. Other soldiers were shaking the frost off their mail and preparing to join him. A tight group of plate-armored Knights of Armadale, moving with improbable swiftness under their heavy burdens, almost jogging, creating a cacophony of jangling and clanging as they passed by the soldiers.

"Don't move around, Dill. I'll do the aiming here."

The tinkling sound and sharp smell of urination assailed Val's frayed nerves.

Will this never end?

With one stubborn pant leg still caught on her boot, Corporal Alwena struggled to keep her balance as she urinated on Dill, barely missing his face with her stamping feet, stepping several times on her own pants, peeing on them a little too. She caught Val's horrified stare and narrowed her eyes again. "This is *your* handiwork, wizard. Take that gizzard look off your face or look away!"

"Eight Knights, look away!" Dill shrilled.

Val looked away. There were worse horrors to consider in the surrounding chaos. Flaming debris and smoldering corpses still littered the ground. Reyn's soldiers ran back and forth shoveling dirt onto the scattered fires. She saw with alarm that the Knights of Armadale were now drawing their massive swords.

"Did you see that, Val?" asked Christopher, startling her. He had his arm around Rebecca's shoulders, but was looking at Val, cheeks puffing like a squirrel full of mashed acorns.

"There. Try to pull your arm away from your face now."

"Aaaugh!" Then a wet sound, like lips smacking. The chain links breaking free of Dill's face. "Thank you," he said sheepishly, almost in a whisper.

Another wet thwacking sound, but much louder, made Val return her attention to the knights. They were hacking at the burning carcasses of the skolves. Thwack, whack, thwack. It seemed to take quite a few heavy and enthusiastic two-handed swings to cut through a charred skolve's neck.

"Val? Did you see it?"

"You know, Corporal," Sergeant Reyn said in cool, careful voice. "You probably could have poured your canteen on him and accomplished the same thing."

~

"PRESERVE *THIS*, WIZARD!" The knight's armor was spattered with blood, her voice hollow and alien-sounding as it vented out of her beaked helmet. She thrust the skolve's dripping head at Halwyn, holding it by one short, shriveled ear.

"What?" the wizard said gormlessly. His eyes were wide and darting, his face covered in a sheen of sweat, the skin of his lean, bare arms raised in goosebumps. If anything, he looked even more uncomfortable than Val felt, standing beside him, watching him react to the knight, unsure if Green was sweating or shivering or an unhealthy mixture of both.

"I want to mount it in my tower. But not rotting. You fix it."

Halwyn took a step backward, raising his hand ineffectually to avoid the dripping head. "I—I don't know anything about taxidermy. I'm not that kind of wizard."

The knight took another step forward, once more thrusting the heavy, elongate head at a cringing Halwyn. Val could see that her colleague was unused to dealing with a knight of Armadale and did not know how to respond. He was clearly exhausted into the bargain, at his wit's end. Halwyn Glace was the Elysian's only teleporter, and he was getting worn down quickly. He had been run off his feet moving their piecemeal forces around. There was no possibility of replacing him, which worried Val immensely. If the Shining Knight really was dead, there were perhaps only two teleporters left in the world. And the other one—the greatest of them, everyone said—was Nehring Ardgour, who was very unlikely to step in to help his enemies.

The charred, ragged head, Val thought, was a good metaphor of how the battle—the debacle—had gone. It had been a gross, shocking mess. Fast though. Faster than anything her Heraldry had shown. If she had blinked, she would have missed it. She *wanted* to blink and forget it, make it go away, leave the field herself and go back to the order and silence of her study, but she knew there must be something to be learned from all that had gone wrong.

Everything has gone wrong.

The Renet was unaccounted for, the Deladieyrs were depleted, and this hastily formed Elysian group, her bright idea, was a pitiful failure. Something good *really* needed to come out of it all.

Maybe something good can *come of this fiasco. I need to know what* it *is like.*

"We should take that head and the carcasses for study anyway," Val interjected, excited. This earned a surprised look from Halwyn and an unreadable one from the knight. Who could say what thoughts were hidden by that beaked helmet? Except that now the beak was turned toward her.

"This is spoil of war," came the hollow words at last.

"What good will come of making a hat out of it?" Val joked, smiling and shaking her head. She tried not to sound superior when she added, "I—we—can learn so much about the skolves from studying their physiology."

For a moment, the beak gave no indication of its possible interest in research. Then, the knight turned the head over to show the ragged, ugly cuts through the neck. "We learned that their heads come off." She dropped the head in the dirt and drew her sword, making both Val and Halwyn jump back. "See this blade?" the knight continued, displaying the nicked edge. "It is dulled now from just one head. We need sharper swords if we want enough heads to go around." She sheathed her sword and picked up the hairy mess, now crusted with dirt as well as gore. "Get us more of those Deladieyr blades. That's what we learned."

"There aren't any more." Halwyn said to the knight's back as the armor-clad figure stalked, jangling, away. Vercors had not produced any of those magnificent swords for some time now. The supply had abruptly dried up, reasons unknown, although many suspected that Vercors had begun stockpiling the rare weapons for their own use.

"We need that head!" Val shouted in frustration. This remonstrance achieved two things. First, it turned more silent, beaked, metal-cased helmets in her direction, and second, it proved that once one starts down the road to Absurdville, it is hard to get off.

No one listens to me.

"What next, Val?"

Halwyn's question was apt but unwelcome. Val did not know what was next. Her inexperience was showing. "Uh, good question, Green," she said to give herself time to think, "Very good. We still need those carcasses, but that can come ... later. Right now, I think we need to call in the captains and jump back to Engevelen City, debrief all th—"

"Lady Katherine, a complaint has been made against you." Smooth-voiced Captain Lowri had approached unseen from the direction of the soldiers of Vercors. She was a dark-haired woman of average height, dressed in chain under an officer's tunic. Her gray eyes looked put upon, which Val could understand, but a formal complaint was the last thing Val needed at this critical moment.

I should be the one complaining. About your men not letting me help them, pissing all over each other like savages, about these knights doing whatever the hell they want with no regard for others. For their betters. I should be complaining about these ignorance-worshipping Statician wizards, who also do what they want when they want, hurting whoever they want, not listening *to me. Not one of you listens, you just demand. And now you come complaining.*

But "Me?" was all that Val said. It would be wrong for a Lady of Engevelen to blurt out her thoughts. She did, however, look at Halwyn, expecting at least commiseration if not support. His face was a study in silent equivocation.

"You *are* head of the Elysians, are you not?"

Head of a herd of cats, you mean. Head of a school of doll carriers, rhymers, cheap gesturers. They don't respect logic, why in the hell would they respect my commands?

"That's right." Val straightened her tunic, pulling it through her black belt. "We need to gather the captains, uh, captain and exfiltrate. The after-action report can come later."

"Tell her, Leftover!" came a voice from the milling group of Vercors irregulars.

Lowri flapped a hand irritably back at her soldiers. "I am sorry, but there is still the matter of the complaint."

"Really? It cannot wait?" Val's frustration rose, like a monster. Then, as Lowri stared at her, the monster rose higher, leavened by her recognition that everything had indeed gone badly and her suspicion that, the herd of cats notwithstanding, the failure was hers. Angry and irrationally unhappy that anyone but herself would raise the issue officially, she glared back at the captain.

It should be me who complains, and you who listens.

"This is a complaint that needs to be heard at once," said Lowri, undaunted. Without waiting for Val to respond, she pursed her lips and called over her shoulder, "Sergeant Reyn. Attend us please." She turned back to Val. "The complaint states that you acted negligently, resulting in injuries to several members of Sergeant Reyn's eight. They have made a formal complaint against you." Her hands made a placating gesture. "I'm sorry. You should know that friendly fire always draws a lot of attention, fair or not."

Formal. Complaint.

A formal complaint would be heard in session by the various officials of the nations who had agreed to form the Elysians. Not a good outcome for the mission. Not good for such a fragile alliance.

Val was an inexperienced commander, but her years of study had given her an analytical mind. She shackled her monster and went to work on the problem. None of her force had been killed in the fight. There had been no deaths but skolve deaths. As embarrassed and disgusted as she felt about the proceedings, they could be cast in a favorable light. What were a few injured soldiers and a destroyed grain bin compared to a troop of incinerated skolves? Collateral damage. The doll had been an experiment, and experiments came with risks. This experiment, on the whole, could be set down as a success. A learning experience. It should earn the Elysians another chance to do still better. *She* might be able to do better, save the Elysians, even save Engevelen.

But not, she realized, once a formal complaint was logged. The entire Elysian concept might be cast aside because of that one letter. It could be the beginning of the end for more than just the Elysian force. It could be the beginning of the end for Engevelen, which needed as much help from its allies as it could get. A formal complaint, once on the books, would be a disaster.

Trim, professional, neatly bearded Sergeant Reyn crossed the distance smoothly, saluting Lowri as he stopped. "Yes sir!" he said.

"Tell 'em, Sarge!" came a voice from the crowd.

Captain Lowri fixed the man with a withering glare before turning her attention to Reyn. "Do you really wish to proceed with a *formal* letter of complaint, Sergeant? With all the protocols that would follow?"

Reyn answered in calm, measured tones. "I don't know that I *wish* to, Captain, but two of the lads are going to have scars—or worse—out of this, and no apology out of the wizards." He fixed his steady eyes on Val. She had some trouble meeting his gaze. It was true that neither Christopher nor Rebecca would agree that they had done anything wrong. After the urination had ended, the denials had begun. The truth was gone like piss in the wind.

"You want an *apology*?" Lowri asked, brows scrunched like sewing knots, expressing exactly what Val, amazed, was thinking. "Might an appropriate apology suffice, then?

"I want my eight to be effective. They aren't now. Their confidence is gone." Reyn looked back over his shoulders at his surly crew and continued, "How can we be sure it won't happen again, like such things always seems to happen when wizards are involved?"

"You know that Val did not give the order to attack," Halwyn said to Lowri, finding his voice in defending her. It annoyed Val more than a little that it had taken him so long to step up.

But her list of annoyances had only begun to be written. A rough voice called out with that curious Vercors lilt, "You never saw the Shining Knight kill his own soldiers, did you?"

Harsher, hollow-sounding accents answered it with, "And what did that do for him?" A bluster brewed between Reyn's soldiers and Armadale's knights. The Shining Knight's legend was a delicate point of pride to the sons and daughters of Vercors, his recent immolation the subject of tearful tavern ballads and brittle nationalism.

Captain Lowri did not so much as look toward the sources of the shouting this time. Instead, she raised an unequivocal eyebrow at Val. When she spoke, she did not let her voice betray any of the sympathy that as a commander herself, she must, Val thought, be feeling. "The commander is responsible for the outcome and the actions of her subordinates."

Even if neither Rebecca nor Christopher see themselves as subordinates.

Val closed her eyes, imagining the Elysian movement failing through unjust comparisons, a prematurely busted doll, and unapologetic wizards. It was not fair, it was unjust, it made her shackled frustration-monster roar, but she did not see what else she could have done. Could do.

I need help. As usual, no help was forthcoming. No help would come.

Halwyn could not fix this, would not fix it, did not have the ego or leadership ambitions for it. Neither Christopher nor Rebecca cared enough, if they cared at all. It was not *their* country being torn apart. The other wizards were no different. Except for Alain, but he was in Courant. The Deladieyr and Methueyn Knights were not here to help her either—doing things *their* way, as usual. The Shining Knight, even if he was only half the paragon the songs and legends made him out to be, was gone, transformed forever from solid flesh to smoke and a flash of sunlight.

Where are the leaders?

"*I'll* apologize to your eight," she said, opening her eyes. *There is no one else.* "If that will satisfy the honor of your soldiers. And I will admonish my wizards and ensure there is no repetition of their recklessness."

"We will still need the complaint recorded on paper," Reyn stated flatly. "Signed off."

Lowri nodded briskly and said, "In the unit notes, Sergeant, not as an official complaint."

"And my men don't want to be teleported back with the rest of the force."

Val could not believe this. The main body of the skolves was not far away. *Do they hate wizards so much?* "You want to be left out here?"

"We were talking about sending a messenger to the units in Villiers, weren't we?" Captain Lowri asked Val. "They could clear the pad, carry orders, and be picked up later."

They could be ambushed, killed, and eaten by skolves, probably moments after we leave. The Sergeant looked a reasonable man, spoke as one, dressed as one. His neat beard and erect posture would not have looked out of place in some units of Engevelen. But the request made little sense.

"Why, Sergeant Reyn?" It hurt her to add, "Engevelen is now little more than a few small islands of humanity surrounded by a rough sea of demons and monsters." This was not the dream she had for her country, let alone the Elysian force.

His answer did nothing to revive that failing dream.

CHAPTER 5
THE BEST

We have become an inferior people, looking upon and maintaining our ancestors' works—sometimes failing at even that unambitious task—inventing nothing, adding nothing, only getting worse with each iteration of our small, unimportant lives.

"Come on, Ave, they'll be waiting," Bro said. Escuyer Bryon Boldol spoke with a gentleness in inverse proportion to his ridiculous size. He stood over a foot-and-a-half taller than Ave and weighed easily three times what she did. Every pale muscle was ballooned as if some enthusiastic blacksmith had worked his bellows on them with a team of oxen. Even his neck had extra muscles. Ave had thought that traps had two peaks, but Bro showed that, taken to the absurd, the trapezius muscle had three heads, all of which strained as he lifted his end of their shared burden.

Ave took a forced breath and hefted her end of the long, heavy box they carried. It was far from light, even for Bro. And its twelve-foot length made it even more onerous, if not downright hazardous, to carry down the narrow alley. The dark cobbles of the shadowy lane looked wet, but it was an effect of polishing from foot traffic, not rain.

Summer was wearing on, and the rains, like time and events, had passed behind.

Too much has passed behind.

Bro led the way through the narrow cut between buildings, feet clapping on smooth stone, face hidden by shade. When he emerged from the alley, he had to take several steps onto the sun-bright roadway to make the corner.

"What do you think you're doing, young man? Get back on the sidewalk!" A cane- carrying, hunchbacked old man, meticulously dressed in a dark three-piece suit and bow tie, glared at Bro from the sidewalk. His wheezy voice barely carried back to Ave, stuck in the alley now that her partner had stopped. She had to squint to make out the shrunken, backlit fellow as he admonished Bro. It was like watching a penumbral mouse shaking a minuscule fist at a horse. "Are you trying to get yourself killed under a carriage?"

Ave saw Bro's great head turn slowly from side to side. After an interminably long moment, he drawled, "There is no traffic, sir."

Apparently, this was an impertinent answer. The dapper old gentleman raised his polished walking stick and waggled it at the giant. "Those are the rules, and they are there for a reason. You aren't in Armadale anymore. We do things properly here."

In Engevelen, we do things properly. Even if they are wrong.

"Sir," Bo said mildly, "are you aware there's a war on?"

The old man thrust his stick at Bro but connected with the box instead. His well-polished cane made only a dull thud against the thick timber, but he gathered himself carefully, aimed higher and hit Bro square in the chest with his second attempt.

"And are you fighting it right now?" he shouted.

Another poke. Bro did not move. He stood immobile while the old gentleman continued to chastise him with his cane. Ave could not see Bro's face. The sound of the walking stick hitting his chest was not much different from the noise it had made hitting the wooden box.

"Are you tending the fields?" Poke.

"Are you picking up rubble over by the north tower?" Poke.

"Is that box going to win the war?" Poke.

"Keep our streets clean, miscreant!" Poke. Poke.

A somewhat scruffy eight in the livery of Vercors quick-timed up the middle of the street, their heads turning toward Bro and the old man as they approached. Their leader, a straight-backed man with a neatly trimmed mustache and goatee, threw up a salute, though it was unclear to whom. As the jingling crew went past, the old man stopped poking at Bro and turned his body with some labor toward them. His neck appeared too stiff to rotate at all. "Stay off the roadway!" he shrilled at the eight.

They did not answer, though Ave swore she saw a flash of teeth, a hint of a smile in the uneven rays of sun and shadow. "Verminous sleeveens," the bow-tied belligerent grumbled to himself, lurching in their direction, leaving Ave and Bro to their labors. Bro wasted no time edging farther out into the street now that the old man had found new targets, and Val was able to emerge into the light of the wide thoroughfare at last.

We are so strange, we people. Ave turned her eyes and mind from the retreating form of the strange, not-so-strange old man to the great stone church of the Steel Castle that they now approached, and finally back to Bro. For all the big man's awesome physical dimensions, whenever Ave looked upon him, she mostly felt pity. His most obvious feature was not his towering height, staggering weight, or appalling muscles, it was his palsied face. The right side was a contracted, twitching spider web of flesh. The eye on that side squinted perpetually, and the upper lip curled weirdly, exposing his canine. A little bit of drool always hung off that tooth. When the big oaf attempted a smile, as he was doing now, the effect was more grotesque than cheerful, more threatening than friendly, a tragic rather than a comic mask. Bro's face told the downside of too much surety, too much faith and will.

Virtues, sometimes, are not enough.

"I sure told *him*," he grinned as they resumed their march.

"Oh yes," Ave replied, "stunning wordplay." She wondered what

Bro might have told the old man if he were capable of witty repartee. There was indeed a war on, but the box, in truth, contained nothing of any practical use in that war. Its contents were a symbol, not a weapon. Would this burden she and Bro had come so far with, or the ceremony it was destined for, prove worth the effort or make the slightest difference? A year and a half ago, Ave would have unequivocally said yes, would have punished anyone who even asked that question, but since then she had carried the weight too many times to no good purpose. Now, finally, her faith was wavering. She had begun to suspect that it might all mean . . . nothing

It's a calendar. Like a menhir of old, but signifying a different kind of change in a new sort of season.

Or not.

The box suddenly felt immensely heavier.

It's the weight of these thoughts.

Ave stumbled and dropped her end. It hit the ground with a tremendous clatter, and the wood split from the corners, revealing part of the crossbar of a great, silvery hilt. "Daughter of Nimrheal!" she swore, looking down at the ruined joints.

"Huh," said Bro as he lowered his end of the spilt box with incongruous care. "Well, don't worry, Escuyer Vanier, it'll take more than a little fall to break the Methueyn Treaty!"

They carried on, the twelve-foot-long, five-hundred-pound sword crossways over Bro's monumental shoulders, Ave dejectedly leading the way, feeling more useless than ever. Bro lumbered even more carefully now, inhaling and exhaling with deep, rasping breaths.

Clearing the way—even against the compulsive behavior of old gentlemen and their pointless proprieties—for Bro and his wide load, Ave could not forget the first words she had seen on the great metal blade. "You are Free."

If we are free, why do we carry this burden from ceremony to ceremony? And why does it have no discernible effect? Why is the same thing happening again and again?

"Ave!" boomed the god-powerful yet girlish voice. The stone floor shook as Yeyncie Greene, arguably the most famous and certainly the most diminutive Sir Heydron in history, bounded toward Ave and Bro. As she slid to a stop, Ave thought that the stone of the floor might shatter. "You made it! I thought I was going to have to send Michael out to rescue you." Yeyncie beamed with the guileless, enthusiastic, dirt-smeared face of an eleven-year-old girl, all openness and youthful welcome. Ave felt closed and ancient in comparison.

Ave could see the dirt-darkened Methueyn Knight, Sir Urien, over Yeyncie's head. He was as tall as Yeyncie was short, the gold band across his forehead reflecting light from one of the apses. She did not see Sir Michael, and still holding her end of the ever-heavier Methueyn Treaty, she shifted her head to look past Yeyncie and Urien for the third knight. There had to be a third Methueyn Knight to approve and witness the Rising of a new Deladieyr. It was an age-old tradition, strictly practiced ever since the Cannibal Knight, Sir Seygis, had almost destroyed the order. They needed to be sure no heretic could ever Rise again. But all Ave's shuffling and neck craning did was reveal the presence of Sir Camden, a former candidate and peer of hers who had Risen to the ranks of the Deladieyr Knights only a few weeks ago.

So where is Sir Michael?

"And you brought the big man with you!" Yeyncie continued, still smiling broadly. "When are you going to stop carrying that sword and start hanging off it, Bro?"

Bro's broken face could form nothing that strangers would recognize as a smile, but Ave knew that the crinkled, spasming mess of an expression that he produced for Yeyncie was the best he could do. Best or not, that horrific expression would scare most children, though it only seemed to make this child-sized being happier. "As soon as I am ready, Yeyncie," he replied gently.

Yeyncie and Bro had been candidates together, years in the past, right after Yeyncie had killed her raging father by thrusting him through a stone wall. It was not long after that fateful time when Nehring had brought the demons over and the Methueyn Knights had declared war on him. The nine-year old girl had quickly Risen and almost as quickly answered the voice and crossed the Methueyn Bridge. Bro had not Risen. He had not gone anywhere, then or since, achieved little on earth or Elysium besides ruining his face, but he could still call Sir Heydron by her original name. Ave thought there must be something to be learned from that, looking at the contrast between the child-like, heaven-strong Methueyn Knight and the ruined giant that was Escuyer Bryon Boldol.

Whatever it is, I don't get it.

"Bro is of great help right where he is," Ave said instead of uttering thoughts that repulsed even herself. If the sword got any heavier, he was going to have to carry it himself. "But where is Sir Michael?"

Sir Camden stepped around both Yeyncie and Sir Urien and nodded his head fractionally toward Ave and Bro. "I am here."

It's too soon! He just Rose. It was like a punch in the eye, leaving an afterimage of the last Sir Michael that Ave had known before this new one who had been her peer just weeks ago. Ave was no wizard. She had no third eye, window, gate—or whatever the squabbling sorcerers were calling it—that she could open to see the knight's connection to the Empyreal Sky. She could not directly apprehend that the connection was infinitely stronger now, that a new power shone from the person who had formerly been Sir Camden. She did not wish to look into his eyes and see a different being inhabiting his soul.

~

"I LIKED THAT OLD GENTLEMAN," Bro declared. He was no longer breathing so hard, for Ave had taken up the hilt and preceded him with her end of the Methueyn Treaty as they attempted to navigate the narrow, twisting back stairs of the Steel Castle. "You need to lift your end higher," he advised.

"No," Ave countered. "It's as high as my arms can reach. You need to lower yours." Standing on her toes did not do it. The sword was jammed on a turn of the stairs. "What was there to like about that snob?"

"Grit. Sand. Spice. Unfriendly, yes, but what ruled him still ruled him. He still had ... salt. And a bow tie." The sword shifted as he lowered it to the base of a step. "Has that got it?"

The enormous blade was stuck at the middle. "This thing is too damned long. Why didn't she let us take it up the hanging bridge, for knights' sake? That would have been easy." Ave struggled to turn the hilt so its crossbar was not in the way. "Grit, sand, salt, spice for your food, dirt on your boots, tie around your neck, or just plain stubbornness in the street. I didn't see any good that old fool was doing anyone."

Bro just laughed. "When did you become so sour, Ave?"

Ave had an idea about that. *I've been getting sour since eleven Risings ago.* She knew that Bro had seen more than ten times that many. And there was his ruined face. *How is it that he isn't as sour as me? No, he isn't sour at* all. Wincing with self-loathing, Ave stopped herself. Taking a breath she switched to honesty and said, "That is just how my people are, Bro. We are rigid and orderly." She sighed, "We hide from the truth with an absurd correctness."

"Don't be so hard on yourself, Ave."

The cramped, twisting stone stairwell had the trick of making Bro's words sound soft and for a moment not so deep. "Try pushing it now, Bro," she said instead of responding to the sympathy in that voice. The sword scraped the inside wall of the stair as it sprung free, then arrested itself again when the point hit the next step. "Knights damn it!" she cursed, completing her turn from honesty back to frustration. "Why are we going up this stupid back way in the first place?"

Bro shifted the point of the sword and they scraped their way a little higher, though Ave had to keep turning the hilt to make it around each tight turn. The sword stuck again, though she could not see on what. "You still with me, Bro?"

"Heh," he grunted, and the sword moved again. "I am here for you,

Aveline." The sword came loose with a scraping sound. It stuck again briefly, but then he seemed to figure something out, and they started making more consistent progress upward. A moment later, Bro spoke again.

"Yeyncie saw your face is why. She always has something in mind with her little . . . quirks."

Ave had to concentrate on keeping the hilt of the heavy sword turned just right so the oversized guards would not catch again, but she could not let this go.

"My *face*? What is wro—you think this is some kind of a joke?" As Sir Heydron, Yeyncie Greene was a frighteningly powerful figure, but she was still in some ways the little girl that Bro, though only Bro, called Yeyncie. And little girls like to play.

But if her perverse choice of a route to the landing was a game, what exactly was its object? And who was winning?

Ave glimpsed sunlight just a turn above them. The landing could not be much farther.

"Not a joke," Bro declared as they rounded the stairs one final time and emerged onto the landing. It was a broad, circular vault giving onto a heart-stopping, all-encompassing view of the city far below. The view that greeted the two astonished escuyers, was interrupted only by the vault's narrow supporting beams and a steepled roof thirty feet above their heads. At the center of the vault, a six-foot-wide central cavity was bisected by a rounded metal beam and protected by a chest-high wall. Ave set her end of the Methueyn Treaty carefully down and looked over the wall into the yawning abyss. Ninety feet or more below its center was the edge of the hanging bridge. A fist-thick rope ran through an iron ring that was attached to the metal beam.

Ave stepped back from the view into the depth of the Steel Castle and turned to look back out on the city. The south side of the town of Aurillon was pristine. Orderly stone houses, well-planned streets, elegant, soaring aqueducts. It looked exactly like what that snobby old gent would call a "proper" Engevelen city, she thought, smiling to herself. The north told a very different story. The great north tower was gone, its huge cut stones blown like melting wax from a candle in a great wind. A huge, long swath of burnt grass formed a blackened line like an arrow from the countryside to that ruined fortification. Soldiers and laborers swarmed the area, but they were tiny compared to the destruction they fought. Ave strained her eyes to make out what lay farther off. A scattering of lonely, smaller stone towers rose here and there, off into infinity.

Engevelen was a nation of towers, those symbols of permanence its people had always needed. The country was old beyond reckoning, and they had had time to build their citadels, their symbols of order and achievement. She knew that about forty-five miles to the southeast was the great city of Courant, home to the Harbinger, the library, and the great school of statics, to the country's most ornate fortifications and public buildings and its grandest hugel gardens. To the west, perhaps sixty or sixty-five miles away was the ancient city of Villiers. High as the vault was, Ave could see neither city from her vantage point, but she knew they were there. But for how much longer? That was the question.

The tower is the lesson.

When Skoll—or was it Hati?—shot across the fields, faster than a burning missile, larger than any man, there had only been time to cry out before the impact. The demon had, improbably, been on fire, but when it hit the tower, it was the stones that exploded. Two of her fellow squires had disappeared under rocks the size of carts. It had happened so quickly that even Ave's keen eyes barely registered their obliteration. It had been a lesson. And going up these stairs was a lesson. Yeyncie had sent her and Bro up this cramped, nearly impossible route because she had wanted Ave to recall those memories.

But to what end?

There had been nothing Ave or Bro could do about the demon. It had simply come too fast. And after destroying the tower, after blotting out the lives of her two friends and unnumbered others she did not know, it had left just as quickly for reasons only it understood. Or perhaps for no reason at all.

During Ave's ruminations, Bro had said nothing. He had waited patiently, looking out on the city, content with his own thoughts. Finally, Ave said what she had been thinking earlier, the thing that Yeyncie must have seen on her face, the unuttered feeling that had led to this lesson, to their frustrating, ridiculous trip up a too-narrow stone staircase with a too-long, too-heavy giant sword. "Michael's dead."

"Michael cannot die. You know that."

"And you know what I mean. The *man* died. A new man joined the angel. He will probably die soon too."

"Probably."

"I didn't see his sword."

"He had a sword."

"But not *the* sword. We've lost another one." The Methueyn Knight Sir Michael was the Angel of War. He always carried a great two-handed sword, a Methueyn class weapon, much heavier and stronger than any standard-issue sword. Something that could not break even when swung with supernal strength. The old Michael had such a weapon. It had been recovered from the body of the previous Michael, and the Michael before that, and the one before that. But this Michael had what looked like normal steel to Ave's eyes. Big, yes, near-indestructible, no.

"Looks that way."

"We aren't winning, are we, Bro?"

"Not yet, Ave." She saw the shadow of his massive hand move toward her, then retreat. "You have yet to Rise and save us all."

Ave whirled on Bro and punched him hard in the chest. "Be serious, idiot!"

Bro did not react to the blow. His enormous chest felt like a stone wall. Ave's fist was the only thing that hurt. She shook her hand to distract from the pain.

Bro smiled at her. "I am serious, Ave," he said gently. "It will be you."

The words made Ave dizzy, nearly made her stumble to the little wall and the yawning space beyond. Nearly made her cry. She knew she was not as good as those who had gone before, was, to put it simply, not good enough. Being reminded of the tower's destruction and her helplessness then, had only made this clearer than ever to her. Bro's prophecy was ludicrous. It was kind of him, but it was a fantasy, a childish dream.

"Don't make me hit you again," Ave said. If Bro's prediction was a pipe dream, her own forebodings—prompted by seeing the new Michael as much as by her memory of the tower—seemed only too real. She considered the rope once more and how, very soon, the beautiful and much-loved Escuyer Revenberge would hang from one end of it. She and Bro would have to pull the other end of the rope all the way up to the cupola and tie the hilt of the Treaty to it. "You know," she mused, "I think we could have simply attached this sword to the rope on the ground. Don't tell her I said this, but our Sir Heydron is kind of mean."

~

Ave arrived late to the ceremony, but for good reason. Repeated often enough and to as little apparent purpose, even watching an angel Rise became mundane. It was a sad, low thing to see the awesomeness of Elysium on earth reach such a point, to think of it simply as a woman being hung by a five-hundred-pound sword. Ave scanned the room, first taking in the central transcendent spectacle of the hanging, next the three Methueyn Knights who stood close—almost under the hanging form of plate-armored Revenberge—and briefly to her fellow hopefuls who stood outside that inner circle. They did not compare well to the hanging, suffering Sir Revenberge who drew Ave's eyes back to the spectacle of another Rising. Even with a rope around her neck and a five-hundred-pound sword pulling the noose tight, she was glorious. Her eyes were open, hugely wide, round, and gazing heavenward into the light as she passed through some inner trauma and connected with the deepest interior expression of herself. The weight of that perfect connection was palpable. It made the rope creak, the sword point leave the earth, made the air feel at once heavy and effervescent. It was truth—clean, complete, unobstructed, barely possible in a human being—a moment of mindful unity that was its own infinite yet intimate miracle. Revenberge filled her own cup, was her own woman, and according to this ceremony, would one day connect with an angel. Ave's skin should have broken out in goosebumps, but she had seen Revenberge's glory before, touched heaven through her. To Ave, Revenberge had already been made perfect and no rite could make her more sublime. Even so, Ave's eyes should have been fixed on the spectacle, but they had seen Risings before and were already sliding from heaven back to earth and her earthbound peers.

As Deladieyr Knight candidates, Ave's peers were not the *best* of what was left. They were *all* that was left. Everyone else who *could* had already Risen. Most of those had then crossed the Bifrost to replace the Methueyn Knights killed battling Nehring Ardgour and his twin demons or had themselves been slaughtered in battle. Or had simply aged out, given up, or disappeared.

Lost their belief in clean, complete, unobstructed truths.

Ave thought it likely that Sir Revenberge would be the last of the candidates to try the Rising. The last who could live through having a noose tied around the neck and then being hoisted by the weight of the great sword known as the Methueyn Treaty. Ave knew deep in her bones that her own faith, her surety, her sense of purpose and single-mindedness, would not be enough to equal the weight of that enormous blade. Such grace, such soul magic, as she thought of it, was not hers. And most certainly not her remaining peers' either.

What a bunch of misfits.

They were not the best of the best or the best of what was left, and Ave mightily wished that they really were not *all* of what was left. When the Methueyn Knights had declared war on Nehring Ardgour, all of them, and the Deladieyr Knights and all their knight candidates from all over the world, had been called to the fight. It was a sight not seen in hundreds of years, perhaps never. They had filled up the halls of their faith, and the sight of their host had been astounding. Citizens had wept at the sight. Wizards had proclaimed that heaven had come to earth, that the empyreal sky crackled with the power of their connection. The ground had trembled at their steps. Nehring Ardgour and his demons would be crushed like hollow eggs on hard rocks.

But the miracle did not happen. And now we are reduced to these few. These dregs.

This realization completed the ruination of the moment. Ave looked from the beautiful, the heavenly Revenberge, who floated downward now, her feet approaching the ground toward her peers, who looked as if they might at any moment start rolling around *on* the ground. Her despair made her sick to her stomach—she knew she was being uncharitable and cynical—but she could not stop. There was a poisonous truth here, and an even more bitter lie.

Bro she knew best. He had been there from the start and had never shown the slightest inclination—or ability—to leave. He flexed his palsied face at her in a broken image of hope and whispered, “Ave, now it can truly be a Rising.” Ave had mourned his ruined example often. He might weight the rope with a horse’s share of muscle, but he proved that heart alone could not guarantee entry to the gates of Elysium.

Escuyer Acklyn looked an unalloyed hero in his oil-dark chain mail. He was a tall, sandy-haired lad with rake-wide shoulders and a spare, narrow waist. He said something encouraging to Revenberge, but it was a whisper, lost in the vaulting height of the Steel Castle. And when he turned from watching Revenberge to wave at Ave, she saw that the middle finger of his left hand was grossly crooked, and his gaze flickered away from her. She had seen that look of fear before. It showed up when he thought no one was looking, right before leaving on a patrol or before meeting with a Deladieyr or Methueyn Knight. He could barely look at Ave and sometimes seemed to shy away from his own reflection. It was like an absence, and that absent look on his face was like a quarter step backward, an unconscious vacancy from the present, from action and initiative, from life. Ack might as well have been an old man struggling to breathe or to process the present, because the fear kept him from really being there. He was never going to put a fist-thick rope around his neck. Ave knew that because she also was never going to hang, though her reason had less to do with fear and more to do with simple self-knowledge. *I may doubt myself, but he is afraid, even, of his own doubt.*

Escuyer Soukhmanthath was eating in a place where no one ate. "Well done, Rev, well done," she said lazily with a mouth full of corned-beef sandwich. Some of it was on her mail. A big piece of the mustard-lubricated, pinkish meat fell from her flapping lips and hit the floor with a heavy splat. Souk thoughtlessly picked up the limp wad with her left hand and shoved it into her mouth, a line of buttery mustard trailing onto her ample chest. Souk had been unshakably laid back since the moment she arrived among them. Not even another Ceremony of Rising seemed to get a rise out of her. She would never float on air.

"It is good that you are here, Aveline," declared Catherine Kattar. "She Rises free of earth, floating on the winds of the Idea." Kat was every bit the opposite of both Souk and Ack. Where Souk was slovenly, Kat was trim, precise, and neat. Where Ack was nervous, Kat was intrepid. Where he shied from the present, she invaded it. Her eyes were narrow, as were all those from Neahon across the sea, and now they were raised up, gazing at Revenberge, but her hand was on the hilt of her Neahon sword, ready. Kat was a fantastically skilled athlete who was every bit as determined as Bro had supposedly been when he broke his face trying too hard. And she was a believer. For Kat, the Ceremony of Rising never grew old. But she was even more doomed than all the rest, thought Ave, for Ave had never seen her weight the floor. She had no, or very little, inherent Empyreal strength despite her remarkable physical ability and internal motivation.

Ave found herself looking for Escuyers Woofter and Seyjara, then winced, remembering. They were gone. Blown away when the north tower had been knocked down. They at least had been given a memorial with the other soldiers killed in the cataclysm. With the disappearance of the Renet and the eight escuyers embedded there, the once numerous cohort of Deladieyr candidates were down to five.

It'll be you next. Bro had said this in the cupola, but Ave knew better. It would be none of them, except in failure or death.

*E*VERYONE THINKS THIS IS A CELEBRATION.

After congratulating Sir Revenberge and planting one electric kiss on her neck, Ave climbed the narrow staircase once more, this time alone. She looked out across the city to the broken tower. The swath of blackened grass was a sign, an arrow pointing to the future, to ruin. *We have gone so far out on the ledge that we don't know how to turn back.*

Ave was aware that her empyreal strength had been waning for some time. Ever since she first realized what was happening around her. Since she began to think too much. She had learned that the death of a Methueyn Knight was rarely singular. She had learned there were few singular events in nature. There had been eleven Risings while she stood as knight candidate. And for each Rising, there had been another side of the accounting ledger, a death. There would be more losses among the knights, just as that single fallen tower would soon be joined by others. The day had come, Ave realized, when there would soon be no more left to Rise, no one left to die. The best had all been spent.

Redoubt Empyrean for this miraculous Rising. But it is also a funeral. For our country. Love has Risen high, but now my love is doomed to die.

CHAPTER 6

THROUGH A MIRROR, TWISTED

"The emotions of a soldier cannot be predicted in battle. They are volatile and subject to catastrophic change. Anyone can turn coward in a fight."
Major Peridot to Davignon, outside Charney

"Do you know why we cannot predict the future, Lieutenant Davignon?"

Farrah Harbinger's sharp, green eyes held Dav's full attention, as they always did. There was always a sense of danger when the old lady spoke, for she never spoke without a reason, and her reasons were always serious. *Mysterious too. Her reasons are as great a riddle as Heraldry seems to be.* Much as Dav wished he were back in the field with the Renet—wherever they were, alive or dead—being here with Farah was galvanizing. She was the most engaging personality he had ever met. Even more so than Peridot. And even if she kept pushing him to the center of everyone's attention, the position he disliked most in the world.

They had moved back into Harbinger Hall, into the main library.

Farrah was perched on a large, comfortable chair—another throne—but she was the only one who sat. Her attendants stood all around the vast, beautiful, book-lined space. Tables had been removed, hot water had been rolled into position in huge copper tubs, each the length of a tall man, and a curious mirror-like apparatus on a swinging arm had been positioned just a few paces from the great lady. Strangely, she had asked Dav to kneel in front of her, closest of all.

"Answer the question, Lieutenant," demanded Lady Sylvie. She at least was not mysterious. An old hawk who probably thought this callow young soldier did not belong in such close proximity to the great Harbinger Wizard. She *definitely* thought he should not be closer to Farah Harbinger than herself.

"Sorry, I thought the question was rhetorical," Dav replied. "I am no wizard." He consciously kept his eyes away from his left hand. "And certainly no futurist."

The Harbinger laughed, but it was the controlled laughter of a person who knew the real joke, whatever that might be. The laughter of the wise. It made Dav feel at once both small and singled out, both ignorant and curious. But mostly it made him feel a deep, underlying caution. Nothing here was safe.

"Oh, I think you know something about it, Lieutenant," the Harbinger said, not quite, but almost, purring. "Did you not predict the future at Charney?"

"I guessed what needed to be done. I made a necessary tactical decision. That is all." *All I will admit to.* He remembered the twisted sign in the ruined city and what it had told him. He remembered the piercing truths he had uncovered.

"As I said, Davignon, you know something about it." A stab of cold fear pricked Dav's stomach. She had such a knowing expression on her face that he suspected she knew his secret.

"Well, I will tell you the answer that I believe you already know. Predicting the future is dangerous because we bring so much of our past with us. We cannot help it, young man. Our history informs us and anchors us, creates the pathways of the mind and drives our personality." She winked at him, easing the sharp, cold edge of fear and allowing him to breathe. "I think you know this. But the past does more than just affect our future actions, it also constrains the *questions* we can ask of the future. And if our questions are enslaved to our personal understanding of history, how can our heraldic predictions be anything but some creature, some repetition, of the past? How can we change the future or ourselves if it is always a past-bound version of ourselves that asks the questions? We are locked in by the u-shaped probabilities produced by our yesterdays, a bell chamber of history and thought." She paused then and nodded ever so slightly to him. "But, as I said, I believe you know something about this, Davignon. I believe you have a doom of your own that you wish to escape. Do you want to know how I will transcend this circular problem?"

Dav was spellbound. But still more than a little scared. "No," he replied. It was a both a lie and the truth. It was all he could say.

Farrah Harbinger leaned toward him. "Because *you* are different from *me*, Davignon. You shall set me free."

"Like an anchor!" exclaimed Alain from the crowd beyond Dav and the Harbinger. "Dav is to be your anchor. But the young soldier," he looked Dav up and down, "as heroic as he may be, the Lieutenant knows nothing of Heraldry. Please Farrah, let it be me."

"Yes, perhaps you should let Alain do it," said Barbara Bysshe, her eyes locked on Dav.

"*I* will do it, Lady Harbinger," said Sylvie. "Let me kneel at your feet, hold your hand, tether you to the present."

Farrah Harbinger gently pushed on Dav's chest. He stood and turned to the side so that the great lady could address her coterie. "Thank you for your offer, Alain. And yours, Lady Sylvie. But you have not understood my words."

"You don't want an anchor," said Dav. *I am here for a reason. Her reason.* He could no longer doubt it; she had said as much.

"You see, Sylvie," Harbinger said, eyebrow raised, "he understands already what you refuse to. I must be set free."

Lady Sylvie's face paled. "No."

Farrah ignored her. “The water is getting cold. We must make our future now. Captain Bysshe, roll in the whiteboard to its mark. Sergeant Proulx, draw the curtains. Alain, be ready with the lens.” She gestured to Dav. “Back where you were, Lieutenant. Your reason for being here is about to be fulfilled.”

Dav stepped closer to Farrah again, went down on one knee, and whispered to her, “I understand something of the concept ... the bell chamber ... that you wish to be free of. But I do not understand how I am to help you.”

She took his hand in hers. “Your written test, whose significance was understood by no one, showed that you are different from everyone here. Unique. There is something about you that I have never seen before.” She thrust her chin at the others. “Something *they* cannot understand. I think it can be made to help us. I will use *your* doom to break free from the confines of *my* past.”

She paused and watched him closely for a moment.

“But there is more to this than your ... peculiarity, Davignon. There is also your attitude. You have not been with me for years. You do not see and understand things as I do. You stand outside my bell chamber. You will be the lens by which I see my way through the locus.”

Her voice dropped to a whisper pitched only for Dav. “And while I am sure you like me well enough, young man, you do not love me.” She squeezed his hand. “You will let this go as far as it must. Swear to me that you will not let them stop me when I bare my face to entropy.”

Dav swallowed hard and looked down. He was surprised to see that his hands were steady. Then he looked back up at Farah Harbinger and nodded his assent.

“Before I begin,” the Harbinger Wizard declared to the room, her green eyes hard and glittering “you need to know that Courant is about to be attacked. Imminently.” The words were the equivalent to dropping a glass vase onto a stone floor. Everyone froze in denial, that short delusional interval when, grasping at straws, the doomed imagine that time and entropy can be halted. Into this vacuum, the great lady added, "Sergeant Proulx, take those letters I gave you and see them delivered at once to the military authorities I indicated. Then return here with the rest of my personal guard." After Proulx had gathered up the bundle of papers and departed, Farrah continued. "I don't know if we will repulse this new attack, but you each will have to act, and quickly, the moment I finish. Do as I have instructed without question, for I may no longer be in a position to address your concerns."

She gestured to Alain. "Bring the lens to my right eye and position the hood and lantern." Alain took hold of the strange apparatus. Two lenses were encased in a transparent telescope and held by an articulated device—a kind of arm. A secondary arm held a lantern of a design that Dav had never seen before. When Alain moved the lens close to Farah's eye, Dav scootched out of the way.

"No. Stay where you are, Davignon," Farrah Harbinger ordered him. "There is room for you to look directly into my left eye despite the ocular device."

From behind him, Dav heard a sharp intake of breath from Barbara at the same time that Lady Sylvie said, "What? No one can look directly into your eye during a Far Heraldry. The medusa effect will undo him."

"Trust. Me." Farrah ordered. "The lieutenant needs to see it this way."

I do? Medusa? He remembered in his childhood hearing the old legend of the woman—Medusa—whose eyes showed heaven. And how those forbidden images turned anyone who gazed at them into stone. Dav wanted both to run and to stay. He was in a position of ignorance, entirely lacking in initiative. Being a soldier in the field was similar, but simpler and far less strange. But like a soldier in the field, he would follow orders—he could exert at least that much control—so he remained still as Alain positioned the lantern and struggled to fit a heavy leather hood around Farrah's head and the lens.

"You are going to have to get inside the hood, Lieutenant," he said after a few moments of tinkering. "It was not cut right for this ... exercise."

Dav ducked under the hood and found his face only inches from the Harbinger's. The lens and the strange lantern were almost as close. The lantern's narrow aperture had been opened fully, and the light was bright under what was effectively a blackout curtain. He could see Farrah's left eye as clearly as if it were next to a bullseye lantern. Her right was pressed up to one end of the lens. When Dav shifted, honey-scented hair brushed his cheek. Her breath smelled subtly of parsley. He had not until then thought of Farrah Harbinger as a woman. She had been a figure of respect, an inscrutable wizard, a kind of queen, and of course his boss, but not really human. Here in the bag, her humanity was manifest and unavoidable. They were breathing the same air.

"What is about to happen?" he asked, partly out of simple curiosity, partly because it was so awkward being this close to her, partly from his fear of this ... medusa effect, and finally, partly because he was afraid for *her*. He wondered what his presence felt like to Farrah, knew his hair smelled nothing like honey, and tried to breathe through his nose, hoping this might make his breath smell better.

Suddenly, he felt his hands gripped tightly in hers, but the sensation seemed to come from some other world. "I am going to go into a deep heraldic trance, Davignon. When I achieve that state fully, you will see the images that I see." She squeezed his hands tighter. "They will be strange, twisted as well as inverted." Tighter again. "No one in the past has been able to bear witnessing them. The old medusa legend is just that, but it probably comes from the real experience of some individual in antiquity who had my gift and the unfortunate people that tried to view their Heraldry. I doubt that anyone turned to stone. That is a metaphor. What likely happened *then*— and would happen to almost anyone who looked unprotected through my eye *now*—is sudden, violent, incapacitating illness."

You want me to be brutally sick while we are together under this hood?

He did not say it, much as he wanted to. Farrah Harbinger had already asked to be trusted.

"You, however, will be fine," she said as if reading his mind. "And you will observe the locus better than anyone but me. As for the others, there is the lens, which acts to undo the inversion and other distortions. The lantern shines through the apparatus in such a way as to project a filtered version of the images from my right eye onto the whiteboard. Sylvie, Alain and the Captain will watch this and take notes. You will stay here with me and watch the raw images."

The strangeness and intimacy of the situation dissolved Dav's shyness, lubricating speech. "In this bag? Who would have predicted this?"

Dav now saw what an eye roll with one eye looked like from two inches away. "*I* did, of course," the oracle said, rounding out with words the irony that her ocular maneuver had already conveyed.

Dav persisted. "But what will *happen*?" A part of him knew he was emotionally compromised, more talkative and less guarded than usual, but he could not help revealing what was foremost in his mind. "Will you . . . die?"

"I do not know, Davignon. When I find the locus, I will attempt to break it in a way that favors humanity." He watched her eye refocus on him, serious and steady this time. "Whatever happens, you can make it worthwhile. Stay with me. Do what I tell you. More than anyone else here, you are a man of action. Act on what you see." She swallowed and, in a much louder voice, called out, "Quiet now, everyone."

Dav had watched people give way to sleep before. His sister, once, when she was ill. A lover, all but forgotten now except for the intimacy of that moment, of sleep coming on. Major Peridot as he carried her out of Charney. Her vulnerability was a gift, a kind of trust that instilled or strengthened feelings of protectiveness. Farrah Harbinger was an older woman, far more intelligent and infinitely wiser than he. She knew things about him, secrets known by no one else. They shared that knowledge, but the young man was not at all sure that the Harbinger Wizard was his friend. She wielded her mysterious knowledge for her own ends, whatever they were. Dav could not be sure that it was for his benefit at all that she had called him to her side and placed him there, literally cheek to cheek with her.

All these fears and misgivings fell away as Farrah's breathing slowed and her bright green eyes lost focus. Dav was transfixed, anchored by his position of trust. He felt an overwhelming protectiveness toward the woman who held his hands, shared his air, and who had slowly stepped away from his world of tangible experience into another that he did not understand. The Harbinger was entering a domain of single combat against fate. All Dav could do was bear witness. And hope she survived.

Over a count of no more than three seconds, Farrah's left eye transformed from its unfocused glaze to a brighter green than Dav had ever seen. *I have never seen green before. Not truly, not in all these hues.* The color spread beyond the iris, flooding her entire eye. From so close, it was like watching a green tide wash over the white sclera. The young man had to tell himself to breathe. Within two breaths, a structure began to appear in that green sea, within four breaths, images.

Out of that green eyescape, Dav saw Harbinger Hall as if from above, but changed, transformed somehow into discontinuities and right angles, rotated inward and around, and then twisting in a knot, turning, and then—abruptly—stabilizing right side around. He saw soldiers atop Courant's outer walls. They were strangely blurred ... gauzy. The image moved closer to them, and Dav realized that the gauziness was caused by some kind of vibration. The pictures in Farrah's eye came closer yet, until Dav could see only three soldiers, two women and a man. They were not vibrating—not exactly—they were, each of them, independent of the others, abruptly and discontinuously *changing*. Their positions, hand on hilt of sword or not, shading the sun or on their hips or by their sides or pointing, altered with each instant. Sometimes one of the women was replaced by a man and then, an instant later, she returned, though never quite the same. Dav was reminded of a stone hitting a pond and making a circular wavefront, except that here the effect was like a continuous rain of stones, the wavefronts overlapping, displacing one another, combining and recombining. Was each of the figures a source of infinite potential change, a shell of endless possibility? That *analogy*, as Alain Overbree might say, broke down just as continuously; the transformations of each figure, Dav saw, were subtly altered and constrained by the others' changes, minimized somehow by the proximity of whoever was nearest.

The image shuddered and changed again, zooming away from the walls and into the city. The sky grew darker. *Did the sun just jump ahead toward the horizon?*

It was the ruination he had seen a few hours earlier, the sight that had led to spilled tea and inner anguish, but not precisely the same. The Harbinger's eyes reflected a different vantage point, perhaps a place in the city where the destruction had only begun. Even so, it was horrific. Broken aqueducts, hugel mounds thrown up and scattered, towers buckled, rubble tossed across streets and smaller buildings, across numberless, half-buried corpses. The image juddered and froze for an instant, then ran backward. A titanic armored, humanlike figure —Skoll or Hati, Dav surmised—hurtled in reverse through the city, cloaked in a flickering blue-white fire that sucked up whatever the demon touched.

"This image is stable," declared Farrah, loudly, for the benefit of everyone outside the bag. "What it shows is therefore about to happen with—now—absolute certainty. I'm showing this to you for two reasons. You *must* act quickly once your roles are made clear. You must escape Courant City."

"And . . . the other reason?" It was Alain Overbree. He sounded as if he was gagging.

The images continued to unspool across Farrah Harbinger's eye. Now the demon shot through the hugel fields, sending crops, grass, logs, and compost careening through the air. A flash of the demon's giant face, snarling, covered in blood and half composted sewage, made Dav flinch against the leather hood. A tall man in golden armor carrying a long, massive spear raced past a mass of skolves, moving faster than even they did, far faster than a horse. His breastplate showed a broken sandal etching as he launched himself directly at the demon.

The image stopped and rotated sickeningly, moving from the hugel mounds to a higher vantage point. The whole city was contained in the image now, towers down, soldiers running in confusion, the demon charging and detonating a grain silo this time. An eerie flickering intruded into the moving scene, like an uncertainty, a stutter step in reality. Grain kernels flew in strange wave-like patterns, in sprays and then in segments of lines, pelting reality in wildly different, physics-defying trajectories. Dav saw a tower re-form and fall, then re-form again. The greenscape rotated once more, refocusing on a gray smudge of movement outside the city, almost on the horizon. As Dav strained to make it out, the smudge grew larger until a line—no, several lines—of skolves emerged in it, but shifting, vibrating, moving disturbingly, sickeningly. They were much more *uncertain*, he realized, than the images of the soldiers atop the wall that he had seen earlier. There were thousands of them, each a gray smudge of possibility, a kinetic image of potential violence.

"Oh no, no, bwaa-aa-aaggghh." Someone was vomiting outside the bag. Then someone else. Under the retching, Dav could hear labored breathing and whimpering from all sides.

"Are those skolves?" It was Lady Sylvie's voice, precise but tremulous. *Why isn't she sure?* The gray shapes of the skolves were flickering like lightning bugs in a dust storm, but Dav could easily tell what they were.

"Breathe through your mouth, Davignon," Farrah whispered, then raised her voice once more. "The second reason I am showing you this is to prepare you for the locus. It will be different. Less clear. *Far* less comfortable. Pay close attention now. The informational content will dwarf my ability to narrate. I must choose when and how to collapse the locus on the fly, and when I act, I must act quickly." Dav saw Farrah swallow, then clench her jaw.

"So stay with me," she ordered. The Harbinger lowered her voice to a whisper once again. "Stay with me, Lieutenant, your task will come last."

And do not vomit in this bag.

Her hands still held his. They felt cold and clammy. The air in the bag was warmer now, less honey and parsley, more sweat and fear. *The fear is mine.* It needed to be so. Farrah was in charge, the only one who could be so. Dav did not wish to think of her afraid. And yet she had repeated herself about being ready to act. The twisting, reverberating images unsettled Dav's stomach less than that uncharacteristic repetition.

"Push," the Harbinger whispered. Dav started, then realized she did not mean that word for him. The image collapsed into deep green blankness and lurchingly reasserted itself over the vast expanse of Engevelen City. An envoy, all in black, rode toward the fortress, escorted by the tall, golden-armored figure with a broken sandal etched on his breastplate that Dav had seen earlier. The envoy flickered, steadied, and was revealed as a woman. The scene dissolved and re-formed. Dav watched the envoy and the knight march into the castle to a congress of richly dressed nobles gathered there. The room boiled in argument, a chaos of shaking fists, pointing fingers, cascading wavefronts of hostile poses and gesticulations. A woman Dav recognized as Lady Christine Cressy, princess of Engevelen, stood forward in judgement. She raised a hand and ... the image exploded.

The room detonated into crazy violence, then reassembled into peaceful conversation, back to violence, then emptiness. Dav saw the envoy hanging by her neck from the palace watchtower, and in the next instant conversing amiably with a group of nobles.

"This is the near bound of the locus," asserted Farrah loudly. "We will cross momentarily."

Someone outside the leather hood vomited again. Alain's voice shook as he said, "It's—it's not so bad."

It abruptly got so bad.

Farrah's green eyes revealed the congress again, but this time the speed of the transformations was slower. The lords, ladies, and knights stood arguing with the envoy, with the princess, with each other. Time slowed further, and Dav could saw each figure flicker and vibrate, grow larger in amplitude and import than before, the scene more a fantail of possibility, like a deck of cards spread across a table. Time slowed again, moved backward, then forward to reveal what seemed to Dav not so much a knot as a fulcrum.

It is the princess.

Her stately figure reverberated brokenly between three states: a lady at peace, nodding acceptance to something, a scold flinging her arms in violent slashing motions, a cynic storming from the hall. All this Dav saw clearly. What happened next in each case, he could not. Each moment was like a singularity from which future prediction was, if not impossible, approaching absolute uncertainty. Each instant after the princess either accepted some decision, made some furious demand, or stalked intractably away, the coherence of the image evaporated. For several minutes, moments that felt like hours, all Dav saw was a wash of unimaginable colors. If there was a story in that unsettling play of light, it had been lost.

"I must cut and pare," Farrah groaned. Dav felt her hands cool further and heard a thumping sound from outside the hood. He heard something like the sound of a moth's wings in his ears, felt a heavy pressure on his head and a sharp, painful ache in his sinuses. He fought to keep his eyes open against the pressure and was glad of this as the spray of colors resolved into a visible narrative once more.

Visible, but not stable. Every flickering, fantail-of-images figure in the palace returned, but they had jumped their bounds. They were no longer a useless, painful jumble of impossible colors, but neither did they resolve into a cohesive scene. It was a phantasmagoria of stories that shot off in unconstrained directions, the actors unbound and oscillating wildly. They had lost their center, and the entire scene had become a stomach-churning jumble.

Armies vibrated across waving fields, thousands of skolves shot toward them in roiling masses, in arrow formations, in lines and as individuals, moving in a blur as if fired from great bows, streaking across time and space. Objects appeared and reappeared. Faces and figures strobed irregularly, fluttering across the Harbinger's eye like the wings of a poleaxed dove. Cities rose and fell. Disorder ruled. None of the scenes lasted more than an instant, forming and dissolving at a speed beyond reckoning, defying interpretation, incomprehensible.

A dark, amorphous figure appeared and held the stage for a moment. It was ill-defined but seemed to burn as if with black flames. It held a spear and stuttered across the insecure worlds within Farrah's green eye. *Nimrheal. That is Nimrheal!*

Seeing the storied demon brought Dav's mind back into focus and helped him keep up with the next train of images. A great wheel of stone in the sky, an aqueduct of colossal size, collapsed. A figure in shining armor blazed in the sunlight and was gone. An enormous sword hung from a bell in a ruined city. An old man spoke—no, sang—atop a ridge of rubble as a horde of skolves raced toward him. A huge jewel was thrown through the air and landed, bouncing, in the dirt. A column of townsfolk pulling carts of luggage was engulfed and slaughtered by a spear-shaped phalanx of skolves. Skoll, or Hati, pulled the head off a little girl dressed incongruously in plate armor. The knight with the sandal-etched breastplate stood in a lonely field, surrounded by skolves. Atop the wheel in the sky, a man dressed in black and gold raised an enormous greenstone torus at Nimrheal. The demon disappeared, then reappeared, was incinerated by a flash of lightning, reappeared, was blasted again, reappeared, was blasted again, reappeared once more and produced a flickering black spear with which it impaled the man in black and gold.

Alain's now shaking voice asked, "W-was that Nimrheal? A-and Nehring Ardgour?" He was answered only by more fatal images.

The greenstone torus fell from the wheel in the sky and shattered on the rocks far below. The awful battle ran backward in time, stopped, and restarted differently. Instead of solely involving Nimrheal and the man in black and gold, seven knights—one of them the man with the broken sandal on his breastplate—appeared and fought Skoll, Hati, and Nimrheal below the wheel in the sky. One by one, the knights were slaughtered. All except the smallest two, a little girl in plate armor and a tall pale woman holding a bundle under her arm. The tall woman raced up the stairs, leaving the little girl to face all three demons alone.

"There. That is *it*," exclaimed Farrah. Her hands clutched Dav's. "Now, where did *that* arise?"

The imagery walked backward, through armies in the field and skolves in towns to Engevelen City and the congress in the palace there. To the envoy, the argument, the finger pointing.

"This is the moment," Farrah declared, "and our last worst chance to win. Now we must pare it down further, pour more energy into it, thermodynamic and ... other." The pressure on Dav's skull increased. He felt percussive waves of hot and cold air blowing on him, roughly fluttering the heavy leather hood. None of this affected the Harbinger's voice as she continued speaking. "The woman in black is Marias Garragorah, who acts as the ambassador for Ardgour. Alain, you must go to this meeting and persuade the princess and the Methueyn Knights to do as the envoy asks."

"What does she ask?" Alain said weakly.

"To trust Nehring Ardgour." Dav could see capillaries in Farrah Harbinger's eye silently break as she spoke. The green image was streaked with tiny red threads. "Do this, Alain, and we change probability. We collapse the locus," she added with no hint of the trauma her eyes betrayed.

"I will."

"Well, thank the knights that is over," came Lady Sylvie's penetrating voice. Dav felt the relief as well, and nearly threw the leather hood away. The sight of capillaries bursting in Farrah's eye tugged at his roiling stomach.

"Bwaa-bwaaah. It's done?" heaved Barbara.

"It is *not*," replied the Harbinger. Her voice was steady, but she breathed unsteadily. The stifling air under the hood felt simultaneously hot and cold as the green of her eyes continued flooding red. "There is one thing more. The most important of all. This war has paved the way for the *new* demon I have warned you about. It is of an infinitely more powerful nature, a being of inexorable entropy and inescapable fate: the One True Devil. Nimrheal may kill inventors, and Skoll and Hati may destroy our cities, but this new devil will transform our world into the hell it arises from. You *must* stop it, Davignon."

A new barrage of images flashed across Farrah Harbinger's blood-blotched eye. Dav could not keep up this time. He knew that there was some grand narrative that held together the many tableaus he had watched play out in the wizard's eye, but he struggled more than ever now to keep up and found it impossible to retain any clear memory of what he was seeing. He felt blasts of burning and freezing air wash over him under the leather hood, but trending, he sensed, toward ever-increasing heat. Sweat dripped off his nose, but the Harbinger was shivering, and her hands felt icier than ever. "Where?" Farrah gasped, her eye now more red than green.

Dav wanted to tell the wizard—Farrah, the suffering woman whose eyes were bleeding—to stop, but he knew that this was not his role. She had said that he was not to stop her, nor to let the others stop her, no matter what happened. From what he could gather from the sounds outside the leather hood, none of Farrah Harbinger's coterie were in any shape to stop anything. They were disoriented, nauseated, enfeebled. Dav was in pain, pain that felt dangerously severe, but he was not sick, not physically—not badly, anyway—yet he felt like a coward watching the Harbinger destroy herself. It took all his courage to let her continue, but it nevertheless made him feel more craven than he had ever felt in his life.

Some of the images began to repeat, had been repeating, he realized, for some time. They were twisted, rotated, inside out now, but he recognized them. Dav saw the old man again, the massive sword, and the knight who shone, this time with a pale woman in equally bright armor. The pounding images were becoming blurry with blood. Then they changed again. It seemed as if Farrah was scrying from city to city now, places he did not recognize, though all with the architectural style of Engevelen.

Are these cities in Old Engevelen, the lost Engevelen north of our current border?

The Harbinger's body shook and convulsed, but she managed to grunt, "Th-there. G-go there, D-davignon."

The air in the leather hood stank.

"Where?" Dav asked. Now he did feel sick. He pushed down his rising nausea.

"H-here," Farrah gasped. He saw a city. It was broken and ruined like so many others in this Heraldry. At its center rose an enormous building with a lone, leaning tower. It stood in a body of water, a lake. A backward image shot across the flooded eye, showing an inverted maze of aqueducts and cisterns, then a map to a room and an inscription.

"W-w-w-w-we entombed it th-there-ere-ere-ere. Th-the-the wea-wea-weapon, weapon. The-th-the only thin-ing th-that c-c-c-can k-k-k-k-k-ill-ill-ill th-the devil."

"Where is that? What city is it?" Dav asked. There was no response. Farrah's eye had gone dark.

CHAPTER 7
THE HOUSE ON THE HILL

"It pains me to say that you look surprisingly good, Mick. Also, that doesn't look much like a sword." The words floated out of the stone walls just ahead, carried invisibly by some breeze, shrouded by the dusk.

Approaching the house on the hill was always a kind of entry into evening. Everything there, just about, was old. The walls where the road passed through were neck-high, man-deep stone, crumbly in places but not from whatever had hit the city. These were ruins from neglect, not the sudden life-changing violence that had rocked Villiers. Trouble had not made it this high or far back. They were so far away from the action that the old folks of the house could hardly have heard the sounds of the battle. Mick had slept through it. He was used to the sensation of sleeping away what remained of his long life. That was just the way it was for the folks who lived in the house on the hill. Eat, sleep, wake. Perhaps someone new missing. Every day the same. Napping like children but waking each time to a dimmer afternoon instead of a brighter one. And quiet. It was always quiet. People did not visit much. The attendants always spoke in low voices. The food was served barely warm, never hot.

At the wall, Mick was still far enough away to see the whole main building. The house had been designed as a fortress, and must have looked like one in its heyday. Not today. Today, it slumped. All that was left were the last broken remains of good rock. The big stone mansion had been left behind like the nest of a migratory bird that had flown south and never returned. The people interred there for their benefit were just as forgotten and eroded. Their shouts were not loud anymore, could not shake the halls of Elysium, wake the angels, or lead assaults on earthly ramparts. But there was no mistaking Doog's voice on the cool early evening air. The old man always sounded like his throat was half-closed. His words came at the pitch of crickets.

"I always look good. You don't need to say it." Mick *did* feel better, but perhaps it was just the friendly face. "And it's a dog," Mick replied. "Don't think it would be good in combat."

"Not half dead like that." Doog ambled out of the shadows he had been lurking in by the wall. *Hiding from Roland.* The old man did not move fast. He had grown markedly shorter and more stooped in the last month. He had not been eating much either and said his back hurt all the time. But Mick had the patience to let his friend make his slow way over to the wheelbarrow where Fenris rested on his furry stomach, snout just hanging off the front of the old cart. Mick had gotten the puppy some water at a fountain, but the toll of being stuck under the ruins of a house could not be washed away as easily as the blood and dirt that had matted his fur. Fenris' eyes rolled up as Doog put his hand out to him.

"Oh, he likes me," croaked Doog as he started roughly petting the dog's head and neck.

Fenris' eyes were now closed. "Guess he does," Mick said, something stinging his eyes.

"I thought you were getting us swords, Captain."

Mick and Doog turned their heads in time to see Louis stub his foot on something in the shadows. He hopped for a few seconds on his other foot, then toppled over. "Oh, Daughter of Nimrheal, that still fucking hurts. You would think after living this long, stubbing a toe wouldn't hurt so knights-damned bad. Who is the bastard who put that there? Hey! Is one of you two lazy sleeveens gonna help me up? I'm the victim of a booby trap. A deliberate trap. Someone put that rock there and waited until dark for it to git me."

Doog was shaking with mirth. "I'm petting the dog."

Mick lent Louis a hand, careful not to hurt him as he pulled him to his feet. Louis was missing all but two teeth on either side of his mouth. Mick could not see the gap, normally so comical, in the dark, but he could see the old man's still-sharp eyes as they took in the wheelbarrow and its furry occupant. "That doesn't look like no sword I ever swung." He frowned up at Mick, who towered over him. "Did you *forgit* what it was you were to do? Again?"

"No, I didn't forget," Mick said gently.

"How is it down there?" squawked Doog in his pinched voice, still petting Fenris who had not moved. "Is it as bad as Brigitte says?"

"Let me in there," insisted Louis, limping over to the wheelbarrow. "Oh, he's nice! Who'd you have to kill to git 'im?"

Mick considered carefully which question to answer first. "I didn't kill anyone. Fenris here was left abandoned in the rubble. I dug him out."

Louis' eyes caught some of the light from the house. "Well, you did one thing right." He petted the dog's bony ribs.

Mick looked at Doog. "It isn't good down there. I don't remember ever seeing anything like it."

Doog interjected, "With your memory, that's not saying much."

"It reminds me," said Louis, "of when some sheltered little kid says she's never seen anything so awesome in her life. When she's really not seen much of anything at all."

"Both of you?" Mick continued without waiting for an answer. "They're evacuating the city already. I saw the luggage and empty houses." He turned to Louis. "But I didn't see any dead bodies or fighting."

"Very funny, old man," Louis shot back. "I'm not all about the violence. Now, where are the swords? These damned rocks make for good traps, but I prefer naked metal."

"Please don't put naked and yourself in the same sentence," muttered Doog.

Mick ignored the repartee. It was nothing new. "I got them, but then I found Fenris and couldn't bring the blades and the hound at the same time."

"So where are the swords?"

"I hid them."

"Great! We'll go get them in the morning."

"Yup." *If I can just remember where I stashed them.*

Doog put his long arms around Fenris and said, "If we don't hide this rickety cart, we won't have nothing to get the swords with. Roland will make it disappear." He struggled to pick up the dog, who remained limp except that he rested his jaw on Doog's wrinkly arm.

"You're not doing it right," claimed Louis, pushing in and trying to take over.

"Leave off, I've got him!" retorted Doog. The two old men started to jostle each other, and Louis had to grab the bent lip of the wheelbarrow to keep from falling down again.

Mick came around the other side of the cart and took Fenris away from them both. The dog pushed his head into Mick's armpit. "I'll take him. You two hide the wheelbarrow."

"Well, at least we'll remember where we put it," chuckled Doog, grabbing at the handles. Louis made a play for control of the cart, but Doog hip-checked him.

Louis stumbled and almost toppled over again. Recovering his balance with ill grace, he said, "I know where we can hide it. There's a bramble on the other side of the wall. I found it a couple of days back."

"What, did you fall into it?"

Blah blah blah, blah-blah blah-blah . . .

Dwell in our peoples' thoughts and hearts?
And were the dreams of each angel
In Engevelen's temples carved?

THE SONG HAD NEVER REALLY LEFT Mick's head, but like the other things in there, it was poorly remembered and adrift of its anchor. Mick's voice sounded surprisingly on pitch instead of merely loud as it reverberated off the high stone ceilings. *Am I remembering more of the words?* It seemed so. It certainly felt right to be singing it as he entered the house with Fenris in his arms and Doog and Louis on his heels. Usually he felt depressed when he entered the house. It was different this time.

Roland appeared out of the soft yellow lantern light of a wide side-hallway. "Mick!" he shouted. He winced and lowered his voice. "Where have you been? We have two orderlies out searching the city for you." His eyes widened, "You brought a dog in here? Now? We are *leaving* tomorrow. What are you going to do with it then?"

Mick considered Roland carefully. The head orderly was a man of many questions, a big man too, though still a hand shorter than him, with a wide, oily forehead that always seemed to reflect the light. Roland always wore a formal white coat, buttoned right up to his neck. He took his job seriously. Mick considering ignoring the questions and just shouldering past him when Doog and Louis jumped in.

"You don't *own* us, Roland. We can come and go as we please," Doog said, just ahead of Louis, who piped up with "Better call your henchman back, then, before the skolves come and get them."

Doog did not wait for Roland to respond before adding, "You know Mick always comes back. Eventually. A smarter person would have held off on the goon patrol."

"Ha, that's right," Louis agreed. "Not good trim at all. I guess they're right, you just can't buy experience—"

"Or sell old age," finished Doog.

Mick had long been subject to the endless one-two patter of questions and insults that Doog and Louis excelled at. He seldom found he could keep up with them, but he almost always ended up smiling. He was smiling now. Roland was not. His dark face had turned pale, and a vein throbbed furiously on the left side of his shiny forehead.

"Get that dog out of here!" Roland reached one meaty hand for Fenris, who still sheltered deep in Mick's arms. Mick turned so Roland could not reach the dog and intercepted the man's grasping hand with one of his own. He squeezed Roland's wrist.

Roland gasped, shocked by the strength of the old man's grip. He tried to bring his other hand into the fray, but Mick squeezed the wrist harder, paralyzing him. The younger man stopped fighting and involuntarily leaned back, his knees buckling.

In a voice that echoed as loud as his song had, Mick said, "If you want to take Fenris away from us, you better go get all your little friends."

"You're just lucky we don't have our swords yet!" shouted Louis from behind him.

Roland's eyes had been pain-wide, but they narrowed in confusion at this. Mick released the man's wrist, and Roland took a step back, rubbing at his wrist as if to make sure it was still there. Three orderlies in buttoned-up white shirts—cheaper, less formal imitations of Roland's jacket—had crept up out of nowhere during the confrontation. Mick was aware of Louis and Doog coming up to stand on either side of him.

"Don't worry, Fenris," Doog said to the dog. "We won't abandon you."

"What's all the ruckus out here?" demanded Warley, a cane-carrying hunched-over old soldier with only one more tooth than Louis. "I can't sleep through the card game with all this shouting!"

"Hey, Warley," crowed Doog in his cricket voice.

"We're about to tune these idiots!" said Louis.

"*I'm* not an idiot," Warley retorted, shaking his cane at Louis. "*You're* the idiot." He turned around laboriously and stalked very slowly back down the hallway and out of sight. No one seemed inclined to move while the slow taps of his cane echoed along the hallway.

"Well, are we going to do this or what?" demanded Louis finally.

Mick saw Roland turn to make eye contact with the orderlies. Two of them gave him a silent head shake. Roland's jaw visibly clenched. "We can't have dogs running around in here, Mick. There's way too much going on right now."

"Ain't nothing happens 'round here but people disappear!" Doug shouted.

Roland flinched, opened his mouth, then closed it. "You know, I'm not—" He paused and looked down, his face bunching up furiously. "I give up," Roland suddenly declared. "There's food in the kitchen. Dog looks hungry."

~

MICK WAS SURPRISED to find that he had slept most of the night. His eyes opened before dawn, which was normal, but for once he had not tossed and turned all night, caught in a no-man's-land between true sleep and full wakefulness. His back did not ache either, and his head did not feel foggy. He was aware of his surroundings more than he could remember having been for a long time and sensed suddenly that eyes were upon him. He turned his head. Fenris stared at him from inches away. The dog had slept beside him on the narrow bed. As Mick gazed back at his bedmate, Fenris's tale began thumping against the mattress.

"Windows to a child's soul, Fenris. That's what your eyes are. Hungry?"

Fenris licked his face, which was fine, and did not bark, which was better. There would still be people sleeping. Mick put on his other pair of pants—the clean ones—and a belt and tunic and walked as softly as he could manage out of his small room. There was no door. Fenris followed. The dog had been doing better after more food and water. And attention. Once past Roland and his goons, everyone they passed in the house, at least those who still knew what was what, had wanted to pet the puppy.

The wide stone hallways of the house were mostly empty now. Few of its denizens slept well, and while some, like Mick, got up early, most took all the patience in the world's worth of time to get their pants on. What was there to get up for, after all? Mick had once seen Doog stare at his clothes for a quarter of an hour, eyes glazed over, body unmoving. That was morning for you if you lived long enough. Mick had come down from the fourth floor and had almost made it to the outdoor sitting room before he realized that the floor was cold. And understood that he only knew this because he had forgotten socks and shoes.

"Fenris, get me my shoes."

The dog sat down on his furry bum and looked up attentively at Mick. And did not get the shoes.

It was worth asking.

"Okay. Let's go. What's that?" Mick heard a sound coming from the water closet. The house had an enormous stone water tank on the roof. Once the work of pumping water up there was done, it would flow by gravity down to any of the big community bathrooms located on each floor. The sound was coming from one of these. It was like something scrambling. Mick walked back down the hallway, past the stairs he had just descended, across the wide, still unoccupied sitting room, and through the open door of the baths.

He smelled the ordure before his eyes could sort out what was happening. At first it looked as if the two old women were struggling with a pile of soiled pajamas. A rolling-chair lay on its side a few paces away, but another wave of the fouled air told him what had happened. He had seen it before, or things like it. "Eight Knights, let me help you." Mick crossed the room in a few bounds, Fenris close on his feet. "Carol, Lady Aurorette, it's okay."

Carol turned, having heard him first. Her thin, white hair was askew, and both her scrawny arms were wrapped around the pajama-clad figure of Valence. She was on her knees and in obvious dire straits. "Mick. Thank Heydron you're here. We can't get him up."

"It's okay," Mick said, one hand on her shoulder. Fenris pushed his way in and started sniffing Carol. "Let him go, Carol. I can manage."

"Oh. Mick?" Lady Aurorette had just became aware of Mick's presence. She had long, white hair framing the ebony face and green eyes of the old Engevelen aristocracy, a true lady. Mick could never understand why she had no visitors. "Sir Valence fell and can't get up," she reported unnecessarily.

"I can help him, Lady A. It's okay. Let him go gently now, and I'll take him."

"No one could hear us calling," Carol said. Mick did not wonder where the orderlies were. Despite three of them showing up last night to cause trouble for Fenris, he knew there were few enough of them and each with plenty to do. Calling for them in vain was, sadly, not a rare occurrence. The house on the hill was not filled with monsters—that might have been better, easier to be angry about and to fight—just neglect, erosion, and forgetfulness.

Lady Aurorette released Sir Valence and slumped on the floor. Fenris padded over to her. "Mick," whispered Valence, piercing gray eyes meeting his. "Good morning."

Sir Valence had once been Knight of Engevelen, secular champion of the princess, a fine horseman and soldier, a gentleman of honor and grace. He had also been an eloquent orator, a genuine philosopher. Now he sprawled on the floor in his own waste, barely able to speak. Another day in the house on the hill, the dreariest battlefield Mick had ever endured. He could not remember everything, but he was sure of that. "Always good to see a knight, especially in dark places," Mick said gravely.

"And dark times," Valence said in kind.

"Mick, could you help me? I can't upright my chair." Lady Aurorette could stand and walk—a little—but she could not push the heavy wheeled contraption off its side.

Once Mick had righted the chair, helped Aurorette into it, and escorted her and Carol out of the bathroom with promises that he and Fenris would visit later, he returned to Sir Valence. Other battlefields had required—he remembered in a place outside of mind, in his gut—forbearance and courage. They had been steeped in the stink of fear.

The terror had been like a frozen knife in the gut, people had said. Aggression had been crucial, of course, but discipline also, to balance right action. He could not remember the details of those days, just the impressions of emotions, the fossilized remains of feelings. But he knew it had taken a strength from heaven to get through those fights. *This battle is no different, no easier. It requires a different courage, but courage just the same.*

Mick crouched down beside the old knight. "Mick," Valence said with infinite dignity. "Better not touch me. I have shat myself."

No one is strong all the time. Valence had been, once. Still was in ways that mattered. Few could lose control of their sphincter and maintain their dignity at the same time. Lady Aurorette and Carol were both too weak to pick him up. *They knew that they were too weak.* And yet they had tried to help, and in helping, held off the humiliation that time had visited upon all of them. Too weak to help Valence, but strong enough to try despite knowing their weakness.

Mick got his arms under Valence, picked him up easily, and carried him to the big tub. Fenris followed close on his heels "I know, old boy. It happens. Let's get you in proper trim now."

"Good morning, Mick. How are you? How is your dog?" Brigitte Landry's voice was light and sweet. She wore a long yellow dress and uncomfortable-looking open-toed shoes. Her bright blue eyes shone from her ebony face and its frame of dark, curly hair. Fenris helped Mick decide which question to answer first by uncurling from around his feet and walking over to sniff the manager of the house on the hill. Brigitte smiled and, knees pressed tightly together, crouched to pet him.

"We are both doing well."

"Yes," Brigitte agreed. "You seem better to me than you have in a long time. Does this surprise you?"

"I don't think about it."

She stood up from petting the dog and took a seat on the other side of the table. "What do you think is going to happen with Fenris when we leave tomorrow?"

The move had already moved another day into the future. "We aren't going to leave tomorrow." Mick was certain of that. It would be delayed again. No one else was there on the third-floor deck. When he turned his head, he could see down the hill. A few wagons were already in motion far below, but they were not being pulled up to the house; they were heading out of town. *Leaving in the early morning, meaning to get as far away as they can before nightfall.*

Brigitte was not watching the town being evacuated; she was watching Mick. "Some of the wagons have already arrived," she said, never taking her eyes off him. "We have already started packing."

"Four wagons. That won't barely start it." He could see she was thinking about interrupting him, but he kept talking. There were issues to resolve. "Wherever we are is where Fenris will be."

"No one will take your dog, Mick," she said, briefly laying a hand on his hairy arm.

"Roland wanted to."

"Roland didn't understand." Brigitte's tones were apologetic now, but she still watched her subject carefully. "You scared him, you know. You scared all of us. It isn't safe out there now. The skolves have attacked Villiers twice, and it was dark outside. He was feeling overwhelmed."

"Roland's need for control doesn't need to make slaves of me or my friends."

Brigitte chuckled at this. "You *are* sharp today, Mick. There *are* four wagons, and Roland's fear *is* driving his behavior." She leaned forward and whispered, "Do you remember your name?"

"No" It was Mick, but also it was not. He knew that, but he did not know what it meant or why the forgetting of it was such a loss.

Brigitte seemed to think for a long moment. She had brought a small notebook with her. She opened it and read a line or two before returning her attention to him. "Well, let's try a test, shall we?" When he did not object or get up and leave, she started. "Here are ten words. I'll ask you to recite them for me later." She read the words out slowly and distinctly, pausing carefully between each one. "Purple, bridge, horse, eight, apples, Elysium, rhubarb, harbinger, protect, idea. Okay?"

"Okay." He turned in his seat to look at the sky. It was bright now. The morning was warming up. "When are the rest of the wagons coming?"

"Any time, Mick. They should have arrived already."

"Are you packing people or things first?" Mick did not mind answering Brigitte's questions or taking her test. He had his own questions.

"The first few wagons will mostly have foodstuffs from the storerooms." She added in a reassuring voice, "We have some long carts with benches—six wheelers—coming for people."

"An army travels on its stomach. You shouldn't separate food from your soldiers."

Brigitte chuckled again. "We aren't an army."

"We could be." That felt right. *We need to be.*

"Is that why you went into town? To join the armsmen there?"

"No." He knew better than to reveal what his goal had been.

"Well, Mick, our new home is not far away. Just a little farther south."

"What is the name of the city?"

"It doesn't matter right now." She flapped an arm dismissively at his question. "Lady Genevieve is arranging our accommodation as we speak. Now, let's try another test, shall we? I want you to subtract eight from a hundred, then work your way down. Will you do that for me?"

"Yes. One hundred." A couple of seconds passed as Mick did the work in his head. "Ninety-two." Another few moments passed. "Eighty-five, seventy-six, ..." It took a while to get down to the last number. "Three."

"Thank you, Mick. That was very good."

Mick was not so sure, but he also knew Brigitte would be reluctant to seem critical of the results. He watched her face as she made notes in her booklet. *She's surprised. And disappointed. I was never a mathematician. Not even before I got old and soft in the head.*

"What were the ten words I gave you to remember Mick?"

"Bridge, eight, Elysium, protect, horse, harbinger, idea. I don't remember the rest."

Brigitte's eyebrows went up. She said, "You are always fast with what you remember. Are you sure that if you took a little extra time you wouldn't remember some of the other words?"

"Yes."

"Did you know that you always remember certain words?"

Mick thought about Fenris under the collapsed house, Doog and Louis lurking by the wall, waiting for him to come home last night. He remembered the faces of Carol, Aurorette, and Valence earlier this morning. The horror at lost teeth, weak limbs, loose stool, and falling down. It did not matter that he could not remember everyone who had been in his life. It did not matter that he could not remember anyone who was not of this house. These were the best people at the worst time.

It doesn't matter what words I remember. Things mattered, he knew that. People mattered. Just not words. He did not need to count words or subtract numbers. He needed to *save* people.

CHAPTER 8
DIPLOMACY

"Know less, feel more."

A Statician wizard's summary of Pessicaust's complex, difficult treatise on the eight-cup experiment.

"Fuck her sorry. I don't wanna hear sorry out of a stuck-up, knights-damned wizard-child. I don't *owe* her my forgiveness."

Corporal Alwena might be ranting, but she was limiting her audience to Sergeant Reyn, who listened stoically. The rest of the eight were inside the quartermaster's building doing a little procuring. They had made it from the site of the Elysians' dysfunctional battle on the frontier back to Aurillon and were resupplying so they could proceed southwest to Villiers according to orders.

"What's all that *about*?" Alwena continued her diatribe. "Sorry! An apology isn't an apology, it's a demand for forgiveness. Those wizards do the damage, and *we* pay the price. Just as it's ever been. I'll tell you what sorry is—it's sidestepping an unpayable debt. Is getting together and singing love and happiness to heaven going to fix Dafydd's head or Dill's face?"

"Or bring back Private Eiriol?" asked Reyn in even tones. They had lost her on an earlier scouting mission.

"Damned straight. There's no getting back the dead." She added in a hiss, "Fucking wizards, they just don't get it." No wizard of any kind had been involved in the loss of Eiriol, but Reyn did not bring this up. He sensed that was not what Alwena needed. *She isn't done yet.* Sure enough, Alwena took a breath and vowed, "I'll forgive when Katherine Valcourt, Lady of Engevelen, high wizardess of the Elysians, wears my shoes."

"Do you think he's going to lose those teeth?" asked Reyn, his voice even calmer than before. Along with the blackened, ring-like pattern on Dill's face was the issue of his two sore teeth. They had been flash-frozen when the doll detonated.

"Do I look like a skolving dentist?" Alwena whirled and clenched her fists to the sky, whole body rigid, up on her toes. "Fuck!" She paused and took a breath, slumping a little. "I hope not. It could be weeks before we know for sure."

"What does he say about it?"

"He says he still has twenty-three good teeth." Alwena laughed, somewhat unhappily. "The git can't even count."

"Ready to move on, then?"

"Move on, yes. Forgive, well, you heard me."

"Good," Reyn said crisply. "Now what are we going to say to the lads when they come join us?"

"We are back under our own command."

"Correct. And?"

"We are going to do things right."

"Yes, we are."

"We are going to do this right," declared Marias Garragorah to her sergeant-at-arms. He rode next to her. Fifteen mounted soldiers followed. They were all dressed in the black ring mail and dark cloaks of Ardgour. All except Marias, who carried no such burden.

"Yes, Lady," he said. It was all he could say, but it had to be said, just as crossing the no-man's-land between Ardgour County and Engevelen had to be done. The sergeant could not gainsay Marias any more than she could gainsay Ardgour.

"I've been a part of a lot of bad things," Garragorah continued. "Some were mistakes..." Her voice trailed off as she considered how few were mistakes of the honest variety. "Some were simply things I had to do."

A dark, shimmering mirage materialized far down the road, almost at the vanishing point. Its undefined nature brought Nehring Ardgour to mind. She added, "We serve a dark and powerful master, Sergeant."

"Yes," he said.

"And we must do as we have been told."

This time he only grunted, his eyes squinting down the road at the apparition. Whatever it was, it had split into several poorly defined figures.

"There is a positive side to this," Garragorah said. "We bear no moral responsibility for our actions, we who are His tools. If there is good or evil in our service, the cost is all on Him."

"Will He protect us?" the sergeant asked, still looking at the figures, now not so far down the road.

Garragorah had to stifle a laugh, a new burp of suicidal honesty. Nehring Ardgour protected no one. He only used them up. Instead of laughing or venturing a lie that she knew would not be believed, she said, "See this embassy through to Engevelen City, and *I* will protect you."

The soldiers in column behind Marias started shifting. The sounds of swords being loosened in scabbards sliced through the air like a scab being torn from a wound. The malformed blur of figures in the distance had resolved into three soldiers on foot. They were thirty or forty yards away now. All wore faded, torn Royal Engevelen tabards over rusted chain. One of the men was tall, another young, and the last —the leader, it seemed—had short, gray, stubbly hair.

"Everyone be at ease," said Garragorah. She raised her voice and said, "We are an embassy from Nehring Ardgour."

"Put up yer swords, foreigners!" the gray, stubbled man yelled, though his voice was warbly.

The three men drew their swords, though Marias could see their weapons shaking. They were outnumbered five to one. The younger fellow's eyes darted from soldier to soldier. Gray stubble's eyes did not. He locked eyes with Garragorah and said with less warble than before, "Them's the last words to put anybody at ease."

"Gentlemen, it is quite all right." Marias said, hands raised placatingly. "You may escort us to Engevelen City. There is no need to draw your weapons."

"Knights-damned potlicker!" Gray stubble proclaimed. "Yer standing on land that still belongs to Engevelen! And you drew first. You all just put down *your* blades, not *us*."

In Marias's experience, it was unusual to encounter a citizen of Engevelen with such a parochial manner—they usually prided themselves on speaking and behaving "correctly"—but then again, every country had these types. This particular one appeared to be in a volatile mix of anger and fear.

I've charmed harder men.

"Now, everyone, let's just calm down," Marias said, smiling at the man. "No one needs weapons here."

Unfortunately, Gray Stubble suddenly felt the need to scratch his lean belly. Which was a mistake.

A spear shot over her shoulder and slammed into Gray Stubble's chest.

"Gaahhh!" he replied to the insult, then fell heavily on his butt.

"Stop!" Marias shouted, head swiveling, unsure what had happened. She did not see who threw the spear, but she could guess what had caused it.

Someone on my side is also in a volatile mix of anger and fear.

The tall man charged toward Marias, but a horse came between them, and she did not see what caused the half-aborted scream she heard next. She whirled this way and that and saw only spears flying, swords flashing, arms stabbing.

"Dear Lord!" Garragorah shouted, straining to raise her voice above the clashing of weapons and the screams of pain.

"Stop! Stop this absurdity!? STOP! For the love of *fuck,* stop with the stabbing!"

Instantly her well-drilled soldiers ceased, eyes on her.

"Damned, damned, fucking, knights-damned potlickers," groaned gray stubble, thrashing frantically around on his back, one foot scraping the earth as if finding purchase on some dirt could put the two inches of blue, veiny intestine back where it belonged. His chain-mail had not stopped the spear or kept his blood where it belonged.

Why does armor never seem to work when you need it to?

Gray stubble, she reflected, was probably asking himself the same question.

"Fucking potlickers! Aaaahh!"

No, he's not thinking about the failure of his armor.

"I'm so sorry," Garragorah said, well aware of how lame this must sound. She stood in her saddle to see how bad things were with Gray Stubble's two companions.

The tall one was shorter now. His head was flopping off to the side, hanging on by a small flap of skin and the tenuous surface tension of blood. And on the ground, everyone is short.

"Ghaaaahhhh!" moaned the younger one, holding up his right hand, which seemed to be missing three fingers.

No, they're just bent backward. The pinky is missing, though. How the hell did that happen?

"Damn it, I *am* sorry," Garragorah said, louder this time, contemplating the three unfortunate men, one screaming, one rolling around, and one lying nine-tenths headless on the ground. It was not a pretty picture, and decidedly not what she wanted. *It's really not my fault.*

Marias Garragorah had a flexible mind. She was an able rationalizer. And a skilled survivor. She knew what to do. "This presents a problem for our embassy. I don't think anyone's going to listen to us now," she mused out loud, looking at her sergeant. "Better finish them off."

"No! No!" the young one cried. His formerly tall, now more or less headless neighbor said nothing, understandably

"Fucking potlickers," the Gray Stubble spluttered.

When it was all done, Marias Garragorah paused to explain some things to her soldiers. "This was not well done, ladies and gentlemen. Not well done at all. I am quite disappointed in you."

She looked around at the bloody mess. A disgusting, violent, bloody mess. It was clear that swords and spears had been used. So clear that it turned her stomach.

Tough decisions needed to be made, but that was why Nehring had chosen her. "We need to make this right. *You* need to make this right, as you are responsible. But I will help you." Marias made eye contact with her soldiers, one at a time, slowly, letting the situation sink in. "We don't have time to bury these gentlemen, and animals might dig them up anyway. Best hack off their limbs and scatter them about." She thought about the situation and added, "And string some guts in the trees. Knock out the teeth... Maybe put a head up an ass. Way up there, not just halfway. Make this look more like skolves."

Once the cover-up was complete, Garragorah decided to address her soldiers once more. When she cleared her throat, they looked at her with wide eyes from blood-flecked faces. *This is good. They are learning.* "Next time, remember, *we* are an *embassy*. We need to build trust. *Nobody* stab *anyone*." *It makes for far too much work.* "Unless I say so. *Nobody* do anything crazy."

"Nobody do anything crazy," instructed Reyn. "Aron, take point, but nice and slow. Don't rush us into anything we can't walk out of. If you see a skolve, back us out if you can. If you can't, hold your position and wave Tudor up with the arbalest."

They had all heard the stories of the Battle of Charney, so when Tudor had found the huge steel crossbow among the stores, bringing it along had seemed like a no-brainer. Except that the damned thing was heavy. Tudor ended up needing a special harness that allowed him to rest the butt of the weapon in a holder just above his waist, with the weight mostly carried by his hips and shoulders.

The arbalest was also slow to load.

Never mind what we'll do if we meet a horde of skolves instead of one or two.

"Move it out," Reyn whispered, "quiet now and slow."

Moving quietly was something they were good at. Reyn's eight had been in more than one scuffle with Armadale along the Engevelen strip. Eyes open and mouths closed was the order of the day. Corporal Alwena was still beyond angry at the "damned wizards," but that was not a factor now that they had left Aurillon and were back in the countryside. The roads were open, but they had stayed off them, skulking in fields hundreds of yards away from the pathways of people, trusting nothing to be safe. Cities well south of them had been flattened by Skoll and Hati, while old towns and lone towers farther north had been left untouched. Earlier in the war, the actions of the demons had been precise. Their provocations had made sense. They had taken ground and held it, assisted by Ardgour's men. But that had suddenly changed. Reyn did not know if the skolves and demons had truly broken with Ardgour or not—an assumption that Engevelen had clutched at too quickly and desperately, he thought—but he was unsure what advantage could be made of the theory if proven true.

Either way, it's dangerous here.

A farmer inspecting his field waved to them. The man was in his late twenties and wore patched suspenders, but the shadow of his narrow stone tower lay close by. "You know, there's a road 'bout four hundred yards that way," he said to Aron.

But the young, sandy-haired man on point did not answer. He smiled, nodded, and kept on going.

This seemed to irk the farmer. He straightened his back and muttered, "Do you foreigners lack the power of speech?"

Reyn could not understand the preoccupation that the people of Engevelen had with order and correctness. Since coming in-country he and his soldiers had been lectured several times by citizens on trifling local customs and other trivialities. *Their country is falling down around them, and he wants us to keep to the road?* He saluted the farmer as he passed, though. They were in the field because they wanted some control over their fate. *However delusional that notion is.*

They entered a forest only two miles down the road and slowed down further. It was clear the skolves had a superior sense of smell, infinitely superior, some said. That did not bode well in a thickly wooded area where line of sight was short and inconsistent. *And where it's impossible to be silent at any pace but a crawl.* Reyn called, but quietly, for a tighter grouping of his eight and an even slower pace. When they found a deer trail, they used it.

Reyn breathed in deeply through his nose, comfortable at last to be in the woods. This was what the Vercors Rangers trained for. Silent, quiet, alone, that was their wheelhouse. No politics, no people, no rigid and incongruous customs, no wizards: these noes were the few good ones. The odors of damp leaves, the rays of late-day sunlight through the trees, the careful placement of feet, these were the experiences he loved. These were the risks his people were best suited to endure.

On his next deep breath, the unmistakable odor of rotten meat rolled over the sergeant. It was so foul that he fought to take another breath. He rushed forward four paces and put his hand on Dafydd's shoulder. "Tell Aron to halt," he whispered. Once they were grouped together, they dropped packs so they could proceed at a crawl. When Reyn nosed up to a rotted log, he was tempted to stick his face in the wet, moldy, worm-infested mess. The other reeking odor was that bad. He felt Alwena on his right elbow and Tudor just two paces away on his left. The dark-haired young man had left the arbalest behind with the other heavy weapons; there was no crawling under its weight and bulk.

Resting his cheek on the top of the log, Reyn saw the skolves. There were three of them, feasting on a white-tailed deer. Two of the skolves were violently retching.

Daughter of Nimrheal, what is happening?

The third lowered its blood-soaked muzzle as it attempted to chew up a fist-sized helping of deer guts. If chewing really meant choking, it was doing well. The other two skolves collapsed onto their haunches, panting. One of them vomited again, then the other. What came up, came up purple and dark red.

Reyn pulled his crew back and whispered, "Bring up the arbalest, Tudor. Everyone else, ready spears and walk softly."

I NEED to step carefully here.

A stein is to a bucket what a bucket is to an armored man, the same as an armored man to a horse. Like is to like is to like, and thus we go from what we know to what we thought we didn't know.

The analogic exercise steadied Val as she took her place at the front of the Elysian Wizards' congress. "Let's talk about the mission, Elysians."

Green smiled encouragingly at her from his seat near the front of the room. The others, lurking closer to the back door, remained stony-faced. Val knew they wanted to abandon the meeting and head back to the practice yard.

Or the tavern for some of them.

Rebecca and Christopher were slumped back-to-back.

"We need to tighten up our methods," Val continued. "Make fewer mistakes. Run cleaner operations." *I don't want to be making any more apologies.*

There was no response.

"And figure out how to make better use of the soldiers who accompany us." *Before the rest of them desert us in disgust.* "So they feel more useful."

"And less likely to piss on us," Rebecca interjected, smirking.

A flash memory of Corporal Alwena urinating on Dill—no—Private Dylan made Val shudder.

"I hear it was ... rather ... shameful," came the slow contribution from Samantha Westerberg. Neither she nor Calvaine Chesshyre had seen action. They had been out on the mission but on the other side of the hamlet.

"Why—can't—these—dirt—grunts—just—do—their—jobs?" Every word was stretched out as if from some stage actor. Sam's arms fluttered imploringly with every new word.

"It was a shame we didn't look out for them," Val snapped, her temper suddenly flaring. The words jumped out, surprising her, but feeling right. "Christopher had just dropped the doll on them. What else could they do? They were head to toe in endothermic artefact."

"Endothermic splermic," muttered Rebecca, or something to that effect, still leaning back against Chris. "Don't talk so fancy, *princess*," she spat. "We don't know what it means, and it doesn't impress us."

"Verily, did you indeed drop the doll?" Calvaine asked in his cultured tones, one well-cultivated eyebrow raised. He was another white-skinned wizard. From the west, apparently, though his origins had never been disclosed. He had simply arrived one day and announced that he was joining the Elysians. Val suspected he was from Dearden. Cal was a wizard of incantations who worked his magic in a language he claimed that only he knew. Consistent with his air of mystery were his policy positions; it was rarely clear before or after an argument how sincere he was.

"I did not!" declared Christopher, abruptly sitting forward and dropping Rebecca, who sprawled indecorously, legs all over creation. "Well, maybe a little," Chris allowed. "Just the head."

"*Both* parts," shot Val.

"But I killed *all* the skolves."

"Yah!" declared Rebecca, jumping to her feet like a cat insisting it had landed on its feet. "We blew them up *thoroughly*. What's the problem? It's the results that count."

"We may have been more lucky than good," Halwyn said in a barely audible voice.

Christopher waved that off. "Lucky and good are the same thing when they work, Green. If you knew that, you'd get lucky more often."

Halwyn's face turned scarlet. No one would know what he might have said back to Christopher, because Val jumped in too quickly. "Don't pour that Pessicaust sophistry on this fire, Chris!" she exclaimed.

Calvaine frowned. "I find myself *confused*. If I remember correctly, Lady Valcourt, Pessicaust was among the foremost of the School of Acutists." He switched to a smile and leaned into his words. "*Your* school."

"No, no, no," Val replied, face redder than Halwyn's now, frustration monster bursting loose. She knew better, but the monster was powerful. "Pessicaust founded the *Staticians*, and his eight-cup experiment was deeply flawed. *Deeply* flawed."

"Oh, and does saying it again and again make your argument right?" said Rebecca. "We will make a Statician out of you yet."

"How did we get onto this again?" asked Halwyn mournfully, running his fingers through his shoulder-length hair.

"Halwyn Glace speaks to the point," said Calvaine, nodding sagaciously. "Why do we keep debating Acutism and Statics?" He smiled, turning the knife, and added, "It's all the same in the end."

Val wanted to shout, "*You* brought it up!" but thought better of challenging someone as self-important as Calvaine. She could feel her heart pounding and hot. When Cal said nothing further, she took a deep breath, trying to calm herself, and ventured, "I think you misunderstand the deeper point of Pessicaust's work."

"I like you, Valcourt," Christopher cut in, smirking, "But do you really think you know better than Pessicaust what his own experiment revealed?"

"Yes!" Val would have screamed, but Green grabbed her arm with a

sweaty hand. The silent intervention surprised her. She glanced at him. He was gazing at her with a strange intensity.

"Can't we all," Samantha pleaded, arms waving like a slowly drowning thespian, "just get along?"

"There is a messenger," Halwyn said in her ear, still holding her arm. "From the crown."

~

"I AM A MESSENGER. An envoy. To Crown Princess Cressy," said Garragorah.

"And what's that got to do with the price of wheat in Neahon?" said the dirty-faced, wild-haired man pulling his overloaded cart. An equally dirty and disheveled woman stood beside him, squinting at Garragorah and her soldiers. Her four children slumped on the ground beside the cart.

Not the best reaction, but at least no one's head is off yet. Marias had given her soldiers another stern lecture on diplomacy and the need to "win hearts and minds" before they had approached the ragged column. A few other huddled groups pulled carts ahead. At least one group had stopped to watch.

Too many witnesses for a repeat slaughter in any case. Garragorah had never before been on hand when a killing happened. She had always been off-stage, the unmoved mover.

Nevertheless, she had counted up her crimes against humanity. It had been a way to acknowledge the consequences of her lies and rationalizations and to tell herself she regretted them. She had even used the memories as a sleep aid. That surely showed remorse, did it not? But seeing those people dead had been much worse. So much messier.

I need to stick to diplomacy.

"I need to speak to someone in authority." Garragorah had decided that the sooner she had an Engevelen escort, the better her mission would go.

Dirty-face's wife pointed to the south and said, "The Baron's castle is yonder."

Garragorah squinted at the horizon and made out yet another of the tall, thin towers that dotted Engevelen. She could just see its top over the low scrub, putting it at a distance of several miles. "Thank you kindly," she said to the woman, then to her men, "Let's go."

"Could you help us pull our cart?" the woman asked. Her husband tried to shush her with a hand on her shoulder, his eyes red. One of her children, a girl of maybe seven, poked her head up from the dirt. Her bright eyes shone from a dark face.

Garragorah whirled her horse and said, "We would love to help, but we cannot spare the time. Our mission is vital to everyone's interest. Including yours." Before putting spurs to her horse, she added, "When we get to the castle, we'll send for help."

She did not look back to see the woman's disappointment or take any notice of the mud and dirt her horse's hooves threw into the faces of the other refugees she galloped by.

I would help them. I would. But they are so many now. So many. I'll help them all much better by ending this war.

It was not long before the tattered column had disappeared from sight and mind. Just a bend in the road, and the caragana bushes hid their misery.

"At least nobody else is dead yet," she said to herself.

"Gahhhh!"

What? There had been a flash of something—something fast, from behind—but Garragorah had only seen it out of the corner of her eyes.

"Skolves!" one of her soldiers yelled in a piercing, high-pitched shriek.

Garragorah whirled her horse to see a knot of tall gray bodies twisting and jumping, moving so fast they might as well have been flying. A horse was down, a rider pinned under it, screaming. Then not screaming. A skolve had ripped the soldier's head off like popping a cap from a bottle.

"Sergeant!" Garragorah screamed. But the sergeant was roaring at his soldiers, desperate to form them up, waving his sword. He could not answer.

Garragorah counted six skolves against sixteen soldiers, two, no three, no *four* down. "Hold them here!" she shouted. "I'll get help!"

She put spurs to her horse again, but harder now, terrified, breathing like her head was in a bag. As fast as she galloped, the screams of her soldiers flew faster, overtaking her, frightening her still more. She thundered up a branch in the road. East, the tower, maybe a mile away now. West two hundred yards or so, a stream.

She decided, pulled her horse's head in the direction they needed to go.

I wonder if skolves prefer eating children to horses?

The stream came up fast. It was broad, more of a river. *Will it hide my scent?* She put her heels to her horse's flanks a third time. It splashed thunderously into the creek, drowning out the sounds of the fight.

"How much of that did you hear?" Val asked the page beside her, a young woman in royal blue skirts and darker leggings. Val's face was still hot, one of several ways her body was telling her brain that the argument was far from over. On her other side, Green looked like he had done a better job of putting the row behind him. *He's happy to get to come to the* big *meeting with me.* She knew that Green always liked spending time with her.

"Uhm," the page said, visibly taking time to choose her words. "It sounded like you were debating some wizardly idea. A pessimistic one."

"Not a pessimistic *idea*," Val clarified. "A *person*. Named Pessicaust."

The page pursed her lips and said, "Oh. Is that someone in the war?"

"Yes," said Green at the same time Val said, "No." It almost made Val laugh, but solemnity was required now. The wide stone hallways of the palace in Engevelen City echoed every sound, and this was not a time for levity. Val had important things to say to the military conference being hosted by Princess Christine Cressy up ahead. As their steps reverberated from the high-vaulted ceiling of the walkway, Val examined her feelings. *Am I over that stupid debate about Pessicaust yet?*

No. Some debates never seemed to end. *Why can't people just say they're sorry and agree with me?*

"What my colleague Halwyn Glace and I both said only *seems* contradictory," she explained to the page. "Pessicaust died a generation ago, but her ideas are very much at play in the here and now." Val loved explaining things, and this polite page seemed to enjoy listening, so she continued. "And that is the problem. Human beings have trouble with complex ideas. While most of us are capable of appreciating complexity, very few can actually comprehend it. Pessicaust's eight-cup experiment is a famous example of this. She was a great wizard, a philosopher as well as an empiricist." Val looked at the page. "Do you know what that is?"

The young lady smiled shyly. "I think so. She tested things. She was an innovator. She must have been very brave."

"Yes!" Val exclaimed. "Nimrheal got her eventually, of course. But before that, she carried out a wonderful experiment to determine whether it was better to perform simple acts of wizardry intuitively or through a process of exact scientific reasoning—in this case, the analogic method. The results were to be judged based on heating eight cups of water by eight separate wizards." Val looked over at the page to see what she would say to this. The young woman led them around a turn but did not reveal her thoughts.

She's shy. "Do you want to know what the temperature data revealed?" Val asked.

"Yes," the page said, her voice eager.

"The data showed no difference between the methods."

"Oh," the page said a moment later. "So the, uh ... intuitive ... approach was just as good as the ... uh ... analogy way?"

"No!" Val exclaimed. "No, it wasn't. *It isn't.*" She smiled triumphantly and added, "This is where complexity comes in. First, there weren't enough experimental subjects to prove anything. Eight subjects. Small cups of water. Cheap thermometers. Who knows what the results would have been with a larger sample and more rigorous methods?" Val's eyes shone a brighter green and she spoke more loudly, with more enthusiasm. "You see, it only *seems* like the experiment proves that heuristic methods are the best. The experiment only proves what the experiment proves, that for a small number of subjects under a very particular low thermal exchange, instinctual wizardry *may be* superior. But the experiment failed to consider what would have happened if the load had been of higher magnitude. Changing conditions are where analogic reasoning shines, but this was never considered at all. We over-conclude because most people don't like complexity. They want to think that this one little experiment speaks to more things than it actually tested. And thus the limitations of an experiment end up creating a bias."

The page's face betrayed confusion, possibly frustration. She frowned and asked, "But aren't you biased too? I mean, you don't know what the results would be if there were more, different, wizards, and heaps and heaps more water."

"You aren't listening."

"I think she is," Green said, his hand on Val's arm. "She just isn't diving into your heap of water." Val was surprised to be brought up short by Green twice in one day. And with the same gentle touch. It made her stop in her tracks. "Thank you," Green said to the page. "The door is just ahead. We will go the rest of the way on our own."

The doors were huge. An armed and armored guard stood on either side, vigilant, waiting. Once across the threshold, they would be among the lords not just of her own country, but *all* countries. With unspoken accord, both she and Green stopped. Neither felt ready to approach the threshold just yet.

Val turned her frown away from the doors and looked intently at Green. "Halwyn, why don't you speak up more often with the rest of the Elysians?"

He shrugged. "I don't like crowds."

"Well, that's a shame. You can be quite witty when you do raise your voice." She looked up at the fresco on the ceiling. *Sometimes, anyway.*

Val focused on Green again, trying to decide if she was pleased by him or annoyed. "You know that I have done Pessicaust's experiment on profoundly more difficult thermal exchanges and found her results to be in error. As soon as a wizard tries something of significant difficulty, preparation and process matter. But, oh, no, no one wants to hear it. They all just quote Pessicaust and use it as an excuse to ignore good process."

Green shook his head wryly. "You only did those experiments on yourself."

"And Alain Overbree!"

"Congratulations," he said, shaking his head harder and smiling. "The two Acutists agree. With an "n" equal to two, you have not exactly improved on Pessicaust's experimental design."

"That's why you should join the experiment," Val said.

Green stopped smiling. "I would love to help you, Val. But teleporting is already difficult enough." He moved his hand up and down her arm, awkwardly caressing her. "I don't even know how to teleport analogically. I just do it. There's no framework. And—"

"We could work on one," Val interrupted.

"Do you know how dangerous it is to teleport?" Green asked. "I don't need to enter a fatal framework if you turn out to be wrong."

It might be just as fatal if I'm right. She wanted to say it, but she also did not want to push Green away. He was the only one aside from Alain who supported her. *Why is this so hard to explain? Why can't people just agree with me?* It was so needless, so irritating. Val became aware of Green's hand, which continued to rub her arm. She said, "I'm not a cat, you know."

The hand abruptly dropped away, and Val immediately regretted her peevish remark. "Sorry," she said.

"Do you think you're conflating your concern for the fate of your country with small matters of magical style?" Green asked, looking uncomfortable.

Am I? The question was small and gently put, but it landed like a punch to the gut. Some part of her had wanted to ask the same question. *Am I afraid to?* There was so much to fear. The poor organizational efficiency of the Elysians, the problem of Pessicaust, her stupid arguments with the other wizards, the tragedy of the war, and the failure of her country, perhaps the end of it. Val tried to consider Green's question objectively, knew on some level he might be right, but knowing was not enough to untangle the knot. "I don't know," she sighed.

A stein is to a bucket what a bucket is to an armored man. The failure of my leadership of the Elysians is like the failure of the leadership of my country. And so, we go from what we know to what we thought we didn't. But also from one kind of incompetence to another.

Green put his hand on her shoulder and said, more gently even than before, "You did just lecture a page on Pessicaust's theory."

The comment hurt almost as much as his question, but Val had centered herself with her litany and was able to listen and keep the monster away. "Are you suggesting the page was humoring me?" *Fuck.* It had not occurred to Val until now that she might not only be conflating her worries but that she might just be a bore, a tedious crank. It was an uncomfortable possibility. *But how do I avoid boorishness when no one will listen?*

~

"WHAT A BORE." Halwyn whispered. "I thought you would address them right away."

Val should have warned him. She should have known she would soon be on the receiving end of the boorishness. They had been in the congress for several hours now, and—consistent with Val's whole life recently—no one was listening to her. No one was listening to anyone. They were all too busy posturing. The Congress was in an enormous ballroom, and it was near to full with lords and ladies of Engevelen and similarly lofty representatives from every member nation to the Methueyn Treaty. The room was packed with nobles, so full that everyone had to stand, which must have been painful for many of them, considering how long the proceedings were taking. The princess may have called for Val to be there, but her role remained a mystery.

I can only wait. Halwyn's gentle criticism had reminded Val that she was a Lady of Engevelen too. She must show discipline and grace, even if the endless meeting was driving her insane. She had once been able to tolerate these long meetings easily enough, outlast the stuffed shirts, stand straight until even the posturing blowhards wilted next to her. But the situation had become so dire so quickly she felt she had lost her grasp of the issues. They had given her the Elysians and expected her to make a difference. But that new power had not magically solved anything. Grace and self-restraint grew harder to hold onto with every new day, every new obstacle.

I must listen. There are three hundred thousand drops of water in a stein, and ten steins in a bucket. Thus we go from drops to steins to buckets. It had been a long time since Val had to go through this litany thrice in one day, but the meeting felt interminable.

The current speaker was Lord Liam Laval, a beautiful man with long, carefully styled hair and a melodious, perhaps too melodious, speaking voice. He seemed to be paraphrasing an argument that had already been made a dozen times. Val struggled to pay attention. Drops did not become steins or buckets without time and effort.

"Allowing General Theibidow to march the Renet north has brought us to this impasse, your Highness," he said. Laval was blaming Christine Cressy, but his graceful tone made the accusation sound almost like a compliment. "It pains me to say it, but we must painfully accept the painful truth." The repetition resonated with Val. The meeting *had* been painful. "I fear we must," he continued, "retreat ..." He paused to survey the room, making eye contact with as many of his listeners as a slow, theatrical pan from the stage could achieve before concluding with a solemn flourish. "While we still can."

"Easy to say when you don't live in the north!" shouted a lady in striking blue and yellow. Others piped up in a similar vein, but just as many seemed to support Laval. Someone else howled, "Promises have been made!" Others bawled back that, "People have died." This was one-upped by "Everyone is going to die." *Unhelpful, but quite likely to prove true.*

"We must continue the wall from the Strip," Liam Laval resumed. He was referring to a border wall with Armadale that crossed the entire Engevelen strip. There had been an idea, early on, that the wall should be built across the entire country. But the plan Laval proposed would strand much of North Engevelen on the wrong side of the stony boundary.

The blue and yellow lady shot back, "And abandon most of the country? Treason!"

The shouting, finger-pointing, and diatribes of disapprobation continued. Voices thundered and echoed off the high, vaulted ceiling. They needed to be loud to be heard above the continual undercurrent of muttering and side conversations. While any lord or lady held the floor, scores of others babbled or whispered to confederates. This was expected in such conclaves, and tolerated if kept to a low simmer. Val and Halwyn Glace began to do their own murmuring.

"And I thought wizards were tough to corral," Val said, *sotto voce*, to Greene.

Halwyn snorted and replied, "If there were more of us, we would show them who's harder to herd."

"We would bring the place down around their ears," Val whispered absently. "Where are the Methueyns in all this mess?"

"Scouting, mostly," Green shrugged. "I'm told that when they get back, they'll make some decisions."

And inform us afterward.

The shouting and murmuring suddenly died away. Val looked up to see tall, straight-backed, green-eyed Christine Cressy rapping a sword hard against the polished stone floor. The clanging echoed crisply despite all the hot air in the room. When total silence had been achieved, the princess passed the sword to her cousin, who stood beside her, and said in her clear, bell-like voice, “We must draw our debate to a close. I see that Katherine Valcourt, Lady of Engevelen, Acutist Wizard, and leader of the Elysian mobile forces has arrived.”

“Uh, that was a couple hours ago,” whispered Greene to Val as she bowed to the princess and waved elegantly to the lords standing all around her. She did this with grace even though she was undoubtedly the center of attention, after the princess, and had no idea what was coming next.

Christine Cressy inclined her head slightly and extended her hand in Val’s direction. “Lady Valcourt comes directly from a stunning victory over the skolves. She and her multinational team annihilated a large horde of the creatures forty miles north of Aurillon.”

“It was a handful,” whispered Greene, clearly enjoying himself.

“Their execution was flawless,”

Green continued to paraphrase, whispering, “As flawless as a clown show.”

“Taking no casualties whatsoever.”

“If you don’t count frostbite and a grain bin.”

“Stop it,” Val hissed without moving her lips. It was not like Halwyn Glace to act so silly and probably spoke to how tired he truly was. *And how little pressure* he *feels here.*

Val could not argue with his corrections, but she understood why the princess was making more of the battle than it was. *We need a victory.*

“It was a victory greater even than the Battle of Charney.”

Greene’s eyes bulged at that one. Charney was said to have been a real meat grinder.

“Who better to send to Vercors to plead our case?” the princess said. “Lady Valcourt, will you teleport to Vercors City and represent our need directly to Her Grace, Veronica Brice? We need the Aignen Legion to march to our aid, and should he still live, the Shining Knight. Otherwise, we may indeed be forced to retreat from all of northern Engevelen.”

“I will do so this very minute,” said Val bowing.

"Bow on your way in, Val," Greene said. "And ask nicely."

"Really? After mocking Cressy's entire speech, you are going to tell me to take matters seriously? You really are all over the place today. I would say take a day off, but you have to get me to Vercors and back." They were already halfway to the teleportation pad—an area that was kept clear and only used by Green— and Val was feeling pretty good about the whole thing. Greene's newfound sense of humor felt a bit churlish now. "I heard you earlier about not mixing things up, staying on point, not being a bore."

"I did *not* call you a bore."

"Hmmf. In any case, what you said *here* certainly applies *there*."

"Uh, it's more than that, *Lady* Valcourt," said Greene. "I come from Vercors, remember? You need to be very careful of Veronica Brice." He leaned closer to her and said in a lower voice, "If you irritate her, you could end up locked in the tower."

CHAPTER 9

WHAT KIND OF WAR?

"What kind of war only kills people?" Ten miles north of Aurillon and Ave had yet to see a live human being outside her group of escuyers.

Souk shrugged and tossed a rejoinder over her shoulder, "Wars always kill people."

The town of Lyle was virtually intact. Other than a few broken doors and windows, the city's buildings were undamaged. With one big exception. The magnificent Steel Castle. It had been violated with a remarkable excess of malice. It had not been smashed like the north tower of Aurillon—as if by a fist from hell—but instead assaulted in a thousand small, malevolent ways, carefully vandalized from top to bottom. Statues had been defaced, tapestries torn down and—Ave thought—urinated upon, chairs had been smashed, paintings slashed by claws. It was as if this sacred space had been the object of a temper tantrum by an insane mob. And while that ruined church would be the first news a courtier would give the princess, it was the only ruined building that Ave, Bro, and Souk had found so far.

Bro's face twitched as he whispered, crouching over the headless body of a child, "But these are mostly civilians. Everyone dead. No one injured." Both sides of his face twitched now. Tan pants did not tell if the three- or four-year-old had been a boy or girl. It hardly mattered what the child's sex was anyway. Bro cradled what was left and looked around, appearing confused.

He does not know what to do with the body.

It was little wonder that the big man hesitated. Bodies littered the streets like leaves. They flopped out of windows, lay, torn into pieces, on rails all down the main street, littered the floors of their homes below terrific sprays of blood that told an unequivocal story of rending and deliberate mutilation. More carcasses formed a pattern leading out of town like spray from a violently burst bottle. People had tried to run away and been run down. The ones on horses had also been caught, farther out, horse and rider dead and defiled together.

"Lay the child down, Bro," Ave said, rescuing him from his despondent reverie. "Say a prayer. It is all we can do."

Souk carelessly sauntered down the street, no more mindful of the carcasses than if they were trash. Ave wondered if she truly cared so little or if this was simply her way of dealing with a situation so much bigger than herself. Ave did not know if those walnut-brown eyes revealed the real Souk. Perhaps the casualness was an act, a necessary compartmentalization. Their job, and the job of the other groups out scouting, was not to bury the bodies but to find out where the skolves who had left them there had gone.

They aren't here. It stunk, though, which confused Ave. *Bodies aren't swollen yet. This happened within the last day.* Nevertheless, the smell of rotten meat was everywhere, filling Ave's nose and burning her throat with every reluctant breath. *Why does everything they touch reek?*

Yet even a smell bad enough to make breathing repellent was not the most pressing issue here. Something was not right.

"Why haven't the skolves invested the town? Or at least taken the cattle."

Ave was well used to violence and death by now, but she had not become an emotionless observer. The wrongness of the ocean of death all around her was overwhelming, yet something still more wrong lay beyond even that horror.

"They left," said Souk. "Isn't that obvious?" She blew air out her lips, making them blubber childishly. She had a way of standing, with her hips noticeably forward. Ave could have identified Souk's silhouette from a lineup of shadows. "They just didn't want to take the time to kill or steal the cows. Big deal."

Bro may have frowned at this. It was hard to tell from that face of his. He was holding the hand of a bodiless arm that had been stuck through a fence. "You think it was some kind of lightning war?" He came from Armadale. Their knights liked to fight in quick, decisive thrusts.

"That's not it," declared Ave. "They took the time to kill the people. Every single one. And then desecrate the bodies." She frowned into the noonday sun and swept her gaze up and down the street. "They occupy nothing, even leave the cattle behind. In earlier battles, they destroyed more buildings than people. What do they all want? What do Skoll and Hati *want*?"

"Who cares?" Souk asked. "We sure as Nimrheal aren't going to negotiate with any of them."

Ave doubted she could ever get used to the violence that surrounded her, and so far she was not getting any more used to Souk's apathy. She tried not to let it show when she answered. "Knowing might help us fight them better."

Souk patted Ave's face as if teasing a child. "It's no big mystery—they just want to make us dead. Killing *them* will help fight them just fine. *This,"* she declared, pointing at the dead and twirling in a circle, "tells you *that*."

"We can't keep going as we have been," said Ave. It was a tiny expression of a larger despair. The Deladieyr order was nearly spent. The squires were all but extinguished. Ave's growing desperation over these things had weakened her, made her self-doubting and morose. Standing in Lyle—now a town of the dead—only amplified these feelings. These were the people her order was meant to protect. They had been slaughtered in numbers beyond burial, then mutilated and left to rot. As some perverse form of display?

We must change the course of this war.

Souk acted like she did not care. Bro cared, cared deeply, but his strengths were not strategic. He still seemed to think Ave would somehow fix the problem or supply the answers. Ave did not know how.

"What's that?" Bro pointed at the well. The rope reel was empty, but the rope was shaking, and the bucket was jammed up hard against the pulley. The three escuyers drew their swords and walked cautiously across the town square, picking their way over the detritus of human beings scattered there. As they approached the well, the rope continued to jerk; they could hear splashing sounds.

For all her laid-back airs, Souk got to the stone first. She peered over the edge. "Someone is trying to climb out of the well." She chuckled. "He's not doing very well at it."

"Just hang onto the rope!" called Bro to whoever was struggling down below. He grasped the rope where it tied the pail and started pulling on it. Muscles as big as horse legs hauled the drenched man up quickly. He was shaking, pale-skinned, and had a shrunken look. Ave reached out and pulled him over the stone lip of the well.

"Who are you?" Ave asked.

"I flee Ardgour," the man said in a thick Novgoreyl accent.

There had been refugees from the north, on and off, since the Methueyn War started. Mostly they had been farmers, and most of them had been repatriated citizens of Engevelen, trapped in Ardgour's County since the invasion a generation earlier. But a few true citizens of Novgoreyl showed up from time to time. And they were all terrified of Nehring Ardgour.

"Well, aren't you are the luckiest person in the whole town," observed Souk. "You're the only survivor we've found."

Lucky? "How did you know to jump in the well?" Ave asked.

"I just jumped," he said.

Ave looked at Bro's hand, which was still holding the rope. The big squire looked at the rope too, and his eyes widened. *He tossed the other end of the rope down the well before he jumped in. He thought it through.*

Ave grabbed the front of his dripping tunic. "We just pulled you out of there and now you want to lie to us?"

"No, no, is not how it happen."

Bro let go of the thick rope and stepped close to the cringing, shivering man. "Yehs, yehs," he said, his Armadale accent coming through clearly.

"One more lie and I toss you back in." Ave had never seen Bro do violence in cold blood, but if anyone looked up to the brutish task, it was that gigantic man, his face spasming but in rage now.

The Novgoreyl raised his hands up in a pleading gesture. With Ave holding his tunic, and Bro towering over him he had nowhere to go. He slumped suddenly, seeming to realize this. "What Nehring hate most not Skoll and Hati's power to kill. He hate their *stink*." He looked from Ave to Bro. "I hid in water. Is something I know about."

"Oh, my knights," exclaimed Souk, showing excitement for the first time since they had waded into the slaughter. "This guy is a Vymyty wizard!"

"I'M WORRIED ABOUT STARVATION," Ave said. The last civilian evacuation out of Aurillon had taken place two days earlier, but the city was still, technically, held by Engevelen. Those responsible for that dubious honor had gathered in congress at the Steel Castle. Yeyncie Greene—Sir Heydron—acted by common consent as chair and leader of a diverse group. Sir Michael, Ave, and her fellow squires had been joined by Captain Caceres, the senior military commander in the city, his aide, whose name Ave had not caught, and Lady Gabrielle, deputy mayor of Aurillon. Sir Urien and Sir Revenberge had not yet returned from scouting. The Vymyty wizard, Taratoraff, perched glumly on a stool off to the side.

"I'm more worried about being massacred. We have plenty of food here," said Caceres, his curly mustache moving with a half-smile, "I made sure we stored enough in our strong points to feed my company for a month."

"Let's keep our minds on the fight," agreed Sir Michael, whom Ave had until this meeting still thought of as her peer, Escuyer Camden. But his airy dismissal of her contribution changed that. Camden had truly crossed the Bifrost and become Sir Michael, Knight and Angel of War.

Yeyncie looked up at him, appraisingly. "I don't think Escuyer Vanier means us. What does it matter if we win the war but everyone has starved?"

Thank you, Yeyncie. The myopic focus on fighting that everyone seemed to share repelled Ave. The Deladieyr and Methueyn Knights and their squires were far from the only things on a path to extinction. *This just isn't sustainable. I cannot be silent on this.* "There are thousands of cattle in the pens of Lyle. They need to be driven south."

"If we lose, it won't matter if we are fed. We will all die," insisted Michael. "Skoll and Hati and their skolves will kill everyone, well fed or not."

"No, not right," said Taratoraff from his stool, his thick accent cutting through the sharp, souring atmosphere of the meeting. "Skoll and Hati cannot kill all." When everyone at the table turned to stare at him, he added, "All people of Engevelen, probably, yes. Some of Vercors and Armadale, possibly, but won't kill everyone. Is not possible. There is just two of them. What can they really do?" He shrugged, then added, "And skolves will be spent by attrition if they drive too much further south."

Souk slapped her leg heavily and said, "Well that's a relief, the world isn't ending after all."

"Just *our* world," said Lady Gabrielle, less amused.

"Yes," replied Taratoraff. "We likely all die. Unless we run away."

We will all die. Unless we run away well past their effective range. Unless we do something differently. Ave thought quickly, then asked Taratoraff, "You know Skoll and Hati well? You know Count Ardgour?"

"Yes."

"How well?" asked Yeyncie, clapping her hands in delight, catching on to where Ave's question was going.

"Is not friends, no—the Ardgour has none—but I know him." He curled his lip and added, "Other Vymyty who knew him better are dead. He use them up."

"What do you mean, he used up the Vymyty?" The new voice came from Sir Urien, who was striding quickly across the stone floor with tall, beautiful Sir Revenberge at his side. A ray of sunlight from the cupola flashed off his gold headband and illuminated Revenberge. Her face was momentarily haloed by that flashing light. Goosebumps flowed like wind in grass across Ave's skin. Revenberge looked like a goddess of morning, Urien her male twin. "Used how?" he asked.

Taratoraff looked down at his hands and said, "Food for Nimrheal."

Sir Michael's hands came down on the table with a resounding thud. "We *must* destroy Ardgour!"

He has only one answer to bad news. Fight. Ave looked around the table. Every person there only wanted to promote their own agenda. Gabrielle had only asked when she could bring her people back. Ave could barely credit it. They had only just evacuated, and many of them had yet to reach their destinations. Captain Caceres had argued for Aurillon to be reinforced by a larger group of soldiers. The different interests made it seem like there were a lot of people at the table. And there were if you were waiting your turn to speak, if you were the meeting chair trying to work through an agenda. But it was a pittance for deciding what to do with the city. For deciding any great matters.

"How?" asked Lady Gabrielle. "My city stands, for all intents and purposes, abandoned. How do we destroy Nehring Ardgour, stop Skoll and Hati and the skolves, and keep from starving?" She pointed at Taratoraff. "We cannot just run away until they tire of chasing us."

"Hold that thought, please, my Lady," Yeyncie Greene said. To anyone who did not know Yeyncie, the diminutive little girl would have seemed a strange chairperson. Until they felt her dynamism. "Sir Urien, were you able to determine where the skolves were going?"

"Yes," he said taking a position at the table. He did not sit. "They were heading, in a meandering fashion, to the southeast."

"At least one of the demons is with them," added Revenberge firmly. "The footprints were very deep and quite unmistakable."

This got everyone's attention. Well, not Souk's. She did not react at all. Escuyer Acklyn's eyes widened, but a shadow hung over them still. So far, his feelings of inadequacy had kept him silent. Shame might eventually change that, but Ave could not be certain. Kat smiled ever so slightly, the beginning of professional anticipation. Bro's only reaction was to stare at Ave, but then he always seemed to be catching her eye. Urien was unmoved; he would have seen the extra-deep, oversized tracks too. Michael appeared hungry for a fight as usual. Yeyncie looked thoughtful.

Bro shifted, making his chair creak, and said, "We did not see any tracks like that in Lyle."

"You didn't miss them, Bro," Revenberge assured him. "The demon came from the northeast and joined the skolves a few miles southeast of Lyle."

"And from there the direction of travel stopped meandering," added Sir Urien. "If they were shot from a bow, they could not be going any straighter toward Courant."

"That's where we sent our townspeople!" exclaimed Lady Gabrielle.

Captain Caceres' eyes narrowed. "They will be there soon. Unless the skolves get there before tomorrow—"

"They won't," said Urien. "They have been resting in the fields quite often. There are great indentations in the crops where they stop. With those rest periods, I doubt they march more than twice as fast as a regular armed force, and the refugees have a big head start."

"They should still be warned," Gabrielle maintained, earning a nod from Revenberge.

"What? Warn the Harbinger of Courant?" said Souk. "You really think she doesn't already know? You think she even wants to hear from us?"

"We should chase the skolves down and fight them," declared Sir Michael to no one's surprise.

Ave jumped in. "The knowledge this Vymyty wizard holds is too important to ignore and far too important to leave here or keep to ourselves. He knows Nehring Ardgour. And perhaps something about Skoll and Hati. He needs to go to Engevelen City."

"What about Aurillon?" said Lady Gabrielle. "Without you, the captain may not be able to hold the city."

Sir Revenberge shook her head, "Ave is right. We have no choice but to leave Aurillon, at least for now."

"We should run away straight to Engevelen," stated Taratoraff.

"Enough," said Yeyncie. "We are going to do *everything*." She looked at Ave. "Escuyer Vanier has the right idea. We must move the cattle south to Engevelen City. We know where the skolves are, and we have a window. This needs to be done, because otherwise *they* will starve and then *we* will starve." She smiled. "But the other thing that Ave and Sir Revenberge have come to understand is that we must do something with our friend the Vymyty wizard. He knows things we need to know if we are to change the course of this war. Taratoraff must be escorted to Engevelen City. And lastly, another group must go to Courant and help in the fight there."

"*I* will lead the strike group to Courant," said Sir Michael.

"You *could*," said Yeyncie, "but I think you should come with Sir Urien and me to Engevelen City. The meeting date has been set; our brothers and sisters expect us there. We must, for once and all, act in unison."

"It was promised," Urien said when Michael hesitated. "And perhaps when we meet, it will be decided that all of the Methueyns will march to aid the Harbinger." Finally, the Knight of War nodded his agreement.

"I volunteer to go to Courant," said Escuyer Acklyn, speaking for the first time. His inner fears had, in an inversion of courage, prompted him to demonstrate his bravery.

"I have long dreamt of seeing the suspended aqueducts of Courant," volunteered Kat. "Such beauty should be defended."

If Kat and Ack go to Courant, they will die. Ave was certain of it. She caught Yeyncie's eye and shook her head in the negative. "I *think*," Yeyncie said, hesitating momentarily, "that Escuyers Kattar and Soukhmanthath and Acklyn should take Taratoraff and the livestock. Deliver the cattle to the yards outside Engevelen City and the wizard to the palace."

"Leaving Bro, Vanier, and myself to go help Courant," said Sir Revenberge.

"A light feather to hold back such a heavy wind," observed Kat. Ave heard the dejection in her tone.

Souk jumped on the opportunity. "Bro has not been described as featherlight since he was about two."

Yeyncie Greene shared another quick glance with Ave before responding. "You don't find cattle driving to be worthy. It *is* worthy. More lives depend on this than any other aspect of our plan."

"As you say," came the curt reply from Kat.

Souk did not look impressed. "Yah, whatever. I'll go." She smirked at Ave and Bro and added, "But it would be more fun for everyone if I helped out in Courant instead."

"I will do as asked," stated Ack, probably relieved, "but I don't know much about cattle."

This led to a lengthy discussion of the logistics of driving cattle. Lady Gabrielle surprised everyone by volunteering to accompany the squires. She also suggested that she might be able to talk the holdouts —the few citizens who had refused to evacuate—into joining them.

~

"Thank you for sending them south," Ave said to Yeyncie after the meeting broke up. She did not say who she meant. Saving people from starvation by saving the cattle was an idea the squire was proud of. That it removed three of her friends from risk made her prouder. *Thank the knights for Yeyncie Greene.* The Methueyn Knight fooled many because of her age and size, but she was shrewd. She seemed to know what was going on among the remnants of the squires, who had a chance and who did not.

And who loved whom.

"Escuyer Kattar was right about one thing," Yeyncie said in a quiet voice. "Even with Sir Revenberge, the three of you cannot face Skoll or Hati." She looked over her shoulder at Sir Urien and Sir Michael, who were busy packing. "Everyone wants to fight them head on. Don't."

Ave nodded, a little surprised to hear Yeyncie speaking so acutely to her own thoughts and fears. Yeyncie stretched up to clap her shoulder and added, "See what you can do to help without standing in the path of a falling boulder."

"I will," Ave said. She knew that, for all Yeyncie Greene's shrewdness, the diminutive knight would hold nothing back when she next went into battle. That was as it should be for Sir Heydron, though Ave could not imagine that any kind of victory in Courant was likely. Saving Ack, Souk, and Kat was the only consolation she could hope for.

Some, at least, will survive this war. Out of the way.

Bro and Sir Revenberge marched up to Ave and Yeyncie with packs in hand. "Look up," the knight said.

The meeting had taken place under the still-hanging twelve-foot sword called the Methueyn Treaty.

"Strange that we could get so used to it that no one said a thing," mused Sir Revenberge. She had hung from the great blade just two days earlier.

Flashes of light from the blade played over Bro's palsied face. "Yup," he said. "What are we going to do with it?"

"I think we should leave it here," said Revenberge, "and come back for it later. We need to move fast to get to Courant ahead of our enemies. Can't do that carrying five hundred pounds of steel."

Leave it? The Methueyn Treaty was perhaps the most revered object in the world. The second most, Ave realized. But she knew from personal experience how difficult it was to move. She looked at Sir Revenberge with surprise.

Yeyncie looked like she was in pain. “We *are* in a hurry,” she said, hedging, “but we cannot afford to lose what has been written in steel.”

If Souk had been in this conversation, she might have said that, if it were lost, they could just make a new one. How hard could it be, after all? Just forge a new twelve-foot sword and etch it with the words. Everyone knew what was written there. Except the Treaty was made of an imperishably hard steel. It was Methueyn class, and there had been few in history capable of forging such an object. And etching it—that would be impossible. What could cut that strange metal? And it *was* heavy, far heavier even than it should have been. The damned thing had nearly caused Ave and Bro to give up in despair when they had carried it up the back stairs.

“I know a safe place to store it,” said Ave. She smiled at Revenberge, then Bro. “No one is ever going to get it down from *this* spot.”

CHAPTER 10
ALACRITY

We never know the entire situation, or even that which is just out of sight. This only increases our sense of isolation.

Major Peridot to Davignon at the Battle of Charney

"What city is that?" Dav asked. No one answered, nor did anyone remove the heavy leather hood. *Where is Alain?* The wizard had been so careful with the apparatus at the beginning of the Heraldry that Dav had expected him to break it down just carefully as soon as the experiment was over. But all Dav could hear was the sound of someone softly crying. He blinked, trying to clear the tears from his eyes, and moved his head back as far as he could to give Farrah Harbinger some space. Her eyes were dark with blood. She was not moving. The great lady no longer smelled of honey and parsley. Her hands were clammy and worryingly cold.

Realizing that no one was coming to help—not soon anyway—and that the Harbinger could not wait, Dav released her hands and attempted to gather up the leather hood they were both trapped under. As he tried to push it off, it became tangled in Farrah's hair and the strange, telescope-like optical filter. The apparatus began tipping toward him, but he got a hand on it and arrested its fall. He took a deep breath and slowed down, gently feeling around the leather. Finally, by touch alone, he found the zipper and buttons and created enough space to thrust the entire, sweaty container off.

Then he tried to make sense of the horror now visible to him.

Captain Barbara Bysshe was on her knees, draped over one of the great tubs that had been wheeled into the library. Her head hung limp over the edge, and her black hair trailed into the semi-transparent light green vomit that had pooled on top of the ice. Alain Overbree lay sprawled on his back beside the whiteboard, his eyes closed. He was whimpering. Tears leaked across his face, mixing with a thin stream of blood from his mouth. Lady Sylvie lay beside another tub, her right leg bent horrendously backward, the left forward. The tub was broken down the middle and bent upward like a cracked walnut. Dav could see ice through the aperture.

"Daughter of Nimrheal," he cursed under his breath and moved quickly. He pushed the lens apparatus violently away from Farah, who slumped, sightless and unmoving, in her big, throne-like chair. Dav straightened her, kissed her forehead, and sprang forward to Lady Sylvie. "It's okay, my Lady. I am just moving you," he said gently as he got his hands under her armpits, lifted her off her grotesquely bent leg, and helped her into a sitting position with the heaved tub at her back.

"How?" Sylvie asked in a rough voice, eyes tracking up to him very slowly, head not moving at all. "How are you on your feet?"

"One moment," Dav said. He patted her hand and rushed over to Captain Bysshe. She was trembling, one of her feet sliding backward as she attempted to stand or reposition herself.

"Captain, I've got you," he said, leaning forward and putting one arm around her waist and the other just under her chin. Then he lifted her head out of the tub and helped her stand up. Her trembling hand found his and clung to it. "Can you stand on your own?" he asked and reluctantly peeled his hand away from hers. She began to list to one side, so Dav grappled with her again and carried her across the room to a chair. He did not want to sit her near the tub where she would smell her own vomit. She leaned forward on the chair and rested her face on his chest. "You will be okay, Barbara," he whispered as he gently pushed her shoulders back so he could step away.

"I'll get help," he announced in a loud voice, running across to the library's enormous double doors and flinging them open. Two of the Harbinger's aids stood there, nervous and at attention. One of the women had an armload of towels, while the other held two steaming buckets of water. *She knew.* "The lady Harbinger needs you now," he said. "If there are others you can call upon to help you, do so immediately. Go! I will return soon."

Leaving the ladies to attend to Farrah and the others, Dav sprinted down the hallway, making for the main hall. Servants, a large contingent of tradesmen, and a few armsmen scurried throughout the vast building, but he did not spy the man he was searching for. "Proulx! Where are you?" he roared. Instead of the sergeant, a richly dressed middle-aged man in a purple cape and top hat, carrying a fat leather bag, approached.

"Lieutenant Davignon?" The man asked. "I'm the Lady Harbinger's doctor. Terribly sorry I'm late. How is she?"

"How did you—oh, you received a letter didn't you?" Dav did not dwell on the Harbinger's powers of prediction and organization. There was little point speculating. He stayed on task. "She's in the main library. Unconscious when I left her a moment ago. Please go to her. Quickly now."

Leaving the doctor behind, Dav dashed up several flights of stairs, crossed a suspended landing to the slender tower, raced up its tight circular stairs, and reached the observatory gasping for breath. Just as his feet hit the landing, he heard the call of the great bells of the city. First, one chimed in a vast and urgent voice from the direction of the north walls, then a second from another part of the city, then another and another. They rang out from all sides, building on each other's sound in urgent harmony, and they did not stop.

So her awful vision was true. They have been spotted. The observatory was high enough for Dav to see over the north wall. He leaned forward, against his fears, determined not to lose the commitment he had drawn on when he had looked into the green, predictive eye of the Harbinger. *There.* He saw it, the distant gray smudge, just as he had seen in Farrah's' Heraldry. *Exactly* as he had seen. *The skolves are coming.* There was no forgetting that Farrah's eye had also predicted the arrival of at least one demon. Dav whirled and looked east, then south, then west. There might have been something moving on that western horizon past the gardens, but it was too far away and too well masked by the smoke of many chimneys to tell. *How much time?*

Only the Harbinger knew.

He looked down, scanning the streets, and spotted Sergeant Patrick Proulx trotting up the cobble with five eights trailing him. "Sergeant!" he shouted. When the man looked up, Dav roared, "Double time!" As soon as he saw Proulx wave to acknowledge the command, he whirled and looked south again. *Nothing south. Nothing yet.* He ran for the stairs.

DAV INTERCEPTED Proulx in the great hall. Each of the Sergeant's forty fully armed and armored soldiers carried a pack as well as swords, spears, and bows. "Have the eights wait here, Patrick, and come with me."

"How is the Harbinger?" Proulx asked quietly as they trotted down the hallway.

Dav did not mince his words, "Bad. Very bad indeed," he replied. He saw no point in adding that he—unlike Proulx—had never observed a Heraldry before and had certainly never seen anyone attempt to break a locus. But he knew that Farrah Harbinger was horribly damaged by what she had done.

Proulx was an affable sort from what Dav had seen, but he was not smiling now. "And the others?" he asked after a moment.

"On their asses. All sick. Not one of them capable of much of anything right now."

"Well," Patrick said, "hadn't we better get them talking at least? We need to find out what the Harbinger saw."

"We need to get them fit for action again, Sergeant, and as quickly as possible, but I saw the Heraldry."

"My Knights! Proulx winced. "All of it? You didn't—I don't know—do something sensible? Close your eyes?"

"No."

"How are *you* ... not on your ass too?"

Dav did not like the implication that keeping faith with the Harbinger had been optional. He had never imagined letting go of Farrah's hands and leaving her to it, though he had no idea what he had really accomplished under the bag with her, watching the terrible visions unroll. He doubted he had somehow anchored her, broke her from her bell chamber, or helped her in some other impossible to understand—magical—way. He did not want to think that his devilled left hand or ... other issues related to it had been of any service to the wizard. He had stayed with her to the end, whatever his feelings, and had no desire to explain why. He answered as flatly as he could. "Perhaps that is why she chose me."

Patrick Proulx's right eyebrow twitched upward, but he only replied, "I guess so."

They passed through the library doors. The beautiful room was full of the smell of vomit, and the broken tubs did nothing to alleviate the general air of misery. The purple-caped doctor was attending to the Harbinger, still slumped and unmoving, Captain Bysshe was blinking her eyes owlishly and dabbing a wet towel against her long dark hair, and another attendant was talking softly with Lady Sylvie, who had been moved to a chair. Her right leg had been elevated with another chair and a cushion, but her bloodshot eyes were moving at normal speed again. Alain Overbree still lay on his back, clutching a towel over his eyes and shuddering convulsively. Dav realized the wizard was crying.

Waving the sergeant to stay with him, Dav approached Alain and went down on one knee beside him. “Alain? Can you hear me?”

The crying stuttered to a stop. “Yes,” Alain said weakly.

“Good. Can you drop the towel and speak with me? It is urgent.”

Overbree wiped his eyes and face with the towel and slowly lowered it. His face was red and mottled. He had gotten most of the snot with the towel, but his upper lip was still moist. “Please don’t yell,” he said in his cultured tones. “My head rather hurts.”

“Do you remember what the Lady Harbinger tasked you to do?”

“Yes, I believe so. I mean, of course I do.” He swallowed and shuddered again. “I should talk to her about that.”

“She is unavailable,” Dav said flatly. Then, harder, he asked, “What was it? What are you to do?”

Alain frowned at Dav’s tone but answered. “To—to go to Engevelen City. To see to it that the Methueyn Order aids Nehring Ardgour’s envoy.”

Dav leaned in close and looked carefully at Alain’s eyes. “Yes,” he said. “That is your mission. Can you stand up? You need to leave *now*.”

Alain tried to get up, managed a crouch, stalled, then said, “No, I don’t believe I can go just yet. Can’t quite . . . stand up, you see.” He lowered himself clumsily onto the floor, his hands splayed out on it as if the ground was spinning. His body curled slightly as if *he* was turning.

“Sergeant!” Dav bellowed. “Go and call for two of your men. They are to come and carry Alain Overbree out of here. He needs to be on his way to Engevelen immediately.” He heard Proulx rush out the door.

“I am in no shape for travel, Lieutenant,” Alain protested piteously, hands still pushing on the smooth stone of the floor.

“Do you hear the bells?” Dav asked. Even in the library, they could be faintly heard. “The Skolves are attacking. From the north. Just as in the Heraldry.”

“Davignon,” said Lady Sylvie tiredly, “you could tell the direction?”

"Yes," Dav said, "and I saw it from the observatory. The way south is still clear. He may get free if he goes now."

"How are you on your feet, Lieutenant?" Barbara Bysshe asked weakly, eyelids fluttering as she tried to follow his movements. Dav could barely hear her. It was as if viewing the Heraldry had poured the life out of her.

"I'm not well," moaned Alain. He pushed himself up on his hands and knees and dry-heaved noisily. When he was done, a long thin trail of fluid hanging off his lips, he said, "You—you can't order me. I'll go in a few minutes. When I'm better."

Dav could hear heavy footsteps coming down the hall. "You will go now while you can," he said firmly. Proulx and two armsmen came around the corner. He gestured to them and said, "Pick him up and take him to Engevelen City. Hurry, before we are encircled."

The soldiers bent and grabbed Alain's arms. As they started to hoist the philosopher up, he wailed, "No! Put me down. This *sergeant* can't give me orders—." He dry-heaved again, this time into their arms.

The soldiers hesitated. Proulx rubbed his chin and said, "Uh, he might have a point, Lieutenant. Chain of command dictates that—"

"This must happen, Sergeant," whispered Captain Bysshe from her chair. "Those are the orders of the Lady Harbinger."

"Okay, but—"

"Get on with it, Proulx. The country depends upon it," said Lady Sylvie.

"We're going," Proulx said decisively. He waved the soldiers and their reluctant burden out of the library and followed them. On his way out, he lifted his brows at Dav and raised both hands in a small gesture of peace.

"I'll be right back," Dav said to Sylvie and Bysshe, then followed Proulx, Alain and the two soldiers out the door. He caught up to them quickly and matched step with the sergeant. The head of the column of soldiers was just visible at the end of the hallway. "Prepare to move out!" Dav shouted to them. Turning to Proulx, he said, "There can be no delay now, no balking, Sergeant."

"I'm sorry I hesitated back there. I was just making sure," said Proulx as they rushed down the long hallway toward the main hall.

"I understand," replied Dav.

"And then—"

"We have no time for worrying about feelings or niceties," interrupted Dav. "Literally no time."

Proulx nodded, relieved. "So, am I taking a horse and carriage or what?"

"You can't," Dav said. "Skolves smell horses. They'll encircle the city, then track down every fresh horse scent they find."

"The Battle of Charney?"

"Yes." Dav thought fast, trying to organize the information he needed to give the sergeant. "Put him in a handcart or a goat cart and run for the gate. Take three of the eights with you and go as fast as you can. Don't worry about endurance, don't worry about tomorrow. If you can make it the ten miles to Lareaul, you can get horses there. Tracking won't matter at that point. Stop for nothing. Tell the remaining eights to stand by for orders." Dav nodded to Proulx, then passed him, picking up his pace, racing toward the end of the hall.

"He is going to be sooo embarrassed when he feels better!" Proulx called to his back.

Just get him to Engevelen City! Dav did not bother shouting it down the hall. Patrick Proulx knew what he had to do. And when he recovered from the mind-bending, stomach-churning Heraldry, Alain would sort himself out.

Other exigencies remained.

When Dav reached the soldiers, he said, "The sergeant will be taking some of you with him. Those who remain, make certain you each have food and water in your packs." Then he was past them all and sprinting down the stairs to the main hall. His searching eyes found what he was looking for. A page. The young lady wore a military jacket but no armor and stood near the apse of Sandeyl. A statue of a broken sandal stood in the space there.

He dodged around a column of tradespeople moving dollies of

bricks—another mystery—and approached the messenger. "Page," he said, "I have orders for you to take. Do you have a notebook?"

Her black hair was styled in braids, and her eyes were wide, scared, excited. Alive. The bells were loud here in the hall, and the page was breathing hard, prepared for danger, body ready to act. "Yes, sir," she said in an eager, urgent voice.

"Pass it to me." Dav wrote in the book—thankfully with no interference from his left hand—signed the note and returned it to her. "I am going to tell you the message verbally also. You are to tell the commander of the south gate to allow Sergeant Proulx and his group immediate egress. *Immediate* and *without* delay." He made sure her eyes were on him. "That means to have a postern door ready for them. He is then to order the scorpions on the south wall to be manned, readied, and loaded. When the skolves circle around the south wall, he is to fire on them. He is to fire even if they don't threaten the wall, even if they turn away from the wall. I want them disrupted and disrupted *hard*. This is an order from Farrah Harbinger. Do you understand?"

"Yes, sir."

The lieutenant grabbed her arm and said, "I want you to stand on the wall with the commander and observe the departure of Sergeant Proulx and his men. Stay there until the skolves encircle the south wall. *Count* the number of shots fired at the skolves until one hundred is reached. Count out loud, please. As loud as you can. When this is done, report directly to Lady Sylvie."

She stared at him, her eyes like saucers. "Right, go now," Dav said. "If there's no horse in sight of the doors, run as fast as you can."

"Yes, sir," she said again and dashed away.

Dav raced back toward the stairs. He met Proulx and his men coming off the wide steps as he sprinted across the smooth stones of the enormous hall. "The south wall expects you, Sergeant," Dav said as he passed him. He did not see the salutes that followed him as he bounded up the steps.

He was up the stairs and back to the hallway in another moment. He passed the remaining soldiers stationed there, told them to "Stand to," and was back at the doors of the library a moment later. Crossing the room, he saw the doctor still working on Farrah. Captain Bysshe had crossed the room to sit beside Lady Sylvie.

"Feeling better?" he asked as he knelt on one knee in front of them.

"Not as good as you, Lieutenant," Barbara said with the closest approximation to a smile she seemed capable of producing. Little beads of sweat stood out on her forehead, and her dark skin looked sickly and pale.

Lady Sylvie's right leg was still elevated on another chair, not far from where Dav knelt. Her voice was tight with pain as she spoke, "I never understood why you were called out of the Renet. I *did*," her eyes widened, "see your test results, and I would never have had you here. Never." Her eyes relented. "I should have trusted the Lady Harbinger." She turned her head heavily toward Farrah, then back to Dav. "You are indeed the man who turned the Battle of Charney. Now, what do you need?"

Dav only nodded to acknowledge the recantation. "Alain Overbree is on his way to Engevelen City. There is nothing more we can do on that score. I need to find the weapon that Lady Harbinger ordered recovered, the one that can kill this new devil."

"The One True Devil," said the captain, eyes searching his face, "whatever horror that could be."

"Right," said Dav. It struck him then as curious that no image of this devil had been shown in the Heraldry. Perhaps such a picture would have finished everyone off. "I need to know what old city it was that she showed us. You are both more educated than I. Do you know?"

Lady Sylvie swore under her breath. "I failed where you did not, Davignon. I am ashamed to admit it. I lost consciousness after the Lady Harbinger said you must kill the devil, but before she showed where the weapon was."

Damn it.

"I saw it," whispered Barbara. "But I could make no sense of it as an image. It was all mixed up. Twisted." The captain's face screwed up in horror. "If you set me before a painting of it, and if I could stare at it for a week—if I could survive that—I couldn't tell you what it showed."

I saw it perfectly well. Dav suppressed the thought. It was not a point of pride but of fear. "I can describe it for you, in detail, and you can tell me where it is."

CHAPTER 11

DEADPOINT

We will tonight, neither mete out justice nor bring fairness to an unfair, cruel situation. We are running away, sneaking, quitting the battlefield, abandoning our countrymen. But in so doing, we will provide ourselves, on another night, a chance to face, head on, our true enemy.

Lieutenant Davignon, siege of Courant

The four bells of Courant continued their deep reverberations. The city still held. *Someone must be swinging them instead of running away.* That was a simpler alternative to the other reasons Dav was content to take so much time studying the archives with Lady Sylvie and Captain Bysshe, trying to find the city he had seen in Farrah's eye. *I saw Courant damaged, but it did not fall.* He remembered one of the demons—Skoll or Hati—smashing the hugel gardens and elements of the outer walls, but he had also seen Sir Sandeyl. The other reason he was taking the time, though still not the main, the true, reason, was his trust in Farrah's Heraldry. She was renowned for it, known to be the best at it, the woman with the oracular eye.

And some of the Harbinger's images were identical to those he had seen himself earlier that day when his ... defect had come over him. He had never known his passing episodes to be wrong. But neither did they bring him happiness.

But even this was not Dav's true reason. What drives people is often unknown even to themselves, only discoverable through effort, if at all.

"No, that isn't it," he said. "The hall at its center was in a lake."

"Not Nuage then," said Lady Sylvie. "It was a great city before the first invasion." She unsuccessfully concealed a wince, likely pain from her right leg, still elevated on a chair. "I understand that Nehring Ardgour smelted it into another of his many mines. I am glad you are not going there. It is a very long way now."

A long way into Ardgour County, she meant. A long way through country filled only with enemies.

Barbara Bysshe brought over another stack of books and placed them carefully on the library table. Unlike Lady Sylvie, she had not broken anything during the Heraldry, but she had been deathly ill for some time afterward. She was able to walk now without listing visibly to one side or the other and could drink water without vomiting. The captain was ambulatory, but Dav thought there was an injury in her eyes. They were harder, full of pain and—perhaps—suspicion. She was certainly watching him more closely than ever. "So it's not Nuage, or Arley, Cambrain or Rouyanne, or the other half dozen other candidates we have shown you," she said. "If you have doubts about any of them, speak now so we don't eliminate a place we should not."

"Yes," Lady Sylvie agreed, "let us be certain. These notes, even these maps, are out of date now. The cities may look quite different today as you saw them in the Heraldry than they did when illustrated in these old books."

"I am sure," Dav replied.

Sylvie shifted her leg uncomfortably. "We lost so much when Ardgour invaded. Half of Engevelen, gone. Unnumbered dead, whole cities destroyed, an ancient government overthrown. The people on this side of the new border separated forever from friends and family. On the other side—Nehring Ardgour's side—they lost their freedom too. So many were enslaved to work in the new mines, and on those mad engineering projects." She sighed. "But that was not the worst of it. They lost their freedom to pursue our culture or change it as they wished, Nimrheal willing. We *all* lost history, books, texts, libraries, art." She gestured at the new stack of books that Barbara had just brought and said, "*This* is almost all we have left, Davignon. Harbinger Hall is home to the last great library in Engevelen, and it may well fall and be destroyed tonight or in the coming days. Yet there is more to it than just *this* and *now*. With Skoll and Hati running amok, destroying our cities, we have forgotten Nimrheal. An understandable mistake perhaps, but what we built here in Courant and in all of Engevelen is a marvel. Our gardens, our art, our aqueducts are marvels, and all of them were built from sacrifices extracted by Nimrheal. We have paid for every advance with our blood."

"It *is* a beautiful library," Dav said, not sure what to add. He had seen the raised aqueducts knocked down and smashed, the bodies strewn in the streets. He had seen even Harbinger Hall destroyed. *I am not going to speak of what I saw.* What good would it do? Preparations had been made already by Farrah, and Lady Sylvie had seen enough in the Heraldry. The shock of it had caused the explosion of grief or dismay that had ruined her leg.

"It is, indeed," Sylvie said. "But you should have seen the library at Arsenault. It was perhaps the most amazing sanctuary of learning in the world, a library in a castle surrounded by roaring water right on a ley line. It was an astonishing place."

Dav marveled at how her treatment of him had changed since the ill-fated attempt to break the locus. Before this, she had barely tolerated him, and then only because Farrah Harbinger insisted that she put up with him. Now she treated him like a favored confidant, and despite the horrific pain she must be feeling, she was doing everything she could to help him find his way. *Or it could be the drugs.* The doctor had given her an aggressive dose of milk of morphia.

"Sir? Ma'am?" asked private Marianne, a stocky soldier, but neat and in good trim. "Your packs are ready as you ordered."

Dav did not look at her. Finding the city was the priority. "Thank you, Private. Leave them by the door please, and assemble with Raydell, Tayleur, Harcourt and Darcelle in the main hall."

"I *am* coming with you, Davignon," announced Captain Bysshe. She was flipping pages for him. He looked at her fingers. They were clean, well-trimmed, but trembling uncontrollably. She followed his eyes. "I can travel."

"You should eat something," he said.

She opened a new book. It was large, about two feet tall and perhaps a foot wide. "What happened to the reticent lieutenant I knew this morning?" She narrowed her eyes shrewdly and added, "You took command as well as anyone I've ever seen." She flipped to a new page and city. "It was obvious even in the condition I was in. Makes me wonder who you really are."

Dav refused to wonder what Bysshe was thinking. Was she genuinely mystified by him or just trying to put him in his place? Perhaps her comments—like so many that people made—were simply noise, idle chat signifying nothing. There were other priorities, and time was short. "Major Peridot taught me ... what you saw. Are you really planning to come with me?"

"You need my rank behind you. Too many local commanders will be scrounging troops in the countryside."

Dav could see the reason in that. It would not do to be drafted into some other mission. Farrah's directive was too important. "In that case, you really should eat." *You left what was in your stomach decorating the tub.* Dav still wondered why and how the steaming waters of those large tubs had been frozen.

A hollow booming sound interrupted his thoughts and made him raise his head. The sound was faint and low. It had travelled far.

"That may be the west wall," Dav said, remembering the Heraldry. "We have to find this city at once." He looked down at the page again.

"That one!" he exclaimed, pointing to a tall tower in a square surrounded by an artificial lake. It had been different in Farrah's eye, roughened by years of neglect and defaced by recent violence, but he was certain.

"That is Chamberry," said Barbara, who had flipped the page and found the city. "It is not far north of Villiers, just across the new border."

"A stroke of luck that it is so close. You could be there in less than a week," said Lady Sylvie. "Let's see it on the map." She gestured peremptorily at Bysshe.

The captain pushed the book aside and flipped through several maps before finding one at the correct scale. "We need to go west," she said, pointing, "and try to get back into territory we still hold. Then north to Villiers, resupply, then cross the border and on to Chamberry." She raised her brows.

"And afterward?" asked Sylvie pointedly.

"We will have a weapon capable of killing the One True Devil," said Dav. "Perhaps we can use it against Skoll and Hati too. Or someone else can."

Sylvie asked, "How?"

Bysshe said, "We bring it back to Villiers for a start. Use it there or get it into the hands of a wizard or a Methueyn Knight or whoever this weapon is meant for." She scowled and said, "It could hardly be more straightforward."

"I'll tell whomever I can as long as I can," said Sylvie. "But this plan will not even start if you cannot escape Courant."

"If," agreed Dav. He had an idea of how to escape the city. It was encircled now, he knew that. The page had returned earlier and reported that Alain had been carried out of town and the commander of the wall had helped cover the run south, but since then they had heard reports of thousands of skolves, in depth, all around Courant. A burst of adrenaline made his heart race. Reason and need coalesced.

There will be no going back, no chance to ask later.

Dav did not believe he would see the Harbinger or Lady Sylvie again. "I have to ask you something, Lady Sylvie," he said.

"Ask."

Dav looked past Sylvie toward Farrah and the doctor. He was still working on her. She had still not moved. Turning back to Sylvie, he said, "I *heard* what the Lady Harbinger said about breaking the locus, I *saw* her Heraldry, I *understand*—I think—that she was somehow able to unravel and identify specific moments critical to not one but two separate knots in potential events. What I don't know is what she did to *affect* what will happen. Other than sending Alain to Engevelen City and myself and the captain to Chamberry."

"You wish a technical answer?" Sylvie asked, a harsh smile passing fleetingly across her lips. "I cannot give it to you. You saw the tubs, Lieutenant?" When he nodded, she continued. "The Lady borrowed energy from them to find those critical moments. I saw the vessels cool one at a time as she worked, but I assure you that she poured energy into not just finding but *affecting*."

"And that's it? Three frozen tubs and problem solved?"

Captain Bysshe shook her head warningly at Dav, but Lady Sylvie looked more tired than angry. He could hear the pain and weariness in her voice as she answered. "I cannot explain the *how* to you. I do not know. Like you, I only serve. However, I doubt that a thousand tubs of water have enough energy to alter, by themselves, the course of events. I believe the Lady Harbinger has been working to this end by other means for some time now. Perhaps she has been expending a little bit of effort over a long period. You saw the building materials stationed around the hall? The stoneworkers? There are prefabricated barriers and workmen placed on her orders in extremely specific locations throughout the city. She *saw* some of this siege and *acted* some time ago. And what of you? She ordered you brought here weeks ago, did she not? She brought you into a position of trust. And she has set you upon this path. I believe that this is the calculus by which she means to change the world."

"I told you before, Lieutenant," Barbara interjected, "the Harbinger does not operate by luck."

"So this was all *planned?"* It was obvious that the attendants, the doctor, perhaps even the bricks and tradespeople he had seen downstairs, had been planned. He considered the Harbinger again, still unmoving in her chair. *Not everything goes according to plan.* He thought again. *Some terrible results are simply . . . accepted.*

"Whether I believe it or not, I will do everything I can." Dav remembered the feel of Farrah's hands under the canvas, the capillaries in her bright green eye bursting one after another. "Not because I believe or understand, but for her courage."

"Well," said Sylvie, closing her eyes, "you have declared yourself."

Dav nodded to her, even though she never saw it. The lady had fallen asleep. He rose and whispered to Barbara, "Are you ready to go?"

Bysshe's hands still shook, but she stood up easily enough. "How do you propose to get through the skolve lines?"

"I have an idea," Dav replied. "But I'll need to show you from the observatory." He got to the door first and handed her one of the packs.

Barbara fell into step beside Dav as they started down the hallway. "You made your decision before asking those questions of Lady Sylvie, Dav. You made it before you so ably took command following the Harbinger's fall. So why did you really ask all that about Heraldry?"

Dav dodged the question. The escape plan was more important. He explained what he proposed to do. Reluctantly, it seemed, and only after staring into his eyes for an uncomfortably long period, Captain Bysshe nodded her agreement.

Why? Perhaps because Courant is completely surrounded, lacks the strength to break the skolve lines, and there is no other option.

"Lead it out, Lieutenant," Bysshe said when they had assembled back at the heavily guarded doors to Harbinger Hall. Dav studied the captain and five other soldiers they were taking on the mission. With the exception of Bysshe, they each wore black chain under their tabards. She was unarmored, but carried a short, heavy spear and an arming sword. At Dav's insistence, Privates Marianne, Darcelle, and Harcourt carried the same weaponry. Raydell and Tayleur each carried a short bow and short sword.

Reviewing their kit reminded Dav of Charney. *If we don't time this right, none of us will be alive an hour from now.* "Okay," he said, "the order of the day is close formation. No gaps." He nodded as if to himself and added, "We need to be silent if we can, but if we get into the middle of a fight we have to communicate, and loudly."

"That's confusing," said Marianne.

Dav exchanged a quick look with Bysshe, who had raised an eyebrow. "Right," he said. "As the captain and I explained, this is all about stealth and timing. We are not heading out looking to engage. So, no talking." He smiled. "But if our timing is off and we are forced into a fight, I expect instant and constant communication. Only by working together can we beat the skolves. Make sense?"

"Yes sir," Marianne said. Dav looked at the other four soldiers until they also assented.

"Okay," Dav said, and motioned for the soldiers guarding the doors to open them. It was dark outside, and quieter that Dav had thought it would be. There was less commotion than he had expected. He stepped out onto the street and checked both directions. Lamp light reflected gently off the smooth, polished stones of the cobbles. An eight crossed about a hundred yards to the north. Citizens stood under the lamplight, pointing and talking. He ignored them all and crossed the street at a trot, stopping only when his shoulder found the wall of the café he had patronized earlier that day. Dav looked up and out into the city again. His eyes were already adjusting. He could see a halo of lights shrouding the distant city walls like a yellow smudge against the black of night.

Now, when *are we?*

Nothing that he could see had been destroyed yet. He focused on the table he had been sitting at earlier and visualized what he had seen in his one horrific vision of the future. *The aqueduct. The bodies.* Dav superimposed those images against the ones Farrah Harbinger had shown him and realized something. *Those images did not show events at the same time. My vision from* earlier *was of something* later *in time.*

He listened, trying to determine where the fighting was. He could hear the heavy sounds of the scorpions firing and the blurred yelling of soldiers. He squinted and made out citizens crowded on a roof not far away, some looking north, some looking west. Great waves of sound rolled off them. Cheers or cries of dismay, it was impossible to tell which.

Dav nodded to himself. *We have time.*

He stepped out into the middle of the street and started leading his small troop west at a brisk, quick-time pace. They shifted north at the next intersection, but adjusted west again at the next turn, joining the West Way, a main road going straight to the gate on the west wall. The dusky orange walls could be seen a mile away, and Dav thought he could see the scorpion teams firing. Screams rang out eerily from the direction of the wall. A massive collision rumbled out into the night. It sounded like a colossal boulder hitting solid stone.

That's Skoll. Or Hati. Dav decided he would call the demon Skoll and hoped he would never have occasion to be corrected. Skoll had hit the wall again, but judging from the sound, had not yet broken it. Dav turned north and increased the pace to forced march.

They passed an eight leading a team of tradesmen along the same road and turned west again. A full company of eight eights passed Dav's team going the other way. There was no talking, exchange of greetings, or acknowledgement between the two groups, only the jangling of chain and the breathing of soldiers moving under the load of arms and fear of death. In moments, they had passed beyond even those sounds; the amber night swallowed them up.

It grew brighter.

The wall was much closer now. Drawing nearer brought a keen new awareness of activity. The sounds of the scorpions releasing their enormous steel spears split the night every few seconds. An incomprehensible grumble became detectable, the sound of the siege crews talking to each other. The wall was in sight.

Another massive collision cracked the darkness. It was due west. Chunks of the parapet flew from the wall, followed by single screaming soldier, all landing with muted thuds. An enormous metal plate leaned against the wall perhaps twenty paces south of the fallen armsmen. A group of figures huddled beside it, but none of them moved to help the soldier, who was writhing from side to side. Soldiers who had been nearby on the wall scattered north and south. Dav turned north again, and called out, "Double time," increasing the pace to a fast jog.

One city block later, they turned west again. The wall was just ahead now. The ground began to reverberate as they approached. A faint, deep roar reached Dav's ears, and the rumbling of the ground grew more violent. He could feel the shaking though his feet. A scorpion crew was frantically turning their weapon downward, but they were limited by the winch wheel, which quickly achieved maximum height. They fired, and the sound of the metal spear hitting something as hard as itself rang out at a high, violent pitch.

Dav reached the end of the street with his troop, and the end of cover. He hand-signaled a halt and sheltered, crouching, against the side of the final building, searching the wall.

There. A postern door. Two soldiers stood in the shadows, flanking it.

"Is that it?" asked Captain Bysshe.

Dav turned and held his palm up to her and the soldiers. "Wait," he said, and turned back to the wall, searching the spot where the soldier had fallen. The dying man had crawled a few arm's lengths and sprawled on his face. The wall just behind the downed fighter was grossly deformed. Even from where he crouched, Dav could clearly see the gaping cracks in the rock rising from the ground to the broken section of the parapet where the soldier had formerly stood. The wall itself bulged inward several feet.

Can it take another hit?

A piteous crying sound reached them. Dav recognized the sound of a too-young man in mortal agony. He had heard such high-pitched cries before.

"We should help her!" said Marianne, misreading the injured man's sex. Dav could hear her shifting. "How can they just leave her there?" She could only mean the group huddled nearby in the shadow of the big steel plate.

"Be still, private," ordered Bysshe. "Everyone here has a job."

"But—"

"Watch," Dav said. "Listen." *When will the moment come?* He listened to the sounds of the soldiers on the wall, to the vast, deep roaring he could finally hear clearly now that they were closer, and looked up again to the scorpion team. He saw them adjust their weapon, point it farther out from the wall, and fire. Shouts and curses followed quickly on the sight of the scorpion being shifted to fire downward.

It's charging again.

The ground shook harder and harder. Dav could feel his teeth rattling.

"No matter what happens next, don't move until I do," he ordered.

The roaring grew painful. The wall they huddled beside shook in tune with the ground. Glass shattered in a window above them. Dav thrust his hands over his head as pieces of glass rained down.

It smells like lightning.

The wall exploded with all the suddenness of lightning and the roar of thunder. Dav forced his eyes to stay open despite the instinct to close them against the hurtling debris from the wall. The downed soldier was engulfed in a rolling carpet of rocks and dust.

Skoll sprang forth from the gap. A flickering blue nimbus

surrounded the demon. It stood eight feet tall, and where it stepped, the earth shook. Its all too human face shone with an indescribable fusion of rage, lust, and joy. It was the epitome of a mania beyond human understanding or experience, a mad, murderous, unstoppable frenzy. The colossal, malevolent ecstasy of that face exceeded anything Dav could comprehend.

Yet I know this demon.

This *was* Skoll. Dav had seen the demon at Charney. Its silver plate armor was more dented now, the helm was gone, and it carried a great sword—perhaps a Methueyn blade. The sword was enormous, but it did not look out of place in the giant's hand. Dav's gut roiled. A wave of sickness that was both physical and spiritual washed over him. The sensation was familiar from Charney.

No.

Dav's left hand suddenly fluttered Delphic messages in the air—some secret and subtle language only it knew. He watched the next few moments spray like paint across his fluttering eyelids.

It was over in three unending seconds—an involuntary, stretched, deadpoint of agony—before his mind returned, falling upward from hell to the earth.

"Davignon!" hissed Barbara. Her hands were on his spasming shoulders.

"The Beast is random," Dav said to himself, body and mind coming back under his conscious control.

"What?" the captain's blue eyes were huge. The fine hairs on the back of her neck were visibly standing up.

Dav whispered, "Don't. Move." There was no time for fear of what had just a moment ago happened, of the brief reminder of his doom. The sharp edge of the present had all his attention.

When the last piece of wall bounced off the demon, the blue nimbus disappeared. The roar Skoll hurled into the fragile air could have cracked teeth or shattered eardrums. The monster looked around it for a moment, saw and evidently dismissed the metal plate and its huddling attendants, then seemed to stare hard in Dav's direction. It froze, looked directly at him, took one, earth-shaking step toward him and ... stopped.

Dav could feel Bysshe's hands on his shoulders, shaking him wildly, then heard a whimper from one of the soldiers behind her. Bysshe's spear was on the ground, its spear point not far from Dav's right foot.

The demon's left hand pawed at its face once before it abruptly turned and bounded to the side, roaring away into the city. A heavy, sharp concussion slapped Dav against the wall. Smaller crashes followed. Skoll had hit a building. The ground shook, there was another vast and overpowering roar, and then the sounds moved farther off.

"Daughter of fucking Nimrheal!" exclaimed Marianne. "I thought it was coming right for us."

Someone was whimpering, "Fuck, fuck, fuck."

Another asked, "What is that stench?"

Yes, rotting meat.

Bysshe's hands were still virtually drumming a fearful message onto Dav's tabard, but she hissed, "Shut it."

"Pick up your weapons!" Dav shouted pushing himself away from the wall. Bysshe was far from the only soldier who had ever dropped her weapon in the face of the demon. "Double time." He ran straight for the postern door. The hundred yards in the open, under the orange lights of the wall lamps, were terrifying. They were only about sixty yards north of the hole Skoll had blasted in the wall. The two guards were concealed in the shadow of the inset postern. "Open the doors," Dav yelled as he closed the distance. "Now!"

A set of four heavy portcullises were built into the postern, each just wide enough for an armored soldier to squeeze through. It took time to raise them. Orders were relayed to others on and inside the wall, out of sight. Dav turned to Barbara. She was still shaking. Sweat stood out on her forehead. She breathed in desperate, urgent gasps.

"What *are* you, Davignon?" she asked. Her eyes had always seemed to follow him with a narrow, skeptical gaze. Now they were wide as they searched his face.

Screams sheared the air followed by a hollow crash. Skoll was returning.

"Someone you trust," Dav replied. He looked into her eyes, tried to hold them, and added, "Captain, hold them together on the other side. I'll come through last. *Please.*"

She nodded slowly, broke her gaze, and plunged into the narrow passageway.

There was movement by the metal plate. Shadows moved in its vicinity. Dav heard a metallic groaning. But he had already seen this error in bloody staccato flashes across his eyelids a few moments before. He cupped his hands around his mouth and shouted, "Stop! Not yet! It's coming back! Wait until it passes." The metallic sounds stopped, and the workmen disappeared into the shadows again.

Dav found himself standing alone. Bysshe and the soldiers had gone through the wall. A commotion sounded above, curses and the snap of bow shots. A tight, turbulent stream of two or three dozen skolves shot through the breach that Skoll had made. They charged due east into the city. A sheet of arrows and the stink of putrefaction hung in the air behind them. Two skolves stumbled but got up and kept going. Dav watched an arrow strike one skolve in the back, stand there stuck in its hairy skin for a moment, then fall off. He looked down at the sword on his right hip. His reward for Charney. It could cut through skolve skin, muscle, and bone, he was sure of that. He also knew too well what would happen next with even a small number of the creatures loose in the city. The soldiers were concentrated on the walls. Most of the reserves were up there too or just inside the city near the gates, where they had expected the penetrations to occur. They were ill placed to react to this breach.

He remembered the horrifying images he had seen at the café, images of what might come, of people dead, buildings ruined. Another ear-shattering explosion shook the air.

This I cannot help. It is happening.

Dav stopped himself from contemplating the carnage now occurring and the carnage to come and passed through the postern.

Thirty feet of narrow corridor later, he came out the other side in time to hear Barbara speaking to one of the postern guards, "Just don't shoot us. Pass that up the wall, please."

The ground shook again, the reverberations growing ever stronger and louder.

Dav surveyed his soldiers. They had their weapons in hand and were huddling against the wall. The captain was staring at him. He looked up. Shadows stretched large from the top of the wall. The scorpions cast giant silhouettes in constant motion. Mixed shot from the siege weapons, longbows and crossbows arced up from the wall, visible in the lantern light for brief instants before disappearing into the darkness. He looked out. One hundred yards of dead flat ground from the wall, the ridged hugel gardens began. *Tactically too close, but so far for us.* Skolves had the infested mounds, which spread out for miles from the city. They were using the topography of the gardens for cover. He looked to the southwest and could just see the swath of destruction that Skoll had made as it had crashed through the mounds.

"On me," he said. "Double time."

They ran out into no-man's-land, angling obliquely toward the furrow that Skoll had blasted into the formerly neat rows of the hugel farm.

Loud breathing sounded in his ears. Bysshe's, Marianne's, his own. The ground reverberated more and loudly. A roaring vibration rolled toward him, catching up, louder by the moment. A rough line of skolves sprinted straight at the break in the wall—fifty of them at least—ignoring Dav and his soldiers. A scorpion spear abruptly materialized out of the dark and impaled one of them. It blew the creature and the one behind it off their feet like leaves scattered by a giant footstep. Another skolve was stopped by an arrow. Then another arrow and another and another. Rippling waves of arrows, bolts, and scorpion spears ripped into the skolves, making pincushions of a few more of the beasts.

The roaring grew louder.

They made it to the edge of the hugel gardens. The mounds had steep slopes, five or six feet high, and were laid out in ridges. Grass, cabbage, peas, lettuce, and carrots covered the outer layer of Engevelen's largest compost project. Buried under the grass were layers of humus, branches, logs, then refuse, sewage, and rotted food. The whole thing retained large volumes of water and required no irrigation. It was the organic waste of the city rendered productive, transformed slowly into food.

The hugel mounds had been attractive parts of the landscape until Skoll smashed through them, leaving a stinking, wet swath of destruction. Dav led the way through the hogbacks, drawing closer to the center of the chaos.

A skolve charged around the ridge, surprising him. He heard a metallic sound, a ringing, and then the skolve's head slapped wetly into the ground.

What?

His sword was in his left hand. He had no memory of using it, but he could only assume that he had somehow sidestepped the seven-foot creature, drawn his sword across his body with the wrong hand, and chopped halfway through the grossly elongated head.

He stepped on the head to pull his sword out of it and was brushed by Bysshe's spear, which belatedly connected with the skolve's neck. "Sorry," she said, then frowned at his left-handed grip.

Dav motioned her to follow him and wound his way between the mounds. As they drew closer to Skoll's passage, the smell of offal and rot increased. Dav signaled for them to stop just on the edge of a mound that had been torn in half. Logs, branches, produce, and shit were splashed everywhere. Vibrations made tiny waves in the dark water. He crouched.

Is this it? Is this when?

The roaring and the shaking became even more urgent. Dav knew that Skoll had shot out of the gap in the wall and was charging toward the hugel mounds, making directly for the place where they were crouching.

"Skolves!" Marianne cried. A knot of them were visible in the carved-out valley Skoll had made. They were only fifteen yards away. As one, their heads snapped toward Dav's team.

They were too many to fight.

In one shocking instant, the skolves were obliterated. Skoll had run through them, a flickering blue juggernaut against which the tall, sinewy skolves exploded. Dav caught only a passing glimpse of the snarling face of the demon as it erased its own creatures without a thought or flicker of hesitation. They had simply been in its way. It was too dark to look for whatever leftover pieces of the skolves were flung about, and no one cared to try.

"Whadwedo? Whadwedo? Whadwedo?" was the mantra of one of the soldiers. *Darcelle?*

Bysshe said, "We can't fight that," in the flattest tone Dav had ever heard.

"Let's go back!" said Marianne.

Dav turned, still crouching, and faced them. "This is all according to plan. Now—"

"That is a fucked-up plan," exclaimed Marianne. She stood up and started turning, but Dav sprang from his crouch and grabbed a fistful of chainmail through her tabard.

"Don't move!" Dav ordered. "Listen! It's coming back. Be ready to run."

The shaking again overwhelmed them. Out in the dark, a blue light flickered. Skoll had circled and was racing back the way it had come. Dav remembered the demon's face, covered in refuse, from the Heraldry. He remembered what happened next. He released Marianne, stood, and stepped out into the cut so he could see.

"Davignon! What are you doing?" Bysshe's voice was desperate.

Skoll came bounding straight toward him at tremendous speed, faster than a galloping racehorse. The blue nimbus flicked off as Skoll was hit by a man in plate armor running at about the same terrific speed, carrying a metal spear.

Sandeyl.

The Messenger Knight, the Runner, the Angel of Travel and Long Distances, had timed his strike perfectly and struck the demon at the precise instant its blue nimbus winked off. The spear shattered. A piece of metal flashed by Dav's face faster than he could track and was lost in the dark. Skoll careened sideways into a row of hugel mounds, which burst explosively when the staggering demon plunged into them.

Skoll rose to its feet, shaking bits of lettuce and offal from its face. A long, twisted branch was hanging out its ear. Sandeyl calmly faced the demon. Skoll took a step toward the knight, then frowned at an empty hand. It turned and rummaged violently in the refuse. Sandeyl sprinted past it in a blink, passing thirty yards into the dark, and snatched something from the ground. It was the oversized sword that Skoll had been carrying. The Messenger Knight pointed the sword threateningly at Skoll for a long slow moment, then turned and ran down the cut, away from Courant. Skoll roared and pursued him.

"Okay. Let's go!" Dav said. "The skolves can't smell us in this," he said as calmly as he could considering that skolves were scattered all about the hugel garden, some resting, some trying the walls. He saw some of them break cover and sprint across no man's land toward Courant's walls and could hear others not far away. He took his first step ... and stopped.

No one else had moved, not even the captain.

Bysshe's head was darting from side to side. She had never seen combat with skolves to his knowledge, let alone with a demon. Darcelle was crouched, hugging his knees in the muck, and Marianne's lips were pulled back in a rictus, revealing her canines to their gums. Her face was stained by tears. Dav's people were terrified out of their wits.

There is no time for this.

But Dav knew that they could not go on without dealing with their fear, if only in a minimal way. He had thought they were prepared. It made him think of Farah Harbinger in her hall, perhaps alive, perhaps not. She had attempted to prepare her people, had ordered workmen to the ready, set plans in motion. And now skolves were inside her city. Skoll had charged down the smooth cobble of the wide streets and visited several laps of destruction on Courant. The Harbinger had seen that. She had seen statues turned to rubble, aqueducts pulverized, grain silos detonated. She had seen all this, but she had still thought they could win.

A building falling is not the same as an institution failing.

All the beautiful structures of Courant may be destroyed. There were skolves enough, and demon enough, for that, given time. But Dav realized that even that loss could not of itself destroy Engevelen. The country, the city was more than just its buildings. Engevelen was also an *idea*. He considered Barbara and Marianne and the others. Their morale, the failing health of their country, and its essential idea of it, all seemed the same in that moment. Hanging on by threads.

Even though they had an uncertain brief window now, a temporary respite from the skolves provided by Skoll and Sir Sandeyl and by the covering destruction of the hugel gardens, Dav did not try to call the march again. Instead, he stopped, crouched, and smiled reassuringly. "It's okay," he said soothingly. "I know it's terrifying, but it *will* be okay. This is our plan."

Barbara's darting eyes focused on him. "I never thought it would be like this."

"That's for knights-damned sure!" exclaimed Marianne. "W-we are so small, so damned f-fucking small." The words came out in bursts. "What d-difference can we make, what chance do we have?"

"Alone?" Dav raised an eyebrow. "Not much. But together we can make it."

Darcelle's arms were tight around his knees, but he looked up and said, "Why didn't Skoll kill us? He was looking right at us. Why aren't we dead?"

Dav tried not to look at his left hand. He forced another gentle smile. "It probably had better things to do."

"We can't go back," Barbara said quietly. She stood up and spoke in a louder voice, "We are committed."

"Yes," Dav said. "There is only one way now, and it is directly in front of us." He paused for one last reassuring smile and said, "We *must* go now," then grasped another handful of chain—Darcelle's this time—and turned to Barbara. "Captain! Grab hold of someone. We are going together, and we are going *now*." Pulling Darcelle into motion, Dav turned and began picking his way through the Hugel mounds.

CHAPTER 12

WHAT GOOD ARE WE?

"Don't help me!" snapped Louis. He was sprawled out on the smooth stone floor like a long, decrepit, thorny bundle of sticks. "Which bastard put that floor there anyways?" Fenris ran over and started licking his face.

"Don't know," says Doog, cackling in his frog voice. "Yer older than the stones it's made of, so might be *you* know." He reached a hand down to help Louis, who slapped at it and missed.

"I said, don't help me, fool. I can get up." Louis shifted around and got onto his bony ass, breathing loudly from the effort. "Just give me a minute here. What's the damned rush?"

"There is no rush," said Mick. He felt—and hid—the love he had for Louis and Doog. It was shaping up to be another day full of the same antics as yesterday, as best as he could remember it, but he was grateful. When you are old, no change is best. Louis might be *on* the ground, and maybe he should not be teased for it, but it was better than being *under* the ground. "Just take your time."

"I said don't rush me! It's your dog I'm petting down here," shouted Louis. He pushed the puppy away, making its feet slide on the polished floor, but it came right back and licked his face again. "Bwaah, damn dog! I could've busted my last two teeth out there."

Doog put his hands on his hips. "You've got two teeth? Where are they, I'd like to know."

"You shut up." Louis had made it to his knees, but his face was within reach of the puppy's eager drooling tongue. He successfully ignored all the slobbery attention now in favor of a continuation of his grumpy repartee. "When I get my sword, I'll cut you open from your grimy caterpillar eyebrows to your moldy white pubes." Louis pantomimed slicing motions with his arms.

"Pretty much all my hairs look the same nowadays," replied Doog, putting on a pensive face. "But speaking of being sliced from pie-hole to pubes, are we getting the swords today or what?"

"If you look after Fenris for me, I'll get them. Count on it." Mick had gotten sidetracked the day before, much to Doog and Louis's frustration. "Where did you hide the wheelbarrow? I'm gonna need that."

"We'll show you that if you first tell this horse of yours to hold still!" shouted Louis. He was still trying to get up and was currently attempting to use a squirming Fenris to prop himself up. The old man pushed down on the dog's rump, and it sat, stymying the project.

Doog lost patience. He stamped over to Louis and tried to yank him the rest of the way up. Louis answered the favour with a punch that only brushed Doog's shirt, but that did not deter him. He kept flailing at his friend, while Fenris, caught in the middle, treated this as a game and shoved his tail in Doog's face.

"I gotta rescue my dog from you two," Mick said. He plunged unsteadily into the midst of the melee, got in between the dog and the men, and got his hands under Louis's. Before the old curmudgeon could react, Mick had got him back on his feet.

A few grumbles and curses later, the three old men and one young dog were on their way down the path toward the stone wall bordering the house on the hill. "You could just tell me where you put it," Mick said.

He saw Doog's eyes slide up toward his face. "*We* are *part* of this, Mick."

"That's knights-damned right!" bellowed Louis, "In fact, maybe we should come into town with you instead of sitting on our thumbs here." Just before the shoulder of the hill turned steep, he veered off the path to make his way on untrustworthy feet over rougher ground.

Mick almost told them not to come any farther. The hill was just too steep. He was barely managing it himself. He did not want to imagine Louis tumbling down the slope. He decided to be diplomatic.

"Someone should keep an eye on things here."

"Two more orderlies have gone missing," Doog added.

"You sure they're not just taking someone to the back side?" Mick asked. The broad back of the hill was where the cemetery was kept.

Louis muttered, "No. No new diggings."

That was good news. Four people had disappeared in the last week. But if the orderlies were going missing too, it might mean something even worse.

They are abandoning us. Mick did not want to think so, but it made sense from what he had observed. Watching from the outdoor deck, Mick had guessed that more than half of the civilians had evacuated already. Plenty of wagons had gone south with families and their luggage. None of it had come up the hill. But more soldiers were pouring in. It looked like someone was getting ready to make a fight of it.

"There!" exclaimed Louis, pointing at some caragana bushes. "That's where the wheelbarrow lies in wait."

Doog spit, but he was a poor spitter. The goober hung off his chin. "Damn it. Every time!" He wiped the long trail off his face, then shook his hand spastically to shake it off. To complete his ablutions, he wiped his hand on his pants, then said, "Roland wasn't one of them, if yer wondering."

"I wasn't," Mick said. His instinct was that Roland would stay, no matter what came, though he did not know why he thought so.

"I would've," Louis interjected. "After you slapped him around the other night, I thought he'd leave then for sure."

Mick scowled at that. "What are you talking about? I just grabbed his arm. That was all."

"Uhhhh ..." Doog trailed off with a furtive glance at Louis that Mick caught.

"Not *two* nights ago," Louis spluttered. "It was two or three *weeks* ago. Before the skolves started in around here. Back when everything was quiet. You tuned him up real good."

Mick felt like he was falling. "I don't remember."

Doog made a dismissive wave and hurriedly added, "Don't worry about it, old boy. It wasn't nothing."

"It doesn't *sound* like nothing."

I don't hurt people, I protect them.

"Oh no," Louis cackled, "he was *scared*."

Doog turned on him, "Will you just shut up and fall down the hill, Louis! It's over and done and Mick's feeling better now."

Suddenly, Mick was not seeing very well. The rocky ground found his butt. "I *hit* him? Why?"

"Hey, hey, hey, Mick," pleaded Louis. "It was *Roland*. He must have been bossing us around. He had it coming. Forget about it."

Doog crouched beside Mick, hands clasped anxiously. "It wasn't your fault, Mick! You were *sick*. But yer better now. We *need* you."

Mick's watery eyes cleared a little, and he squinted down the hill in the direction of town. People were still leaving in wagons. Soldiers were moving about, building fortifications, others heading north, probably to scout. To see when the skolves would come again. He could hear grasshoppers, feel the warm sun on his face, smell the grass and wildflowers, feel Fenris sitting beside him, pushing, just slightly, against his leg. He was *alive,* but he could see that it was *all* downhill, had *been* all downhill. He knew, looking at his rough, scarred hands, that he had lived a life of violence. He could not remember that life or the no doubt fearsome deeds of his more lucid days, but he felt sure somehow that it had all been to a *purpose*, to an *idea* that was still part of him, somewhere, if he could only find it again.

But he knew that he had beaten Roland to no good purpose.

~

"THIS COULD BE MY LAST CHANCE," said Sir Valence as he tossed the stick. With an enthusiastic "Ruff!" Fenris shot off after it, scrambled to a stop, picked up the stick, and ran straight to Mick. He shook his head at the dog and pointed back to Valence. Fenris padded over to the other old man, who was sitting comfortably in a chair on the deck overlooking the city. Mick could not help but smile at dog and friend. "Last chance?" he asked.

Valence was a rawboned man, lean but grown frail. His whispery voice suited his appearance, though it could not really be described as weak. Just quiet. Considered. "When you're young, life lies ahead. You get lots of chances." He chuckled. The last time Mick had seen Valence, the old knight had soiled himself, but he seemed to have recovered, and not just in body. "Or you think you do, anyway," Valence said with his old acuity. "If you fail at something when you're young, you at least get to try again with the hope of doing better."

"Unless you're killed."

Valence tossed the stick again. Fenris leaped in pursuit. "Sure, but you never consider that possibility when you're young, not seriously anyway. And for a while it's true. And that is pretty good, Mick, as far as human beings go."

Mick pointed at Valence before the stick-bearing Fenris got to him, saving the puppy a stop. "How can a temporary truth be good? Truth should last forever."

"The immutability of truth, hey?" Valence looked up at the sun and said, "I used to be a pretty good knight once, you know. Fast and sharp. And more important, implacably just." He looked down toward the city, putting his face into shade. "Now, not so much. You *saw* me yesterday."

"I have a short memory," said Mick.

Valence chuckled. He accepted the stick once more from Fenris and threw it again as the dog demanded. "Your memory has improved, Mick. Do you know that? Anyway, back to your question. Laws of the universe, those have universal truth. They last. You're right about that. Truth for people, though, that may be temporary. The truth of their feelings and capabilities."

This hit to the heart of Mick's worries. He had not asked the old knight if he knew what had happened with Roland, but it was as if Valence were speaking directly to his personal crisis. "We fail ourselves," Mick whispered.

"What?" said Valence, then, "Yes, that's right. Our bodies and minds fail. Here, look at this." He held a shaking hand out for Mick to see. The thumb and two of his fingers were bent inward at the metacarpal joints. They looked double-jointed. It looked as if the joints had bent backward and the hand had turned in on itself in some arthritic inversion of purpose. Some agency of time and the temporary nature of humanity had ruined Valence's hand. *When did this happen?*

Mick did not ask that question; it was not the salient point. He said instead, "I'm sorry, sir. Does it hurt?"

"Only when I pick up things," Valence laughed, picking up the stick and throwing it again for Fenris. "At our age, anything we do could be our last chance at it. Everything we do could be the last thing we do."

"If only," Mick said ruefully, "we were in better shape for it."

"If. Ha. The thing that happened yesterday. The thing you say you don't remember. It could happen again. At any time. I'm ashamed of it." He caught Mick's eyes with his own and did not let go. "It's like our quiet, unremembered, unspoken-of deaths. We don't—I can barely talk about it, but we need to. They're the same: the ultimate death or the thousand little deaths of dignity."

"You kept yours," said Mick.

"Thank you. You helped. I wish you had never seen it. I wish *no one* had, but if I lived in fear of it and said no to my narrowing opportunities, I would never get a chance at anything good again." Valence accepted the stick from Fenris once more and cocked his skinny arm and his time-mangled hand to throw one more time. "So you see why I must accept your proposal? *Yes*, is my answer, I will do it." He threw the stick. Fenris chased it. "I will look after your dog while you go down the hill and get us our swords." He smiled unreservedly at the puppy. "This could be my last chance to play with a dog. Did you ever think I would say no?"

Will I have another chance to do better? What if I do worse again and don't even know it?

~

Experience trauma, and every instinct you have leads you to avoid more of it. You may try to forget it or try for revenge to cancel it out. Some people talk about it, as if reliving pain somehow relieves pain. Maybe it is so for a few, but most choose avoidance. Some flee into catatonia, seeking a state of nothingness in which to bury the too much that has been done to them. Others thrust themselves into new business, avoiding the trauma through busyness.

Mick would have gladly endured knowing *why* he had beaten Roland, but with no memory of the incident he could only rely on others' stories. They had told him he had been emotionally overwrought, lost control, overreacted. They told him it was a thing he had done more than once. They told him he had been sick, that it was because he was old.

The house on the hill had a huge water reservoir. It had been put there because the house was . . . on a hill. The people living there would need water, and it was a big hill. What if the aqueducts failed in town? The house was designed to be a military fortification, one more citadel in a country of citadels, so the engineers had overbuilt the tank. The pump was meant to be run by a geared wheel and a donkey, but it also had an eight-foot-long lever that normally took two or three men to push.

Mick chose that as the lever of his self-reflection. He was not yet ready to go and find the swords. Something told him that the idea behind arming his friends might be tied up with his shame. The same instinct told him he should not acquire the weapons until he had come to terms with what he had done.

He could not remember performing the brutish acts of violence and insanity that his friends reluctantly described. He was horrified by the idea that it had happened, memory or not. Pushing the heavy pump could not take that horror away, but the work was satisfying, all the same. He could change the position of the water, apply his kinetic energy and his pain to change its position and give it potential. Mick did not think that shifting the water from its place in the town's aqueduct to a new place in the tank would change him. That was too trite for anyone with his scars and his honesty. Pushing a pump and filling the reservoir was simply something he could do that would not hurt anyone.

"Mick?" It was Lady Aurorette. She was in a pale autumn dress, one hand clutching the doorway. Someone was beside her, holding her free arm. Carol. Dressed in flattering imitation.

"Ladies," he said, and released the long handle on his pain. It would be more work starting the pump up again if he stopped, but he knew how difficult it must have been for Carol and Lady Aurorette to climb the stairs to the roof. He imagined the two old women trying to prop each other up, grabbing each other's arms, grasping fragile skin that would bruise from each touch. "Let me help you."

With a little patience and time, Mick helped the ladies to a seat on the stone bench that went around the circumference of the roof, below and part of the parapet. Lady Aurorette sat primly, hands crossed over her lap. Carol mimicked her. Mick looked at them expectantly.

"We want swords too," Aurorette said, eyes bright. They looked like spring. They were so green they made her look young, even if just for a moment.

"What?" Mick blurted before he could compose a more gentlemanly response. He was glad they had not come to speak of his mad violence. He did not want to feel better about it. He needed to be *cured.* But *swords?*

"Swords," said Carol. Her thin hair had been carefully styled, fluffed up artfully to conceal its paucity and her gray scalp. Mick remembered how wild and exposed it had looked the last time he had seen her, when he had found her and Lady Aurorette trying to help Sir Valence. "We want to help."

Both women together would be lucky to lift a heavy stick, let alone a longsword. *They tried to lift a fallen man.* "I'll see what I can do."

Sometimes one must swallow even reasonable objections.

"But if these evacuation carts come, please go."

"Why?" Aurorette asked. "What is there left for us?" But she was not really asking, she was showing. She was a lady of impeccable manners, an aristocrat. Of ancient lineage. She had, throughout her long life, always stood or sat ramrod straight. Mick *knew* that. Like Valence's hands, he could not *remember* it, but he *knew* it. She was a woman with a straight back. Always. And it was straight now, though it quivered. Beneath her courtly self-possession, she was in spasm. Mick could see by her shaking, her thin lips, her tightening green eyes, that she was in pain.

He retrieved his rolled-up jacket from the ground near the pump, brushed it off, and held it behind both women against the parapet. "You're right," he said in answer to that spasm, "the wall is dirty. Lean back on this."

Lady Aurorette slid back, but kept her upright posture. Carol was content to make more of a relaxed puddle of herself, pooled up against the jacket, the wall, and her friend. There was no fantasy Mick could conjure in which either lady could lift, let alone wield, the shortest sword, and no hell in which he would tell them this.

"What good are we in the world, Mick?" Carol asked, perhaps seeing the pity in his eyes.

Mick blinked away tears for the second time that day. "I've been asking myself that very question, but I will never ask it of you, Lady."

Carol looked at Aurorette and gushed, "See? He called me *lady*."

Lady Aurorette shrugged, "Of course he did. His eyes still work." She thrust her chin at the pump and said, "What are you doing up here, Mick? And where is Fenris?"

"The hound is playing with Sir Valence. I—" He hesitated. "I am doubting myself."

Aurorette's eyes narrowed, "Come here, Mick."

He knelt in front of her. The lady smoothed the collar of his shirt, and without warning, slapped him across the face. He nearly cried at the blow, not because it hurt him, but because he knew it had hurt her hand.

"It is wrong for a knight to doubt himself," she said.

Mick stayed on his knees. He hung his head. "I beat Roland for no reason. I don't remember it, but I know I did it. It would be wrong to have done this and not doubt."

"You are confusing regret with doubt." She raised an eyebrow and said, "Though if you can't even remember the event, I'm not sure regret makes sense." Her eyes blazed with spring again, and she added in a commanding voice, "You were ill, old man. Move on and do better, if you can."

Carol smiled sweetly at him. "And get us the sharp metal, dear."

Mick stood. He smiled wryly at Carol. "Whatever you wish."

She called me a knight. He looked sharply at Lady Aurorette, "You've seen what I have done. In the past." He did not mean what he had done to Roland a few weeks before.

"Yes."

"Do you trust me?" *Do you trust me now? The present me?*

"I know you from . . . before. I know who you were."

"What is my name?" Mick had thought only Brigitte knew him from before. He had suspected that Valence might also, but had never dared to ask. But Lady Aurorette had slapped him, so he could ask her.

"Me saying it is meaningless." Sometimes Aurorette's eyes were the green of spring, and sometimes they were dark. This time they were dark, a night green. "You can only remember it for yourself. But it inspires trust. I trust you, Mick."

CHAPTER 13
ACHIEVABLE GOALS

The wheelbarrow creaked along the street, much like it had only a few days before, pushed by the same old man, thinking the same old thoughts.

He knew he had done wrong.

Doog and Louis had said that he had been sick, that it was not his fault. Aurorette had said she trusted him and that he should move on. Valence had reminded him that every chance could be the last and had to be seized while it was still there.

But should I take this chance? The journey down the hill had been long enough to ponder that essential question. It was not as simple as throwing a stick for a dog. He had scared up enough metacognition to realize his mind could not be trusted. He might not know his name, but he knew somewhere beyond the naming of things that he was dangerous. He also knew that to be himself, all he had to do was act, to let slip who he was, allow the *idea* of himself to take over.

With the skolves literally at the door, the opportunity to ease all constraint would surely come. *But should I?*

I still have time to decide. The city still stood. The house was on the hill.

The private at the armory had directed Mick to the barricade at the north end of the city to talk with Sergeant Havard, who was supposed to be on duty there. To his surprise, he also realized he was curious about how the soldiers were conducting their defense of Villiers.

There were plenty of soldiers marching about town. They passed by in eights and sixty-fours and some mixed units with uniforms Mick did not recognize. A few small groups were still helping citizens load wagons and evacuate. It took time to move people, especially if they did not want to move. As he pushed his squeaking wheelbarrow north, Mick saw fewer and fewer citizens and more and more soldiers. The rubble from damaged houses had been hauled away to barricade the ends of city blocks or build up the north wall of the city. The wall had been only a little over six feet high and two feet deep—more decorative than defensive—but now a rough ledge had been built on the backside for the soldiers to stand on and look over. Those on watch were armed with a motley assortment of weapons: pikes, spears, some very light make of crossbow, huge, recurved longbows. Stacks of arrows, pikes, and shields lay at intervals along the ragged barrier. There were no real siege weapons, which was just as well since the wall could not support such heavy equipment. From where he walked, Mick could see three crudely patched breaches in the wall and a gate that had been repaired and rehung. These might stop the skolves from what Mick had heard about them but would make little difference to Skoll or Hati or whatever it was that had blasted through the walls so easily.

Now where is Havard?

Mick rolled his handcart up to the gate, close enough to eyeball the soldiers there. None of them appeared to be Havard. *But they all look the same.* Mick wondered if he would be able to pick the sergeant out. The chain mail made it difficult to distinguish individuals, and when Mick first met him, Havard had been dressed like most of the armsmen he could see at the wall right now. *I guess I have time to look.* He did not want to head back to the armory without giving the place a good look. His newfound sense of restraint made this a necessity. He turned east and walked along the wall, watching for the sergeant, dodging piles of rock, a few tents, and some hastily constructed supply kiosks.

"Can I help you, sir?" asked a female soldier, eyeing him curiously.

"I don't know," Mick replied. *Knights, she's young.* She looked fourteen. Smooth, unblemished skin, and large, almond eyes that looked impossibly blue against her dark skin. "Do you know where Sergeant Havard is?"

"Yes, I think so, sir. Should be at the front gate with the major."

"I was just . . . th—thank you. I'll take another look." Mick turned his wheelbarrow around and started winding his way back down the rubble-pocked street toward the gate.

"She's wearing plate armor!" the female soldier shouted.

Mick stopped, turned his neck, and asked, "She?"

"The major! She's wearing plate armor."

"Thanks," Mick said, his slow brain making sense of what he had just been told. There had not been much in the way of full plate, so he was pleased with this information. And the walk back to the gates gave him time to consider what he was doing. His self-mistrust did not apply directly to the mission of arming his friends at the house on the hill, but there were other concerns. Sir Valence's arthritic hands and the various weaknesses of just about everyone there could not be ignored any longer.

And yet they need a chance.

No one should just disappear overnight. Mick knew what had happened to the disappeared. They were dead. He knew it could not be prevented. The very old lived in a fragile equilibrium with life, one that could end abruptly, without warning, at any time. Valence had said that you never know when your last throw of the stick will come, and of course he was right. But no one should go quietly, without word or ceremony. As if death were a shameful secret or human beings past a certain age were incapable of knowing about what waited so close by for them.

If our deaths are a secret, the memory and meaning of our lives is lost.

Mick knew that he had to arm them. No matter what. Even if they were incapable of lifting those arms or giving their foes more than a good laugh.

"Havard!" Thanks to the young soldier's tip, he had spied the brawny sergeant beside a shorter figure also in shining plate armor.

The sergeant was not wearing a helm. He whirled around at the sound of Mick's voice and seemed to struggle for a moment to remember the name of the old man pushing a wheelbarrow. Then something clicked. "Mick," he replied, then aside to his companion, "Major, this is the man I was telling you about."

The major turned. Her femininity was prominently displayed by the cut of her cuirass, but it advertised her strength just as clearly. It took muscle to carry such a weight in metal. Seeing Mick, she froze into immobility. Then her hands went slowly to her great beaked helmet, and she gently removed it. Black hair with long white streaks fell from that heavy basket, and bright eyes locked onto Mick's. "Do I know you, sir?" she asked in a loud, clear voice, eyes searching his face.

Mick had no idea. "You might, but I am sad to say I don't remember all that I used to."

She blinked slowly. "You live in the . . . place up there?" She pointed an armored finger south, toward the hill. "The . . . home?"

"Yes."

"And you've come for more weapons. To arm your . . . colleagues there?"

"I have."

The major shuddered. It was abrupt, like a hiccup, but it came from her eyes. She turned quickly away, giving Mick her back but still speaking. Her words sounded strange, less clear than before. "Take whatever you need." She began walking away, heavier in her armor than before. "The sergeant will help you."

Mick watched her walk away, saw her put her helm on much more quickly than she had taken it off, witnessed her stop at the wall, and look down into it. "Is she okay?" he asked Havard.

The sergeant clapped him on the back. "She has a lot to worry about, Mick."

"There have been no skolves for a while."

"That's true," Havard said. "*Here* there aren't, *this minute* they aren't. But they *are* in the area. We just don't know what they are up to. Got some scouts—Vercors Rangers—way out there looking for them. Kind of an interesting group. Showed up here with orders and were supposed to get picked up by some wizard. Wizard was delayed, so we started using them. Probably our best scouts. They've been out for a few days, which aggravated their wizard no end. The fellow has been here three times and keeps missing them." He raised his eyebrows and added, "Truth be told, they've been out too long. Supposed to have been back this morning." As if dismissing Mick, he turned abruptly and walked toward the wall.

Mick did not take the hint, if that is what it was. He left his wheelbarrow in the road and followed Havard. They ended up standing together looking over the wall, not far from the major, whose name, Mick learned, was Serres. He also learned it had been the demon called Hati that had ruined so much of the city. And all in a night while its army of skolves watched from the tree line three hundred yards north of the city. Hati had then disappeared—off to ruin someone else's city, maybe—leaving the skolves behind. Some of them, anyway. How many, and where exactly, was what the scouts were supposed to figure out.

Sergeant Havard kept an eye on the tree line as if expecting the rangers at any moment. Two companies of longbowmen stood by, fingers on their quivers.

"So what do you need, Mick?" Havard asked, still watching the ground beyond the wall. "We have short swords beyond the wildest reserve requirements, so you could have more of those, as many as you like. And some armor, maybe? Shields? We are using all the metal ones, but I have two rooms full of old wooden heaters that no one's going to miss."

"Pikes would be a good idea," Mick said, noting some leaning against the wall a few paces away, "but they might be too heavy for my people."

The sound of a horn blared out from the north, the notes too crisp to have carried far.

"That's it!" roared Havard. "Be at the ready!"

"At the ready!" was repeated along the wall. Soldiers shifted up and down the line, pulling arrows, loading crossbows, drawing swords, hefting spears and pikes. The ground trembled slightly as a full company quick-marched to a position behind the gates. The sounds came as a familiar thrill to the old man. He wished he could remember why.

To Mick, Havard said, "The horn means they're pursued."

"Remind them not to shoot our scouts," said Major Serres to Havard. Her voice sounded hollow from within her beaked helm.

Havard bellowed, "Make sure of your targets before you shoot!"

Again, there was a repeat to the left and right. "Make sure of targets!"

"How fast did you say skolves are?" Mick asked.

Havard scanned the tree line. "A lot faster than us. Fast as a galloping horse. Maybe faster."

Three or four times faster than a tired scout. Mick looked at the tree line and tried to calculate how much of a lead the scouts would need to make safely it to the wall, but he really had no way of knowing. *Halfway?*

"Come *on*," whispered Havard, eyes locked with increasing intensity on the dark boundary between what he could see and what he could not.

Mick thought he heard the same exhortation from hundreds of other mouths up and down the line, "Come *on*."

There was only stillness at the tree line.

Major Serres had moved closer to Mick and Havard at some point. She said, "Tell the longbowmen to shoot on command. Tell the crossbows to wait."

Havard again relayed her orders with a shout, "Longbows, you're on the call. Crossbows, hold up."

"Longbows on. Crossbows hold," was repeated up and down the wall.

Still, nothing moved.

They watched, hardly daring to breathe. Then, as if buffeted by a sudden wind, something stirred among the trees. An instant later, the movement resolved into soldiers, running, seven of them, bursting from the trees. It looked like someone in the group might have stumbled and been helped up by others.

The horn called a single note, which cut off almost before fully forming.

"Run!" shouted the major.

"Run!" shouted Havard.

The call echoed up and down the line, but to Mick it did not look like the soldiers were running fast at all. *It almost never does, when you're watching someone impatiently, and absolutely never does when they might die if they're too slow.* He wondered how he knew this.

The image of Sir Valence playing fetch with Fenris blazed like the sun in Mick's eyes.

Last chances.

Mick did not shout "Run!" but suddenly, unaccountably, he found himself over the line with a pike in his hands, running toward the struggling rangers. He did not remember grabbing the pike or leaping over the wall. He did not remember if landing from the six-foot height had hurt his ancient knees. Mick did not remember his earlier self-doubt, never worried if he would get to the rangers in time, never speculated that he might not be needed, or if his effort was a fool's errand, the futile histrionics of a mad, old fool from a house of fools, never wondered if he might do more harm than good or fretted that a wall of monsters might come out of the trees and dwarf any effort a hundred of him could muster. He never considered in any way the question of leaping the wall or not. There was no thought or speech involved at all.

He simply ran.

"Mick, get back here!" bellowed Havard. "For knight's sake, stop!"

But Mick was gone.

The ground sped by quickly as the rangers grew closer and closer. Two huge, strange shapes broke out of the trees, aiming straight for the soldiers. Mick had never seen a skolve before, not that he remembered, but deep in his flow state, he did not react to their size, speed, or horrific symmetry. They were simply what they were. He tightened his grip on the pike, lowered his head, and charged.

The rangers abruptly stopped and formed a semi-circle. One of them limped on as the rest rotated their spears and planted them, gleaming tips pointing up and back toward the trees. An instant later, the skolves hit them, hard, pushing recklessly into the rangers' spears, swiping at them with their rusty swords. For a moment, the spears held them there, but could not turn them back. Mick could see the skolves shake from side to side, paws, swords and bodies trying to dislodge the spears from the rangers' hands and get inside their arcuate line.

As Mick rushed toward the battle, one of the spears broke. The rightmost skolve lunged forward with a roar and was immediately hit on its horse-length head by an overhand sword stroke delivered by one of the rangers. The creature reeled back and fell.

Mick broke left for several long strides, then sharply right into the flank of the skolve still held at spear length. "*Last chance!*" he roared as he lunged and thrust his pike straight into the chest of the beast, taking it off its feet so suddenly that its sword flew out of its huge paw, tracing a spinning arc through the sky before disappearing into the grass. Ferociously, the old man twisted the bladed end of the pike, which had penetrated a foot-and-a-half into the creature's chest cavity, and step-pulled it out. Dark red blood sloshed out of the ragged wound, but the beast was done. It could only collapse and curl weakly around itself.

The other skolve was struggling under spear thrusts from four of the rangers. With an incomprehensible roar, Mick leaped forward and rammed his spear into the skolve's head, just missing its eye. It skittered along skull until it caught at the base of where its cheekbone would be. Mick pushed harder, forcing the skolve's head roughly to the earth, and the haft broke, making him stumble forward with seven feet of wood in his hands. He stepped between the rangers, shifted his grip, and speared the skolve again in the snout with the broken end of the pike haft. It tried to scramble up but collapsed, bleeding from dozens of wounds, but the soldiers kept slashing at it. No one was certain when it would be safe to stop stabbing. Another ranger was rolling around on the ground, hands to his leg, blood seeping between fingers.

"Pick him up," said one of the rangers at last, a man with a rough goatee.

Mick shouldered his way in, whipped off his belt, slapped the man's hands away from his leg, and wrapped it tight twice around, just above a large gash oozing red. "I'll take him," he wheezed, picking the soldier up and slinging him over his shoulder.

"Run!" a female ranger screamed. "There's more coming!" Her voice dropped. "All of them."

Mick did not bother looking back, knew that there was no looking back once over the wall once the chance was taken. There were, however, consequences.

A vast, high-pitched wail passed overhead. *A sheet of arrows.* Mick knew the sound from somewhere in the distant past. A storm punctuated by the pounding of arrows as they struck their targets. Mick did not look back.

"Look out!" cried the man he was carrying, and an instant later something heavy struck the back of Mick's leg. He stumbled and went down. The soldier flopped off his shoulders with a scream. "Ahhh. Fuck me," the man groaned. "Why?" he cried piteously as he rolled weakly, one arm over his face.

Mick staggered back up, hopped, found that his legs still worked, saw nothing was sticking out of himself, shoveled the ranger back up into his arms, and started running again.

"Grandpa," the ranger whispered. "Grandpa ... don't drop me again." Mick looked down at the man. Rings from his chainmail had been ripped and driven deep into his leg just above the knee.

Another sheet of arrows scudded above them and rained down behind them, closer now, loud, the impacts loud like thunder.

"Run, Mick!" It was Havard's voice. Mick saw the sergeant standing at the open gate, beckoning desperately with his arms. Pikemen crowded around the sergeant, but they left a hole. The other rangers were a handful of steps ahead and passing through.

A short, quick scream of arrows and bolts passed just over Mick's head. He felt the wind of the storm as much as heard it. Then he was through the gate and stumbling, almost dropping the ranger again. He caught his balance and took a few more steps to make sure, fighting for air like a stiff bellows. His heart fluttered in his chest like the wings of a small, scared bird.

"Hey," came the barely audible voice of the wounded ranger. "Hey, you're the toughest grandpa *I* ever saw."

The sound of men shouting, accompanied by a pounding noise, made Mick whirl around. There was a skirmish at the gates now. Pikemen were thrusting and spearing out from the last few feet of open gate as dozens of other soldiers tried to force it closed. Soldiers on the wall were firing arrows and bolts. Havard was roaring into the busy air. Mick spotted the major in her armor up on the wall, pointing at something.

"Sir, you can put him down," said a female medic. She and another medic had a stretcher on the ground.

Mick laid the man out on the stretcher. A crowd formed—the other rangers from the troop, panting and slapping backs and looking down on their injured companion.

"Hey, did you see that?" said the injured man in a weak voice. "Grandpa pulled my bacon out of that one."

"Shut up, Error," said a female ranger. Her eyes glided sideways to Mick. "What's your name? I'm gonna assume, just out of my elbow, that you are not, in fact, Private Aron's grandfather."

"Are you sure? I went to some trouble over him." Mick said.

They erupted in laughter, though if not for the man's Vercors-pale skin, Mick would have had no idea if he were speaking of his own son.

"His name is Mick," said Havard, marching into the group. He caught Mick's questioning eyes and added, "Skolves are driven off. For now." He shook his head in amazement at Mick. "I can't believe what I just saw! What the hell were you thinking, old man?"

"*Wasn't* thinking."

"Huh," said Havard as if that settled it. "How's your leg?"

"My leg?" Mick replied. "Oh. I don't know. Still works about like it used to."

The female medic left the stretcher and crouched behind his leg, saying, "That could just be the excitement, sir. Let's take a look." He felt her hands on his leg. "That's funny," she declared, "your pants are ripped pretty good—almost in half—but you aren't cut. Just what might be the start of a bruise. Huh. What were you hit with?"

"I didn't see it," Mick replied.

"A spear," wheezed Error, from the ground. "Hard and flat, knocked us on our ass."

The chuckling that followed took the attention off the old man, which pleased him.

Havard blew out a huge breath and shook his head just as theatrically. He looked at the rangers. "The Major is going to want your report," he said.

"I'm gonna want a beer," said the female ranger.

"Well . . ." said Havard, "I think we could talk her into accepting your report at the tavern." He thrust his chin at the old man and said, "Mick, you come too. Get some food and a beer."

~

INTRODUCTIONS WERE MADE ALL AROUND, real names and the childish nicknames that the Vercors rangers all seemed to have, and that Mick knew he could not possibly remember. Beyond his lacerated leg, Private "Error" turned out to have received several other wounds in the few seconds of combat with the skolve, including two broken ribs and some sort of head trauma. He would be out of action for an indeterminate period. Weeks, possibly months. The rangers had been out on patrol for days and showed it by their greasy hair, unshaven faces, restless fidgeting, and general air of exhaustion. Cheese, bangers, bread, and beer kept them happy enough in their seats at the tavern.

"How do we look, Mick? Ranger hard? Road hard?" asked one of the rangers named after human waste. *Turd? Yes. No, Tudor.*

Corporal Alwena, the most talkative of the group, saved Mick the trouble of answering a silly question by saying, "Hammered shit, idiot. Leave Mick alone before he slaps you off that stool like a skolve."

"I wouldn't slap you," Mick said in a low rumble. *I wouldn't.*

"All right," said Sergeant Reyn, coming back to their long table with Major Serres, still in plate armor, though helmetless, beside him. Reyn was the serious, quiet member of the rangers. Mick guessed, somehow sure that he had seen such behavior before, that being the sergeant meant Reyn had to play the straight man. Sure enough, the man pushed aside some plates and pulled a notebook from his jacket. "We got about twenty miles into Ardgour County and—"

"How deep are the skolve lines around Villiers?" interrupted Havard.

Reyn exchanged a look with Alwena, who was quiet for a change, then said in a slow, careful voice, "To call the skolve deployment geometry a line would be an exaggeration. They're in a sort of arc around our north half, but scattered and poorly organized. Or they can't be bothered to organize . . ."

Serres held out an arm in a commanding gesture and someone put a beer mug into it.

"Whoa," said Turd. "I wish I had that power."

"Everything has a cost," she replied enigmatically before returning her attention to Reyn. "What are they *doing*? What does Hati *want*?"

"Yet to be determined on both counts," answered Reyn. "But we got a pretty good view of Hati flattening Chamberry from the mine on Guijaumet. Hit it like a regiment of trebuchets."

Private Dylan—Dill—interrupted Reyn. "Damnable brute stood there on top of the rubble afterward like a street performer waiting for applause." Dill was a lean young man whose otherwise good looks were marred by several unattractive necrotic circles on his cheek. Two blackened front teeth completed the appearance of ruined beauty.

"It was showing off?" Serres asked.

"Oh yeah," answered another of the privates. This one had a stubbly, unevenly shaved head with a scattering of scabs on the dome. Mick was having trouble keeping track of the lot of them. *Dafydd!* Yes, that was the lad's name.

"It squashed a few people all right," said Dafydd, "lots of them. But it also stood around, arms in the air, while the townsfolk who hadn't scrammed already made a run for it."

"Like this," said Turd, and he jumped up and started comically punching the air above his head.

"It wasn't quite as funny-looking when Hati did it," said Alwena.

"*Anyway*," said Reyn with exaggerated patience, "we think the demon has been reducing towns and cities in Ardgour as much as here in Engevelen. Which fits the prevailing political theory."

"And the skolves?"

Reyn gave no answer, but Alwena jumped in, "Holding territory, maybe. They don't seem to advance much when the demon's away, but they get right pissed when someone steps on their turf."

"They're territorial?" asked Havard.

"Oh, yeah," said Alwena.

Reyn squinted and shook his head uncertainly. "Or they might just be looking for food. Remember when we first arrived here, and we told you how we ran into a couple of them on the road? They were trying to eat a deer. It made them *sick*."

The conversation went on for a long time after this, as beer-filled, post-mortal-danger discussions often do. Mick mostly just listened. He needed to know what he could do to help his people at the house if they ever had to fight a skolve. Two things seemed certain though: the skolves were stronger than just about any soldier, and his people were far weaker. Eventually, most of the privates fell asleep at the table, spent from their ordeal. Private Eurion, who had also not said much during the conversation, left to go look in on the injured Private Error.

"I will come and visit you on the hill, Mick. If I can," said Serres as she and Havard got up to leave. Her eyes were strangely watery. "Thank you for your help today, sir."

Mick nodded to her, got a clap on the back from Havard, and started to think about leaving himself. *I still need to find those swords.* He also remembered that he had to recover his wheelbarrow before someone at the wall found a use for it.

"So what's next for you, Mick?" asked Alwena. "Back to that castle of yours on the hill?"

This surprised Mick. "You know it?" he asked, forgetting they had spoken about the house at some point in the conversation.

"I got eyes," she answered. "Looks to me like the most defensible place around here. That's maybe where we should all be."

Mick grunted. "You got to be old to be there."

"Old like you?" Alwena winked at him. "I'd take that."

"Hopefully not for a long time," Mick said. "We all got worn down somehow."

"Don't we know it," Alwena barked, satisfied with herself in the way the young do when talking about the old, not understanding Mick at all.

"Thank you for coming down and helping us," said Reyn, reading something in Mick's face. "Can we do anything for you?"

"I'm okay. I just have to bring back a load of swords," Mick said. "Though I'm worried my friends won't be able to use them." He dropped his head. "They aren't very strong."

"I see," said Reyn soberly.

"You gotta work with what you have," said Alwena, undeterred by anyone else's mood. "Look at these knuckleheads," she pointed at Dafydd and Dylan sprawled face forward on the table.

"Hey," one of them said, though the voice was muffled by its face being on the table.

"See?" Alwena said. "They knew who I was talking about. They were never that great and—"

"Hey," came another muffled voice. The other one, Mick guessed.

Alwena barely paused before continuing. "And then we ended up working with a team of reckless wizards, the worst kind of idiots you ever saw. This one moron threw a creepy doll right at us. Some kind of spell to combust these skolves we were setting an ambush for." She shook her head theatrically and sneered, "Burnt the skolves all right. But froze our boys half to death. Froze the armor right to them. Dylan's going to lose two teeth. They're loose already. Killed them at the root." She waved at Dylan and said, "Show him Dill."

Dill did not move. Mick was fairly sure he knew which teeth.

"Usually there's a moral to this kind of story," said Mick.

She pointed at Mick and turned her head just slightly to Sergeant Reyn. "See?" she said, "I told you this old warhorse knows what he's about. *He* should be in charge." She slapped her pants and continued ranting, "*Course* there's a moral. And it isn't just about not working with wizards. No, you have to work with people you *trust*. And you have to work within their limitations. Those wizards never practiced working with us, never consulted, never trained. Zero chance of improvement." She held up her fingers in an O. "Only way to get control was to get transferred." She looked at Reyn again and asked, "Am I missing anything here?"

Reyn's face looked somewhere between bored and disgusted.

He's heard this rant before.

"You peed on us." This came from either Dafydd or Dylan, but the voice was muffled. In any case, the remark did not make sense to Mick.

The sergeant, after a moment's thought, said something that did make sense, at least in a general way. "Achievable goals."

"That's right!" crowed Alwena, "achievable fucking goals. You gotta pick something you can handle, train up to, or otherwise prepare for."

"THOSE DON'T LOOK LIKE SWORDS!" Doog said as Mick pushed the squeaking, fully-loaded wheelbarrow into view at the top of the hill. His words came out almost exactly as they had a few nights ago when Mick had carted Fenris up the hill.

Louis was right there beside him, leaning against the stone wall. "It ain't dogs neither."

"Nope," said Mick. "Already stocked up on those. These here are crossbows. Easy to load with these levers they have. Easy to pull the trigger."

CHAPTER 14
THE WAY OF FOOLS

The Shining Knight evaporated in flames and light. We took the fight to Nehring Ardgour in his home and paid the price. It is ever the way of our enemy to take advantage, to outmaneuver and set his enemies against themselves or greater powers.

Sir Volsang, Methueyn Knight of Vengeance.

"Why aren't we teleporting directly into the Citadel, Green?" asked Val as they materialized with a "pop" onto a flat stone square in the middle of a long, high-pillared chamber, yet another place she had never been before.

Halwyn Glace could not yet answer. He was completing his Statician-wizard whole-body gesture. His legs spread wide in a powerful squat, he pushed his arms out and up from his hips as if the gesture alone could move a mountain. In a way, it did. Teleporting was a rare ability that did not conform well to the analytical methods of the Acutists. No cost comparison, let alone a cost function, could be calculated for the vast improbability of moving a person from one location to another with no visible means of transportation, let alone instantaneously. Somehow, Green made it work, though he paid a price. The tall, young man shivered violently as he completed the movement, his entire body covered in a mist of condensation. The air around him blurred and shimmered as if some vast thermodynamic inequality were struggling to find a new equilibrium.

He did not speak until the distortion passed. "Security," he answered.

Green led Val off the platform toward a nearby table and a pair of silent guards, who showed no signs of surprise at the sudden arrival of two wizards out of nowhere. The guards wore full plate armor, and their hands were on their sword hilts. "Knights of Vercors," Green whispered. He took up the fluffy white towel that lay folded and ready on the table and wiped off his face, neck, arms, and shoulders.

"You may not enter the Citadel, Halwyn Glace," said one of the knights. The voice out of his helm reminded Val somewhat of a tuba.

Green looked wryly at the twin metal figures and said, "I will escort Lady Valcourt to the gates only. There are things she must hear."

They emerged into the streets of Vercors City, accompanied now by the knights. Ahead loomed the great stone Citadel, the palace of the Duchess of Vercors. In the late afternoon sun, its shadow almost reached them.

"Do not *look* within either." It was the knight who had spoken before.

"Fine," replied Green in his haughtiest tone

The strange exchange puzzled Val. She was familiar with the politics of Vercors. She had met their ambassador and been fully briefed, and she knew the general history of the country, but she had never acted as an envoy to them before. Her feeling had always been that Vercors was a good ally, if a little less advanced than Engevelen. A little *backward*. Provincial, perhaps. A simpler, cruder people. She remembered the boorish rangers in her Elysian group, rolling in the dirt, peeing on each other. Apple-knockers, all of them. A small voice in her head reminded her that the shameful scene had really been Christopher's fault, and that she bore, well, *some* responsibility. Then again, she had not peed on anyone.

Whenever Val took the time to really think about that day, she was able to push herself to take the difficult, the rational steps needed to acknowledge her responsibility. She had engaged other wizards in debate over it, even apologized to them. In her best moments, Val was reasonably fair-minded. But whenever she wandered from that disciplined, self-aware state—which was most of the time—she slipped back into her normal state of attribution error. In other words, she had a monster, and that monster was prejudiced.

And so the teleportation site and the strange knights had surprised her. The reception suggested a perplexing refinement. "Why cannot Halwyn come with me?" she asked.

Hollow words in tones of steel trumpeted the answer to her, "No teleporter may see past the Fool's Way."

Green cleared his throat and said, "It is because of what Nehring Ardgour did, oh, twenty years ago. Before either of us was born, Val. He tried to steal the Methueyn Bridge."

"I am aware," Val said loftily.

"Of course," Green said with a polite smile. "And you also likely know he almost got away with it." Green stopped and stared at Val with bright eyes. "Because he *teleported* into the Cardinal Steel Castle in Engevelen City. Almost into the same room the Bifrost is displayed in. But you can only teleport to where you see or where you have *seen*."

"So you aren't allowed into your own Citadel?" Val said. "They don't trust you?"

"They don't trust *any* teleporter," Green corrected.

"The Shining Knight was trusted," said the knight. The talkative one, Val decided.

"And we wish him peace," said Green quickly. After a moment's pause, he continued, "I must deal with a list of outstanding Elysian issues anyway, Val. Besides checking on various dispositions and passing orders to local commanders from the princess, I really have to find our rangers in Villiers. It's been a week now, and Captain Lowri is starting to think we abandoned them."

Our princess trusts you. There was no one Val knew more dependable than Green. "Can you stop by Courant?" she said. "I would like to speak with Alain Overbree if he has time to make a visit."

"I'll try," said Green.

The talkative knight said, "We are at the steps."

Val looked up. The steps led up, way up, to what must be the first gate of the Fool's Way, she surmised. "That came fast," she said.

"Time always passes quickly with you," Green said. His eyes were not on the grand stairway or the great keep that seemed almost to hover above them.

It might have been Val's imagination, but it seemed like the two inscrutable, steel-clad figures on either side of them turned ever so slightly away from her and Green, as if to give them a small private space for a moment. "You will come for me tonight?" Val said, in a smaller voice than she intended.

"Yes." Before Val could turn and start up the wide stone steps, Green spoke again. "Remember what I said about caution, Katherine."

Don't end up a prisoner in the tower.

And she realized something new, something he had left unsaid in his advice earlier.

I cannot part the distance to you. Not there.

She imagined Halwyn saying this and wanted to curl up and die around herself and her cutting words earlier about not being a cat. Val took a step toward Green and reached a hand up to his sharp pale jaw. "I *expect* you," she said gently.

It was the best a Lady of Engevelen could do with two onlooking steel enigmas and no privacy. She turned away from Green and started up the steps.

The Fool's Way cut across Val's low opinion of the sophistication of Vercors. Mammoth gates and labyrinthine twists were the least of it. She spotted yet another skybridge from which archers could rain death on an invader and could not help but comment on the martial majesty of the citadel.

The talkative knight said, "On the Fool's Way there is no line of sight, no single straight path to victory or destruction."

"It looks like nothing but gates and steps and traps," said Val.

"Indeed," the knight said. "To our enemies, the path leads only to uncertain, unsafe answers. Even Halwyn Glace cannot pass through here. Only a friend could hope to bring down the duchess in her citadel."

"Has a friend ever tried?" Val found herself asking.

"No."

He is opening up to me. "That is *really* interesting. So ... speaking of that ... is anyone kept prisoner in the duchess's tower right now?" Val did not know why she asked this, except that Green had kept bringing it up, and now she had to know.

She expected—no, hoped—for a laugh now that they were becoming such good friends, but she received silence instead, which made her fear the rumor was not a joke after all.

A sharp hammering sound reverberated off the stone walls ahead. They crossed under another portcullis, then up a set of stairs, and around another sharp curve. The sound came again and again. *It is a stone cutter. It must be.*

Just past the next portcullis, a man kneeled on the polished stone floor, a heavy short-handled hammer in his right hand, a massive iron chisel in the left. He struck the floor. Hard. He was cloaked in gray, his head shrouded, and his hand protected by heavy gloves.

As Val and her two escorts drew close, the knights abruptly stopped, and Val found a vambrace-covered arm blocking her way. Though startled, she looked down at what the cloaked man was carving. It was a motto, almost complete, missing only a T, she presumed. It read "Know the Cost".

"May we pass?" asked the talkative knight cautiously.

"Pass," came the man's raspy voice. And they passed, but she noticed that the knights shuffled as wide of the engraver as the passageway allowed and made sure she kept well away from him as well.

Fuuuuck, that's weird. Am I being played? Eerie encounters with gravel-voiced, cloaked men seemed just a little too rich to Val. And why would a knight in armor be so deferential to a mere workman? Was it a performance for her benefit, perhaps to put her on edge before the meeting, part and parcel of the disorienting architecture of the whole Fool's Way? She consoled herself with this theory for the time it took to pass through another portcullis, the eighth, and therefore, she knew, the last. The hallway straightened and widened now, the ceiling rose transcendently above them. There were no more undulating, constricting stairwells. The image of the two plate-clad knights giving the cloaked figure such a wide berth flashed across Val's mind. Cloak. Hood. Gloves. All covered up. *Maybe he has leprosy. Did I touch him?*

She could not take the notion seriously, not consciously, not rationally. It made no sense to have a man with leprosy carving philosophy into stone. Yet she carefully reviewed what had happened, tried to remember just how much space she had given the man. With the mindset of a person flitting unpredictably between the deeply felt need that had brought her there and the foolishness of the girl she had not completely left behind, Val completed her passage through the Fool's Way and found herself before a vast, heavily guarded double door.

"Not the main hall," said one of the faceless, armored men who stood in a file there.

The talkative knight pointed to the right and said, "The duchess has chosen to meet you in her private council chambers."

The knights led her down another long hall to a heavy iron door. This entrance was guarded by eight knights and a ton of polished steel. A female knight opened the door. "You are expected," she said.

Val's escorts preceded her into the council chambers, which appeared to be little more than a sitting room. And not a very impressive one at that. At its center, a handful of people sat crammed around a plain, none-too-large table. They turned and gazed at her as she approached. Val made out a narrow flight of steps that led up to another door at the poorly lit back of the room. There appeared to be an alcove concealed in the shadows there, but she restrained herself from using the empyreal sky to see if anyone inhabited the curtained space. Given the prohibition against teleporters, she had decided to be very judicious with her wizardly skills. Her imagination conjured an image of the cloaked stone carver hiding up there, chisel in one hand, hammer in the other, listening and watching. *Move on, Val.* She suppressed the image. One silent observer—however potentially leprous or strange—would not matter.

The small number of personages around the table surprised Val. She was familiar with the elaborate ceremonies of Engevelen politics, where courtiers abounded.

We are going to get this done.

She quickly took in the people she needed to convince to save her country. The duchess, Veronica Brice, was identifiable by the wooden throne she sat in.

"Welcome, Lady Valcourt of Engevelen," said the duchess in a melodious voice.

Brice was dark-haired, pale-skinned, and preternaturally alert. On her right sat a gray-haired, bluff-looking man whom she introduced as Gethyn Brice, her brother.

"Always are we pleased to see our friends from the north," said Gethyn Brice just as smoothly.

Beside him sat a short red-haired woman, the duchess' advisor, Amanda Afriyat. She gave Val an appraising look but said nothing.

On the other side of Veronica sat General Fayne Angharad, who even seated was clearly a very tall woman. She was the only one in chain armor, over which she wore a bright blue surcoat.

"We trust our soldiers are proving helpful in the ongoing conflict," said General Angharad solicitously.

They're doing great. Well, the non-peeing ones, anyway. I just need about ten thousand more of them.

"What do you want?" asked Amanda in far less pleasant tones

"Why didn't any request that you may have go through Ambassador Celyn?"

This abrupt challenge gave Val a mental hiccup, which she did her best to conceal. She knew that diplomacy always entailed a double game, a hand of friendship and a club of coercion, a good and a bad girl. She remembered the stonemason's nearly completed inscription about cost.

Val knew these things, and the truth of them worried her now, for she had nothing concrete with which to pay, nothing of value to monetize. *Only a choice between uncertain futures.*

"The Ambassador felt our request exceeded her mandate," Val answered smoothly.

"Oh dear," said Gethyn, which in his basso profundo came out almost like a joke.

"Yes," the duchess added, "that is rarely a good sign,"

"She didn't even want to come to this meeting," observed Amanda softly. Abruptly, her tone became hard, "What is it you have come to sell us?"

"I have nothing to sell," said Val. "I have come only to ask."

"Everyone wants something," replied Amanda. "And they all want more, need more, *demand* more." Val had been to court dozens of times. She had witnessed what happened there, had even made jokes about it. She had expected resistance. That is why she had admitted to the nature of her visit immediately. Best to deal with the awkward parts early. Nevertheless, every word from Amanda was like a knife in the gut. Val was finding—not for the first time that day—that she much preferred when people simply agreed with her.

The duchess put her hand on Amanda's arm and said, "What is it that Engevelen wants?"

Val took a deep breath. "We need the Aignen Legion."

She had feared gasps or laughter, but the stern figures crowded at the table just stared, defying Val's talent, in her own mind at least, for reading faces. General Angharad broke the silence.

"What happened to the other troops we sent you?" she asked in an even, unreadable tone. Her long face was unreadable too.

"They are doing fine," Val replied, a little too quickly, perhaps. "We simply need more."

"So there have been no casualties, then?" said the general.

"Some have died," said Val. She added, too quickly again, "A few," then winced, wishing she could reverse time.

"Some?" said Amanda exchanging a look with the general. "How many of our sons and daughters have given their lives for your land?"

It did not matter that Val understood her mistake. There was no easy remedy. *I'm in it now. And unready.* The feeling was too familiar. She had an idea of what the result would be, but she had no choice but to speak the damning words, "I don't know."

"You don't KNOW?" Amanda roared the final word.

"She doesn't know," said Gethyn in what could have been a calming voice. He had the tiniest of wry looks on his face. He looked piercingly into Val's eyes and said, "You do not know, and yet you ask for more."

Never mix a cringe with a request. Val knew this, but it was a difficult combination to avoid at this point. She did her best, all the same. "I fear I must."

"Of course," said the duchess cryptically. "Do you know where our troops are?"

"Our command is aware of current troop dispositions to the limit of current communication," said Val in what she hoped was not too obvious a fudge, then thinking fast, added. "We would like to thank you for the loan of Halwyn Glace in this regard. He has been invaluable in gathering reports from across Engevelen daily."

Amanda Afriyat jumped back in. "So you know where the Renet has ended up at least."

Knights damn it. "No. Ahem . . . they are north of our current borders, beyond safe teleportation for Halwyn or easy heralding due to the locus."

"They are weeks overdue," said General Angharad. "The Renet has almost certainly been destroyed."

There was nothing for Val to do but backpedal. "Perhaps it is as you say, though we hope no—"

"Isn't it a poor leadership that governs by hope?" This was Amanda again.

Val's heart had started pounding several questions earlier. Now she felt her face burning, but she could still recognize a rhetorical question when she heard one. Amanda's sarcasm seemed to slide into Val's perforated stomach, filling it with bile, but she had to try a return sally.

"It might be a mistake to hope," she replied. "But the loss of the Renet, if true, makes our need for your Aignen Legion all the more exigent."

Amanda took another stab. "What *exactly* do you want the jewel of our army for?"

"Defense against the skolves."

"Where will the Legion be deployed?" poked General Angharad. She rolled out a heavily annotated map on the table and spun it to face Val. "Show us where you propose to position our troops."

We have no plan for that. Val buried the damning thought and only replied, "I am not privy to that information."

"What then," said Angharad, "is the *general* plan? Are you . . . privy to that at least?" He almost smirked. "Do you intend to emphasize the wall-building strategy in the south or to hold your northern cities, if you can?"

"This matter is under debate," Val said. "In either case, we will need your help."

The duchess leaned forward, her eyes sharp and gleaming intensely in the dim light. "But we will not give additional help for *either* case. We have to know."

"Perhaps you should return when you have these answers," said Gethyn. "Or send someone who has them."

It was a parting comment, meant to sound polite, but it was no less sharp and straight to Val's viscera than the other ones. "I fear there is no time," she pleaded. "It will take a week at least just to mobilize the Aignen Legion, I assume."

Amanda sneered, "No time? You have had all the time between the start of the war and now to decide what you should do. Don't blame us for your lack of preparation."

Val could barely hear over her own thumping heart. Her skin felt hot everywhere. And tight. Itchy.

"Do you have a plan to deal with Skoll and Hati?" Angharad asked.

"The Methueyn Order will deal with them," Val asserted in a tight voice.

"Lady Katherine," the duchess said sympathetically, "you should know that if the Methueyn Knights could not beat the demons early in the war, they certainly cannot now."

"Why not?" Val said helplessly.

"Because they are weaker now," the duchess said. Veronica Brice was reputed to be academically inclined. Some said she was secretly a bit of a wizard. Val did not know about that, but the duchess showed her acumen with her next question. "Do you know what a log-normal distribution is?"

"Yes," Val said.

"Good," said the duchess. "Imagine that. As you know then, it is a rule of nature that the best candidates are found first. From a large cohort of squires, the best become Deladieyr Knights, and the *best* Deladieyr Knights are the *first* to become Methueyn Knights. All the best graduate first. But all of these have died. And with each new draw from a fixed pool," the duchess continued, "the candidates are weaker. I assure you, Lady Katherine, that we are way out on the tail now. The last hopes are always the worst."

"But Yeyncie—"

"Yeyncie Green is an exception, and you must admit that she herself became a Methueyn Knight long ago. They all conform to the *idea* of their angel well enough, but these new knights lack the *capacity*." The duchess smiled sadly at Val and said, "The Methueyn

Knights cannot save Engevelen. You need a new idea, Katherine, not my soldiers, enslaved to old, failed ones."

Moments later, Val found herself being escorted back down the Fool's Way. In her despair, she could barely remember how the meeting had ended, but she knew she had brought the disaster on herself. She had been unprepared, had once more gone into battle unready. Her failure was one of planning. *Well, that happened damned fast. I walked right up the Fool's Way and did what fools do.*

It was mortifying. Val was an Acutist, a wizard who used rational methods to do her work. She prided herself on preparation, but she kept not preparing. *Why do I repeatedly make the same mistake?*

Anger mixed poisonously with her shame. *My own court set me up for this!* It had not provided her with any of the answers she needed. There was no agreed upon plan, no strategy, to deal with the skolves. Some wanted to retreat south and concentrate on extending the walls. Others wanted to defend what was left of northern Engevelen. No one seemed to have a plan of any kind for Skoll and Hati. Val had always believed that Engevelen was the most advanced and wisest country in the world, but this day had shone a hard light on that false pride.

No one listens to me. But I see now that some of them have reason not to.

The walk back to the teleportation platform went by slowly in a shame-fueled dilation of time. This time, the two Knights of Vercors said nothing as they escorted Val. They encountered no strange, hooded—possibly leprous—stone cutters. The streets were quiet. The failing light and falling darkness reflected Val's mood.

"You can just leave me here," she said when they had entered the building.

"We cannot," said the talkative knight. "The duchess must know that you are safely away."

I bet.

The air above the platform abruptly blurred and popped, startling Val. In the next instant, Halwyn Glace materialized, arms once more pushing from his hips as against the weight of a mountain. Little vortexes of condensation, the children of unequal enthalpy, coalesced about the blurred form of the tall wizard. The volatile air shimmered around him, then clarified into a halo of snow thrice his size, little flakes exploding out from him, floating free for a moment, and lastly, slowly falling.

"Green," Val said, miserable, looking nowhere, not truly noticing the spectacular thermodynamic effects of this latest teleportation. She was too busy wallowing in her wounded pride. She said, "I failed." It hurt. The shame of it hurt, and although her injured pride was less consequential than the real-world, future consequences of failing to secure more aid from Vercors, the pain of failure was personal and immediate. She tried to make a joke of it. "At least I didn't end up in the tower."

Green staggered, shivering violently on the platform, twisting and huddling about himself. His face was slick with condensation, and his jaw moved sharply several times, but the only sounds that came out were, "Auggah." Then, "V-v-v-v-Val-l-l-l-l"

"Green?" Val asked, realization that something had gone wrong dawning on her, yanking her out of her self-absorption at last. She looked more closely at her tall friend. His squinting blue eyes were shaded red, and some of the wetness on his face, she saw now, was tears. *Something more than a difficult teleportation has happened.*

She rushed to him as he faltered on the flatform, slipped on the suddenly iced stone, felt a moment of conflict between comforting him wordlessly with a hug and demanding to know the bad news. She chose the latter and grabbed him by the shoulders. "What has happened?" she asked, staring into his spasming face.

Halwyn started at her. He swallowed and seemed to choke. "C-Courant. I-it i-i-i-is-s o-over-r-r-run."

CHAPTER 15
WHAT SHINES?

"Most wizards act entirely under a delusion of validity."
The Shining Knight

"What do you mean, *overrun*?" Val asked. She found she was shaking Green. No, *he* was shaking her. The man was shivering, but more violently than she had ever seen. She touched his face with both hands. He was cold. His lips were blue. "What have you done to yourself?" she cried. "Get him a towel!" she shouted to the two knights. "Get all of them!"

"Sit down," she said, pulling Val to the edge of the platform. He staggered, trying to obey, and crashed as much as sat. There was a lot of clanking of armor and then a moment later the arrival of a large pile of towels. "Help me," Val ordered. "He's freezing. Get his clothes off and wrap him in the towels."

"N-no, V-Val," Green protested, "You c-can't s-see me—" He didn't say naked, but Val knew—had always known—that he was in love with her.

"Your dignity doesn't matter next to your life," Val said, incredulously. She ignored the annoying small voice that reminded her that moments ago she had been moping over her own hurt pride. To be human is to judge yourself the winner in every tie, to see only yourself in the best light. It was fundamentally unfair, but to be human is to be a hypocrite.

And sometimes even the most egotistical human beings surprise themselves with unexpected empathies. For the third time that day, Val felt herself enter a larger world when she looked at shy, shivering Halwyn Glace.

"B-but, I—"

He's embarrassed about how he is going to look, of what I will think of his naked body. Val knew Green had fantasized about them being together, and assumed that none of those fantasies had included the humiliation of hypothermic shrinkage. "Green, this is how it's going to be," she said firmly. "Don't fight us." She looked sharply at the knights and said, "Help me with his buttons and drawstrings." Green's fingers were shaking too much for him to help or to resists. Val grabbed one of his palsied hands and said, "Don't worry, we'll laugh about this later."

"I-i-in a g-good w-w-way?"

THEY LAUGHED EVEN before they were done, and the Knights of Vercors joined in. Green had said, "I f-feel like a d-dog," as one of the knights toweled off his dark hair.

"I feel like your mother," replied the knight. The quiet one, this time.

The talkative knight had returned with two attendants in blue-and-gold livery carrying plates of lamb stew. He said, "Let us all hope you don't *look* like her."

The repartee did not exactly sizzle with wit, but stress either sterilizes or unleashes humor. In this case, they were all laughing. Green was the worst with his runny nose and shakes. The sound of the knights' laughter in their steel helms was strangely musical.

The tall wizard recovered steadily after being toweled off and getting into dry clothes, though his shivering became strangely violent just before subsiding.

"Eat!" said the quiet knight, pushing a plate toward Green. "Or your mother shall be wroth."

"You too, Lady Katherine," said the talkative knight. "You should not take it personally that you have been run roughshod over. It is how the duchess is. Find the truth. Whatever it may be."

Even if it hurts.

The stew did not hurt. Halfway through her plate, Val felt ready to quiz Green again about what had happened.

"I teleported to Villiers, but I missed Reyn's eight again. The commander there had sent them off on a scouting mission." He frowned. "She seemed quite impressed with them, you know." He sighed and continued. "Then I dropped orders off at Aurillon, which was well received, as the commander there doubted his ability to hold out any longer."

"They are evacuating?" Val asked.

"While they can," replied Green. "I did some line-of-sight jumps." His lips curled back, and he added, "A *lot* of skolves in the area."

"What, did you ferry them all out of there?"

"No, thank the knights. I found them a route and left them to it."

"How many soldiers can you teleport in one jump?" asked the talkative knight.

Green answered quickly because he had done it a lot for the Elysians. "I can take an eight. Maybe a few more." He shoveled in a spoonful of the thick stew. "As long as I am fed, warm, and not too worn out."

Val said, "How many could the Shining Knight move?"

The talkative knight's helm turned toward her. "More. Many more. Though he did not like to."

"Why?" Val asked.

The talkative knight did not reply.

"After that," Green continued when it was clear that the Knights of Vercors would say no more, "I jumped to each of the *many* towns south of Aurillon. By the time I jumped to Courant, I was on my twenty first tunnel and just about ice-sickled, but the princess wanted to know if Farrah Harbinger had any new messages for her." He scraped up another spoonful of the stew. His plate was empty. Val slid her half-eaten plate toward him. "The first thing I saw on arrival was Skoll or Hati hurtling into a stately building across the street from me—a bank, I think. It was a large stone building, but the demon went right *through* it."

"What did it look like?"

"Big," said Green. He frowned. "Eight, maybe nine feet tall. All of it in some kind of armor. Some unusual alloy when I observed it in the empyreal sky. And the creature is very powerful. Like a Methueyn Knight but *more*. Much more. Just as it hit the building, it got this blue glow. It looked like some sort of empyreal effect. Something entropic, I think." He looked hard at Val. "I was terrified. Cold, alone, and a long way from Harbinger Hall. I tunneled back to Engevelen City and gave my report. Most of the Methueyns are there now. I thought maybe I could jump back to Courant with them, but they had some reason not to go yet. Then I jumped here."

"You could have delayed coming for me," said Val.

"No, I could not."

She reached out for his hand, held it, and said, "You're not a cat." She could sense the two Knights of Vercors looking at each other. Green smiled and gripped her hand. His skin was still cold.

It is going to be a little longer before he can teleport again. Val realized something else. She turned to the talkative knight. "I need to speak with the duchess again."

"It is late," said the talkative knight hesitantly. "The duchess will be in her tower."

"It is night," said the less talkative knight.

Green's cold hand tightened on Val's. She remembered his advice about not going to the duchess's tower. *Fuck it. My country is just about done. What have I got to lose?*

She clapped her hands decisively. "Excellent," she said to the knights and then turned back to Green. "How will we meet up after I come back?"

~

VAL THOUGHT the Fool's Way would seem shorter this time. It did not. The two Knights of Vercors took her to a new set stretch of twisting hallways after emerging from the way. They crossed a dimly lit open square filled with gardens and pools. She looked for the shadow of the duchess' tower, but there was too little light. Val cheated and opened herself to the empyreal sky, piercing through the darkness, and spotted the narrow spire looming ahead.

Who has been locked up here, anyway? She was not going to ask her escorts. Not much talk had come out of their shiny helms since she had asked to see the duchess again. They had sent an attendant running ahead, reminded her once more that it "was night," and then led the way in silence. *I think the Shining Knight was imprisoned here.* He had obviously been released to defend Vercors on a multitude of occasions, up until the final, unfortunate fight with Nehring Ardgour. Or the story was a lie.

Val could not imagine how someone like the Shining Knight could be locked up. Thinking further back, she remembered Sir Jennyver Coslett, the Winking Knight. *What was the problem with* her*? Some story about an alliance with Novgoreyl?* Val also recalled Ike Ithell, the story-teller who had apparently told one story too many. *Lady Kira.* She had married a Knight of Vercors without permission. *Sir Breckon?* Val had no idea if any of those legendary heroes had ever actually existed, but the tower certainly did. She released the empyreal sky when they had passed through the tower's great room and were approaching the great central stairs. The lighting was better here, and she did not wish to give offense.

The knights led Val up the stairs. She heard a hammer striking somewhere above. It tapped a double beat that reverberated down the wide stairway, then back up off the hard stone floor of the great room. The metallic clangor grew louder as they ascended, punctuated by a low-frequency whooshing sound that had to be a bellows. At the next landing, they came to a guarded door. A full eight stood there in plate armor. There was a long delay as her two knights spoke with the new ones in muffled tones. Abruptly, the hammer strikes ceased, and all ten knights turned and looked at the closed door.

A few moments later, two heavily built men and one stocky woman, all dressed in heavy work clothes and aprons, emerged from the door, and closed it behind them. They smelled of metal and carbon, though their hands and faces were clean. Val noticed a few drops of water falling off the woman as she passed.

The not-as-talkative-as-he-had-been knight turned to Val and said, "In a few moments, the door will open. Pass through and climb the stairs to the next room. Wait there."

I guess I am on my own.

The door opened soundlessly. It was held by a woman in a blue-and-gold page's uniform. Val walked through but ignored the broad stairs. She noticed a subtle trail of water leading down a hallway to the right. Curiosity drove her to walk in that direction.

"Not the forge, Lady," said the page in a delicate voice. "You are to ascend to the duchess's anteroom."

"Why don't I smell the forge?" asked Val.

"Ventilation and draught were designed carefully," said the page.

The duchess's tower seemed a strange place to build a forge, to say the least. *Why?* Val was not going to find out tonight. The page was standing by the stairs, one eyebrow and one arm gracefully pointing up.

"Thank you," Val said and began climbing. Each polished step made a sharp clicking sound as she ascended. This time she had a plan.

She knew what she needed to say to the duchess. It would be an emotional message, fueled by her rage and sorrow over Courant. She would *make* the duchess listen to her! It did not matter that Val lacked all the answers. Answers were beside the point. Something needed to be done *now*. Otherwise it would be too late.

She emerged into a softly lit oval chamber whose beauty, after the plainness of the private council chamber, astounded her. The walls and ceiling were entirely covered by one vast, magnificent fresco depicting the allegories of the Methueyn religion in all their rich complexity. Only one of the hanging lanterns was lit, but she saw enough to know she was in the presence of a masterpiece. Most of the room was in shadow, and her eye was drawn to a subtly shining object near the lantern. It was some sort of plate armor hanging from a wooden rack. She crossed the room, walking around a set of high-backed padded leather chairs, to take a closer look.

Yes, it was plate armor, made for a man, but damaged. The center of the breastplate had been melted right through.

What happened to you?

The metal was unusual. It was glassy, reflecting the light in every direction. Val looked more closely at the breastplate. The metal adjacent to the six-inch hole in the center was marred, as if it had dissolved and reformed. An inch away from this metal scab, the steel shone again. Val moved her face closer and saw that the breastplate was not a single piece of metal. It was made of tiny rectangles set in a fine grid. She touched one with her finger. It moved very smoothly, though she had to press firmly to make it do so. “It’s pneumatic. How?”

“Look closer,” came a gravelly voice from the shadows.

Val whirled. She recognized those roughened tones. It was the stone carver, the cloaked man, the figure that her escort had asked leave to pass, the possible leper. He stood at the back of the room, shadowed but unmistakable. “Look closer,” he repeated.

“I can barely see the grid around the squares,” Val protested.

“Look through the window,” he instructed.

What? Oh. Val opened herself to the empyreal sky. She pushed and pushed, drawing the resolution of her empyreal sight tighter and finer. The little squares and grid, she now saw, were formed without the slightest imperfection. The lines were faultlessly straight and fitted together down to a scale of a thousandth of an inch or better. Far beyond the tolerance of anything that she had ever seen. The pieces fit ... perfectly. They slid perfectly. They trapped air, making little bubbles of kinetic insulation.

"Closer," the cloaked man said.

Val had never considered using her empyreal sight in this way. There was no purpose to it that she knew of, but the enigmatic figure's hoarse command compelled her. And Val was curious. Her days had followed a path of dogma, politics, and argument. Her discussions with the other Elysian wizards, the Staticians, had not been scientific. They abhorred complexity, loving only the embrace of comforting heuristics. No peer of hers—not even Green—really wanted to discuss the underlying causes and methods of empyreal manipulation.

They wanted to be wizards.

As for the politicians at the princess's court, they only wanted to pose and talk. To spin narratives and score debating points. Their objective was subjective power. They were courtiers. They wanted nothing more than to argue again the next day, not to solve problems, not to find accord, but only to hear their own vain voices. When Val had entered the tiny star chamber of the Duchess of Vercors earlier that day, she had been ill prepared for real questions.

At *this* court, there was curiosity and a call to discover. A sharp pivot to a profound difference. She concentrated, forcing her empyreal sight down to a small, truer space than she had ever visited before. She saw down to the layout of the metal itself, to its essential crystalline structure.

"Only there *is* no structure," she observed. "The four parts are randomized." She looked up toward the melted edge. "Except near the hole, where it takes on a regular shape."

"It returns to its crystalline bias." The rough voice floated in air like an apparition.

A sudden insight rocked Val. "This was the Shining Knight's armor!" she exclaimed. She touched the rough hole in the center. "The story from Sir Volsang was that he flashed away to nothing." This was not a narrative that Val had ever examined critically before. She knew of no wizard who could instantly evaporate the easiest metal, let alone this work of profound metallurgic art. Obviously, Volsang had been exaggerating, but incongruously, the melted core of the breastplate told a harder story.

Nothing and no one could have lived through such an assault. "What could have done this?" she said, turning to face the stonecutter.

The sound of his voice fell to the floor and grated like little rocks, abrading. "Even entropic tungsten can be defeated if enough energy is used."

What? This metallurgy was laughably over her head, but Val was still sitting in the window of the empyreal sky. Quite by accident, she saw the man under his cloak. He shone in the empyreal sky, a brilliant light to heaven. Like a Methueyn Knight, he was connected to a power from elsewhere, reality bending subtly around him. And yet, despite that maelstrom of incandescence—or *because* of it—he was horrifically burned. His chest was melted, his hands sloughed, and his ears drooped like a candle burned too long. Her stomach heaved, but instead of vomiting, she exclaimed, "Daughter of Nimrheal! You're *him*. The Shining Knight!" The realization was a sharp, wet slap in the face of Val's righteousness. Such suffering raised an internal mirror to her earlier pedantic behavior.

Abruptly, her hold on the empyreal sky came unmoored, and all she could see was the cloaked man once more. *Did he do that?*

"Yes," he said roughly, "I shone too brightly."

"You're the Duchess's prisoner," Val said with sudden insight, then regretted her gaucherie.

Improbably, little pebbles made the sound of laughter. "Veronica Brice takes no prisoners," he said when his chuckling subsided.

"I apologize," said Val. "But you're supposed to be dead."

"I was more nearly so when it happened."

Val knew the story. Sir Volsang had returned to Engevelen City to tell the tale. He and the Shining Knight had fought Nehring Ardgour and been defeated. Soundly. They had thought to take him by surprise, but Nehring had been ready for them and used some terrible new power against them. Volsang had no language to describe what had happened, only a warning to avoid the green torus.

He was burned worse than he is now? The Shining Knight was a once-in-a-hundred-year phenomenon, a powerful wizard and empyreal knight both, a teleporter. She wondered if he healed like the Methueyn Knights did. And if so, how little of him must have come back from the assault on Ardgour to still be so badly hurt now, months later.

A multitude of questions went through Val's mind. About Nehring Ardgour, about what had really happened in the fight with Sir Volsang, about the nature of the demons Skoll and Hati and of the skolves, and whether this amazing man could see through the locus. *Does he know what we should do?* But like most people, her mind followed familiar patterns and she asked the lesser question. "What is your school? Are you an Acutist Wizard?" she asked.

He said, "I hope to make ideas work for *me*, not the other way around." Before Val could fall all over herself in embarrassment at this curt remark, he made it worse. "Lady Valcourt, I try not to limit myself by forging a narrow and constraining cage. Giving myself labels can only separate me from ideas. And people."

"Oh." Now Val felt like a fool for the second time in the day. *Small. I am small.*

Perhaps he sensed her distress—though his rough voice conveyed little emotion—because he added, "I am not so wise. Nehring defeated me."

This small overture made Val smile. "And yet here you are. Still alive and not even a prisoner of the duchess."

"No."

She said, "You are acting on her behalf, though?"

"Always."

You are her gatekeeper.

"I did poorly in congress with the duchess earlier," Val said.

"Yes."

"Courant is under siege," she said. "I need to speak with her again." *And you will decide if I get to. Just as you did the first time in the Fools' Way!*

He said nothing for a moment. This made Val listen closer to the rasping voice of the Shining Knight when he finally asked, "Do you understand your error?"

So many mistakes. Val could have made a grocery list of the things she had done wrong, with the Elysians too, not just with the duchess.

I did not go from what I knew to what I thought I didn't know. I only brought what I needed.

When Green told her about Courant, she had decided that her previous mistakes did not matter. The stakes of the war were reason enough. She had walked the Fool's Way a second time, filled with righteousness. She now realized that speaking from a sense of high-minded indignation would also be an error. Seeing the ruin of the Shining Knight did not remove or dampen her motivations—the burning and ungentle need she felt—but it did bring to consciousness a new and different modesty. She said, "I brought no details and no plan. I came in ignorance, asking favors."

"True. But that is not all. And do you understand why?"

Val said, "Probably not." Caught between horror at what had been done to the Shining Knight, admiration for the immensely intelligent man, a desire to speak at length with him and learn from him, the burning exigency of her situation, and her impatience with riddles, she spoke the truth. "We—I—needed to do *something*."

"Yes. Something. You face a terrible crisis but unconsciously substituted easier problems, such as asking for our help, in place of your true issue."

"You believe that we don't need additional help from Vercors?"

"You do," he said.

"But ..." Val paused, hoping the Shining Knight would speak more fully. "What am I missing?"

"You were reinforcing your own illusion of certainty."

Our incompetence with a larger force would be like our incompetence in the village north of Aurillon. Like is to like is to like, and thus we go from what we know to what we thought we didn't know, from pissing on a couple of soldiers to pissing away an army.

"I think I understand," Val said. "May I speak with the duchess?"

He pointed to a door in the shadows behind him. Val took a step forward, then hesitated. She did not wish to pass the Shining Knight. It did not seem fitting. Nor did she want to open what for all she knew might be the door to the duchess's bedroom. The Shining Knight paused for only a second before he crossed to the door, knocked twice, and opened it. Val followed him into another, smaller antechamber, this one with a lit fireplace and four deep, padded chairs. Veronica Brice sat in one of the chairs, reading a ledger.

"Courant is besieged," rasped the Shining Knight after announcing the visitor and indicating that Val should take the chair opposite the duchess. He remained standing. "The Harbinger is still there."

The duchess watched Val for a moment, then said, "The pressure to act has increased. In such situations, I have observed that most people yell more loudly rather than think more deeply. However, my knight has brought you here, so I am prepared at least to listen. What new argument will you make?"

"Halwyn Glace is nearly dead from hypothermia on your teleportation pad," said Val, forcing herself to look steadily at Veronica Brice, "but he suffers from more than that. He is a good man. He feels a great anxiety for my country as well as for people like him who have already been so badly spent by this conflict."

She glanced toward the cloaked man, but her words were meant for both. "I was going to give you a speech about Engevelen and what will be lost if you do not help us. Do you know that there were once a thousand towers in my country? They were like your stone castles, symbols of order and our civilization. Half were lost a generation ago. The people who lived within their shadows were taken, their liberty stolen, their libraries burned, their history excised. Now the other half are threatened. Many have already been destroyed. We don't know what Nehring Ardgour wanted back then. He didn't get it, that we are sure of. We don't know what Skoll and Hati want now, and we are quite sure we never will. But this time, the enemy may succeed in getting what it desires."

She took a deep breath before making the point she had been building up to. There was an acute risk that the duchess would be mortally offended. *Last chance.*

"I was going to talk about how unwise it is to sit here, smug and comfortable, confident they won't come for you next."

The duchess had listened calmly, but now she seemed to stiffen. With a wry expression, she said, "Smug? I might have locked you in the tower had you . . . actually said that."

"I wish I could be sure you're joking," Val replied. "I *was* going to say that Skoll and Hati might come for you next. That if they did, we would not be here to help you because you would have left us to die and be forgotten. I even fantasized about finishing by saying I had walked the great Fool's Way, but ignoring this war is the real Fool's Way. If we can be forgotten, so can you."

"So why have you decided *not* to say this?" asked Veronica Brice, smiling more broadly this time.

"Because blaming you and shaming you are . . . unproductive," Val said. "I don't believe you *can* be shamed. *And* it might have gotten me locked in your tower." She allowed a smile to flit across her own face now. "But also because you *did* send troops to help us." The memory of Halwyn shivering made Val wince. "And because you sent your Shining Knight against Ardgour." She looked at the cloaked man again, this time addressing her words to him directly.

"Why do you stand, sir?"

"You know why," came the almost whispered reply.

It hurts too much to sit. Her mind recoiled from considering a life in which such a simple comfort was impossible.

Val nodded to him—it was all she could do—and turned back to the duchess. "I know you want to help, whether for your sake or ours."

"I don't get out of bed for only one reason," replied the duchess.

"Though I am surprised that the Harbinger has not already informed your court that our Aignen Legion is massed on a quiet road just south of your border, ready to cross at my command."

"Really?" Val's heart leapt. A week, at least, had been saved. *She did not tell me this earlier. For a reason. For several reasons.* She asked, "What will it take for you to give the command?"

"A reasonable chance of victory," said the duchess.

"For us," said the Shining Knight, "victory means the death of Nehring Ardgour, the death of Skoll and Hati, and the destruction, or secure containment, of the skolves. *You* too want all that. And your country back."

"We have tried to achieve all of those things, starting with Nehring," said Val.

"And failed," said the Shining Knight.

More than the rebuke in these words pained Val to hear. Every word that had come from the cloaked man's mouth hurt her to hear. His tortured, stiffened, horribly burnt vocal cords told a story of agony in every hoarse, rasping syllable. Every time those heartrending notes perturbed the air, Val wondered at the power that had been used against him. *Perhaps, like him, in defeat even we may find victory.*

"How were you beaten?" she asked him on an impulse, then instantly regretted her impertinence.

The Shining Knight showed no sign of taking offense. "Nehring Ardgour," he replied, "is a most powerful wizard. Perhaps the most powerful that has ever lived. He has, of course, a natural endowment of talent. But it is his knowledge that puts him so far ahead of us. Through study and fearless experimentation, he has found a way of evading Nimrheal's hatred of invention. This has allowed him to make fundamental discoveries in interdimensional breakdown and the harnessing of energy. Vast amounts of energy." He raised his arm, allowing the sleeve to reveal the hideously burned skin of his hand and wrist. "He has a mineral, a transformative rock, that holds power enough to destroy . . . almost anything."

Val could hardly breathe with excitement. She forced herself to take a long, slow inhalation before asking in what she hoped was a steady voice, "Enough to kill Skoll and Hati?"

"Possibly. If you knew how to use it."

"Surely that's the key, then," exclaimed Val, no longer able to disguise her elation. "Let's just go get it!"

"Do you seriously imagine that we have not tried?" said the duchess. "Ardgour's is an extraordinary intelligence, and he has ambitions we know nothing about. He is no mere butcher or conqueror." She paused and looked at the Shining Knight. "We have no idea what ultimate purpose he has for this material, this greenstone torus, as he calls it. We knew, once, where it was stored, but we do not know now."

Val's excitement deflated as quickly as it had arisen. "So before we can even think about dealing with this . . . torus, we need to know where on earth it is ..." *And if only Ardgour knows its location, that means breaking the locus.* Val was a mediocre herald at the best of times, but even for the greatest heralds, the locus, if unbroken, made seeing into the future with any certainty an exercise in frustration. "Can *you* break the locus?" she asked the Shining Knight.

"Once, perhaps, I could," he said. "Now my body could not tolerate the strain."

Val could only imagine the thermal effects of a deep empyreal exertion on skin so severely damaged. She shuddered visibly.

"But surely," the duchess said, "your Harbinger has made the attempt?"

Val imagined the Harbinger sitting in Courant, besieged, with all the answers and no way to communicate them to anyone outside its walls.

~

An hour later, Val arrived back at the teleportation platform. Green sat on the edge of the stone, no longer shivering, his long legs swinging. "Did you succeed?" he asked, trying to read the expression on Val's face.

"Not . . . exactly," she replied. Veronica Brice had said a great many things after asking about the Harbinger, most of them about the decisions that Engevelen would need to make. She had made no firm promises regarding her own decisions. Still, Val felt much better now that she knew what she needed to do. "We have to make contact with Farrah Harbinger before it's too late."

"You were right about her coming back," the duchess said. She and the Shining Knight sat in chairs facing the fire. The effort was agony for him, but it was worth it this time. Her hand was on his.

His cowl was still up, and his voice still sounded like the popping of burnt embers. "It was the only prediction I had any confidence in."

"We could have told her about your heraldic dream," Veronica said.

"About the old man on the hill? The left-handed devil? The slaughter of the Methueyn Knights?" he said. "It was a knot I saw poorly and understood worse."

"But the locus has changed? You saw Farrah's influence on it?"

"That is why I said nothing." The Shining Knight paused and added as an afterthought, "That and one other thing."

"What else?"

"You cannot just *tell* people things. However terribly this turns out, it must unfold on its own."

CHAPTER 16

RED PIE

"I thought we would understand a lot more when we saw it," Ave said, looking down from the hill at the amber glow of Courant. That glow was fading as the morning sun ate the darkness. "I cannot really tell what is going on there at all."

Bro's face twitched. He said, "It's a big city." He was not wrong. On a hill or not, they could only see one small section of the walls and what had been done to it. They could not see through the stone or into the buildings. They could not line up the soldiers on those walls and speak to them one at a time. Not from a hilltop.

"It is certainly besieged," said Revenberge. "That we do know."

"I suppose," said Ave. She could see smoke rising from the city now that it was lighter, though not in great quantities. A ray of sunshine illuminated a ragged hole in the west wall. "So much for warning the Harbinger about the attack. We should have gotten here sooner."

"I think she knows now," said Bro. "Anyway, this doesn't seem so bad to me. No demon in sight at least."

Sir Revenberge, who had been listening silently, pointed at the damaged section of the wall and said, "The demon was there. It will be back. In the meantime, the skolves seem to be resting." The wolf-like beasts had moved on Courant much quicker than expected, not stopping at all after the point to which Revenberge and Sir Michael had tracked them earlier.

Ave declared, "We need a plan."

"Make for the walls," replied Revenberge. "Find a postern door. Get inside and help the defenders fight the skolves, and the demon when he returns. What more can we do?"

More of the same, the same results.

Ave looked at her companions, wondering which of them would die first.

Bro was by far the biggest and strongest man that Ave had ever seen, a giant whose size and musculature defied all expectations of what human development could be. He was as tall as a skolve and probably stronger. The veins that cut across his skin looked sharp enough to cut a throat, and flint, she knew from experience, could be struck against his hard, angular sinews to make fire. But that twitching, ruined, perpetually wincing face told the other side of the story. It announced that Bro was doomed. He had lost before, after all—lost his face—and things were worse now. He was the perennial squire, never to be a knight.

Sir Revenberge was not nearly as large or tall as Bro, though she was tall enough. And she *stood* tall in her shining plate armor. Her face was no twitching mess. It was beautiful, strong-jawed, perfectly framed by long, dark hair. She could make an atheist believe in Elysium, could catalyze hope from despair. Revenberge was everything a Deladieyr Knight should be, calm, sure, in absolute alignment with her Idea.

But also static, unchanging, *unable* to change. And therefore doomed. Everything her Idea spoke of had already failed a dozen times over, but she could not change, could not adapt, because she was perfect. She would die too. Probably after Bro, but her fate was just as certain.

But I will be first. I no longer believe. I have too many ideas, too many doubts. I have become jaded and faithless.

The only good thing about the order of our deaths is that I won't have to see her die.

"Can we not consider something different?" Ave blurted out. She was sick of her morbid, self-defeating ruminations, ashamed of imagining harm befalling Revenberge or Bro.

Bro looked at her. He tried to raise his eyebrows in a silent enquiry, but of course he could not.

"What do you have in mind?" Revenberge asked. She did not look surprised or skeptical.

Is she open to new ideas after all?

"I don't know," admitted Ave, "but it feels like we always do what we always do. Go fight some skolves, kill a few, get a few of us killed. Meet Skoll or Hati, fight them, and for sure get killed."

"Should we let them just destroy Courant and kill everyone there?" Revenberge asked. "I cannot do that."

Ave shook her head. "I know you can't. Neither can I." She looked at Bro. "Byron, what about you?"

"I'll do whatever you want," he said guilelessly, gazing at her like the biggest and most fucked-up dog in the world.

"Don't—" she started to say, but Revenberge's warm hand was on her arm and she reconsidered. "Thank you, Bro," she said, smiling at him.

"We take you seriously, Ave." Revenberge said, removing her hand, leaving goosebumps behind. "We just don't know how what else to do."

"We need to be smarter," Ave said. *I wish I had spoken with that Vymyty longer.* She put that thought aside and continued. "You know what we always do. Go in and do our thing. With little or no consultation with the regular forces. Yes, I know we are trying to protect them. We think we're the bravest and the toughest, but it's also because we are so knights-damned sure of ourselves. We don't consult with anyone. We don't want to." She scowled. "This war is called the Methueyn War because we've carried it entirely by ourselves for so long. The treaty nations dragged their feet a little, and so we just declared war on

Ardgour ourselves. And then we didn't even fight it together. Volsang is still out there on his own somewhere, trying to kill the count all by himself. We have, for the most part, died alone and in vain."

Sir Revenberge blinked. "I suppose we have, Aveline, though it's a bit hard to hear you predict that I'll end up in a lonely grave too." She opened her eyes wide and smiled. "You draw too sharp a line between arrogance and conviction."

"The Methueyn Knights are gathering in Engevelen City," said Bro. "Perhaps this time we will find out what they can do when they act together."

"Perhaps," said Ave doubtfully.

"In the meantime," Revenberge said, "we have a city to save. Let's take your advice ourselves. Let's go find some sort of command authority and work with them."

~

THEY FOUND a wide channel in the hugel gardens outside the west wall and charged down the fairway, running faster even than skolves could. They hurtled through air that smelled of shit and rotten meat: exposed hugel gardens and skolves. They were not spotted immediately and were deep into the skolves' lines before there was any reaction. Not that skolves formed lines. Some of them were curled up in the grass of the mounds, others rooted around in the remains of the gardens. *Eating?* Ave could not be sure, nor did she care. With her homely fellow squire and her beautiful Deladieyr Knight, all with Deladieyr-class swords in hand, she focused on the element of surprise. When the first skolves saw them, she was ready.

Bro carried a heavy, five-foot-long, two-handed sword, but he swung it easily with just his right hand, parting the air with a whine, cutting through a skolve's axe handle and straight through six inches of snout and teeth. It yelped like a panicked dog as teeth and blood exploded from its mangled face.

Most arms would break when connecting with as much force as a Deladieyr or Methueyn Knight could generate, so of necessity the order had over millennia accumulated a collection of superlatively engineered arms. Blades that were harder and sharper, yet less brittle than others, often by two, three, or more times. Few alive could forge such swords, so each rare weapon was treasured and venerated. Most had been lost in this war, broken—because anything can be broken—or lost in the dirt with their fallen wielders. Skoll and Hati had captured some of these swords as well, such as Sir Michael's great two-handed sword.

A huge, eight-foot tall skolve reared up in front of Sir Revenberge, swinging what looked like a six-foot length of heavy pipe. She swung her sword while stepping to the side and intercepted the pipe, shearing through it. Three feet of separated metal flew end over end like a windmill blade and hit Bro, making a metallic clang as it bounced off his forehead.

Bro!

He staggered but kept his feet. The skolve stumbled as well, and it and Bro collided. A taloned hand ran down Bro's face and was caught by his hand. For one strange instant, Ave saw long nails scrape, then tear on a ripple in Bro's squinting face. A snapping sound followed as Bro's hand shattered the forearm of the wiry creature. It mewled sickeningly. Bro growled and hurled it by its broken arms into another skolve.

"North! Come north!" shouted someone from atop the walls. Ave looked back and saw a group of soldiers urgently gesticulating, waving their arms and pointing northward. Ave was surprised she could pick out the words. The wall was a hundred yards or more away, and she was buried in the sensory overload of battle.

She blocked an axe blow from a skolve, her sword taking a big chip out of the haft, then swung wide and cut through the creature's abdomen right down to the spine. "North!" she called. The skolve went down like a marionette with its strings cut. Ave grabbed Bro by his chainmail, yanked him in that direction, and started running. "Come on Revenberge!" she called.

"I dropped my sword," Bro said, breaking away and fishing around in the muck of shattered hugel mounds.

Fuck! Ave changed direction and leaped back to defend him as he floundered among the cabbages, sticks, and shit. A contorted mass of gray was funneling through the garden toward them. They had taken the skolves by surprise, but more and more of the beasts were becoming aware of them. "Let's go, Bro!" she roared, knowing that skolves seldom gave up once they engaged an enemy.

"Got it," he declared and sprang to his feet just in time for a skolve head to hit him in the chest. Revenberge had neatly decapitated the animal. "Aaagh," he said as blood splattered across his surcoat and into his mouth and eyes.

They charged toward the wall, Revenberge in her plate armor coming last. Ave looked up as she ran, trying to follow the gesturing and waving. The heavy report of scorpions sounded, and the zipping of their shots buzzed in her ears. A wave of arrows flashed overhead. Ave looked over her shoulder and saw a skolve with three arrows sticking out of it, screaming in fury and charging at Revenberge. There was flash of reflected light from the knight's sword and the skolve disappeared. *There!* Ave saw the postern ahead. A soldier emerged from the heavy iron door, waving and shouting something unintelligible. Ave ran diagonally, as fast as she could toward the portal. The soldier disappeared inside.

"Stay on my heels, Bro!" she said and dashed toward the door. She pulled her sword in and up as she hit the corridor, passing under numerous portcullises before she came out the other side. She turned to look back, but could not see past Bro, who took up all the space in the narrow passage. Once he squeezed through, face and tabard streaked in red blood, Ave was able to see through the passage to the other side.

Sir Revenberge had not entered the postern yet. Ave caught glimpses of her, still fighting on the other side, could envision her trying to disengage from the skolves, could imagine more and more skolves crowding in. Revenberge was strong, but enough of them could take her down. How many could she face and survive? Three? Five? Perhaps ten? But not twenty.

A sheet of arrows zipped past the opening, Ave's narrow lens to the world on the other side of the wall. The arrows made a short, furious sound, like the breaking of a wave. Another sheet shot past Revenberge. Then another and another. She saw Revenberge's sword swinging in a furious blur, rotating like a windmill blade in a gale. Another sheet of arrows, and another, then Revenberge was through the first door, pulling it shut, not getting it shut, stabbing out with her sword, then finally slamming it to. Heavy crossbeams dropped from above, securing the door. Revenberge sheathed her sword and walked briskly but calmly under each of the portcullises, which slammed down behind her in succession.

Sir Revenberge's face was orange with blood and sweat. She smiled broadly and said, "The sun is rising."

Ave had forgotten that Revenberge was a disciple of Urien. A lover of mornings and sunlight. Of action.

How could I forget, even for an instant? That bright smile burned from a pure optimism that could turn any idea into love.

"Let's see who's in charge around here," said the Deladieyr Knight with the glory of life in her eyes.

Quickly they found a back stair up to the top of the wall. There was a lot going on along the walkway between battlements. Each of Courant's walls were thirty feet deep, their tops mostly filled with soldiers, armor, barrels of water, boxes of food, and bundles of arrows and bolts, leaving only a narrow passageway at the rear. Every forty paces, there was a scorpion crew. Stairs near the postern gates led to the interior of the walls, and—in areas with higher battlements—reserve eights and sixty fours were assembled. When Engevelen bult something, they built it well.

"Where's the commander of the wall?" shouted Revenberge. A group of soldiers pointed south, but Revenberge, Bro, and Ave had not marched far in that direction before they encountered a break in the wall with a huge metal slab covering it.

"We need to get the masons working on this right away, not later. Whatever they do needs to set, and that takes time," said a man in plate armor. His helm was off—the better to shout orders—and his thick, black, curly hair made a halo about his head.

"They won't come out, sir," said a man in chainmail. "They sa—"

"Commander," said Revenberge, "perhaps we can help."

"Stand to," said the commander to his subordinate. He turned to look Revenberge, Bro, and Ave up and down. "You are welcome indeed. Glad you made it inside. We need your help. The last knight didn't come inside the walls."

Revenberge asked, "What is the situation here?" Simultaneously, Ave pitched in with, "Who was the last one?" Bro only peered at the gap in the walls, which must have been about ten or twelve feet wide. Revenberge looked at Ave and laughed, eyes still bright in the morning light, then made introductions.

The commander's name was Major Desjarlais, but he went by Des, he said, now that they had been up fighting since the day before. "Late yesterday, a force of anywhere from one to ten thousand skolves surrounded the city. Led by a demon, which we are taking to be Skoll."

"Why is your estimate for the skolves so wide, Major?" asked Ave.

"Yah," said Des, looking out over the wall. "Because they don't fight like people do. No siege weapons, don't form lines, only attack when Skoll is about or if someone's outside the walls. Most of them are out of arrow or scorpion range right now. They seem to be eating or sleeping, or hiding under cover in the gardens." He grimaced and said, "I told them a hundred knights-damned times this hugel garden was going to be a problem."

"It's about two thousand, based on their tracks," said Ave. "Unless they were joined by others. We followed them here."

"Huh," he said. "There are more than two thousand soldiers under arms in Courant, but we can't beat half that many skolves if they get inside the walls. They are a real bastard to kill." He gestured sharply toward the city behind them. "Less than a hundred got inside the city last night, and we still haven't dealt with them all. That's why I can't get this wall patched properly. My masons are holed up and won't come out."

"We should go kill the skolves," declared Bro, twitching face seemingly contradicting his matter-of-fact tone.

Ave put a restraining hand out toward him and said, "Wait. What about Skoll? Where is the Harbinger Wizard? Who has overall command of the city? And who was the 'last one'?"

Des raised his eyebrows at the list of questions. "Skoll has come and gone twice. Last night we had a breakout—some mission of the Harbinger's—and a knight, had to be a Methueyn, came out of nowhere and walloped Skoll. Put the demon right on its big, evil ass. Took off after that with the demon's sword, if you'd believe it. Skoll chased him. Came back, we think, but has not led a charge yet." He pointed at the damaged section of the wall and said, "Which is a good thing, since it's Skoll that did *this*, and right now he could probably knock down this steel plate in about a minute."

He turned to the soldier he had been speaking with earlier. "Take a sixty-four and go get those masons. Bring them if you have to drag them. Tell them we got three knights that are going to take care of the skolves." After the soldier saluted and left, Des continued, "I don't know where the Harbinger is. Rumor is she's dead, but I don't believe it. Lots of orders came out of her hall last night. General Diamond was in overall command, but she, I'm pretty sure, *is* dead because I haven't had orders from her since the skolves broke through. How's that for answers? Now would you mind finding and killing what skolves are still running around the city?"

"Where will we find them?" asked Revenberge.

"Head east and follow the carnage." Des smiled darkly. "That's combat, you never know everything. If you find them, let me know. If you find General Diamond, let her know I'm still here."

The first thing that falls is coherence.

Soldiers double-timed down the streets, passing randomly, heading in different directions. Citizens darted between buildings, panicked or dazed. No one knew who was in charge, where the general was, or whether the skolves might be on the rampage around the next corner. As crazy as it all was, it made sense. Other things did not.

"Is it over? Can we come out?" a woman shouted to Revenberge from her window.

"Stay inside," was all the knight could say, as if the flimsy door and fragile window would protect the woman.

We will only know it's over after it's over.

"You can't keep me locked up!" shouted a red-faced man the next block up when Revenberge gave him the same advice.

Do whatever you want. Ave almost yelled it, but then she saw three little kids crouched behind him, not red-faced or red-necked, but very teary-eyed. There was nothing she could say that would soften their fear and sorrow.

There was also no looting—yet—no overall disorder, but Ave was struck by how little anyone seemed to know. Or how little their behavior made sense.

"Have you seen any skolves, ma'am?" Bro asked a middle-aged woman, who was sweeping glass off the stoop of her shop.

She looked at him like *he* was a skolve, silent, staring, judging the freak-faced big man who was trying to keep her safe.

Another elderly lady stood on a stone sidewalk covered in the debris of someone's door, holding only a dustpan but no broom. "Ma'am," Bro said, nodding respectfully, face twitching. "Have you seen any skolves?"

She, too, only stared at him—stared too long—until her long bony arm came slowly up, and pointed a bonier, wrinkled, shaking finger toward the next block.

They felt their way, as blind to what might be just ahead as they were to the overall situation, but groping by questions, sound, and the spoor of destruction for an estimate of what might lie just ahead, just out of sight.

Bro rounded the corner of the block that the lady had pointed him toward and narrowly avoided stepping on a man's head. The unfortunate fellow's skull was cracked already, and his apron was blood-soaked, a decoration that covered every other part of him as well. No one had tried to sweep him up yet. His blood had not even congealed. Ave drew her sword and went around the corner. Fifteen yards away, another body lay in a doorway, a torso really, missing its arms and legs, reminding Ave of what she had seen in the town of Lyle. Sounds came from inside the doorway, a scraping on wood and a stomach-churning slurping.

The big man charged the door, screaming, "Aaaaahhh!" This meant nothing but told everything. His right shoulder hit the doorway and broke the molding off in an explosion of shards and splinters. Ave slowed to avoid crowding Revenberge in the doorway and peered through a large broken window.

It was a bakery.

She saw Bro charge a skolve, which had buried its head in a three-foot-deep mixing bowl, rooting around and sucking up the dough. The big man cut diagonally at the skolve, meaning to cut it in half at the waist, but his massive sword caught on the ceiling. Still roaring unintelligibly, Bro released the hilt and tackled the skolve before it could get its snout out of the dough. Both of them disappeared in a cacophony of sound and fluttering flour behind a stout oak table.

From Ave's right, a blurry movement in her peripheral vision solidified into a skolve, unarmed as far as she could see, charging Revenberge. She stepped forward and swung her sword—more carefully and with more wrist and less shoulder than Bro had—and took off both its long arms at the elbows before it could reach the beautiful knight. One forearm and paw landed on the table Bro had disappeared behind, and the other flew back out toward the front of the shop, hitting and cracking the window Ave was looking through. Ave leapt through the doorway to forestall other threats. She did not see any new skolves, but two immiscible odors assaulted her nostrils: raw dough and rotten meat.

Bro and the skolve both sprang to their feet, the skolve now wearing the iron mixing bowl over its head. Bro swiped massively right with his huge hand, hitting the bowl hard enough to make a loud "gong" ring off the skolve's head.

Ave hugged her sword and charged past her friend, aiming for the door to the back room, where she could now see shadows moving on its threshold. She burst through into a huge, airy, multi-level stock-room filled with shelves of sacked wheat-flour and flour-feasting skolves, maybe ten of them. "A little help here," she shouted, stepping farther into the room to give space to her companions.

Ave never thought about clearing her mind. She never consciously decided to set aside her many questions and misgivings, her fears of her own weakness, of the failure of the Methueyn Order and all that was Engevelen. But she *did* set all this aside. It slid off her, instantly sublimated by the flow state that she entered. The change was attended only by a brief moment of joy as fear and anxiety were transformed into perfect action. The floor creaked under her new weight.

When she stepped to meet the first skolve, the building shook.

Her sword, as light as a blade of grass, whistled through the air, shattering skin, jaw, and spine as it went through the first of the creatures. A spray of blood and teeth traced an arcuate path through the air, but not as quickly as Ave turned, her feet leaving grooves in the wooden planking, her sword slicing around faster yet into another skolve diving toward her from the split-level platform at the back of the room. She cut straight down through this one's face, splitting it in two to the chest. A sledgehammer, which it had wielded in its left hand, flew off and hit the wall behind Ave with a terrific concussion.

A fifty-pound sack of bleached flour hurtled into her from the left and exploded on impact, filling the air with white dust. Two skolves followed it, swinging metal.

"AVE? YOU OKAY?" shouted Bro. He was caked in white flour mixed with streaks of bright red blood. His eyelashes were so heavy with the powder that they stuck together when he blinked.

Ave could not remember when he had joined her. Just past his shoulder, she saw Revenberge, her armor similarly caked in flour, her sword so grimed with flour and blood it looked more like a long pastry stick.

"Yes," she said, though she had to pat herself down and shake out her arms and legs to make sure.

I have been battered in flour, sweat, and blood. She was as caked and ready for the baker's oven as her two companions. The room had been painted with white flour, red blood, and the body parts of skolves. It looked as if the beasts had been run at triple speed through a grain auger and sprayed across the flour-lined stock room.

"Ave? Ave?" Bro said again, eyes still blinking heavily. The flour on his face was broken into grotesque ridges by his palsied twitching.

She fumbled her sword back into its scabbard, reached up, and pushed clods of dough out of each of his ears. "I'm fine," she said. "Let's get out of here. I need to speak with the Harbinger."

Revenberge would not leave until they had found rags to wipe their grimed swords off and thoroughly checked each other over. The Deladieyr Knight's breastplate was dented, and her left pauldron was cracked, her shoulder bruised from some blunt trauma she could not remember. Bro was limping badly, and the joints on his right hand were bloodied gruesomely, though they had now stopped bleeding. The broken skin around his knuckles looked like the crust of a cherry pie.

"That was a close one," said Revenberge in a calm voice. "If there had been eight or ten more of them, we might not be walking out."

"I feel such pity for the soldiers," said Ave, imagining how dreadful it must be to square off against skolves without the strength advantage she and her companions had or their Deladieyr-class swords.

They had all heard of Harbinger Hall, the storied palace of Farrah Harbinger, but did not know where it was and had to rely on people they met for directions. An old man, dressed in an old fashioned but fine dark suit shuffled up to them. He stopped directly in front of Bro and held up a small hand towel.

"Thank you," Bro said gravely, taking the cloth from the old man. It was not much bigger than his ham-sized hands, but he used it to dab gently at his ears, which were still caked heavily with dough and flour. The old man refused to take his hand towel back, so Bro thanked him, and they continued their journey across the great city of Courant, getting directions as they went along.

Most buildings were still intact. The aqueducts were still standing, water still flowed. Only once did they come across a building that had been blown down by Skoll. Ave knew it had been the demon. She had seen the same thing happen in Aurillon. As horrifying as it was to see a massive stone structure turned to rubble by a force beyond comprehension, it was the smaller buildings with their doors broken in and people ripped in half that were more viscerally upsetting. No matter how awesome Skoll might be, it was still a singular threat, at best dual if Hati was included. The uniqueness of Skoll's terrifying menace felt containable. Not so the skolves. There were too many of them, and Ave, Bro, and Revenberge had just found out how dangerous even a small group could be.

As they approached the towering, stately hall of the Harbinger, Ave was preoccupied. *How in the knights' earth will we ever get rid of them all?*

CHAPTER 17

HOPELESS IGNORANCE

"You look like the biggest, bloodiest pastry in all Methueyn," came the voice. It leaked through a narrow slot in a recently bricked façade, a barricade of sorts hastily thrown up several paces in front of the main doors to Harbinger Hall.

"Open the door," said Ave, tired and unamused.

"Okay," replied the soldier after a moment's hesitation. "Slide two steps right, and we'll open up." It turned out they had built a little maze of brick, as the soldier explained when they entered, "to confuse the skolves."

It might even work. In her experience of them, Ave had not observed much sign of deductive capacity in the beasts. *They're territorial and food-oriented, driven by instinct, not reason.* And unrelentingly murderous and dogged, seldom, if ever, retreating. If they had any larger intentions, those must be driven by Skoll and Hati.

How do we beat them? Must we kill every single one? She knew that this was a failing strategy.

"You're here for the Harbinger?" the soldier asked as they emerged from the maze into a light, airy hall. He looked the three of them up and down, practically goggling at the gigantic, grotesque Bro. "She is up in her library," he said after this open-mouthed pause. "Walk softly, she suffers."

Ave was treated to a strange medley of sights as they crossed toward the stairs. Groups of soldiers knelt in apses and prayed even as workmen bricked over the magnificent stained-glass windows above them, and groups of civilians—families, mostly—huddled randomly in the great open spaces of the hall. Random people pointed at Ave, Revenberge, and Bro as they passed but whispered when they spoke—an effect of the majesty of the hall.

They trotted up the stairs and down a long hallway to a closed door with the sign of books upon it. An elegant, severe lady of uncertain age opened the door just as they arrived. She gasped when she saw them and said, "They sent you up like this? Eight Knights, what were they thinking?"

"We need to see the Harbinger urgently" Ave declared.

The attendant's lips thinned. "Not like that, you will not." When Ave made as if to step past her, the lady put up a hand. "There are things you need to know before you see the Lady." She lowered her voice and said, "She is not well. Follow me."

As she led them down the hallway toward a bath, introductions were made. When Lady Sylvie learned that Ave was only an Escuyer and not a Deladieyr Knight, she asked, "Why do you lead and not Sir Revenberge?"

It was a barely veiled put-down, an appeal to hierarchy, but Ave was saved from answering by Revenberge.

"You don't know the nature of our order, do you?"

Lady Sylvie picked up a stack of towels and turned to the knight. "I know your nature very well, and I must say I am surprised to see members of the Methueyn Order coming to us for advice. You have a history of going your own way, absent advice or interference from others." She thrust the towels at the knight. "Use these, please."

Then surveying all three with a skeptical look, she added, "I'll have food brought up. You look as tough as rocks and as broken down as sand. I wonder when you ate last."

"A day or so ago," said Bro.

It was both comforting and incongruous to clean up in a marble bathhouse and eat a finely cooked meal in a city under siege in a time of war, but Ave was impatient to speak with the Harbinger. She felt that if anyone had an answer for her concerns, it would be the great wizard. But for years now she had been fighting in town after town, first in Ardgour County and then in Engevelen, always on independent missions, always moving from place to place, never resting properly. And always, it seemed, on a failing trajectory. Taking pause before rushing to the next fight did not seem like a bad idea.

It would be better to make a difference than run off to further ruin. Ave hoped the Harbinger could help her find a way.

"You look more like proper knights now," said Lady Sylvie, though with a sidelong glance at Bro, when she rejoined them in the sitting room after they had eaten.

"Before I answer any questions or take you to the Harbinger," she said, looking steadily at Ave, "tell me why you have come."

"Because we are out of time and out of ideas," replied Ave, knowing as well as Lady Sylvie evidently did, that it was up to her to respond. *It is I who feel dissatisfied, I who have the questions.* "Because this war is long and late and going badly. Because we need to make a difference. We need to know what the Harbinger has seen."

Sylvie's hard face was impossible to read. She only said, "The office of the Harbinger rarely hears from the Methueyn Knights, as I said before. Usually, you draw swords and run into battle, spurning consultation of any kind. And now an *escuyer* comes with pressing questions, demanding answers."

Only in Engevelen, do we trip on rank when the country is burning down.

"And as I said before," Ave boldly replied, undeterred, "we are out of time and options. And tired of losing the lives it has cost us working separately," she added. "Let us please set aside whatever cold protocol or warmer animosity has placed you in our way. These old attitudes aren't working, neither yours nor ours. I *need* to speak to the Harbinger. I *will* speak to the Harbinger, whatever my rank may be."

Sylvie's jaw tightened perceptibly. "You are out of order, *squire.* Perhaps you should stop where you are." She looked past Ave to plate-armored Revenberge. "I would not wish to get Escuyer Vanier in trouble with you should she push me further."

Sir Revenberge replied flatly, "We came here to warn you and to help you relieve this siege. Why are you making it difficult for us to discuss how we can contribute with your Harbinger?" She glanced at Ave and added, "You assume that Aveline serves me, because *I* am a knight and *she* an escuyer. But the opposite is true. *I* serve her, hoping that *she* may Rise." She fixed Sylvie with her preternaturally calm gaze. "There is nothing you can say that would get Ave into trouble."

You are beautiful.

"You want to speak with the Harbinger so you can Rise?" Sylvie sneered, looking at Ave.

Ave saw something brittle in the lady's cold face. *Hurt? Fear? An unrequited love of her own?* She reminded herself that she was not the only person traumatized by the horrors of this war. She softened her voice and replied, "I doubt I will ever Rise. I ask only so that we can help."

Lady Sylvie's iceberg face shivered for a moment and then broke, spasming almost like Bro's, before quickly reassembling as hard as before. "Perhaps there is hope for us all yet. If so, this will be the second time recently that I may have been wrong about someone. I will tell you what I can, but you should first know that the Lady Harbinger is dangerously ill, and your . . . consultation is unlikely to bear fruit. She has not been able to speak for some days. There was a shock and . . . well, I will tell you everything."

She told them how Farrah Harbinger had heroically attempted a heraldic operation meant to break the locus—that volatile but stubborn knot in probability—to illuminate a path to salvation, if there was one. Her goal was to find a way to end the Methueyn War at last, but the Heraldry had been overwhelming for everyone involved. Lady

Harbinger had collapsed and was still insensible, and her entire inner council had been incapacitated for several days—except for a mysterious lieutenant, one Davignon Delatam—who was completely unimpaired and may have seen the Harbinger's vision clear and whole.

"Why is that name familiar?" asked Revenberge.

Sylvie said, "Because he was feted as the hero from Charney."

"Oh."

"Without him, the Renet could never have made the case for invading Ardgour," said Sylvie, "which now seems to have been a terrible mistake. You may not know that his reliability was later called into question after a shameful, a frightening performance on his officer's written test. He would have been drummed out of the Renet, except that the Lady Harbinger, for reasons no one can fathom, plucked him away and brought him here." She sighed. "He seemed a stuffed tabard to me, and in his short time with us had hardly said a word without prompting. But he changed after the Heraldry. He became a different man entirely. He took command like a general when the rest of us were helpless."

"It sounds like he was hiding something," said Revenberge. "People don't change that much."

"I no longer question him," Sylvie said severely. "He does the Lady's bidding."

The quaver in her voice when Sylvie said *Lady* confirmed something to Ave. There was such a warmth to that word, that word alone, in Sylvie's otherwise cold delivery. Her feelings for the Harbinger went beyond her station. At that moment, Lady Sylvie darted a sharp glance at Ave. *She fears she has given herself away.*

But Sylvie recovered without missing another beat and went on to describe how the Harbinger had apparently seen two critical paths, one involving an envoy from Nehring Ardgour and the other a quest to find a weapon to destroy some new and still more powerful devil, the "One True Devil," according to the Harbinger. "So if you wish to make a difference," Lady Sylvie concluded, "you can either join the Methueyn Knights and aid them on whatever mission they and the envoy agreed upon, or you can find Lieutenant Delatam in Villiers and seek his instructions."

"Do you know if both missions got away?" asked Ave.

"Davignon made sure that Alain Overbree, the Lady Harbinger's confidential advisor, escaped before the skolves surrounded the city," said Sylvie. "The lieutenant left a good deal later, in the midst of the siege, I'm afraid. I have no idea if he made it."

"All of the Methueyn Knights are gathering in Engevelen," said Revenberge, "but this Davignon fellow just took a handful of soldiers with him?"

"Tell us more about his mission and about this One True Devil," said Ave.

~

"THE GROUP that tried to break the skolve lines? The ones led by that guy out of Charney?" asked the private. "They're all dead."

"Dead?" repeated Bro lamely.

"Oh yeah, deader than Lessingham," said the private, a short, good-looking young man with wide sparkling eyes, "deader than Nimrheal's mother, deader than last year's turnips. Rotting in the garden like a headless, stump-for-a-tail, stump-for-a-head mouse. *Dead.*"

Night was falling, perhaps in more ways than one. Ave needed sleep, and she did not need to hear that the enigmatic Lieutenant Delatam was dead. After speaking with Lady Sylvie, Bro and Ave had gone to the wall to see what news they could pick up about Davignon while Revenberge had responded to a new report of skolves inside the city. They were speaking now with a soldier who claimed to have witnessed the exit from the city of Dav and his small troop.

Has one of the missions already failed?

"You saw this?" Ave asked, pointing over the wall at the hugel gardens. They now looked as if they had been mulched by a combination of demon, skolves, and scorpion shot. Turned over by a rotary tiller from hell.

"Oh yeah. They got outside awright, but they didn't get far. Skolves piled onto them right quick."

"Was this before or after the knight attacked Skoll?"

"Uhh," the private said. "That was . . . after, I think. That knight, he came running faster than anything—well faster than anything 'sides the demon itself—and hit it like a lightning bolt." He made an expansive gesture with both arms and said, "The racket of it knocked me right on my ass."

"And that's when the lieutenant and the others died?" Ave asked.

"Yes, right then. Skolves everywhere. Bunch of them were trying to come through the breach."

Ave's eyes narrowed. "You were knocked on your ass, but you saw what happened?"

"Yes."

"But you were fighting skolves at the breach."

"Yah."

"So how did you see what happened to Delatam's group?" *In the dark.* "Are you sure they're dead?"

"Oh, they're dead, awright." He looked out over the wall to some point in the churned-up hugel garden. "Can't imagine how frightening it would have been to be out there right beside the demon when the knight hit it. I saw the hero of Charney stand up and face Skoll. Looked right at it. Like staring down a tornado. Knights-damned hell of a scary situation, yeah, they're dead for sure. Probably." He paused, eyes rolling around in their big sockets and finished with a whisper, "I'm pretty sure. Maybe."

You idiot. Ave narrowly avoided saying it.

Bro's twitching mess of a face gave nothing away either. He only said, "Did anyone get a better look?"

The soldier frowned incredulously. "It was *dark* out there. They were a long way off. *Nobody* got a good look." He smiled, bowed his head, and started walking away. "Heh, maybe they got away."

Ave looked at Bro and said, "Does anyone know anything in this city?"

~

"NOPE. No one knows much of anything," said Ave the next morning on the wall. Overnight, they had split up and cleared out the last of the skolves inside the city. "Not even who's in charge."

"I will impress it upon the major to declare himself commanding officer *pro tem* and centralize command," said Revenberge.

"Following dead bodies is poor defensive strategy," said Bro. The scattered pockets of skolves had been painfully difficult to find with no clear or coordinated command and communications.

"I am worried about this devil mission in Villiers," said Ave. "Do you think we should go there and help?"

Bro whispered, "I will go where you go, Aveline."

"And *your* thoughts?" Ave asked Revenberge. Bro's declaration was unsurprising, but it meant nothing to Ave if Revenberge could not be shifted.

"We must stay and help the city stand," the Deladieyr Knight said. "It will take all three of us."

Damn it.

Revenberge did not see Ave's reaction. Caught up in her own Idea, she smiled wryly and said, "I am sick of bakers being murdered."

The air trembled, softly at first like faraway thunder, then quickly grew stronger and louder. Loud enough to make some of the soldiers look for lightning in the sky. Louder still, it got, loud enough to feel in the bones. The ground shook. The walls shook. A stack of swords leaning against the parapet rattled and fell over. Soldiers pointed west into the trailing dark of the morning. A cry went up along the wall. "Skoll!"

Ave turned to follow the pointing and saw the dark figure cloaked in a blue halo. It did not charge. It *advanced.* Deliberately and steadily, stamping the ground, reveling in the noise and quaking of its measured passage, taking its time as it approached the wall. The closer the thing got, the slower it seemed to come on and the harder it stamped. Mucky wastewater from the hugel garden exploded upward with each step and sizzled off the blue nimbus. Then Skoll stopped, turned north from where it had been heading, and aimed itself toward where Ave, Bro, and Revenberge stood.

Fuck. It makes Bro look like a child. The demon was monstrously large, yet it looked like a huge, furious man. It was as if everything hostile, arrogant, malign, and unreasonable that could grow in a man was filled to bursting in this titanic figure. This was the wild drunk, the malicious bully, the wife beater, the evil bastard who waits in the dark alley all rolled into one and exaggerated, expanded into something beyond pity or disgust. Ave could feel, with every step, its demonic, unearthly power. It was, she sensed, ego, rage, and selfishness made manifest. The demon was everything bad in humanity, and looked something like a man, but was something more, something far worse.

The demon's once-silver armor was drenched in brown waste, and its breastplate was emblazoned by a huge gash running sideways right through its center. The heavy section of plate looked as if it might have broken in two if the cut were only just a little wider. She also saw that it carried Sir Michael's great sword—the one that Sir Sandeyl had taken two nights previously—in its right hand. A mass of skolves were gathering behind the demon. She looked north and south and could see them streaming toward the monster's wake.

The skolves have come to watch.

I AM SKOLL. MAKE A FLAG IN MY IMAGE AND LET IT FLY. THEN BRING ME YOUR HARBINGER TO BOW TO ME AND YOU MAY LIVE. DO THIS AND I SHALL TELL MY SKOLVES TO EAT SOME OTHER CITY.

It pointed the huge sword up at Ave, Bro, and Revenberge.

SEND YOUR KNIGHTS TO MAKE OBEISANCE AND BE PROTECTED BY ME.

The words rolled like thunder through the air. No one said a thing, no one fired a weapon. No soldier moved except to tremble, no skolve except to hunch behind the demon in submission.

Ave knew something then, something important. She understood *why* the siege had failed when Sandeyl had arrived and struck Skoll, stealing the great sword of Michael. She understood why little had happened since and why Skoll stood before the walls now. Skoll *needed* to make a show for the skolves. It needed to *dominate* to *lead* them. It craved obeisance for its own sake.

Skoll was a dumb brute, an idiot. No different from a drunk, angry man-child except for its staggering power.

And the eight-foot-tall ego it needed to feed.

She would have laughed at it, turned her back on it, dismissed it as pathetic except for the scale of its power. Another thought occurred to her. *It* should *be laughed at.*

No Methueyn Knight ever trash-talked. Nor any Deladieyr. Not that Ave knew of. Their Ideas did not require it, would have disdained it. There was no insecurity to be fed, no ego-serving satisfaction to be sought. Ave had no satisfaction to feed, but taking something away from Skoll seemed like an excellent goal just then. She cupped her mouth with both hands and roared, "We might consider it, but presently you are covered in shit, mongrel!"

The soldiers exploded with laughter, their fear finding instant release.

Pivoting even as the laughter continued, Ave turned her back on Skoll to speak to Revenberge. "We should go now! Over the wall and into the hills. Lead it away! Staying and fighting is what it wants."

Revenberge was aghast. "You want to run away after *that*?"

How much time do we have? She had no idea how long it might take a demon to process that humiliation, but she doubted it would take long. "Yes!" Ave said, riding the wave of insight Skoll's actions had given her. "Let's do what Sandeyl did. Run away. Distract the thing. Get it away from the city. Don't give it the spectacle it desires. We cannot beat it in a fair fight, but we might still frustrate it."

"AAAAARRRRGHH! I WILL MAKE YOU ALL DEAD NOW!"

The ground shook with more heavy steps, rapid ones this time. Then came the full explosion of sound and fury as Skoll hit the wall, punctuated with the yells of soldiers shouting, and bows, crossbows and scorpions firing.

The wall shook a second time. Right under where Ave was standing.

"Let's go!" she said.

"No."

"Why in Elysium's name not?"

Sunlight flashed off Revenberge's plate armor. She spoke like a flower in a still meadow, "I have filled my own cup, Aveline. I will not leave the city. You and Bro should go. Take my love and *go*."

Ave knew that Revenberge meant those last words literally. A flash of memory—of the beautiful woman on an earlier morning, lacking armor and not needing it—nearly choked Ave with frustration.

The wall shook again. Bro caught a soldier by the arm who would have fallen over the parapet. He flung the man back to safety.

"Clear the section!" shouted a sergeant.

"We are never going to beat them if we don't use our heads!" Ave said to herself, her frustration struggling toward nothing good. But she bit down on the thought, even though she knew it was the truth. Skoll was obviously an idiot, but knights . . . knights were not idiots, though sometimes they seemed like slaves to their ideas. Not simpletons, but simple. Single-minded. Pure.

Revenberge could only fill her own cup, could only be herself. It was morning and sunlight was on her. She had a joy of the world—of life—of the new day, and she would not abandon the people of Courant even if, rationally, she should. She could not imagine an indirect way of opposing Skoll. Ave's idea suggested that leading the demon off might save them all, but it was only an idea. It was not Revenberge's *Idea*. If they left and the demon did not, no one in the city could stop it.

It was a logical conundrum, but Deladieyr Knights never suffered such a quandary. They always knew what they valued most. The conundrum proved to Ave, once more, that she would never—could never—be such a knight.

But she could not leave Revenberge to protect the city alone. Not for anything. Even if it was the wrong thing to do.

The wall shook again. Great cracks opened beneath them. The soldiers had moved off north and south, and two formations of sixty-fours had assembled on the ground behind the walls, ready to fight. Eights and sixty-fours rushed along the top of the wall to reinforce the soldiers at the section Skoll was attacking.

"Where do you want to meet it?" Ave asked Revenberge.

She smiled and pointed. "Down there."

"Bro and I will keep the skolves from following it in, then come and help you."

Revenberge nodded, and they raced along the wall, looking for stairs. Their feet had just touched ground when Skoll broke the wall. The demon had not even bothered re-opening the old damage it had done. That hastily patched breach was only about forty yards to the south. A demon obviously did not care about efficiency.

Or cares more about creating a grander spectacle for its audience.

Or it just enjoys smashing things.

The demon strode carefully through falling stone, waiting with a theatrical sense of timing until the dust cleared before emerging fully into the city.

It was hit by five scorpion spears on its first step inside the walls, followed almost instantly by about two hundred arrows and bolts. Every object bounced off the demon, but the scorpion shots made it go down on one knee and roar at ear-popping, hair-whipping volume.

Revenberge hit it crosswise in the face with her sword before it could recover. Skoll fell backward onto its butt with a seismic thud, although the knight's sword did not bite deep and Revenberge was thrown off balance as well. There was one brief instant when Ave was sure she saw surprise, pain, and new humiliation cross Skoll's murderous face. Revenberge had made it pay for its theatrics. She shot off down the city block. Skoll roared again and pursued her.

Was there even blood? A blow to the face with a Deladieyr-class weapon should have ended anything short of Nimrheal, but Skoll had seemed barely hurt.

She is going to die.

"I will help her," said Bro as if reading Ave's mind, and was gone.

She nodded to thin air and sprang toward the gap Skoll had opened in the wall. The first knot of skolves had just emerged from it. Arrow and spears fell on them like driving rain, pin- cushioning the beasts. One skolve stumbled out of the arrow storm, took three stumbling steps, and was decapitated by Ave. She noted that three arrows were sticking out of the flying head.

If only that had happened to Skoll.

Ave stepped back quickly as more skolves pushed through the gap and were met by another sheet of arrows, bolts and scorpion shot. Bolts and spears bounced off stone, shattering, pelting Ave with some of the pieces. She turned her face away from the debris and saw the first soldier of an eight just ten steps away from her. She made eye contact and shouted, "Is there another patch? Get it!"

Another skolve made it alive out of the hail of missiles. Ave jumped forward and bludgeoned its rusty sword in two with her shining one, then cut halfway through its torso to its spine, and kicked it back into the growing pile of skolve carcasses and broken projectiles.

"Aaii!" A bolt had struck her on the top of her left shoulder, broke the rings of her chain mail, and spun off her in an explosion of metal and wood. She took two steps back and waited for the next skolves to emerge.

~

Ave had no trouble tracking Revenberge, Bro, and Skoll. They left a trail of ruin behind them. It was said that wizards left only ruin in their wake, but Skoll had both knights and wizards beat in the wreckage stakes. Having held the gap until a new metal patch arrived, Ave had left the soldiers to it and raced off in a desperate search for her friends. She hoped there was time yet to prevent their deaths.

One ruin might seem as good as the next to die in, but perhaps we can yet make a difference. Perhaps something can be saved.

The how of it, Ave did not yet know. She was sure of *where* she wanted to go, where they might make that difference, but had no idea *how* to change Revenberge's mind. It seemed hopeless trying to change the direction of an obdurate Idea, but Revenberge was her friend, and so much more than a friend. She had to try.

And Bro was like a pet or a child. He only wanted to help. That was his sole agency. Ave felt responsible for his fate.

The ground shook and the air trembled, but Ave hardly seemed to notice. She wondered if she still had dough in her ears from the fight in the bakery. But there was no dough, only shock from violent concussion after violent concussion, from mindless rage, transcendent power and violence. Ave rounded a corner as Bro slid across cobbles to lie, bleeding at her feet. His nose was smashed, and tears blinded his eyes. His tabard was torn and his sword, Ave saw, was thirty yards away on a pile of rocks.

"Bro!" Ave cried, trying to pick him up. A two-foot-wide swath of broken chainmail slipped out from under his tabard and fell to the ground as she wrestled with him.

How?

"Revey," he groaned, pointing.

Ave looked across the square. On the opposite side stood a big, stone, three-story building, a magistrates' court by the look of it, and beside it, on the far edge of the square, Skoll lifted Revenberge above its head and smashed her into the ground. The demon did not simply drop her, it *hurtled* her into the road, cracking cobbles, breaking plates in her armor.

"Where does the love go?"

Ave did not know who said it. Then she said it again as Skoll smashed Revenberge's broken body again into the stony ground. It was the breaking of her heart, the denial of sunlight, of morning, of hope. Of love.

"Revenberge!" Ave cried. Skoll gazed right at her. The demon's eyes were an unnaturally bright cyan blue.

POP. A burst in the air from the roof of the magistrate's office broke the moment. A knot of soldiers and civilians had abruptly materialized there, one of the figures deep in an athletic pose. The air shimmered around them. A second later, Ave felt successive waves of hot and cold air pass over her.

A woman emerged from the mess of people, arms spread wide and singing in a loud, indulgent voice:

People of Engevelen
Let your hearts be leavened.
Set aside all of your fear,
The Elysian wizards are here.

The instant she finished her juvenile ditty, the air rippled from her to Skoll, a cyclone that blasted the giant from its feet, skidded it, flailing, across the cobbles, and smashed it into a stone bench on the other side of the street.

Wizards!

Ave was buffeted by thermal winds. She swiped at her eyelids, which were inexplicably frosted, and tried to make sense of this new turn of events. Skoll had broken the big stone bench, but it had not broken the demon. It shook its head violently, and with a roar, sprang to its feet and charged toward the building that the wizards had teleported onto.

A man walked close to the edge. He wore a long, brightly colored scarf, had a voluminous bag slung over his left shoulder, and carried something in his arms. "Say hello to my pretty little friend," he shouted and tossed a small object off the roof toward Skoll. The demon skidded to a halt, brought up short as the thing—no two things—described a hyperbolic path through the air.

Ave squinted. It was a garish pink, porcelain doll, or the head and body of one. With an impossible swiftness, Skoll lunged and caught both pieces, one in each hand. Lightning exploded from the sky above him, from the ground at its feet, between the demon's head and shoulders, flaring around its enormous body. Ave jumped as an invisible electric blow jolted her. Before she could recover, thunder hit her ears like a blow from a hammer as the afterimage of the lightning flared across her eyelids. When she forced them open, she saw that Skoll had been knocked into a sitting position. Its face was covered in dark soot, and fragments of the doll were husks in its hands, one blackened, the other frosted. The cobbles all around the demon were covered in baroque patterns etched in black soot and reflective ice. The gash in the demon's breastplate had at last been widened, and the lower half had slid off. With an unintelligible roar, Skoll staggered to its feet, twice almost slipping back onto its behind, grabbed a huge piece of frozen rubble, and hurled it at the knot of people on the roof.

The scarf-wearing, doll-throwing maniac shrieked and tried to duck. The rock, which had to be at least three feet across, missed him but hit someone else—a soldier—with a sick meaty sound. A moment later, a second meaty thud was heard.

He fell off the roof.

Ave could not see where the body ended up. The group on the roof exploded into motion like a murder of crows, running in every direction a rooftop would allow, away.

Skoll roared, as loud as the thunder from the doll, and ran straight toward the building, colliding with it in another violent, ear-splitting explosion. Roars and the sounds of falling rocks followed for a moment, then dissolved into silence.

Ave and Bro found themselves alone with Revenberge. Only days ago in Aurillon, Revenberge had Risen, bright, triumphant, shining. And not many days before that, she and Ave had last been alone. They had each sought a different idea—filled different cups—but they had on that day shared love. Ave remembered Revenberge's perfection in the dim candlelight. Always she had been wondrous, alive, joyful.

Triumphant. The tall, beautiful woman now lay unmoving. Broken. The glory of life had left her eyes. She was covered in dust, no longer reflecting the morning light in any sense

There were no words. Ave only felt shock at first. Then pain and fear and disbelief coursed through her. It was the kind of shock that makes people eat their own fist. And why not eat your own fist? This was the datum that no act could cure, no idea remedy. Love and light, and the morning, lay broken in the square.

And there was no reason for it. It had not needed to happen. Fighting Skoll had not saved any lives, only guaranteed the end of one. *We cannot win like this.*

Seeing goddess-like Revenberge laid out in the rubble, her mangled body now the worst ruin in the whole ruined city, Ave understood the hopeless ignorance of violence.

It was an understanding only made worse by its absolute lack of surprise. This had already been the fate of almost all the knights and squires of the Methueyn Order.

Bro turned toward Ave. For once, his stricken, twitching, tear-tracked face did not seem out of place. He said, "Should we go find Skoll?"

"No!" Ave had been on the tipping point of a decision for weeks. Months. There was an insanity to the Methueyn Order. A changeless commitment to pure, internalized Ideas. They were perfect, authentic agents of their separate Ideas. They each filled their own cups, but none of them could conceive of cooperating or acting strategically. *And so we do the same thing again and again to the same result. Death. Failure.*

Revenberge's smashed corpse tipped her into decision.

I have questioned, but I have not acted. And now Revey is dead.

"Do you think I am the worst escuyer the order has ever had?" Ave asked aloud. The words passed her lips before she could censure herself.

Bro's eyes were wet but unwavering. "I have always thought you were the best of us all," he said.

I know you do. She knew it. Question herself, yes. Question the order, its ideals, yes. Question history, yes. But she did not question Bro's unquenchable faith. She could not answer that faith by letting him die repeating the same mistake as all the other knights and squires. She could not answer that faith without some of her own.

"Then it is time to end this insanity," she said, tearing her eyes off broken love and roughly grabbing Bro by his ripped tabard.

PART TWO
HOPE

CHAPTER 18
MAKING IT WORSE

"When your soldiers feel safe, beware the most brittle break."
Major Peridot at Charney

"I'm here!" exclaimed Alain Overbree, leaning on Proulx. "Escaped from the siege at Courant . . . like Sandeyl himself, outran an army of skolves . . . have vital knowledge for the princess." His sweat-stained tabard and breeches, once so elegant and expensive, now reeked of fermenting vomit, pungent sweat, and sour fear. His face was shadowed by untrimmed, wild growth, and his red eyes brimmed with the tears of the broken triumphant. Proulx's soldiers crowded behind Overbree, looking almost as wretched. Their clothes were not as rich as Alain's, but they lacked the splashes of barf that the wizard's sported. The horses, left farther back, looked on their last legs. Salt stained their brown hides, and they breathed in rattling gasps.

Alain took a few noisy gasps himself before he was able to speak again. "You must send a runner to the palace at once, straight to Princess Cressy. Tell her that she must *not* execute the envoy!"

"Who?" said the sergeant-at-arms in charge of the gate, staring at Alain as if he was insane.

"The envoy of Nehring Ardgour!" shrieked Alain, his voice cracking, his dirt-crusted fingers scrabbling at the soldier's tabard. "The fate of the world depends upon it."

"There have been no envoys, sir," the sergeant said.

Alain's face grew wild, his voice desperate. "No one has come?"

"No one."

"No one do anything." said Val, "be careful. Just go in, look around, and get out."

Green nodded. He looked better than he had the night before, firmer, less scared.

Take some food with you. Val almost said it aloud before catching herself. Green had always been thin and fragile-looking. He was not about to pack on any saddlebags with all the teleporting he was doing. But she knew better than to say something so motherly with the rhyming Statician wizard Rebecca Laurie and the creepy doll-thrower Christopher watching. *What a pair!*

Not for the first time, Val noticed how much they resembled too-close siblings, or even a long-married couple, with their pale skin and dark hair but also their shared love of reckless action and irreverent sarcasm. They were wizards of the old kind, the kind that some called impetuous monsters and reckless ruminators.

"Courant is one of the greatest cities of Engevelen," Val said. She smiled at the wizards but warned, "Be careful with it." She wanted to say more. Val housed her own reckless monster. It had gotten away from her too often recently. It was a pedant, a lover of trifling distinctions and verbose explanations, big on detail, short on wisdom. It loved to give lectures, pick fights, and obsess on minute issues so that the big, uncomfortable problems could be avoided. Seeing the melted armor and brunt husk of the Shining Knight had shocked her into fully recognizing the monster. It had grown fat on the stress of Engevelen's plight, but that meeting had given her the self-awareness needed to leash it. For now.

"Oh yeah, Valcourt," Rebecca said, "we've got it covered."

Christopher added, "It's just scouting anyway. We'll pop in there with old Green here, eyeball the situation, and pop back out. No skolves or demons the wiser."

"Quiet as an owl," said Rebecca, smiling at Christopher. "Or a bear."

"Owl?" asked Green. "Are owls and bears quiet? Why not a mouse?"

"I don't want to be a damned mouse," retorted Rebecca, eyes wild. She shook her head at Green and said, "No one gives them any respect."

Val almost lost her grip on the monster. But she bit down on its leash and only said, "Just as long as your simile is quiet, you will have my respect." She lowered her voice to a whisper. "*Quiet.*"

"Three quiet and super sneaky owl-bears," declared Christopher, almost in a shout, hefting his bag of painted dolls. "They'll never know what hit them, uh, I mean they'll never know we were there."

"I wonder if I could write a poem about these three bears," mused Rebecca. "It has a ring to it that might do some damage."

Val narrowed her eyes, wondering if it would make things better or worse by cautioning her incautious colleagues yet again. *Worse.* "About ready to go then?" she asked in what she hoped was a patient tone.

Running footsteps sounded in the hall, growing louder as they approached the teleportation platform. A page raced through the opening, her ringleted dark hair bouncing as she ran, then settling again as she slid to a stop just before colliding with Val. "Stop! Please, Lady Valcourt, wait a moment," said the page breathlessly. She had a scroll in her hand which she proffered to Val. "From Princess Cressy."

Rebecca stamped a foot and said, “How come *we* never get scrolls from the princess, Chris?”

Christopher’s eyes slid conspicuously to the left and then to the right before saying, “Because we’re as quiet and inconspicuous as three bears?”

“It just isn’t right!” exclaimed Rebecca, pouting. “We bears need better representation.”

“I’m not a bear,” muttered Green, watching Val read the scroll.

Val finished reading, met his eyes, and looked at the other two wizards, thinking quickly. Everything Christopher and Rebecca said worried her, especially after reading the scroll, but she had promised herself not to be distracted by trivialities.

“We have changed your mission,” she announced. “Alain Overbree has arrived from Courant, speaking of some dark and confusing Heraldry by Farrah Harbinger.” She looked down at the scroll momentarily. “But . . . well, it sounds like he is not . . . well.”

“I’m sorry to hear that, Val,” said Green with genuine sympathy. He knew that Alain had been Val’s mentor in the Acutist school.

Rebecca’s eyes sparkled with excitement. “Whoo hoo hoo. What *dark* Heraldry?” she gushed.

Val pulled the scroll to its full length, but the effect was anticlimactic. It was only a foot long. “It does not say,” she said. “But we are instructed to immediately retrieve the Lady Harbinger so she can speak to the princess directly.”

Chris said, “We get to go to grandma’s house and literally *kidnap* her?”

“Do not call the Harbinger ‘grandma,’ Chris,” Val said, horrified. “Lady Sylvie will, *literally*, kill you.”

“First of all, I don’t know who that is. And second, kill me? Come *on*. We are going to save grandma from the skolves.”

“I don’t see what difference this makes,” said Rebecca. “We were going to talk to Grandma Harbinger anyway.”

Val told her monster that all this “grandma” talk was just their usual harmless way of speaking, that it was meant in fun, bad taste and all. But the beast gnawed ferociously at the chains of her Engevelen poise.

A skolve's mass to a man's mass is approximately one point five. On average. To light a man on fire requires four barrels full of water. To light a skolve on fire should take six. Like is to like is to like, and thus we go from what we know to what we thought we didn't know.

It calmed her, the Acutist method of figuring out how to burn something down. *It would help if I didn't have to make an educated guess at the relative heat capacity and flammability of a skolve. I really need a fresh carcass.*

Green shook his head, "No, no, this is a big deal. We were going to talk to gra—the Lady Harbinger, but we weren't going to bring her back with us." He looked at Val and said, "Right Val?"

"Huh?" Val said. She was still absorbed in her mental exercises but quickly came back to earth. "Right. It is a material change. A significant one. You are going to have to take at least two soldiers with you as a contingency in case the Lady Harbinger requires help." She looked at Rebecca and Christopher, who looked as irreverent and unpredictable as ever, and hoped that their childishness was all an act, a pose of nonchalance. She had also wanted time to work with the Elysians on protocols and best practices, but it could not be helped. Events had once more turned their plans upside down, as if determined to limit their options.

"Just do the minimum there. Avoid fighting. You are scouting, locating, and retrieving. That is all."

~

"That bit of scouting worked. They have room for us," said Captain Bysshe, coming out of the inn she had reconnoitered and facing Dav and the other soldiers. Streams of men and women, mostly armed, pushed by their little group. The town of Argenteul was crowded with soldiers marching in every direction, mixed with a trickle of citizens pulling or pushing carts full of their belongings moving south toward safety.

"Fuck my feet, that's a good thing," muttered Marianne. Her face was blackened from the hard route that Dav had led them on.

"Your feet?" asked Darcelle, drunk on exhaustion and relief at not being dead and added to the garbage field of the hugel gardens. "I could be talked into fu—"

"Not another word!" Dav growled. Long experience had told him which issues to deal with harshly, even to exhausted troops.

Darcelle jumped, so startled that he hit the hitching post with his own dirty face and fell onto the street. Dav's face screwed up as he assessed the soldier's reaction. It was not comic, and not entirely due to fatigue. The man was terrified. Of Dav.

Why?

He remembered their brief encounter with Skoll, the ungentle splash of epileptic vision, his left hand moving of its own volition, and the demon passing them by.

Did he see?

As much as Dav did not want the man to be in such a state of fear, he could not apologize and risk compromising discipline. And he certainly could not explain away what had happened that night. Even for himself, Dav had only guesses, none of which would make anyone feel at ease.

"On your feet," Dav said in even tones. "We made it. One more day and we will be in Villiers, and the day after that, knights willing, at Chamberry. But tonight, you each get proper beds. You saw all the tents on the outskirts. The captain did well for you."

"We're really going back?" Marianne asked, eyes shining big.

Dav knew she meant going back to the lines, fighting skolves or demons, that her mind was anchored on memories of the terror she had just escaped.

It was awful.

Running through the hugel fields had been a nightmare, every step taking them farther from the orange light of Courant's walls.

Another hundred yards into the mulched ruin of the gardens, and it was all but pitch-dark. Dav knew by instinct—and by a seizure flash of jumbled space and time and violence—where to go, but the soldiers could not have had any idea. They followed his sudden turns and abrupt stops and starts on faith. And because they had no other anchor. They were way out in the deep, dark water, and Dav was the closest thing to a life raft they had. Twice he killed skolves before any of the soldiers had even seen them, his prized sword cutting their tough carcasses easily. They had come through all that horror and uncertainty with little protest, and *now* they seemed afraid.

Did I use up all their faith and trust?

He remembered something that Major Peridot had told him at Charney about the downside of victory. His soldiers were disarmed by success, their courage used up now that the danger was past.

"First thing," said Captain Bysshe, not looking at Marianne's eyes. "They've got a bath hall down the street. Let's get cleaned up first, then eat."

"What are we going to change into?" Marianne said. Their clothes were caked in mud, filth, and sweat, and stank like rotted vegetables mixed with shit. Their chainmail had its own sharp odor, the oxidation of rust.

~

What has Alain changed into?

Val set up the three raisins, the orange, the small pumpkin, the watermelon, and the large pumpkin in their respective positions over each chalk mark in the Elysians' practice yard.

Across the yard, Calvaine babbled in his mysterious wizardly language. It was a tongue he claimed that only he understood, though Val was pretty certain it was gibberish even to him. He faced a huge, man-and-a-half sized scarecrow, attempting some effect that for sure only he was privy to. Samantha had just left, having utilized vials of some new sulfurous concoction against the stone walls of the yard, burning them clean of moss and dirt.

There were no other wizards left in Elysian headquarters.

Green had left for Courant, taking two obedient, silent soldiers and the recalcitrant, bantering wizards with him. Val finally had a few minutes to practice the high science of analogic wizardry known as Acutism —and probably only a few, for how long could it take to teleport into Courant, quiet as bears or badgers or whatever Rebecca had said and bring back Farrah Harbinger? This was the first moment Val had had to herself, free from the mental noise of her many distractions and responsibilities, for weeks. And yet it was so exceedingly difficult to take her mind off her former mentor, Alain Overbree, and her very brief encounter with him moments earlier. He had been on his way to quarters—they had met by chance and exchanged only a few words—but the meeting weighed heavy on Val.

She had never seen Alain even slightly out of trim before, never mind the disarray she had found him in. The Alain she knew, and admired profoundly, would never have allowed himself to be seen in such a state. Yet there he had been with vomit all over his shirt, unshaven whiskers on his face, stained teeth in his mouth. And worst of all, raving.

I live in a world where Alain Overbree makes the neighborhood rummy look good. What is that like?

Bad.

It had made Val's stomach drop almost as much as seeing Green half frozen on the teleportation pad in Vercors.

Do these images hurt so, discomfit so, set me so adrift because I have depended so unthinkingly on these two men? She considered Green. *Because I use him just as thoughtlessly?*

She looked at the vessels of water, from small cups to large barrel, all sitting one pace from each of her organic test subjects, their sizes varying in proportion to the mass of water in each container. She reminded herself that she *knew* the relative masses of each object, from raisins to pumpkins, had *felt* their differences, their weight, and capacity.

Like is to like is to like. I practice the feel of one thing I know, compare it to the feel of another thing I know, to yet another, thus to be ready for that which I don't know.

Val opened herself to the empyreal sky, felt the resistance that Huygens had written about, tasted it. She smiled and broke through, once, twice, three times, four times, and a fifth.

The orange popped, the pumpkins cracked, the watermelon bubbled foully, and the raisins sizzled sweetly. She was buffeted by winds, first hot, then icy cold.

Waiting for the danger of vegetative explosion to pass, Val closed her eyes and savored the feeling of changing the world.

Like is to like is to like. I must remember this. It must become natural. I must take it for granted.

Turning her back on the baked vegetable and fruits, Val marched out of the practice yard.

It was time to figure out what had happened to Alain.

~

Organizing clean clothes and baths took hours. Captain Bysshe and Dav scrounged cleaning oil for their armor and new padded undergarments from a quartermaster on the tented encampment on the south side of town while the other soldiers bathed. They cleaned up last, sitting in long, deep copper tubs separated only by a thin dressing screen. The other soldiers were sent back to the inn to eat.

It was strange being alone with the captain again. And nice, in the now quiet baths to have this time. Getting from Courant to Argenteul had required tremendous faith and trust on her part under the worst conditions. In the few weeks that they had known each other, Dav had often noticed her eyes on him. With suspicion, he had thought. But when the situation had called for it, she had acted with complete confidence in him.

"Thank you for getting us out of Courant," Bysshe said. Dav could hear soft splashing and see her silhouette through the screen. One of her arms was raised. He imagined the clean, bubbly water running down it.

"We were lucky," he said, looking away from her perfect shadow.

"Were we?"

Dav did not answer. A silence stretched between them in which the gentle sounds of bathing were suspended. Dav found himself looking back through the screen at Barbara's unmoving form. "Yes," he finally said.

Dav imagined her looking back at him. He was sure of it when he heard her next words. "You were curiously unaffected by Farrah Harbinger's Heraldry, Dav. I'm still not sure I can walk straight."

His first instinct was to prevaricate, but the captain had called him "Dav" instead of Davignon or Lieutenant. It made him want to be more open. But he did not have a good answer for her, was not certain he had a real answer at all.

He could see the profile of her face through the screen. The effect of seeing her in outline somehow her words reach deeper into him.

"How did you save Major Peridot at Charney?"

"That is a very long story."

"Hmmm," she said. "Of course. You are a man of secrets, Dav. Quiet for weeks, and then giving orders like a general."

"I was a sergeant ... before," he said. "We give orders when we must. Loudly and clearly."

"True," Barbara said. "But you were always right-handed, were you not? Until we fled Courant. Then you fought with your left. Before that, you stopped Skoll with the same hand. I saw it. I wondered if you were some god, from Elysium maybe, or even . . ." she hesitated and spoke more softly, "or even the One True Devil that the Harbinger sent us to find." There was a smile on those shadow lips. He knew that though he could not see it. "*Are* you a devil?" she asked.

She did not mean it. Not exactly, he told himself.

"I hope not."

"When are you going to tell me your secrets, Dav?"

"Here, naked in this tub, you want to share secrets?" he said, trying to disarm her questions and conceal his nervousness.

She laughed. It was a richer sound than he expected from the always-in-perfect-trim captain. "Don't you think we should, here, naked in this tub?" she asked. He could hear her sigh, smell the perfumed water, and see her flawless silhouette lie back with sublime, unconscious art. "We certainly cannot do it when the others are around. Right now, I don't know if I trust you, love you, or am terrified of you. Only one of those feelings is appropriate, but we have passed all that, Dav."

He remembered her after the Heraldry, sick, helpless, then running fearlessly through the dark nightmare outside the walls. Sticking with him, following his lead, trusting him. She had no real reason to do that, not with his mixed reputation and their lack of history, but she did. Surviving those things had brought an intimacy that, conflated now with the privacy of the baths, had unexpectedly transformed their relationship. Dav felt his skin heat. He said, "Thank you," but did not say what for.

"You are going to have to tell me," she said softly.

"I will," he said, surrendering to her silhouette, her languid voice, and the release of fear and anxiety it produced. And for love of her trust.

Her voice floated up once more. "Are you going to come over and join me?"

Their relationship had been confined to the single dimension of function. It had been no deeper than her silhouette was through the thin screen. She was the captain, and he her subordinate, though not one of her choosing. To each other, they had been but simple objects.

I cannot bear to see only her shadow any longer.

Dav stood up, soapy water streaming off him, and crossed the screen to—for the first time—see and appreciate Barbara fully.

"I AM TRULY sorry if I did not take the time to appreciate the situation fully when we met earlier," said Val, sitting in a club chair across from Alain.

He still looked more rummy than Acutist wizard. The man—normally the model for urbane humor, analogic reasoning, and gentle, civilized deportment—now had the burning, otherworldly eyes of a prophet. He seemed drunk on some delusion, filled with fanatic purpose yet broken by some ineffable pain. For Val, looking at him was like a punch to the gut of reason.

"No, no, no," he said, speaking too quickly. "How could you? We were passing in the corridors of power, and I hadn't slept in days. Days! Not since Courant." His tumbling words stopped long enough for Val to catch up. He leaned forward, hot eyes brimming wet, holding Val's for too long. "It was unlike anything I'd ever seen, Lady Valcourt. Nothing to compare to it at all."

A change of clothes could not change a traumatized mind, nor could a shave cut away all the wildness that the trauma had put into Alain Overbree, but he at least looked like he belonged in Princess Cressy's guest room now. He was free of dirt and vomit, but his febrile way of speaking tempted Val to pass him the polished copper wastebasket that sat beside the desk to her right. *He looks like he is going to be sick again.*

"It was like watching—no pushing—a hundred armies, a hundred demons *backward* through my eyes. It was like *eating* the vision with my mind, but eating too much, wrong, rotting. Like shitting out my eyes." He sighed like sore dogs whine. "It was the greatest intellectual assault I have ever been part of. Like being raped by a thousand awful futures."

Val loved analogic reasoning, but she wished his similes would cease. *Shitting out his eyes? No wonder the princess wouldn't just take his word for it.* She hoped Green would return with Farrah Harbinger soon and add her testimony to his, because Alain was not improving any too quickly. She had been pretty certain before today that he would never have been caught dead shitting, let alone letting the word pass his lips.

What has happened to him?

"There is a cost, Lady Valcourt, to seeing the future," Alain supplied pityingly.

He has seen his country ground to dust by Skoll and Hati, by armies of skolves, and apparently by this alleged new demon. The One True Devil.

Like is to like is to like. And thus we go from a disaster we feared to new ones we have heralded.

"And you have paid it, Alain," Val said. "When this envoy arrives, the princess will surely take your advice."

"She *must*."

Val nodded, avoiding his needy eyes. "But what about the new devil? What is it? Where is it? When will it come?"

Alain clutched his head with both arms as if to curl into them or perhaps to put himself in a mad headlock of his own devising. "I don't know. I didn't see it. I think it comes *after*." He dropped his arms and added, "Davignon saw it. He saw it all, right there under the hood with her. And he was fine! If anything, he was *better* than before. How can that be?"

"That's the lieutenant who got you here?" Val asked. *Why is that name familiar?*

"Yes ... you know, he saw a demon before. At Charney." Alain frowned. "Suspicious, now that I think about it ..."

Val remembered the story of Davignon now. He was the soldier who had charged in and rescued his major from Charney. "So where did this Davignon go?"

"I don't know." Alain blinked. "I could barely see or hear by that point in the Heraldry." He gestured vaguely. "Somewhere in Ardgour County."

We really do need the Harbinger back here. Val could not understand how one lieutenant, however brave he might be, could be expected to brave demons and skolves and a new, more terrible devil. *He should have Methueyn Knights or wizards with him.* If ever there was a job for her Elysians, finding and retrieving this weapon was it.

"What I don't understand," said Val, moving on to other mysteries, "is why this Heraldry showed Princess Cressy ordering the ambassador to be executed. That is not how diplomacy is carried on in Engevelen."

"Huh," grunted Alain, a trace of humor peeking through his madness. "It was Garragorah."

"Mother of Nimrheal," Val swore. "How could she dare show her lying face again here?"

"And yet she will," said Alain wearily.

"And we have to listen to her?"

"We do." He winced and said, "If we don't want our world to end."

Rapid steps sounded on polished stone, followed by polite but firm knocking on the heavy oaken door. "My Elysians must have returned!" said Val, happy to set aside thoughts of Garragorah and stepping quickly to the door. "They'll have the Lady Harbinger with them," she said over her shoulder.

She opened the door, to find a page standing there.

"Lady Valcourt, Lord Overbree, you are summoned to the court of Princess Cressy," said the young woman tremulously. "An envoy has arrived."

"Farrah was right," said Alain, straighter now, cloaked in a renewed façade of confidence now that his claims had been given credence. "Let us go meet Marias Garragorah and place ourselves once more on the road to victory."

As they walked briskly down the wide hallways of the palace, Val wondered what road they truly followed. Everything Alain had said, and every sign of emotional damage that he had unintentionally revealed, suggested that nothing but further destruction awaited them on the horizon. Garragorah's coming may have been heralded, but her name was antonymous with hope.

The woman who killed more people with a lie than Nimrheal with his spear.

Have matters just gotten better or worse?

Or both?

These happy thoughts were interrupted by the rapid, echoing footsteps of another page. No—not a page—Captain Lowry of Vercors, one of her senior military advisors in the Elysians. "Lady Valcourt!" she said, sliding to a halt on stone more polished and perfect by far than her rough boots. "You must come immediately. Halwyn Glace has returned."

"With the Lady Harbinger?" Alain asked.

Lowry's head swiveled to regard Alain, whose eyes were febrile once more. "No." A pause. "There have been losses."

"I must see to this," Val said.

Alain swallowed. "You must."

Val looked Alain up and down and said something no past version of herself would have uttered, "It's up to you to convince Princess Cressy and her council not to execute the envoy out of hand." On the heels of that improbable charge, she added another thing she never would have expected to say to her mentor. "But you need to present yourself properly and speak coolly. You are a court wizard of Engevelen. Cloak yourself in your old formality and good trim if you expect to be acknowledged and heard."

~

WHEN BARBARA and Dav returned to the inn—buttoned up, formal, and in fine trim—their soldiers were nowhere to be seen. "Must be out exploring the town, Dav," Barbara said.

"It's not that big." Dav was happy enough to have a little more time with Barbara before she had to become Captain Bysshe again. He could not express, and would not try, how much he liked hearing her calling him "Dav" instead of his full name or title.

She had not even pressed him for his secret again, apparently confident that they would have time to share that too, now that they had shared so much else. Her feelings had been the most pleasant surprise of his life. "Let's go see if they trekked back to the quartermaster," Barbara suggested.

"Sure."

An old, too-familiar weight of doubt collapsed upon Dav. *They cannot bear to be around me.*

"CAN your skin now bear its weight?" asked Veronica Brice, gazing at the shining armor.

The cloaked man turned from the gleaming, newly repaired metal to the woman who had always shined brighter to him. "At a cost," he rasped.

She stared at him. "What cost?"

"Draw sword, sheathe certainty."

Veronica's thin, drawn lips revealed her feelings before her words confirmed them. "I know we cannot predict the future with any certainty. The locus has been split in two, you say, and one part is with the Methueyns, the other in Villiers. That does not concern me. I just want to know if *you* will survive should you take the field again."

"I saw an old man on a hill," he said, his words like sawdust in her ears. "*The* old man. But I did not see who lived."

Her mouth might have shaped the word, "Fuck," but no sound troubled the air between her and the cloaked man. The Duchess waited for him to say more. When nothing came, she asked, "So you think we should go?"

"History will happen with or without us," he replied harshly, pitilessly.

"But if we want any control at all, we need to be part of it." She gave a minute shake of her head. "I know the truism, but it isn't *all* the truth. We could wait on events here, where we are strong, and face them on our terms, *or* we could go to Villiers and fight there. Our internal advantage matters too. Why should we give that up?"

"I do not say we should."

"But you saw the Harbinger's hand on events?"

"Unequivocally."

"And she has aimed us all for Villiers."

"Us."

Veronica ran her fingers down the armor, making a bell-like tinkling as the tiny plates gave way under her touch. Stepping away from it, she said, "So will you don the shining armor once more, guard me in the wild, protect me, lead my armies, slaughter my enemies?"

The cloaked man turned his attention to the shining metal. Each of the armor's thousands of perfect little plates reflected light as if they were the thoughts of an infinite mind. "Will you release me from your tower?"

For the first time, Veronica laughed. "Oh, you're a prisoner now, are you? Just like in the stories? And you just want to go back to your farm? You?"

"I have spent too much of my life stalking your enemies."

"My enemies are yours. That will never change." The Duchess clenched her jaw and faced him. "I just wish I knew if our actions were going to make things better or worse."

~

This has gone from bad to worse.

Dav looked at Barbara. There was no sign of their soldiers, no clue to their whereabouts. Except for her, he was now alone. And he did not know what she thought. He doubted it was the love and admiration he had felt from her in the baths. Not now in the cold, reassessing light of abandonment. Barbara was once more unreadable. Whatever doubts or fears she felt were locked away by soldierly discipline. For all Dav knew, she still thought he had a sinister secret.

Which he did.

I can't be the One True Devil, can I?

CHAPTER 19
SCHEMES

"It kept after us, jump after jump after jump." Green said. Blood trickled from his scalp, reminding Val of the condensation that had rolled off him in Vercors. The headwound was from a ricochet—a tiny fragment, luckily—of the much larger rock Skoll had hurtled at her Elysians.

It had killed one of them. A Knight of Armadale whose name Val did not even know.

Rebecca nodded sagely. "Totally. And we were quiet as three bears too."

Green frowned at her and mouthed "Really?" before adding, "Every time we jumped to a new line of sight, Skoll charged right at us. We could barely stay ahead of it."

Why such persistence? The demons Skoll and Hati were known for their insane ferocity, but in the situation Green described there seemed little to be gained by pursuing the Elysians so ruthlessly when easier prey lay all around. Val had always felt frustrated by how little was known about what motivated the demons. Ruefully, she had to admit that in some ways this gap in her understanding felt worse to her than the loss of the knight or even the failure of the mission.

If we stay ignorant, we will keep failing.

Her monster growled, but she stared it down.

"And that's why you gave up on reaching the Harbinger?" The question, almost shouted by a scowling Captain Lowri, interrupted Val's reverie

"We were in sight of Harbinger Hall," Green said apologetically, "but the demon was right on top of us. It would have been suicide to have persisted."

"It was really quite a brisk chase," said Chris with an exaggerated Engevelen accent. "I'll be surprised if Grandma Harbinger is still alive in there. Old Skoll seems to have a bit of a . . . er, hate-on, to use the vernacular, for us wizards."

Rebecca jumped in, eyes wider and brighter than ever. "Yes, even more than it hates Methueyns and Deladieyrs!"

"What?" Val asked, catching Captain Lowri's confused look, which matched her own. They had not mentioned any knights from these illustrious orders in their first, hurried report.

"Oh, yeah," Chris said. "It was right in the middle of stomping three of them when we arrived."

"Who were they?" demanded Lowri at the same time that Val asked, "Were they okay?"

"I have no idea," said Chris nonchalantly as Rebecca simultaneously quipped, "If smashed into broken cobbles is okay, one of them was *very* okay."

Val's monster growled a second time. Louder. "*Who* was smashed?" Her voice rose. "The Princess is in congress only a few hundred yards from here. And the Council of Knights is not much farther away. They will *all* want to know. Did you see him? Can you describe what he looked like?" *Do you FUCKING care?*

Captain Lowri's hand gripped Val's shoulder, and she took the hint. In a calmer voice, she said, "I can take a description to the Council."

"It was Revenberge," Green said hurriedly. He had teleported many of the Deladieyr squires before joining the Elysians. He probably knew all of the small number that remained. "*Sir* Revenberge, I should say. She was all in plate. Must have Risen."

"Revenberge," Val breathed, her anger warring with her grief. *I knew her.* A memory came unbidden. Revenberge crossing some square near the palace, tall and smiling in dawn's light. It had been a smile to outshine even the gleaming towers, halls, and squares of Engevelen City. "Woman of grace, angel of the morning," she said aloud, surprising herself with the warmth in her words.

"Not anymore," Rebecca said with all the grace of a thrown pail of vomit.

"Rebecca!" Val shouted, her body shaking with rage. The world blurred around her. Anger broke through, and she found herself in the empyreal sky. Fire waited.

Like is to like is to like. Oh, am I like Rebecca*?*

Val closed her eyes as tightly as she could, and the window to hell closed with them. Her anger, along with the ensuing analogic litany, and the possibility of fatal action faded with the embarrassed realization that, only a week before, she had treated injuries to her own soldiers with a similar lack of concern. Memories of the shameful scene flashed through her mind. Lowri's soldiers on the ground, frozen, being pissed on. Green in a cloud of snow. Shattered edifices and cities. The long and growing list of dead Methueyns and Deladieyrs. And finally, Revenberge, the brightest star of all, fallen, extinguished. She realized that her embarrassment over the urination had not been Engevelen snobbery. It had been a self-defense response. All these things, even the urination farce, were not just absurd, they were heartrending.

Like is to like is to like. Great institutions fall, great knights fall. From one loss to another we move from a position of greatness to something lesser. And thus, we know both what civilization was and what savagery might lay ahead.

What savagery must not *lie ahead.*

Ideas formed with the speed of a boiling thunderhead. *If what they are saying about Skoll is true, there may be an advantage to be had.*

"Rebecca. Save your misplaced humor. You're going to need it. We are going back to Courant."

"Noooo..." said Chris and Rebecca together.

"When?" was all Green said.

"Tomorrow? The day after? As soon as we can consult with the Princess?" asked Captain Lowri.

"Today. But we are *all* going. Every wizard, and as many soldiers as we can move. I just need a little more clarification on the tactical value of something." Val locked eyes with Chris and then Rebecca. "Tell me more about how much Skoll hates wizards."

~

"Is her head still on her shoulders?" Val asked. She and Alain Overbree were huddled together in an antechamber to Princess Cressy's private meeting room.

"Just," he answered with a trace of the old Alain's I-know-a-secret smile on his face. It was a relief to see that the old pedant might still be in there. Val had not been sure when she had left him, earlier that morning, on the threshold. His eyes were still hooded and his skin sallow, but a semblance of his characteristic confidence was returning. Her mentor had always liked politics and the telling of stories.

Val was not so sure *she* did.

Where heroes fail, cooperation must succeed.

She needed to report her team's failure and gain approval to launch a new intervention despite the collapse of the previous attempt.

It will work if we *work together.*

"How much time do we have?" Val's eyes shifted to the copper door.

A true smile erupted now, brightening Alain's dimmed eyes. "Enough, if I keep it brief and to the point."

Little chance of that. The world was ending, Val was as tense as a drumhead, full of what would probably sound to the princess like mad schemes, and constrained by a soul-crushing schedule, but incongruously, she felt almost relaxed. Her old mentor was going to tell her one last verbose and overwrought story.

~

I MUST SAY that Princess Cressy really upped her game on this one, for instead of having Lady Garragorah, the liar of Novgoreyl, rely on the uncertain hospitality of the Council of Knights, she entrusted her to Sir Sandeyl, and that fleet-footed golden knight brought her straight to our secular court, the congress.

Sandeyl was young, tall, and graceful, but I noted that the left pauldron of his plate had been crumpled as if it were paper, and his breastplate was entirely absent. Though he carried himself with the appearance of good trim that only the heaven-sent can manage in such circumstances, the more discerning among us must have noted that these anomalies made for a ... mismatched look. I've never been quite sure why Methueyn Knights wear armor anyway. Their skin is like steel, so why wear more steel?

In any event, when Sir Sandeyl spoke, it was like some mighty birdsong, beautiful and startling at the same time. "I bring you," he said, "the Ambassador of Nehring Ardgour, Lady Marias Garragorah, to speak to us about an end to the conflict between us."

Alas, these pretty tones were wrapped around the wrong words. They dropped like a damp handkerchief onto the polished floor of the congress. There was no . . . bounce in his message. It just . . . disappeared. Attenuated below the level of sound or thought, as one might say.

But there was shock, certainly. No one spoke. No one moved. The princess had clearly expected this, thanks to me. Her eyes scanned the crowd cannily, and she waited. A moment later, some old lord of a forgotten tower slowly turned his back. Another old man followed, then his lady. But most of the crowd of nobles did not turn away. A whispering began to rise from the heretofore silent starers. It transformed into a murmuring of sour discontent that rose further, swelling to a barely restrained cacophony that now included booing and hissing from various quarters.

Garragorah was unfazed by any mutterings, boos, or hisses. Her eyes were sharp and unsurprised—and don't repeat this— in the same way that Cressy's were. The envoy seemed to view all the nobles with the same cool, astute regard. Her thin, self-assured smile took it all in. Then her clear, commanding voice rang out.

"It has been far too long since I visited Engevelen, and sadly it is once more in deeply tragic, indeed, heartbreaking circumstances."

"You have no heart!" someone shouted. This was repeated like an angry echo by others.

Someone else shouted, "Point of order!" but was ignored. Another elderly noble—it might have been the Baronet Calencieux, I didn't get a good look at him—roared, "Circumstances that *YOU* caused!"

The envoy found a way to smile at these entirely accurate statements, but she changed her tactics. She turned to golden Sandeyl, standing only an arm's length away, and said, "Thank you for bringing me here, glorious Sir Sandeyl." Then she turned to the crowd again. "Are not the Methueyn Knights magnificent?"

The crowd could not boo that. They fell silent, as if unsure how to respond to a statement they could not dispute from a messenger they detested.

"I have been sent to you by Nehring Ardgour."

A new, awful buzz flew around the room at this statement. Someone shouted, "We don't want anything else from that evil bastard!" And another, "We'll send you back to your skolves!" It is possible they added "In a sack," but that really could not have been what I heard. The Engevelen nobility does not speak so.

Lord Liam Laval strode to the front of the assembly, stopping just a pace or two from the stairs to where Princess Cressy sat in state. Ignoring Sandeyl and Garragorah, he addressed her directly.

"Why are we listening to this faithless liar? She is renowned only for deception and betrayal. She serves the prince of perjurers himself. Why are we wasting our time when we need to take action? We should hang this *emissary*"—here his voice dripped with contempt—"on the spot!"

The crowd roared approval. Garragorah stood expressionless. Cressy's face showed only cool poise. She waited until complete silence had returned before replying.

"Because, my Lord Laval, the Lady Farrah Harbinger has said we should. The fate of our fair country, she has assured me, depends upon giving Marias Garragorah a respectful hearing." Then the princess pointed at me. "And because Lord Alain Overbree has dared an army of skolves to tell us this." She turned hard, cold eyes on Garragorah and added, "The Harbinger has bought you a moment's reprieve from our just wrath, envoy, but do not try the patience of this body further. Speak your mission with alacrity."

"You are right to be angry," said Garragorah. "I truly regret what has happened and my own part in it." She even managed to look contrite. "I set out with sixteen of my own personal guardsmen to bring you my news—my contrition. Along the way, we tried to do good deeds, make amends, and show faith. Skolves ravage the north. This, your curse, is our fault! It was an awful sight and a terrible penance to see the great and many towers of Engevelen brought low. We fought the skolves when we could. And we saved many fleeing citizens, families, of Engevelen." She looked down then and produced precisely two fat, glistening tears. "My heart was broken in two at the scenes of death and destruction I witnessed, the separation of families from homes, and life from limb. My faithful guards were all lost in noble acts of defense, sacrificed on the road to this apology and the possibility that your world can yet be saved."

"*How*" asked Princess Cressy in ringing but icily unsympathetic tones, "can Engevelen be *saved*?"

"By sending the Methueyn Knights north to meet with my lord, Nehring Ardgour, and to send Skoll and Hati back to hell."

Laval stamped one polished boot on equally shiny marble and roared, "He has made this claim before! Through *you*, liar, and all we got were tens of thousands of skolves!"

"It is true," said Garragorah in a mournful tone. "It is all true. But this time, it will be different."

A poisonous laughter washed across the congress.

"I am so sorry!" Garragorah wailed.

Tears rolled down, beautiful on her striking face. I don't know quite how she did it, but that woman cried like a goddess. I mean look at *my* face. I look awful after Courant. My embassy was barely heard, my narration doubted because of the tears and hardship written here. But Garragorah's tears did the impossible. They stilled a room of haters.

Had she bewitched us out of our senses? Certainly her words could have convinced no rational listener.

"This time *is* different!" she cried. "For we are all lost if we do not work together, if we do not reach for trust, however impossible it may seem. We are at the end of all hope, but you are Engevelen, the greatest nation on earth. You are greater than all my failings, and you alone can save the day by trusting me one last time."

"Why should we?" asked Princess Cressy. "Why should we believe that this time will turn out differently?"

Garragorah pivoted and pointed one elegant, slender, dramatic finger at Sir Sandeyl. "Because of *him*. Because of the other Methueyn Knights. Because of the power of the Bifrost, which they will bring with them."

"The Bifrost!" Calencieux shrieked.

"Yes!" Garragorah replied quickly, as if eager to stem some tide. "The Bifrost, but also the entire Methueyn Order to safeguard it. The Methueyn Knights have never, since this war started, acted as one. But if they do now, they will end this conflict."

"Do not believe any word that snake hiss!" bellowed a new voice in a thick accent. This new speaker stood between three mis-matched Deladieyr escuyers. This man was quite a site, I can tell you. Starved, shrunken, deflated. Hollowed-out cheekbones and taut, papery skin made his thick eyebrows look like paste-ons from a mummer's circus.

Lady Garragorah flinched for the first time . . . and perhaps ever.

Well-coiffed Lord Liam Laval, though he obviously agreed with the sentiment, was less impressed by the wild looks of the Novgoreyl noble. He sneered, "Who in Engevelen is this *new* envoy? The ruffian king?"

"That," boomed Sir Heydron, with the rest of the Council of Knights at her back, "is the Vymyty Wizard Taratoraff. He knows what Nehring Ardgour really wants."

"AND THEN WHAT HAPPENED?" Val asked eagerly.

"Well—"

The copper door opened, interrupting the lengthy continuation of the tale Alain must have hoped to give.

"The princess will see you know," said a page, holding the door open for them.

Alain winked at Val and whispered, "To summarize, a return to finger pointing and an escalating argument over who had the right to relieve Garragorah of her head. Sir Michael seemed particularly keen, but Heydron restrained him. She's senior on the Council of Knights, if that herd of cats can be said to have any real structure." His voice dropped even lower, and he added hurriedly, as they reached the doorway, "It always seems to be the Heydrons and the Volsangs that have the most power. I wonder why that is? But Volsang has not been around at all. He didn't come. Still out hunting Ardgour. Or dead."

They found the princess seated at a small oval table in her inner chamber. On one side of her sat Liam Laval and on the other Lady Severine, her principal advisor.

Alain continued whispering, though even more quickly now, as he and Val approached the table. "Perhaps both protective love and violent hate are two sides of the same diametric coin." He looked up, saw that he was almost within reach of a chair, and added, even as he bowed his head to the princess, "In any case, I reminded everyone of the Lady Harbinger's Heraldry, there was more shouting but no head chopping, and nothing was resolved."

As one would expect of our court.

As soon as Val and Alain had sat down, the princess, who had watched them in silence as they entered the room, began to speak.

"Lady Valcourt, I don't see Farrah Harbinger with you," she noted wryly. Val realized the princess had already guessed the failure of the Elysians. The Lady pursed her lips and added, "Well, it was a tough mission. No one expected a miracle."

"You may yet get one, Your Highness," said Val.

One sharp, curved eyebrow rose on Liam Laval's forehead. "Katherine Valcourt has another plan, I take it." He sighed theatrically and said, "You had better, because despite how bad things have gotten, I have failed to sell the Castlereagh Line to the court. Why do I have to be the bad guy?"

"Because it suits you," replied Lady Severine.

Val had always liked Severine's practicality and easy management of the nobles. *Severine is to Cressy what Sylvie is to the Harbinger. Like is to like, and so we go from being alone and having to do everything ourselves to having an ally and workmate.*

Lady Severine continued, "No one wants to abandon the northern half of what is left of Engevelen, especially since doing so is not guaranteed to save us. How can we organize a retreat, hold off the skolves, and build a wall all at the same time? What does a wall matter when Skoll and Hati can punch a hole in it any time they please?"

Laval's hands went up in a mock surrender that Val knew he would never expose in full court, while the princess shook her head but only said, "How can your failing Elysians save us now, Lady Valcourt?"

"By returning to Courant and the Lady Harbinger." She paused for effect, then added, "But retrieving her this time." She smiled, showing bright, white teeth. "We know something now that we did not know the first time."

"And what," asked Cressy, "may that be?"

"We know now that the special hatred Skoll has for knights over citizens is like his hatred for wizards over knights." She then proceeded to tell them what Halwyn Glace was currently doing and what her plan entailed.

HER LISTENERS SAT silent for a few moments after Val had finished explaining. They exchanged glances but made no move to respond. Val fought the urge to justify her ideas further. She had made her case. Alain Overbree had been silent throughout and seemed content to remain urbanely aloof. For now at least.

"Your scheme seems incredibly risky," said the princess at last.

Val said nothing. Lady Cressy was right.

"The key that turns the lock may break inside the door," said Alain cryptically.

Laval's cultured face screwed up most uncouthly. "What?"

Severine proved herself the sharper advisor. She translated Alain's riddle for the rest. "If Halwyn Glace is lost, there will be no way to extract the surviving elements of Katherine's force."

"Does anyone think the Methueyn Knights will accede to Garragorah's embassy?" asked Cressy.

"The Methueyn Knights are alike to the court in this regard," said Alain.

"Do you mean they don't trust Garragorah or can't make a decision?" said Lady Severine.

Laval snorted. "Both, surely."

The princess ignored her courtier's poor attempt at humor. "They won't work together," she conceded, then looked at Val and seemed to come to a conclusion. "We cannot succeed as we are. We lack the unity required for decisiveness."

"Perhaps because we lack the knowledge for unity to be anything but a foolish delusion," said Severine.

Cressy's eyes stayed on Val. "If the Lady Harbinger has seen a solution—even with its risks—we need the knowledge directly from her, and we need it now."

My thoughts exactly.

"If you fail, Lady Valcourt, we are no worse off. Go then and pull the Harbinger from out the demon's mouth. If you can."

CHAPTER 20

WHAT WIZARDS DO

"Eat something, Green," Val said under her breath. "While you can." Halwyn Glace nodded, looking flushed. He was dressed in heavy gray wool and was probably feeling more than a little warm as well as excited and definitely ready to go.

Val was not ready to give the order.

Not yet. Not this time.

She had been here before, about to begin a mission or a key action in a mission, not quite ready but forced to go. Or choosing to go unready. And thereby failing.

Like is to like is to like. We have made this mistake before, rushing in. Let us look one more time and hope to go from what didn't work to something that does.

Val reviewed the plan and the layout of Courant, a city she had lived in for years. She thought about the vital importance of retrieving Farrah Harbinger, who had been a mentor almost as important as Alain Overbree.

She took a slow, deep breath and surveyed her forces as they stood grouped on the teleportation platform and walkway beyond, awaiting their turn:

Captain Lowri with five Vercors irregulars and doll-carrying Christopher Carlyll. He had brought a bigger bag in addition to two larger female dolls with exaggerated, disturbing red tears painted rolling down their white porcelain cheeks. These two dolls were pinned to his tunic for easy reach, but they gave him a clownish appearance. A maniacal clown.

Six Knights of Armadale in full plate armor, bent on revenge for earlier losses, with slow-talking elemental wizard Samantha Westerberg stood ready also. Val had suggested they leave the armor behind so they could move faster and make teleporting them easier on Green. Green, however—a Statician wizard who had always refused analogic testing—could not back her theory up. *The knights probably wouldn't have listened anyway. No Knight of Armadale gives up her armor on the battlefield.*

Seven Guardians of Kames, with the wizard of incantations, Calvaine Chesshyre, waited patiently and with significantly less drama than the honor-armored knights.

Eight elites of the Princess's Light Guard and the unruly rhyming wizard, Rebecca Laurie, were positioned to reinforce Christopher's team.

And finally, Val's own group of seven, led by Patrick Proulx, who had demanded and received the privilege of making the extraction of the Harbinger while the rest distracted Skoll.

"Is everyone ready?" Val asked in as loud a voice as she could muster in her nerve-taut state. "Remember the plan, remember your extraction location. We must all move quickly, especially in stage one." She looked directly at Rebecca and added, for her particular benefit, "Remember, Courant is the pride of Engevelen. Be careful. As of an hour ago, people still lived there."

Rebecca smirked. "Hey, don't worry, Val, this is what wizards *do*!"

"What wizards do!" shouted Christopher, making his dolls clap their eerie, humanlike hands together, one doll to the other.

"Indeed," drawled Samantha Westerberg. "What we all do. When do we begin?"

Val jogged back to the pad, stopped in front of Green, paused, then gave him a quick, chaste hug. His dilated pupils and too slow release of her waist told of more than his surprise.

He was not the only one surprised. Captain Lowri's face tightened unnaturally, Christopher's eyes widened to a size approximating teacups, and his mouth gaped open.

Someone farther back in the lineup let fly a crude "Woo-hoo." *Rebecca.*

A metallic voice emanated from one of the armored Knights of Armadale. "Where is my embrace? For is it not the same danger that we face?"

Val ignored him. She composed herself.

I am a Lady of Engevelen.

And this is going to work.

With exaggerated care, she produced the sand clock from a chain around her neck and held it out from her chest. "Sand clocks out," she commanded.

Her clock had one thin mark on it, set near the bottom of the empty top half. The others' clocks each had between three and five marks. Val paused, making sure everyone was displaying their clock. "Ready... turn them." She turned her sand clock, nodded to Green, and said, "Go now, Halwyn."

"Step close," Halwyn said to Lowri and her crew as Val moved farther away. He squatted. His hands went to his hips, then pushed slowly away as if moving a mountain. A popping sound preceded an explosion of hot and cold air, reverberating across the platform, leaving a pattern of frost, condensation, and steam.

And they were gone.

"Move!" Val shouted, waving at Samantha Westerberg and her Knights of Armadale. Even before they could make their clattering way to the center of the platform, there was a "pop" and another rolling, percussive disturbance. Green had returned, arms pushing empty air as if pushing the world, cool condensation dripping off his fingers, cheeks red from heat.

Val waved the knights on and yelled, "Get in closer!"

Her ears popped again as Green pushed the mountain of probability over its indefinable edge, and the entire party disappeared in a thermodynamic explosion, a mounting inequality fed by the fact that nothing could be perfectly efficient, especially the extremely unlikely.

"Run!" Val exhorted the lighter-armored Guardians, the next group to go. "In tight as soon as he appears. The rest of you move up. We cannot fall behind."

The process continued until the platform was coated in graceful, arcuate ridges of ice and all the groups were through.

"Do we go now?" asked Patrick Proulx, touching his eyebrows tentatively, one of which was crusted with ice and the other glowing red from the ungentle movement of alternately supercooled and superheated air.

"We have a moment," Val said. "Halwyn is moving each of the groups once more from within the city before he drops us off." She scowled at him. "You were at the briefing, you know this."

"Yup, but I haven't slept yet, since the road." Patrick said. When Val scowled at him again, he smiled and added, "We can still run faster than any of these others, and we know where the Harbinger is. We're *hers*. We'll get her out if anyone can."

"Good." Val looked at her sand clock, wiped condensed water off it, and looked again. "Get ready."

Green returned in a detonation of snowflakes and fist-sized funnel clouds—a new and frightening phenomenon. He was shaking uncontrollably. She jumped right at him—through the awful, ripping power of one of these twisters—and wrapped her arms tight around his lean, cold, shivering body. "Embrace him!" she called.

Arms and bodies squeezed in on all sides, tight and hard.

"Aaaaahhhhh!" Green roared as he pushed his arms past hugging limbs and put his wizardry to work once more.

In a new explosion of air and snow, they appeared in Courant. *Right where we need to be.* Val knew the rooftop, knew precisely where Harbinger Hall was, and could just see the tip of Farrah Harbinger's observatory. Not far away, really, but far enough not to draw the demon there.

The group hug sprung apart like a spring unloading or time reversing. Val stepped away from Halwyn last.

"Th-thank you," Green said, then pushed a hole between worlds once more, popping out of Val's sight, leaving only falling snow and gusts of wind behind.

"Let's go!" Val commanded, heading toward stairs she had trod frequently in earlier years.

In the far distance, a rooftop exploded, and a vertical cloud formed, a tornado of error from one of the other wizards.

A great roaring rolled over the air. *Skoll.* It was screaming in rage at the wizards flitting from location to location, unpredictable thanks to Green's teleportation.

One curved branch of a vast, suspended aqueduct improbably tilted and began to fall, slow as cold honey and as inevitable as the falling stone it was built from. The sound of the extended, tortured crash arrived several steps later.

Proulx's soldiers formed up on Val, with Patrick himself not an arm's reach away. "Wizard Glace is going to kill himself before this is over," he observed as they started down the stone steps.

Irritation flared—more than irritation, faster, hotter—but Val suppressed the monster. "Green's tough."

"Uh huh," said Proulx in an unreadable tone. "Why do you call him Green anyway? I don't see the connection between Green and Halwyn Glace."

Val almost stumbled on the stairs. *I don't know either.* An image of Green's ice-rimmed eyes and heat-burned face came and went as fast as the stairs.

I need to save my country.

I need to prioritize.

He's tough.

Val stumbled again but kept going.

They hit the streets. Fifty yards across the square, a line of spearmen in Courant livery struggled to hold their position against a band of skolves.

"Ignore it, lads," Patrick Proulx said in a calm voice. "Keep moving."

They moved at a fast trot out of the square, leaving the spearmen to fend for themselves. The ground shook with a heavy pounding off to the north, a roaring, then some strangely amplified but muddled rhyming, a flash of light, and a long trailing percussion of sound with a hint of groaning metal.

Rebecca.

Tall buildings, long evening shadows, and scattered rubble prevented Val from seeing what had happened, but she knew who was responsible.

The plan had been to use Skoll's hatred of wizards against the demon. Val had deduced that Skoll could sense empyreal manipulation, and so she had devised a strategy of continuous movement of multiple groups of wizards and their supporting troops through teleportation to pull the demon first one way and then another.

But always away from Harbinger Hall.

The ground shook again. The explosion was farther away now. Val wondered if another section of aqueduct was about to fall. The sounds of destruction—true harbinger of what wizards did best—seemed to go on and on.

The plan is working.

Val had reluctantly given up on subtlety in favor of effect. "There it is," she said. Harbinger Hall loomed ahead, one building away.

A clanging sounded behind them. Val whirled and saw the armored forms of Armadale's knights emerge from an alley, Samantha Westerberg behind them, her arms extended as if emoting.

They're not supposed to be anywhere near here.

Some trick of acoustics brought a fragment of Westerberg's words to Val's ears, "Why can't we all just follow the plan?"

A howl of skolves sounded down the alley followed by a flash of light along its dark length.

"Run!" Val said. "Skoll might have felt that."

Knights damn it!

Val and her crew charged toward the makeshift, bricked maze that had been mortared over the old Harbinger Hall entrance. A soldier waved them in.

"The Lady Harbinger!" Val said. "Where is she?"

"Is she in the library?" Patrick asked.

"Uh, no." said the soldier, hesitating, "In her chambers."

"Follow me," said Patrick.

"Wait!" called the soldier. "Let me get Lady Sylvie first."

He was ignored. They ran across the great open chamber on the main floor and up the stairs, past other soldiers, more than a few stoneworkers, and even a few citizens who seemed to be taking shelter.

"She's not well!" came the faint call of the soldier as they reached the top and turned down a long hallway.

"Last time I was here," said Proulx, "a whole roomful of wizards were sick from her Heraldry. I think we sh—"

Val cut him off, saying, "Is this it?" at a door she thought she recognized.

"Yes."

Val knocked twice, hard and fast, and stormed through the door.

Farrah Harbinger was sitting in a padded, high-backed chair not far from a large four-poster bed. She did not look sick at all. She was dressed formally in a green riding dress, and her eyes were open and intent. Val rushed up to her.

"Lady Harbinger. We have come for your wisdom, to use it to save Engevelen."

The Harbinger did not answer. She seemed to be gazing directly at Val, but there was something strange in the green of her large, wide-open eyes, something like a moving shadow, Val thought.

"Farrah?" Val crouched down closer to her.

"Don't look into her eyes, Lady Valcourt!" hissed Lady Sylvie, appearing from somewhere to the side and rushing to clutch at Val's shoulders. "She has been heralding continuously."

The awfulness of that statement made Val hesitate, but she did not look away from the Harbinger. Not in time. For an instant, she made out the image in the Harbinger's eyes. It was a city, a ruined city, but twisted as if reflected in a warped mirror, turned inside out and backward, distorted in other, ineffable ways. Wrong.

"Bwaaaaw... waaah. Woooh."

She twisted away from Farrah to vomit, painting Sylvie's open-toed shoes with bile. As she heaved a second time, she heard Sylvie and Proulx exchange words she could not make out, and then the first haunting words of the Harbinger.

> It is all
> down a hole.
> Buried whole,
> Kept secret
> Against some
> Great fall
> Against some
> Unknown kairos.

The room spun. Val teetered, struggling to keep a precarious balance and prevent herself from falling into her own puke. Sylvie had let go of her to save her own feet and shoes from additional vomit baths.

"W-what?" Val managed to produce.

Eerie words sang back in cultured tones. "What happens when we forget, when the One True Devil treads through the dust of our living? What is left when poetry is burned, books are shattered, the writing of small moments and large feelings are lost? Where does love go when love's harvest is tilled under, salted, and seeded with the broken stones of libraries?"

Arms out, wobbling, Val tried to stand up against a dangerously spinning room.

"She's . . . heralding . . ."

Sylvie was scrubbing her feet with a towel. "Yes, as I warned you," she said querulously. "It started again just an hour . . . no, a half hour ago. Perhaps it is a sign of recovery, perhaps not. It's prophetic, though difficult to make sense of." She tossed the soiled towel to Val. "Sometimes she sings, sometimes speaks in rhyme and meter, sometimes in riddles, sometimes in a prose that seems mostly rhetorical questions."

Like the harbingers of old, of legends. There had been prophets of Heraldry in ancient times, but they, it was said, were attended by interpreters who translated and tidied up their messy, distorted visions.

"We have to get her up," said Val. She gestured to Patrick Proulx, who waited by the doorway with his soldiers. "Get her up! We have to go. There is no time." She lowered her voice and added, "Just don't look in her eyes."

Proulx nodded as if he had not attempted to warn Val of this just moments earlier. Two of Proulx's soldiers lifted Farrah Harbinger to her feet, even as her green-eyed gaze continued shining a scene of madness and her commanding voice prophesied doom.

The Book of Memory
Burns. It burns
As our season turns.
The fires of forgetting
Are the immolation
Of terrible mistakes,
The annihilation
Of knowledge earned
The denial of human hates,
The too-short unspooling
Of all we have learned.

When tall walls crumble

And hopeful time drains,
When thunder rumbles,
And shattered stone rains,
Who takes all they have left,
Plants a flag, unfurls a totem,
Draws sword, stands in pain,
Accepts a lonely death,
For a book of love poems?

The true end of a people
Is the erasing of memory
And all the tiny, trivial stories
Of vast and costly feelings

The end of meaning and time
Is the erasure of history,
The hobbling of philosophy,
The utter annihilation of mind.

"Whhhooooaaaalll!" said the soldier on Farrah's right arm, hurling vomit with awful power but little precision.

"I told you not to look," said Proulx evenly, pulling the reeling man away and waving a female soldier in to take his place. "Don't look in her eyes, not for one second," he instructed. "Better than you have been poleaxed by our Lady Harbinger." He considered for a second and added, "And don't listen either. It's all very important no doubt, but we need to move quickly now and in good trim."

How did this Lieutenant Davignon fellow stand up to it? Val's stomach still lurched, and she struggled to keep a straight line. For some reason her feet veered continually to the right as she trotted along at the head of the group

"Where are you taking her?" asked Lady Sylvie, following anxiously, her authority degraded. "You can't escape the city now. It's too late."

"We have a plan," Val said in the muffled voice of the nauseated. "And a teleporter. We just need to get to the extraction location."

As they crossed the great hall, ignoring the soldiers, tradesmen, and workers who stared incredulously after them, a new thought occurred to Val. *I wonder if demons can detect Heraldry too? Or is it just the big, energetic manipulations? Like is to like is to like. Probably. Did we arrive here just in time?*

"Can everyone c—?" Lady Sylvie seemed to think better of her question, perhaps realizing that they were about to abandon everyone left in Courant.

"Lock it up behind us," Sylvie said to the guard as they rushed through the door to the street.

"How many sol—" Val began, then stopped, realizing that the others had fallen behind. Farrah Harbinger, like a sleepwalker, could be led along, but apparently not faster than a moderate walking pace.

"I don't know how many soldiers we still have in the field," Sylvie said, struggling for breath, unused to walking fast, limping horrendously, old before her time. *War will do that.*

"Major Desjarlais still holds the west wall," Sylvie gasped. "Junger last reported a few hours ago. I don't know about the others. Courant needs help."

"Green is going to try to lead Skoll outside the city as our last action here," said Val as she looked south, trying to orient herself to their destination. "Perhaps that will make a difference to the defense."

Probably not.

Just then, there was another roar, a hint of rhyming on the wind, and the muted, distant sounds of great rocks or stones falling. A dark cloud rose to the north.

Val pulled out her sand clock. The grains were almost at the marking. *We're behind! How did we get behind?*

"We have to move faster, sergeant," she said to Proulx.

Patrick winced. Then his expression hardened. "This isn't working. Pick her up, lads and ladies. We have to run with her."

With some reverence, a soldier took each of Farrah Harbinger's legs while two others took her arms.

"Don't look in her eyes!" Proulx shouted. He had run out of ambulatory soldiers and had none to spare. Under his breath, Val could hear him repeating, "I'm sorry Lady Harbinger, I'm so sorry." She pretended not to hear.

Love always surprised her.

They ran down the rubble-sewn streets at a fast trot now, carting the Harbinger like a sack of flour.

"Oh, thank the knights," said a new, slow voice. It was Samantha Westerberg, standing ahead of them. Alone. There was no sign of her escort of Knights of Armadale.

"Keep moving," Val instructed Patrick Proulx.

As they passed Westerberg, Val said, "Well, keep up if you're coming. There is no waiting here. Not today."

"If only we could all escape alive," Samantha said in her drawl.

"Why are you here?" Val asked, watching Westerberg out of the corner of her eyes as she tried to run a straight line. She looked unhurt, but there was a great deal of dust on her tunic, face, and hands. "This is nowhere near where you should be."

"Those Nimrheal-damned knights wouldn't listen to me," she complained, wheezing.

"Where are they?"

"They wanted to kill Skoll."

"And?"

"They didn't even get past the skolves."

Honor! Is there a more useless thing? A more selfish thing? None of it surprised Val. After all, a particularly rigid version of the same knightly honor had constrained Engevelen's progress for centuries. "Well," she said, "I'm glad that you didn't die, too, in some misplaced gesture toward an idea of how things are supposed to be."

"Pick it up," said Proulx, his voice charged and brittle. But Val knew why he was out of sorts. She had seen it before, men falling in love with Farrah Harbinger's green eyes, her sense of purpose, her power and poise.

Val pulled out the sand clock once more. The line had been crossed. "Faster!" she shouted. Green could not afford to wait. There was a reason that each group was teleported to a different location in the city, a reason Green had scouted those locations in accordance with Val's map while Val had arranged the plan with everyone else, a reason that another teleportation happened somewhere else right on the heels of the last, and a reason each group needed to leave their arrival location as quickly as possible. If Skoll hated empyreal manipulation, if the demon was a hater of wizards, then it would particularly hate teleportation, the costliest, most power-hungry manipulation of all.

Green could not wait for them.

"There it is!" she said. The pale gray stone museum formed the corner of the next city block.

Val lurched, off balance from some new shaking of the ground. One of the soldiers carrying Farrah fell on her ass but kept hold of the great lady's leg, and they did not drop her. The shaking grew louder.

And louder.

Sharper.

Skoll.

They were almost at the broad, shallow steps of the museum when Val saw an armor-clad knight step out of an alley, just a block behind them. One of the Knights of Armadale, one of Westerberg's escorts, someone who was supposedly dead. She did not stop, kept running, hit the stairs, but she did speak. "What the H—"

Stone exploded like flour behind the knight, and a dark, fast-moving shadow obliterated her.

"Faster!" said Val, charging into the wide, shadowed entrance, eyes searching for the stairs, mind trying to forget the easy, instantaneous obliteration of shaped metal and the human being inside it.

The stairs shook as they ran, gasping and panicked. Up and around, up and around.

The building lurched as something hit it, something below now. A thing they could not fight, only distract and keep off balance.

"Keep going!" shouted Westerberg urgently, her slow drawl gone now. She had a large glass vial in her hand. Val knew that it was filled with an acid. "I'll take out the stairs. Let's see it catch us then."

Samantha was an elemental wizard, a Statician who could take objects or people down to their elemental components, who could work entropy until all connection was lost, all aggregation broken. The acid in her vial was used in that process, though there was no possibility that such a small amount could really do much. It was yet another mystery to Val. *When there's time.* She kept running, found herself ahead of Proulx, his soldiers, and Farrah Harbinger.

Where is Lady Sylvie?

A great, hollow concussion hit her as she reached the roof, followed by a powerful burst of hot, then cold, now dusty hot and alternatingly cold, wet air. The concussion buffeted her, and a terrible suspicion shot through Val, that Westerberg had abandoned her escort and had now collapsed the stairs while Sylvie was still on them.

But she didn't look back. They still had the Harbinger and, emerging from the rooftop door, she saw Green standing alone at a far corner of the building. His eyes were half glued shut with ice, but they were trained on her. Even as she ran toward him, a paper-thin sheet of ice broke from his thick cloak and shattered on the stone floor.

The building shook again, hammered by a new and still more powerful shockwave. *Did the stone floor just tilt? Yes, it's not my balance.* Val raced toward Halwyn Glace, glancing out upon her falling city. A patchwork of fires, broken stonework, twisted bodies, and collapsed aqueducts burned themselves into her mind.

It's what wizards do.

She turned away from the wave of skolves that ran like a poison tide down the streets of the great city below.

Lady Sylvie came limping toward them with Westerberg beside her, one of her arms around her back. Not abandoned, after all.

Val's feet hit ice and she slid into Green. He opened his arms and caught her. He was cold, so cold, and lean, too lean, like a man made of frozen pipe and cold rope. The others slid in close too, a tangle of arms and legs.

She heard him swear under his breath. There were too many of them.

"Gather in," he shouted and bent his knees.

The building shook with another collision. They lurched, all except for Halwyn Glace, who began pushing with both hands from his hips as if he would lift the world.

"Yaaaaarrrrrrggghhhhhhhh!"

In an explosion of ice and wind, they appeared on the teleportation platform of Engevelen City.

"Towel!" shouted Val. A towel appeared in her hands, and she lost no time in aggressively, desperately rubbing Green's hair and face, knocking off the ice and drying him, warming him. "Now go!" she said. "But don't lead Skoll away. It's too late for that. Just bring our Elysians back. The ones you can."

Another scream, another sharp pop, one last sphere of falling snow, and Green was gone.

"That boy loves you more than any man I have ever seen," said an exhausted Lady Sylvie, one hand on the Harbinger's cheek. "I never saw a man cry from being dried off before."

CHAPTER 21
WATCH

"Valence!" roared Doog. Or tried to. His croaky old voice carried about half as far as a fist-sized frog's ribbit. "Valence! Your watch is done. Come on in for breakfast."

"Never saw a man stand—well, slump—at watch so long and without complaint," observed Louis.

Doog scowled at him. "Well, we can't all have your good trim, gimpy."

"Do you want to go again?" Louis took a lurching step toward Doog, probably meant to be threatening, but since he stumbled on a crack in the flagstones and almost fell down for the eighth time that morning, it failed to impress.

"Any time, old man!"

"No more fighting," said Mick, joining them on the breakfast deck. He had a buttered scone in hand. "Where's Fenris?"

Doog pointed vaguely. "Down there with Valence at the wall. Been with him all night, far as I can tell."

Mick saw the old knight now, slumped in his chair on the wall. He had built the stone platform and steps so Sir Valence could sit with the top of the wall at about stomach level. A loaded crossbow rested, pointing slightly sideways, next to Valence's arms and head. Fenris was under the chair, head in paws like the old man above him. The other platforms Mick had constructed were empty.

"Eight Knights, how can he be stand being out there so long?"

"Shut your loaf hole. He's sitting."

"That's what gives the piles, eejit. From the cold stone. Everyone knows that."

"He's on a chair!"

"Do you want to go again?"

"You asked that five minutes ago."

"Again, again!"

"Knock it off, you two," Mick growled. Everyone wanted to fight, but no one wanted to sit a watch. Except for Valence.

"Valence!" Doog croaked once more. The effort started him coughing onto his own buttered roll, scattering butter-softened bits into the air like a thick morning snowfall.

"We're gonna run out of scones."

Louis cackled at this and shouted, "Yah, you and Mick are eating them all up."

"We can always make more," said Lady Aurorette. She was seated in her wheeled chair at a nearby table with Carol and Brigette.

Mick looked past the slumped form of Valence, down the hill to the other wall, the one around the town. The soldiers there were scrambling. More skolves had come, and there had been at least one skirmish already.

"What happens when they break through?" said Mick.

"*You're* fulla poo!" shouted Warley, shuffling laboriously by, both hands on his cane. Roland loomed behind him, carrying a plate full of eggs and unbuttered toast and trying unsuccessfully to hide his impatience at Warley's thumpingly slow progress.

"What are you on about now, Warley?" croaked Doog.

Warley fell into his chair with a heavy thump that made Roland wince. The old man thrust his cane belligerently at Mick. "He said poo at me!"

"I didn't," said Mick. "I said, what—" He stopped himself. *What* will *happen if the wall fails, and the line is broken?*

His gaze fell back to the wall around their house and to Valence sitting his watch. *They will come here.*

If they can.

Mick thought about the wagons of provisions that had sent ahead, when Brigitte had thought they could be persuaded to evacuate the house on the hill. The food stores had gone, but the wagons for the people had not arrived. "We don't have enough flour."

"We have enough for more than a month," said Roland, having delivered the plate of food and taken his station behind Warley's chair like some sort of hawk watching them all. His white coat was buttoned to the neck again, and he stood stiffly, as if at attention. As if attempting to project some aura of professionalism or gravitas. "Six weeks."

"Do we?" growled Mick.

Roland flinched.

Brigitte cut across the tension. "Mick, what are the words?" She had been watching quietly with Carol and Lady Aurorette. And carefully, like a real bird of prey, not a transparent, paper kite like Roland.

"Purple, bridge, horse, eight, apples, Elysium, rhubarb, harbinger, protect, idea."

Brigitte's eyes widened, and when she spoke, it was like the hawk diving. "Do you remember the other words? Do you know your name?"

Mick thought. The words were close. He could *feel* them. But instead of fumbling for lost ideas, he addressed the problem he could see more clearly. "If the soldiers retreat to our house, we'll be out of flour in a few days."

"They—they'll bring food with them," said Roland, gravitas slipping away in a stutter. Looking worried. Or scared. Trying not to, standing with his arms crossed now.

"They'll be running for their lives, eejit!" said Louis.

"Yah. Eejit," said Doog, slapping hands with Louis.

Roland's face darkened.

Brigitte stood up, carefully arranged her neat, yellow dress with her hands. "I don't know what can be done about our stores at this point," she said. "The winter reserve in the west fields may well have been emptied to stock the provision wagons, but even if they weren't, I doubt anyone would be keen to go check."

"Well, at least the big water tank is full, thanks to you, Mick," said Lady Aurorette.

Carol amplified this by gushing, "You were *so* strong."

"All that talk about water reminds me I have to take a pee," declared Doog.

"Me too," said Louis. "Come on, you can hold my pants up."

"Yah," shot Doog, "and you can hold my—"

"Gentlemen," interrupted Mick in a low voice.

Louis's face split in a grin. "Sorry, sorry, old man, but someone's got to hold it, heh, heh, heh."

"Knights alive," croaked Doog, thrusting his head out toward the wall, "how has Valence held it so long?"

A terrible feeling shot through Mick.

"Where are you going, old man?" said Doog.

"Use the stairs, Mick!" added Louis. "Don't just jump off. Roland here will have a conniption."

Roland did look like he might have a conniption, his face even darker. But Louis's warning came too late. Mick had already leapt the low wall of the patio, landed with a groan on the lawn, and was running, which is to say, hobbling quickly, toward Valence.

The old knight was stiff and cold. His arms were locked on the stone wall. Too stiff and too cold to throw another stick for the dog.

Fenris licked Mick and the old knight both. He was a puppy and did not know about old age, death, and failure.

~

"Keep up, Roland, for knight's sakes," said Doog.

Roland had been helping Louis get up after tripping on his feet. His indignant expression showed how unfair he thought the comment was.

"Everyone all right?" asked Mick.

"Fine!" chirped Louis. "Why wouldn't we be, dammit? It's not like any of *us* have up and died."

Mick had carried Sir Valence down to one of the cold storage rooms, the one with turnips, and laid him out there. Brigette had tried to talk him into taking Valence to the infirmary, but Mick wanted the old knight safe from the heat.

Safe from the temptation of quietly burying him while I am away, unspoken over, unremarked, forgotten.

Like all the others.

"Yes, why do you do that, Roland?" asked Mick.

"Do what?' Roland replied. His formal white uniform was sweat-stained now and dusty from the walk down the hill. And only getting sweatier and dustier.

Mick stopped and looked at him. "Cart us off in the night, bury us in secret?" he asked, though he knew—perhaps he knew —what the answer was.

But those that bury my friends in the night, absent ceremony, should answer for it.

Sweat rolled down Roland's wide, greasy forehead. "Brigitte says it's for the best."

"Why?" said Doog. "Why try to hide death from those living in the closest proximity to it? You think we don't know we're dying?" His weak voice found greater strength from somewhere. "You think old Valence didn't know?"

"Nah," Louis interjected, pushing away from Roland who had been holding him steady, and continuing toward the town. "Them sleeveens ain't hidin death, they're hiding our lives—what's left of 'em —from us."

Roland's hand went up as if warding off a blow. "No, no, it's not like that. We just don't want you upset. There's so little time left. Why should you spend it in fear?"

"You don't get to decide that!" growled Louis. "Death," he said more quietly, "that ain't what we fear."

Roland's face mottled, turning red, puffing up. Then he went still, and a moment after, seemed to deflate. "I'm sorry."

They were passing through the town now, crossing barricades, tents, neatly ordered piles of equipment, and soldiers everywhere. Many of the soldiers stopped and stared as the quartet walked slowly by.

"It's Grandpa!" someone shouted.

A young private pointed at Mick and said, "Grandpa."

A low rumble of "Grandpa" rose up from all around.

"What are they saying?" Roland asked, coming forward to walk beside Mick.

"Nothing," said the old man.

"It sounds like they miss their grandpa," said Doog, smiling.

"Hah!" Louis exclaimed, a gleam in his eyes, "they should've just come visited us at the house. We're all somebody's grandpa."

Closer to the north wall, the soldiers' curiosity faded. The situation was exigent here. A skirmish had apparently just ended. There were wounded, some screaming, others moaning. Stretchers went by with armsmen who could no longer do either. One woman was missing her head and shoulders. Another soldier had a face that had been mangled beyond recognition.

No one had thought to cover up the grim spectacle.

The sight of so much suffering and violence set Mick's blood afire. He felt suddenly lighter and nimbler, as if filled with some powerful, as yet undirected energy, an answer to the pity he felt for the dead and wounded. An answer to death and old age and Sir Valence dying on the wall.

"Grandpa!" said one of the soldiers on the wall. That word rose and fell like a wave on either side, down along the wall.

"Who d-do we talk to?" asked Roland, looking worried. The broad man's façade of confidence was utterly shredded.

"Mick!" said Sergeant Havard, as he jangled over to join the group, trailed by two younger soldiers. "Major Serres was hoping you would come. She says we could use some of your help."

Lightning buzzed through Mick's veins.

"What is he talking about?" said Roland.

"Quiet, sleeveen," barked Louis. He and Doog and some of the others had heard Mick's account of his role in the battle days earlier. It was a story not shared with the orderlies, though Brigitte had somehow found out.

Mick clapped Havard on the shoulder. "We need to borrow four wagons from you. Just for the day."

"Sure," said Havard, straightening up, wincing, pretending to be hurt. "We aren't going anywhere at the moment. What for?"

"There's a grain reserve about a quarter mile west of town," Mick replied. "We are hoping maybe it wasn't emptied during the evacuation."

Havard nodded. "Okay. Could be it wasn't. If the skolves haven't gotten to it yet."

"They still facing your north?"

"So far, but there's a lot more of them now." Havard lowered his voice. "A lot more."

"We gotta try," said Doog.

Havard took this in, then gestured to one of the privates and whispered in the man's ear. The soldier saluted and took off at a run. "You lads almost out of food up there?"

"No," said Roland. "We have six weeks."

Havard frowned at Roland, then looked to Mick, eyebrows raised.

Mick gestured with his head in the direction of the hill and its house. "It's for when you lot come join us."

~

"Just about loaded, Grandpa," wheezed Aron. Havard had sent Reyn's eight to scout the quarter-mile stretch to the storehouses and help load and drive the wagons. Aron's ribs were wrapped up tight, and he could not take a deep breath. He had been assigned light duty, so he had sat in the cart with Doog, and was still sitting in it, talking to Mick every time the old man came out with sacks of flour.

"We have a problem," announced Alwena from the roof. "Skolves are attacking the town again." She had a telescope in her hands. "A lot more of them. A couple of groups are filtering south along the walls."

Reyn appeared as if out of nowhere, head tilted. "Okay, I can even hear it," he said, "I'm calling it. We're loaded enough."

They had come west from Villiers up to the collection of wooden storehouses on a narrow dirt road, but there was another route south, a track that led through tall grass to the west side of the hill. Mick turned and considered it. "Agreed," he said, turning back to look north and east. He too could hear the sounds of battle now, attenuated but getting louder. A moment later and the sounds were unmistakable. Shouts, screams, the shrieking release of massed projectiles. The piercing howls of thousands upon thousands of skolves.

More of them than before, always more.

People will be dying now.

That strange energy coursed once more through Mick. An image of Sir Valence sitting at his post came to mind.

Raise up the Bridge to Elysium!
I will not end my holy fight
Nor shall I stop paying the cost.

"What's that you're singing, old man?" asked Alwena, down off the roof now.

Mick realized that he had lost time while he sang the words. The other rangers were at the wagons now. Roland was sitting in Mick's cart, ready to drive, whip in hand, eyes wide. He wanted to go.

Alwena said, "We need to haul ass. And more of this flour too."

"Ass first," said Louis. "I don't feel like gittin' 'et."

"Do they eat *people*?" croaked Doog, clambering slowly up beside Aron, who shook his head.

"Doubt it," said Alwena. "Doesn't stop them from killing you, though."

Screams rolled like a cold wave across the warm air, chilling Mick. "I'll meet you there," he said. "Take my seat with Roland, Sergeant Reyn. Look out for those in the house on the hill."

Reyn's goateed face told no story. He only said, "Yes."

Roland's frown fought with a look of frozen fear, telling everything. "W-where are you going, Mick?"

"To help."

"B-but you're my responsibility." Roland was shaking. Howls cut the air. Closer than before. "You h-have to come back to the h-house."

"I don't."

"I can't go back without you."

"You've never even been off the hill since this started," shot Louis. "You think he needs you?"

Doog had to get in his own jab. "You just can't get over being our jailor, can you, Roland? Can't stand losing control."

"No, no, no. I have a job to do." Roland swallowed, looking about for support. But the other orderlies had not come. "I didn't know. It wasn't so dangerous then."

Louis sneered, "You don't *own* us, eejit. Or our risks."

Roland gave up on Doog and Louis and directed his gaze back to Mick. "*Please*, Mick."

Mick was filled with energy now, ready to go, needing to go. He stopped and looked back at Roland. The big man's white coat was gray with dirt and dark with sweat. His hands were shaking. Mick had to resist shaking his head. Roland was surprising him.

He is truly in the same house as the rest of us now. Just as endangered, just as scared, and—perhaps—just as desperate for his own sense of meaning. "I'm sorry I hurt you, Roland. I had no excuse."

Roland's eyebrows shot up and he sat backward, confused. "Hurt me?"

"A while ago. I hit you."

"You remember?"

"No," Mick replied. "But I know it happened. I'm sorry."

"It's okay," said Roland. "It's my job. To try to help."

Mick looked into Roland's eyes. They were full. "Take the flour up." He thrust his chin in gesture at the others. "Take them back safe on that south path. Complete your watch and fulfill your responsibility. I'll come later."

"I—I will."

To forestall objections from Doog and Louis, Mick added, "Take your posts, gentlemen, after the flour is stowed."

"Alwena, Dafydd, Eurion, go with Mick," said Reyn as he got up into the wagon beside Roland. "Eurion, take the arbalest."

"But we just got this one," whined Dylan from his wagon.

"There'll be another," said Reyn. "Mick. Take my sword." He stood and unbelted his longsword.

Mick took it, let the belt out, and closed it over his hips.

"We won't let 'em bury Valence, Mick," said Doog, clearly wanting to say something.

"Not 'till you're back," added Louis. "Make those fuckers remember you, old man!"

Doog chuckled and added, "That way you don't have to remember this yourself, heh, heh, heh."

Mick had nothing to say to this.

"Come on now, youngster," said Doog impatiently to Aron, "give them reins a flick."

Mick jogged away, leaving the wagons and his friends behind, heading toward familiar sounds. *But familiar from where, and when?*

~

"THEY'RE COMING, GRANDPA," hissed Alwena. "It might have been better to skip the chitchat and just get going."

"Stay behind me." Mick said, drawing Reyn's longsword. A moment later he whirled, sensing that no one was behind him. And he was right. The three Vercors rangers had spread out to flank him, low in the tall wild barley to the side of the road.

A howl cut the air, close, sharp.

"Say hello to hell, fuckers," grunted Eurion, loading a heavy metal quarrel into the oversized crossbow.

Dafydd said nothing but gripped his spear tightly in white knuckled hands.

A stench like rotted meat drenched the air.

"Stand firm, boys," whispered Alwena. "There's no running now."

Mick saw them then, cutting the stalks like a flight of geese. *No time to run.*

With a shout, he bounded forward to intercept the skolves. In the voice of a young man, he sang, "Raise up my shield, sun's light will warm!" and collided explosively with the lead skolve.

Dust and barley hung still in the air for a frozen moment, a dead-point in time. Mick looked down at the skolve crumpled at his feet, its head crushed, he knew not how.

Another skolve charged.

"Raise up my maul!" he roared and brought his sword down on its head, ignoring the metal bar it swung at him.

A terrific report cracked the air. A piece of metal flew off to Mick's right. The skolve was cut through the middle of its head down to its heavy spine.

"Thwack!"

A heavy quarrel flew from behind and went through a third skolve. The howling beast careened sideways, only to encounter Dafydd's spear as the young soldier charged through the dust and chaff.

Mick shook his sword free and went after the fourth skolve. He swung ferociously, but missed his target, hitting the top of the creature's axe. The axe planted itself in the dirt and the skolve stumbled over it, but Mick's sword was cracked through the middle. The old man tossed the ruined blade aside and tackled the skolve.

There was a confusion of stabbing and punching, rolling and yelling. The air filled with dust and sprays of blood.

"Grandpa!"

"Grandpa!" It was Alwena. She stood staring at him, agape, Dafydd and Eurion beside her, looking just as gobsmacked. Her short sword was bloody. Mick let go of the wet mess that had been the skolve and staggered to his feet.

"Are you okay, Grandpa?" Dafydd, gasping for air. "Your shirt's ruined," he added lamely.

"No, it isn't."

Eurion was trying to reload the arbalest, but he paused and frowned in exaggerated disbelief. "It's hanging in *strips* off you, Grandpa, and you're trying to say your shirt is fine?"

"Maybe you should wear armor next time," mumbled Dafydd.

"I think that's it for now," observed Alwena, eyes scanning the tall grass around them. "Not sure where the other ones went."

"They're scared of Grandpa," said Eurion.

Alwena shook her head in mock disgust. "Leave him alone, Urinate. Grandparents are grumpy and don't like to be hectored."

Mick could hear fighting farther north at the wall. If anything, it was louder and more desperate than ever. "Our watch isn't over. Let's get up there where we can do some good."

CHAPTER 22
SUPPORT

"They want the support of the Elysians, or of me at least," said Green. "Conceptually."

Val was due to rejoin the nobles, but she was happy to speak with a warm, dry Halwyn Glace. He had risked his life to bring all the wizards back alive from Courant but had almost immediately been called in to the Council of Knights meetings, which were taking place simultaneously with Princess Cressy's emergency congress. "So what's the concept?"

Green shrugged, "Take the Bifrost to Nehring Ardgour's machine."

"They want you to teleport it?"

"You would think," he said with a mischievous smile, "but no. There's a secret." He lowered his voice. "Well, two secrets. The first is the location, which Yeyncie Greene is not allowing talk of."

Val was short of time now. She had to reign in her monster. "They are going to have to tell us if they want our help, but okay, what is the other secret?"

Green's smile grew wider. He leaned in and whispered, "The Bifrost *cannot be* teleported. The Methueyn Knights will have to run it to Nehring Ardgour."

"What?" said a shocked Val. "Have you confirmed this? Why didn't we know already?"

"It's a *secret,*" Green replied. He lowered his voice again. "Remember when Nehring tried to steal the Bifrost?"

"You mean before either of us was born?"

Halwyn laughed, then turned conspiratorial again. "Yes, *then*. He teleported to the room, hall, or cathedral it was kept in and tried to take it. But he couldn't! It will *not* teleport. Ardgour had to leave without it. Not even he could fight all the Methueyn Knights. But that's why no one knows exactly where it's kept now. In case Ardgour tries again."

"I wonder why it resists teleportation," Val whispered back.

Halwyn was still giggling. "I bet you could figure out why, Val. I might even let you design an experiment for me. Later, of course."

"I have never seen you so excited," said Val. "This is actually not great news, you know."

"Well, what is?" said Green, still smiling happily. "At least we are still alive."

Val started turned from him. The nobles were in conclave, and her duty was there.

"Thank you for sharing the secrets. I better get back. It looks like we are finally going to make the big decision."

"To listen to Lady Harbinger and abandon the northern half of what's left?"

"Like you said, Green, what good news is there anymore?" Val started to walk away.

Green reached for her shoulder and said, "Wait, Val."

She stopped, impatient, struggling against the feeling.

"Val, I—I love you," he blurted. When Val said nothing, he added, "You must have suspected it. This isn't getting better with all the best decisions being so dark. I need you to *know*. Know for sure."

What do I say to this?

The timing could not have been worse.

"Thank you. I know that you love me," she said. *No time, no time, no time.* Her frustration was more felt than thought. Competing anxieties and pressures—and the old need to achieve control—compelled her to divert. "I need to get back now."

"Val," Green said, an edge to his voice now. "How do you feel about me?"

"I love you as much as I can with my country falling down around me. Can we speak to this properly later?"

"Yes." His tone was a dirge.

Like is to like is to like. When all decisions are bad, nothing good is coming.

"ARE we really to give up our lands? Our castles? Our peoples? The *children*." The old man was stooped and skinny, fighting and failing to maintain that perfect Engevelen posture he had been famous for in better years. He kept looking around for approval as he spoke, and despite getting none, he did not stop there.

The children need no more words wasted on them from men who will do nothing concrete to help them.

Val clenched her fists. Like most of the lords and ladies present, Lord Calencieux was only practiced at form and pretense, not initiative or substance. "Should we just give up the *children*? Abandon them?" he demanded theatrically. "Walk away and hide behind some new wall? Are we lords not the wisest and best of this great country of Engevelen? Are we not the ones that others look to for solutions in crises like this? Are we not the intellectual shield of all citizens, the metaphoric parents of all their children? We have a responsibility. We must be cautious. Such a decision should not be rushed."

Calencieux spoke with all the exaggerated enunciation and forced volume of a stage actor pretending to brilliance while the stage burned down around him.

We have only been talking about this for a year.

From her seat near the door, Val could keep her irritation hidden from the other lords and ladies, but the struggle was becoming more and more difficult. They had been talking for hours, covering the same ground as they had since the war started and still getting nowhere.

"It's too late for my castle with all this dithering!" shouted a lady in the assembly, obviously feeling as impatient as Val.

"Point of order," someone else called.

Unnecessarily, it turned out, as Calencieux went on, undeterred by either comment. "And this is to my point," he said, the oversized throat knuckle on his overthin neck bobbing like a cork in the long neck of a bottle. Even with his big words and expensive robes, that neck looked more like the long, pallid, drooping gullet of a plucked turkey.

Val lost track of his endless droning. She blinked and remembered the aqueducts falling in Courant and the frost on Green's eyelashes. And his declaration of love. She blinked again, forcing her attention back to the ballroom, wondering if she had missed anything, but of course Calencieux was still talking, still making the same otiose arguments.

"Your highness," interrupted Lady Eileen of Lavender, a recently abandoned town near Aurillon, "I would like to speak."

She wants to speak because she doesn't want to hear.

"It's too late for Lavender, let us move on!" came a shout from across the room.

"Point of order! Point of order! Point of order!" rose from all sides.

This only seemed to encourage Lady Eileen. "We *must* march our armies north to retake Lavender. There are still people trapped in farms and towers throughout my lands."

And likely all dead by now. Val remembered skolves pouring through Courant's streets as she was teleported away. Smaller, weaker Lavender could have fared no better.

One argument dysfunctionally followed another.

There was no agreement, only more arguing and posturing. *This is the uselessness of overrefinement.* Val felt a pang for Green and his pure, naive, poorly timed expression of love.

She sat and listened through three more pointless speeches before leaving.

~

"May I be admitted?" asked Val at the threshold.

The Methueyn Temple was not as big as the ballroom, but it was certainly beautiful. It was a Steel Castle without all the space those sanctuaries required for congregation or a priest. A round table with eight intricate carvings on its surface sat at the temple's center. It was surrounded by two outer rings of chairs for the Deladieyr Knights, and beyond those by eight apses, one for each of the Methueyn Ideas. Each of these alcoves was lit by sunlight through a richly coloured stained-glass window. Each window told the story of one Methueyn Knight's Idea.

Green sat in Volsang's place, at the spot on the table with a great axe carved into it. The Knight of Vengeance was off hunting Nehring Ardgour, a quest he had pursued for two years now. Green met Val's eyes as she entered. He nodded slightly, his normally open face unreadable.

Beyond the table, seated as far away from each other in the closest row of Deladieyr seats as they could, the Vymyty wizard Taratoraff, and the infamous diplomat and liar, Marias Garragorah, stared in opposite directions in silence. At the exact center of the table rested the great crystal known as the Methueyn Bridge.

"Yes, of course," said the diminutive knight sitting at the shield symbol. She beckoned Val to enter the room and approach. Sir Heydron, or Yeyncie Greene, could not have been more than eleven years old by Val's reckoning, but she was the bright fire at the center of the meeting. Tiny and slight, yet filled with a dangerous potential and a brilliant mind.

"Though you and Halwyn here must both leave when we discuss the location," she added. Then she pointed two fingers in a stabbing motion toward Garragorah and Taratoraff. "Neither of you will say anything of that either, unless we give you express permission."

Taratoraff said nothing, but Garragorah's smile washed over her face like oil on a pan. "Of course, Sir Heydron. I will follow all your rules to the letter."

"And do not approach the table!" shouted Sir Michael. "I don't mean you, Lady Valcourt," he quickly clarified in a normal voice. "You may approach."

So . . . no one trusts either emissary from Novgoreyl.

"We don't trust either of them," said a tall, dark-haired, extremely pale woman sitting at the crescent moon position.

Sir Leylah, Val realized. She had seen them all before, walking the halls, crossing the short green between the castle proper and their stone temple. *Or have I?* Val tried to remember if the Sir Michael who sat at the place with the great sword sigil was the Michael she had seen last. *It is not him. He died. And now here he is again in new form.*

"What news from the congress?" asked Darday'l, a dark-haired, dark-skinned woman in smokey plate armor.

"They have not yet invited Farrah in to speak to them," said Val.

"And she's just waiting on the stuffed armor? That doesn't sound like the Harbinger to me," replied Yeyncie.

Val sighed. "She is not altogether well. Yet." *For all I know she is sleeping. Or still raving prophetic poetry.*

Darday'l's eyes grew large. "But you heard some of what she said while still in trance, did you not? How I would have liked to have been there!"

"It was unbearable both to see and hear." Val doubted she would ever forget vomiting after one brief look into the twisted, impossibly moving images painted in the Harbinger's prophetic eyes. "And it has clearly hurt *her*."

"Such is the pain and joy of knowledge."

"Indeed," said Val doubtfully. She smiled to herself. Arguing about the value of knowledge with the angel of learning would probably be a waste of time.

"And what have you learned here?" Val asked. "Have you decided upon a course of action? How can the Elysians be of help?"

"I fear the sun will rise again before we make any decisions," said tall, golden Sir Urieyn, a flicker of disappointment on his normally joyful face.

"Let us decide now then," demanded Sir Michael, clearly angry. "I say we go to Courant and confront Skoll."

"I would go with you," said Sir Sendeyl of the damaged armor, who had escorted Garragorah into the city. "Perhaps the two of us can prevail where I alone could not. I am sorry I could not hold onto your sword, brother."

"We shall get it back!" returned Michael ferociously.

Sir Darday'l shook her head in exasperation. "Please. We need to know more before we act."

"The Treaty was left in Aurillon," said barrel-chested Hervor. "I should retrieve it. In these difficult times, we need a symbol to rally the people. They have lost hope, I fear."

Pale Sir Leylah smiled ruefully. "I would like to attend one of the battlefronts—Villiers, perhaps—and heal the injured. While we talk, people are dying."

So this is what they are like when together.

Val had heard it said that the Methueyn Order, individually peerless, could not as a group have organized a bun fight in a bakery. They were notorious for their extreme individuality, but she had seldom spoken with more than one of them at a time. She had not seen them in conclave until now, with the willfulness of each on full display.

Are they like the lords and ladies in congress? No. They disagree not from pretense, but from the fundamental differences in their Ideas. It is almost child-like.

Val met Green's eyes. She realized he had been staring at her through the entire conversation.

Like egos in a congress, like competing ideas with voices but no ears, our essential problem is laid out. Like is to like is to like, and thus we go inex-

orably from our failure to work together toward the failure of Engevelen as a whole.

And miss the cooperation and love that have always awaited us?

Yeyncie struck the table a tremendous blow, an impossible blow from such a small person, making the entire chamber ring with its reverberation. “No, no. No!” she roared in a voice larger than her body, larger than the room. “Not this again! It has happened enough. Far more than enough. It can happen no more. We must solve this problem together, or it will not be solved.” She pointed to Garragorah and said, “Marias, tell Lady Katherine your proposal. The *short* version.”

Garragorah stood up from her chair, assuming a posture not unlike that of the lords in congress, but the considerable and continuing pressure of Yeyncie’s volcanic glare seemed to wilt her pretense. She started to speak, then stopped, and shrugged. “Nehring Ardgour wishes to send Skoll and Hati back whence they came. He needs the Methueyn Bridge to do so. He proposes that you bring it to him before you are all dead . . . and before Skoll or Hati just come and take it.”

“That is what the envoy said to Congress,” Val confirmed for the others. She turned to Taratoraff. “Is this story true?”

The wizard did not shift in his seat. His body was crumpled into the chair like an old, threadbare blanket, tossed and shrunken in place. “Never trust Nehring Ardgour,” he said in a surprisingly loud, deep voice. “Or Marias Garragorah.” He cleared his throat loudly. “But that is one of Nehring’s plans.”

“One?”

“Wait,” said Yeyncie. “We are saving the Vymyty for last. As a check. Question Garragorah further.”

Val traded a look with Green and then addressed the envoy. “How does the Methueyn Bridge rid us of Skoll and Hati? And if the demons can come and take it later, why don’t they do so now?”

“I am no wizard,” said Marias blandly. “I can only repeat what I am told, acting in good faith for the executive power I serve.”

“And thus take no responsibility for your lies,” said Michael harshly. "You are just like a boat bringing grain down the river. It's not your fault if the kernels are rotted."

Marias nodded in exaggerated fashion as if to a child. "Exactly so! I am merely the conduit for this news. As I have ever been."

"The wizard is right," said Michael. "You are a liar." He turned to the others. "Why are we even listening to this scoundrel? Her embassy of lies is done."

"Is that true," asked Yeyncie in a whisper. "Can you give us no more?"

Sir Leylah, the pale woman, asked, "Shall we pass judgement then?"

There was a curious silence after these words, a tension that Val did not at first understand. *Oh. The angel of night and renewal. Her hands are life or death.*

The diplomat's eyes roved the cold and unsympathetic room. Something beyond surrender crossed her face. "He hates this world! He thinks it is a dirty, disgusting, low, foul place. To him, *this* is hell, filled with a stinking fleshliness he hates."

"*That* is no lie," said Taratoraff. "I am a Vymyty wizard. He made us bathe thrice a day and always before seeing him. Even after I escaped him, I hid in water."

"He is more spirit than man now," Marias continued. "He leaves his body and teleports his soul in preparation for his great journey."

"This will not work," said the Vymyty in a voice like moving earth. "But is true. Ardgour has tried many things. Learned many things."

"I don't understand," said Halwyn Glace. "If he has learned so many things, how has he escaped the wrath of Nimrheal?"

~

ON A STILL, sunny day, not far from a highway in the clear blue sky, near a castle, downstream from long and treacherous suspended wooden bridges, in a narrow and steeply rising canyon, a dark form abruptly materialized.

An instant after the cloaked figure manifested, a dark, towering thunder cell appeared in the sky behind him.

The man's cloak rippled in the sudden gusts of wind. A hand with long, lean, well-trimmed, immaculately clean fingers reached up and pulled down the cowl to reveal a handsome, though sharp-edged face. He turned to observe the anvil cloud. Fingers of fast-turning air seemed to reach out from the dark, roiling mass toward him. He smiled and turned away from this horror to gaze down the empty canyon once more.

A sound fought to be heard above the escalating gusts of wind. It was a metallic jangling. Lightning struck, close and violent, the report deafeningly loud and only an instant behind the staccato flash. The dark, cloaked figure did not flinch. His attention was fixed on the trickle of sound from far down the narrow canyon. A more sustained gust of wind blew his cowl against the back of his bald head and pointed the edges of the cloth downhill in the direction he was looking.

The jangling grew louder.

Lightning struck again, thunder broke, and the wind screamed.

A plate-armored man appeared, running up the canyon at great speed. He was enormous and held a long-handled, double-bladed axe tightly in one massive, gauntleted hand. The knight did not slow or deviate in his approach. He came on at the speed of a racehorse, and as he neared the dark-cloaked man, he raised his axe to strike. The hooded figure held up a hand.

The knight ignored the cloaked man's raised hand and swung down ferociously. The axe struck deeply into the rock of the canyon. The cloaked man had vanished.

And reappeared instantly thirty yards up the canyon. "Wait, dread Volsang!" he shouted in a voice that was as dark and strange as the storm falling upon them both. "Cease these childish attempts at violence. I must tell you something."

Volsang pulled his axe from the canyon floor and walked unhesitatingly toward the other man. "What?" he asked in harsh tones.

"I have solved the second-to-last problem! This is an excellent day."

"Fuck your day, Ardgour."

Ardgour only smiled and said, "But I wanted to thank you."

Volsang raised his axe again. "For what?"

"Paying my debt."

A bizarre sound like boiling liquid rose out of the storm. It came from an opaque, malformed haze just up the canyon and ten yards or more high and wide. The cloud shrunk, coalescing into a form very like Nehring Ardgour but less defined. Screams rose from deep within it.

A flickering, bone-like arm reached out from the cloud and stretched heavenward, and in a crack of lightning, a dark spear appeared in its vaguely defined hand.

The cloud moved in uneasy stutters toward Volsang and Ardgour, not so much stepping as slipping judderingly across space in uneven measures.

"Goodbye, Volsang," said Ardgour as he disappeared.

~

That works?

"That works?" asked Green, echoing Val's horrified thoughts. "Ardgour sacrificed the Vymyty wizards to Nimrheal for each new discovery he made?"

"Yes," said Taratoraff, "Nearly all of us were . . . spent in this way."

"And others," said Garragorah. "His wife, his servants . . . Nimrheal will manifest and stay in this world until *someone* dies by its spear."

Can that be true? If so, if Ardgour had confirmed this by sacrificing others—and repeating the experiment multiple times—it was monumental. It changed *everything*.

"And Nehring Ardgour pursued this knowledge in order to learn how to leave this world?" Val asked, struggling to balance an equation with so much death on one side.

Taratoraff was about to reply, but Yeyncie silenced him with an impatient gesture. "You, diplomat, will answer."

Garragorah's face was pale, but she spoke with a firm voice. "Yes. It started with his attempted theft of the Methueyn Bridge in younger days. Then, later, bringing Skoll and Hati here. Mistakes. The skolves. Another mistake. But now he has abandoned this plan and uses all his resources to build a ... device ... to weaken the demons. It is an extension of the machine he used to bring them over. He has almost completed this new device, but it requires the Methueyn Bridge to work properly." She took a deep breath. "You must bring him the Bridge before it is too late. Before the demons take it from you."

"They shall *not*!" spat Michael.

There is a question here. "If Skoll or Hati also want the Methueyn Bridge, why haven't *they* tried to take it?" demanded Val.

"I do not know," said Garragorah, spreading her hands.

"Is fear," said Taratoraff. He looked at Yeyncie for permission to continue. "When first arrived, Skoll and Hati fight Nehring. But he have power of device, as existed then, behind him. It contain deadly power. He chastise and master demons, make them pets. They are cowards once hurt, doubly so when . . . embarrassed, as they were in front of skolves."

"What is it? This thing that can tame Skoll and Hati?" asked Green.

"A poison only Ardgour understand," replied Taratoraff. "But they fear him greatly, unknowing that away from machine, he cannot overpower them. They only learn limits of his power this much later."

Darday'l squinted at him. "And how does that bear on the Methueyn Bridge?"

"Is also object of great power. They feel it. Instinctively. They know is here, but not what it is or what can do. They fear walking into trap and being hurt as Ardgour did to them with original device."

"Fascinating," mused Darday'l. "I must learn more about this device. How it works. *Why* it works."

Well, I'm curious too.

"We lack the time," said Yeyncie. "We must, I think, decide if we are going to try this or not, and if so, who will go on this quest."

Michael spoke first. "Why don't you, I, and Sendeyl run the Bridge to Ardgour? Then we can *smash* Skoll—a weakened Skoll—at Courant."

"I could help the wounded in Villiers," said Leylah. Hervor and Urieyn were muttering their own suggestions at the same time.

Val noticed the excitement in Garragorah's eyes. She could see the woman's body tighten with new life and hope.

"Can we trust Nehring Ardgour?" Darday'l interrupted. Her face betrayed greater caution and less excitement than the other knights' eager countenances, than Yeyncie's even.

"No," said Taratoraff, "Never trust. And you must *all* go to have any chance of success."

Yeyncie's face glowed red with frustration. "Why? Why must all of us be there?"

Taratoraff looked at Garragorah and sneered, "Because Nehring always have more than one plan. He will try to use Methueyn Bridge to leave this world he hates. This he will do if he can. Only if you prevent him, will he enact the more . . . cooperative plan this liar tells you of."

"I am only repeating what I was told!" said Marias passionately.

"What else?" asked Yeyncie with a sigh.

Taratoraff slumped. "Demons will know if you move Bridge. I think. And they will overcome their fear, try to take from you or prevent it to reach Nehring." With downcast eyes, he added, "It will require all of you to fight them both."

"You know what I think?" said Michael in a rising voice. "I think you don't know any of this! How could you?"

Good question. It sounded like a great deal of supposition to Val. But a new question occurred to her. "How many Vymyty wizards and others did Ardgour sacrifice?"

"Everyone?" asked Taratoraff.

"Everyone," said Yeyncie.

"Over one hundred and thirty must be."

So much knowledge. "And you were close to him through all of this . . . sacrifice?" Val asked, head reeling from the monstrous enormity of it.

"For much of it."

Michael pounded the table. "You're as guilty as her!" He pointed at Garragorah. "You're as guilty as *him*."

~

VAL and all seven Methueyn Knights entered the ballroom, but surprisingly the unquiet arrival of the god-like knights did not immediately galvanize the attention of the lords and ladies. A new presence had preceded them by only a moment. Lady Farrah Harbinger sat like a queen on a throne beside Princess Cressy, straight-backed and stately.

But wearing an iridescent black blindfold. Val found that, though unable to see Farrah's eyes, her own were drawn inexorably to the shimmering blindfold.

Besides the powerful and magnetic, the eerie, presence of the Harbinger, there had been other changes to the room since Val had left it an hour earlier. The chairs had been stacked along the back wall, and the nobles were on their feet, crowding closely around the raised dais. Above them all and set back from the stairs of the dais were Christine Cressy, her brother Peter, Lady Sylvie, and the Harbinger.

Is she well?

The blindfold argued no. It could only be there to protect the crowd from the eyes of the Harbinger, heraldic eyes that everyone in the chamber had been warned about.

Unless this is just theatre.

Val would not put such a performance past the Harbinger or the princess. Farrah was the most intelligent person she had ever met, honest but with wisdom above the strict letter of truth. And she looked better. Her hands lay on the armrest, relaxed and composed, and the way she held her head suggested she was watching the audience, and weighing them up, despite the blindfold. She projected, even from behind that barrier, a powerful, riveting charisma.

"You will not understand what you hear," Lady Sylvie said in ringing tones. "This is Heraldry, this is prophecy. It is not easy, and it is rarely kind." She kneeled carefully beside the Harbinger's chair and whispered in Farrah's ear.

The Harbinger's gesture, a nod, was barely perceptible.

She is better! It is theatre. Or partially so.

"I see an old man upon a hill, surrounded by skolves, encircled by memories. The future of Engevelen lies within the circle of his arms. A heavenly woman falls from the sky, riding on the blade of the gods. She collides with the earth and journeys alone across the wilderness, carrying an impossible burden of questions and the weight of the future. A man with a sinister secret dives in the dark for the truth and catches a riddle. The Shining Knight blazes his last before the gates of midnight. The Methueyn Order fights its final battle beneath a bridge in the sky and the doorway to heaven. A young girl is both saved and doomed because no one listened.

"A country is abandoned. A great wall is built to save what is most precious.

"The One True Devil comes for us all. It is a being of anarchy and inevitability. Brutal, relentless, leaking entropy. This being will utterly destroy us if these things do not come to pass."

As she said the last word, Farrah's head lifted theatrically as if she was looking at the sky, and she went still. Sylvie rose from her knees and announced, "The Harbinger has seen every event foretold here. They have already been set in motion and will happen with or without the help of this congress. Our task is to evacuate our people southward and build our wall."

"Really? Run away? Hide behind a wall and everything will turn out all right?" said Lord Calencieux in a voice dripping with sarcasm. "Is that what we are expected to conclude from this . . . cockalorum? All I heard were riddles. Where is the proof?"

Alain Overbree, who was in the crowd with the nobles, shouted back, "I have already told you of the Harbinger's other prophecies. I *saw* them at Harbinger Hall. I paid the price. This vision but augments what I have already reported. We must commit to this wall. The Methueyn Knights will destroy Skoll and Hati so that the wall can hold the skolves and not be broken. And some vital battle will be fought—I'm now told—in Villiers. It is really quite plain."

Further questions were interrupted by the thundrous sound of tiny Yeyncie Greene's foot stamping from the back of the hall. "There *is* proof," said Yeyncie.

The lords turned, shocked, toward the plate-armored little girl and her entourage of blazing Methueyn Knights, as if only noticing them now.

Princess Cressy had not spoken at all during the long day of debate, but seeing her chance, jumped on it. "What says Sir Heydron concerning proof?"

"No one knows a certain fact—or knew," said Yeyncie. "Escuyers Aveline Vanier and Bryon Boldol hid the great sword known as the Methueyn Treaty at the top of the bell tower of the Steel Castle in Aurillon. *Hanging.*" She made an expansive gesture with her arms. "Hanging from a great height in the heavens. The Harbinger has *seen* Aveline Vanier retrieve the Treaty. Just as she has seen the wall built and has seen our order of knights fight a final battle in the north. The Methueyn Knights will go. This *will* happen."

CHAPTER 23
INFINITE VESSEL

"She filled her own cup," muttered Ave bitterly as she gazed hopelessly out the window of the tower. Heartbroken and exhausted by the long run from Courant to Aurillon, the flavor of her grief had been ground into something bitter. And now having achieved the great city and approached to within a few city blocks of the Methueyn Treaty, she and Bro found themselves thwarted. A sea of skolves milled about the old town just north of them. The rotted-meat smell of those bodies was no worse than the stench of their failure.

"What?" said Bro.

"I said she filled her own cup," Ave repeated in a forlorn voice. "Revenberge. I loved her, but she filled her own cup. She didn't need me. Did you notice that, Bro?" She looked at his big, ugly, twitching face. The sympathy she saw there irritated her, grinding her resolution and sense of self into something rare and rancid. "No Deladieyr or Methueyn Knight needs anyone, I know. They are all their own . . . source. They *all* fill their own cups." She turned away from his ruined face and pathetic, naive projection of solace. Out there, tantalizingly close yet unattainably far away, she could see the great tower of the

Steel Castle. When she squinted, she could make out the great sword hanging from the bell tower. Exactly where they had left it.

"Perhaps we all fill our own cups and dig our own graves. Cooperate? Rarely. Love? It cannot last if ever it existed." She turned back to him with an expression like a blow. "No wonder the best of us are dead and the rest skidding into loss."

Bro shifted. He stared at her from two feet away, his eyes filling. The tears made her want to put out those eyes. If he saw the hostility in the red windows of her soul, it did not deter him, but then Ave had often told herself that Bro was simply stupid.

"You think love takes up space?" he said as gently as a man his size could.

Something buried in her resonated to this simple question, but she was too splenetic to address it. Instead of exploring the feeling, she said petulantly, "I question everything."

Bro surprised her by laughing. He did respond to the volatile look this engendered, saying, "You are a child of Darday'l, of course you question everything. Yours is the only Idea that has real complexity."

Something hot burned the back of her throat. She bit down on it. "Then why do I feel so weak and defeated? And so bitter?"

"You aren't weak," Bro said calmly. "You led us back here to the Treaty. You have a plan."

"Ha!" Ave said, a little too loudly. "Look at those skolves. There must be a thousand of them, and that's only what we can see. We can't get through that. My plan fails here." *Dead on the cobbles, smashed like Revenberge.*

Bro's eyes only scanned the gray horde for a moment before he said, "Something will change. I believe in you, Aveline."

Bro's faith was immiscible with Ave's grief. She could not look at him and whispered to herself, "She fills her own cup, and now mine is empty."

Ave had expected Bro to say that this moping and bitterness was unlike her, because it was. She had left murdered Sir Revenberge lying broken and unburied in the streets of Courant with a terrible, new insight.

The long path of defeat needs to change.

She *knew* that. The thought had galvanized her, protected her from paralytic shock at seeing something so beautiful so broken. But tens of hours and more tens of miles of labor under grief had eroded her fragile aspiration. Years of the loss of the best and most loved had already drained her reserve of purpose and hope. A part of Ave was aware that Revenberge's death had not been the worst moment for her. The weakest point was now, alone except for the big idiot, far from *her* cold ruined body, tired and in shock, in the realization that her hopeful little plan was impossible. An army of skolves was seeing to that.

Her newfound resolution had, by poisonous diagenesis, transformed into despair.

Bro had been there through it all with her, had sat through a war's worth of failure and death. He must, on some level, understand this sour transformation of morale. However, instead of making the expected excuses on her behalf, he simply said, "Someone you loved has died."

"What did you say about love?" she said, the question coming without warning out of somewhere deep, unconscious, elemental.

"You loved Revenberge."

"No, not that. *Before*. You said something before."

"I said love takes up no space."

Like a pail of cold water on a hot face, this stopped her in her tracks, but grief soon flowed bitterly once more, drowning whatever nascent epiphany had struggled briefly to be born from her exhausted, aggrieved mind. "Oh really? Doesn't that sound *nice*," she hissed. "There was room for *my* love in *her* full cup, was there? The heart is big enough for love, is it? Well, look at *you* and *your* face! Look at what love did to *you*."

For once the twitching half of Bro's face went quiescent. It was a shock to see, if only for a moment, the whole handsomeness he had once had. So shocking—and she knew her words had been cruel—that Ave expected the next thing she would see was rage. *Will he throw me out the window now? I deserve it.*

Bro leaned forward, massive hands reaching for Ave's neck. Then resting them gently on either side of her wet face. "My love was not too strong. It was my body that was too weak." He looked down at his plate-sized paws. "And I wear the consequences."

Ave wanted to hate Bro, to rage at him, call him stupid and ugly. But underneath her weary, foul mood, she could not hate her old friend. His twitching face had never really been ugly to her, and she knew he was far from stupid. He was the one person who had always stayed by her side, followed her, believed in her. Bro was, *literally*, the only person in the world that Ave could speak her frustration *to* and take it out *on*. She resented and loved him for this in outward reflection of her inner conflict. "Do you fill your own cup?" she asked him.

"Yes," he said. He turned his gaze from his giant, vascular mitts to Ave's glistening eyes. "My Idea fills me."

"Then why do you follow me? Do you want to fill *my* cup?"

Bro's face reddened at this innuendo, but the half of his face that could smile did. "You will save us all Aveline." His smile evaporated. "With or without me."

Rage, frustration, and grief had caused Ave to say many things that were not exactly true, to miss truth, but finally her passion found something pure. "It is not about being needed, is it?" She looked down on the skolves below, some lit by mid-day sunlight, others hidden in the shadow of ruins. "It never was," she breathed. "I think I always knew that."

Like a bolt of lightning, a new idea filled Ave's mind. Words came to her all at once, each with the sound of chiming bells. Her face flushed, her eyes filled once more with tears, and she spoke the poem that had arrived like magic—eloquent and fully formed—in her heart.

In Elysium is a sign,
That every cup is full,

Every angel divine.

Does heavenly love grow
In the field of *eidos*?
Does your idea
Deny my love?

Perfect ideas are
Perfectly miscible.
They are not proud,
They take no space,
Breathe no air,
Perfectly fill,
But never crowd.

A metaphor of Heaven
Is an ever-filled vessel.
Your cup may be full,
But my love yet fits
In your endless heart,
Your boundless soul.

Ave opened eyes she had not realized were closed and looked out, smiling upon Bro and the city of skolves and ruin. *We will find a way.*

A sharp report of thunder shook the tower. Then another and another.

What was that?

A shadow darkened the window. Thunder detonated again, close by now. A sheet of lightning staggered across the open window, blinding Ave, its sound like a knife in her ears. The tower shook violently. Chunks of rock tumbled past the window.

Ave jumped up and incautiously stuck her head out just in time to see the black, roiling thunder cloud reach down toward the tower like a vast, spinning claw.

"Oh knights! I've killed us! My poem has brought Nimrheal."

Bro joined her at the window. He looked down and pointed at the skolves, who were milling in a frenzy.

"No, Ave," he said, wonder in his voice, "you've done something the rest of us never could. You've had an original thought, something our certainty won't allow."

Ave opened her hands in confusion. "We are about to *die,* Bro."

The big man's palsied face tried for a smile and failed like a shattered mirror. "Skolves fear Nimrheal too," he said. "The demon kills whoever it finds." He saw her look of confusion and added, "This is our chance to get the Treaty."

~

"Which way?" shouted Bro from the open patio, forty feet off the ground, second floor from the top. Skolves churned in a mass below. There were several abandoned buildings between them and the Steel Castle, plus an open square, all full of the animals. Bro and Ave had used the uncertain stonework of a fallen aqueduct, still partially suspended, to move from their former perch to this building and had hoped to avoid the skolves until the last moment. But the skolves remained as thick as a sea.

Where is Nimrheal?

Thunder shook them. Winds buffeted them like shield strikes. The skolves were howling in terror. Thousands of their high-pitched voices fought with the sound of the storm.

"The stairs?" Ave said. The wide, rubble-filled stairway would definitely take them down to the crowd of skolves and probably to their deaths. Twenty or more feet of empty air distant, the walls of the next building. A cracked, stained-glass window split, staggering light into eight colors ten feet below.

A bifurcating flash of lightning hit the side of their building only paces away. Ave felt a sharp jolt and saw, through half-paralyzed eyes, electricity arc like angel's white fire off the rings of Bro's mail.

A sound of screaming filled Ave's ears. *Bro!*

No. Bro wouldn't scream.

Ave fought to control her fluttering eyelids and looked behind Bro. A smoky black mass roiled there, filtering like black poison from the vast space of the funnel cloud, rotating like unreason on perception. A sound like boiling oil, tortured lambs, and angry bulls emanated from the seething, revolving conflagration. A spear materialized, swinging from a too-long arm, rotating with the cloud. The limb was made of smoke or gray bone, dark cloth or unsubstantiated nightmare—and it vibrated as it turned—hurting Ave's eyes, making her viscerally ill.

"Nimrheal!" Ave shouted, pointing.

Bro's sword was still in its sheath at his back, but the big man did not try for it. He unhesitatingly shot forward, cracking cobble with each step, before the evil cloud could wholly manifest, flying on long, thick legs past Ave, to the edge of the stone patio and into the air.

She followed him without hesitation. There was nowhere else to go.

Nimrheal came into being—fully—thunderingly—with a noise to split sanity and a form to annihilate vision.

Ave never saw that appalling moment. She was dropping through the air, paces behind Bro, who smashed through the stained-glass window of the adjacent building, caught both legs on the stone rim, and tumbled inside. Ave pulled her legs into a tuck and rolled through the opening, colliding with Bro's grotesquely oversized back. Her sword hilt, sticking out of its sheath, slammed into her ribs painfully in the roll, but she sprang to her feet with a force of will begotten from the knowledge that death had arrived.

A flash of splitting light through broken glass and the too-close, teeth-rattling shaking of thunder told them that lightning had struck again. Close by.

"Up!" Ave said to Bro, tugging on his monolithic arms. "Forward!" she shouted pulling him into motion. Her eyes darted. Lightning struck again, and an invisible, electric paralysis jumped through the air, faster than awareness, coming and going like a blow to the mind.

"Down!" she said against the howl of wind and rain and skolves, when she spied a set of stairs. Feet blurring across two steps at a time, smashing though a fallen painting, jumping the last fifteen feet.

Instinct made Ave draw her sword and turn the instant her feet hit the hard, broken stone of the landing. A black spear thrust at her face from out of the darkness. All her strength and good fortune combined to push the impossible weight of it just outside her radius. Screams and the sounds of boiling, misplaced energy assaulted her ears.

Whatever Nimrheal was, it moved without stepping, sliding eerily across space, unbound by reality, collapsing the spacetime between life and death.

Bro's massive sword cut the air and bent the spear in a terrific concussion. The black lance fell from space, marred, abandoned. A dark, shrouded claw reached out of the darkness, up toward hell, for new weapons.

"Run!" Ave roared.

Down another flight of stairs, across a wide, paper-strewn hallway, one oversized cover page revealing in big letters the bolded words:

"Remember Engevelen, nation of the righteous."

Below, in far smaller lettering, it read:

"We do what is right."

A blast of lightning and another round of thunder propelled an explosion of pages into the unquiet air.

A page with the words, **"Keep in good trim"** fluttered past Ave's eyes as she smashed through double oaken doors into the blasting winds and darkness of the day.

Five steps from the door, she hit skolves, decapitating one and bulling into another. An instant later, Bro smashed into them, just as tall and heavy as they, his sword swinging in a blur. Blood, raindrops, severed paws, and green viscera detonated from the path of his blade.

The ozone-saturated air reeked also of rot.

Lightning struck again, directly in front of Bro, and Nimrheal boiled into existence, its spear skewering a skolve, its ghastly screams silencing—finally—the howls of the beasts.

The rain fell heavy, but for an instant no being moved.

Nimrheal, a shade of ugly unreality.

Bro, paused in mid-swing of his enormous sword.

Ave, about to shout something.

The skolves, fixed in place with swords, bars, pitchforks, and axes in their long paws.

The eerie moment passed, and violent motion resumed as suddenly as it had stopped. Nimrheal blurred, a moving wave of death and a raw supernal force chewing through the skolves. Standing on some fortunate amphidromic point, Ave and Bro were untouched. Knots of skolves seemed to revolve in one direction to flee from Nimrheal. Some of these collided with each other and fought. Many of them dropped their weapons and reverted to claws. Other knots revolved in the other direction and attacked the demon, feeding its blurring black spear and fueling the flight of new blood and limbs and heads into the air.

Other skolves crouched on paws and knees, their long snouts pressed voluntarily down into broken rock.

"Let's go," said Bro, charging away from the carnage, dodging a tumbleweed of battling skolves. Ave had already been in motion before he spoke, leaping some who rolled in rubble, slashing at others, careening through the storm and the unpredictability of events. She hurdled an overturned cart and emerged from the debris field of a fallen tower into the square before the Steel Castle.

Ave locked swords with an unusually large skolve and held the beast for an instant before Bro annihilated it with a ferocious overhand swing and a barreling run through the parting remnants of what was left, turning him red and blue from the spray and viscera. He stumbled, spinning, and was passed by Ave.

Rolling thunder shook the ground, raised a haze of dust, and rattled teeth. Screams and howls erupted close behind. A roiling, boiling disruption cut the air, a scream without words, a rage against reason. Cold fear washed through Ave. She turned her head and saw

Bro shift to receive Nimrheal's black spear in his back. It had been aimed at her.

He grunted and skidded across wet pebbles, falling, sword flying with a rude clang. Rings of shattered chainmail tinkled as they tumbled gracefully across stone—freed from their coat, having failed to protect the big man—rolling through rainwater to some new fate.

Without thought or hesitation, Ave turned to help Bro, to face Nimrheal, to die.

The dark, malformed cloud seethed ten yards away, pausing on the threshold of her death as if evaluating her. A moment of stillness, and a long, clawed hand reached upward once more to hell.

"Go!" Bro wheezed, trembling on two oaken legs and one shaking arm, trying to stand with the tip of an eight-foot spear protruding from one of his massive pecs.

An ugly mass of skolves struck Nimrheal with a sound like tortured metal, carrying it instantly away, behind a massive stone.

"Hold still," said Ave, yanking the spear out of Bro's back.

Blood shot grotesquely from both sides of his body, but he retrieved his sword, stood fully and said, "Thank you. That thorn was beginning to irritate me."

Ave ran toward the open doors of the Steel Castle, turning to watch Bro, praying he could keep up, slamming the heavy door behind him as he passed. The sounds of screams, howls, thunder, and roaring followed them into the church.

Sliding across the polished stone of the interior felt like entering cool water after the rubble of the streets. Ave looked up at the great sword of the Methueyn Treaty. It hung there, high above, point facing down. Five hundred pounds of unearthly metal in a position of utmost potential.

A massive thump against the hinges of the right door told of an inexorable force just missing some awful expression. "The stairs!" shouted Ave. "You first, Bro."

Bro's face spasmed. He was as pale as death. He slowly shook his massive head: "You know we don't put the biggest person first up narrow stairs. Lead the way, Ave."

Up four turns, and Bro was a turn behind. Up another two turns and something entered the choking, tight, steep stairs below.

A metallic wash sounded behind Ave.

"My chainmail fell away," said Bro. "Most of what was left."

A howl reverberated up the stairs.

"Come on!" shouted Ave.

Bro labored up, caught Ave, turned, and peered around a corner. "They're coming," he said, trying to find a way to draw his huge sword in the confined tube of stone and stairs. Ave helped him work it out, and he stabbed down with it into the face of a skolve, using it like a spear down the inner turning of the well.

"That jammed them up," he said, and labored upward, huffing and wheezing, slow and slower.

Ave pulled on his torn tabard, trying to haul him up, but with each turn he became slower and heavier, his voice lower and deader. But he kept talking, talking like he never had before.

"I thought skolves would do, you know," he whispered. "I thought they might eventually satisfy him."

"So?" Ave said

"Disrupt him," he laughed weakly, using a hand to help himself up the stairs. "You don't know. I forget almost no one does. Nimrheal will keep coming back until it kills *someone*. Usually a lot of someones." He now used both hands to help himself climb. "But if you hit Nimrheal hard enough. If you hurt it, disrupt it, and if it has made its kill already, it goes."

I did not know that. How does he?

Instead of asking this, Ave pulled harder on his tabard. "Shut up and climb."

"But skolves don't seem to count."

A panicked howl rose up just as they mounted the final landing. A howl followed by a boiling, an inexplicable screaming.

Nimrheal is on the stairs.

The great sword of the Methueyn Treaty hung just out of sight, below the edge of the stone circle. It was held by fist-thick rope, tied to the hilt and secured around and around a metal bar. The rest of the rope was flaked out in a neat pile. Ave looked down at the hilt, six feet below.

What now?

"Get onto it," Bro said, examining the loops of brown rope. His great sword was gone. Abandoned somewhere on the stairs. The realization made Ave sick.

"What?"

Bro unwrapped one loop. "Stand on it. Grab the rope. I'll lower you and the sword, then follow."

"You can't hold the weight, Bro," Ave protested. "You don't have the empyreal weight." She looked at the sword and the rope. "The sword and my person would be a lot to ask even of Yeyncie. And you're hurt."

Bro's face looked like cow's milk, he was so pale and white now. But he laughed.

Howls, screams, and an awful screeching came from the stairs, close. Closer. "We need a new plan, and soon." Ave whirled, looking for some new solution.

Bro's hands went onto her shoulders. Heavy. "No, this plan works. I can hold you. Climb on to the hilt."

You've never hung! Bro was the longest-standing squire. He'd been there from the start of the war, longer than Ave by far. "You don't have the weight, Bro!" she said angry and scared. The crashing was closer now. "You've never Risen, can't Rise." Her voice dropped, and she said, "You're too weak."

"Jump on," Bro said, smiling.

Not knowing why, except there was little else to do, Ave swung over the lip of stone, hung committed from her fingers, stretched her feet, felt for, and climbed onto the sword hilt, one foot on either side, and held the rope at eye level. The hanging bridge and the floor of the church were far, far below.

“I Rose years ago, Ave, but never took the title,” said Bro, loosening the great looping ties.

“What? Why?”

Bro unwrapped the final turns, and his massive arms bunched. His breath came in gasps. Veins squirmed, his entire pasty white face spasmed, not just the ruined side. “I knew someone would come. Someone who could make the difference. I needed to be there for her.” The stone floor creaked under his feet. “I knew *you* would come.”

“Me?”

“*You* are the infinite vessel,” Bro whispered, and with a twitch of his massive hands let the rope move between his fingers. His voice rose, “An infinite vessel. A full cup that can hold anything.” A gleam erupted in eyes that had seemed dead moments before. “You can think anything, *do* anything!” he shouted, life returning to him.

The sword swung minutely. Ave gripped the massive rope more tightly.

A howl and another simmering scream erupted close by, from the stairwell.

“Fall to earth!” Bro bellowed, louder and deeper than any bell. He opened his hands wider, and the rope burned through his skin, wafting the smoke of human sacrifice into the atmosphere. “Take my love!” he roared, a hurricane of sound. “You are heaven! Save us all, Aveline.” And he smiled again.

Ave dropped away—riding the five-hundred-pound sword of the Methueyn Treaty—with one last memory of the smoke from his hands and the smile on his face, somehow at the end not spasming.

CHAPTER 24
FAMOUS WORDS

"I thought there would be a speech," said Val. "Something rousing, inspiring, and then everyone would agree." She was in the ballroom with Alain Overbree, Liam Laval, Lady Sylvie, and Farrah Harbinger. The Methueyn Knights and various lords and ladies, princes and princesses, had all left.

Alain raised an eyebrow. He had regained much of the poise he had lost after viewing the Harbinger's mind-twisting Heraldry. "I certainly tried to make one," he said. "Well, several, but it was like they had gotten themselves into a pattern of talking and meeting and that had become all they could do."

They didn't want to listen. All the famous words in the world won't matter if no one is listening.

No stranger to the process, Liam Laval shook his head. "When the meeting becomes about your sense of self instead of *good* sense and the problem at hand, nothing is likely to be solved."

"Not that this was an easy decision," said Alain. "No one wanted to admit that we are beaten."

Lady Sylvie's lips were thin and her eyes hard. "Those fools wouldn't admit the sun was hot until they were burned."

"But where is the leadership?" asked Val. With the Elysians proving so hard to steer, leadership never left her mind. *Another group that doesn't like to listen.* Courant's aqueducts had been destroyed, and the city lay in ruins after their mission to retrieve the Harbinger. And yet their action had been called a success, and the Elysian wizards had strutted about like conquering heroes. Christopher and Rebecca were still roaming the palace hallways shouting, "This is what wizards do!"

Distract demons, that is what we wizards seem to do best. Like leading a bull to smash a fence.

"We have been victims of our own history," said Farrah Harbinger, breaking her silence.

Liam and Alain traded a look, perhaps both surprised that the great lady had spoken at all. No one knew how fragile she might be after her ordeal, no matter how straight her back and hard her green eyes. "How so?" asked Liam.

"Jaded sophistication. Process without good will or cooperation. Caught up in the little things like clean streets while the big problems pass us by. In love with social structures but forgetting *why* they were created." She raised her chin. "We have not been a brave people, not for a long time. When was the last time that Nimrheal came to punish a daughter or son of Engevelen? When have we last taken a chance? In our long, slow decline, we have forgotten who we are as a people."

Val felt her breath catch. *Like is to like is to like . . .* But she could not finish the thought, she was too replete with guilt and sadness over her arguments about Acutist and Statician wizardry or her hurry to watch old nobles argue over points of order instead of really listening to her Elysians. Or responding to Green's declaration of love.

And worse, she knew that she had been shown the error of her ways before, but did not know if she would ever be capable of doing things differently next time.

"And besides that," said the Harbinger, "until there was a plan to defeat Skoll and Hati, until the Methueyn Knights finally agreed to work together, nothing else could happen. The plan to build the wall—this Castlereagh Line—was until then infeasible. The demons would have simply smashed it. It is timing more than anything that a leader must look to, especially when reason or principle fail."

"You knew, didn't you?" said Alain with vast admiration. "You knew that Yeyncie was going to sell the plan for you."

Liam Laval's eyes sparkled, and he laughed aloud. "Why make a great and eloquent speech when you can get someone else to do it for you?"

Farrah Harbinger only answered with a hard-edged smile.

At that instant, Green opened the far door and called, "The Methueyn Order is about to leave, Val. They have a few last words for you."

~

AVE RODE the great sword of the Methueyn Treaty toward the distant, polished stone floor of the church and a milling mass of skolves, carried by the gravity of Bro's words.

"Take my love!" he had roared. *"You are heaven! Save us all, Aveline."*

And she had dropped away, or he had risen up. It felt the same to her. A jumble of thoughts coalesced in her mind: the loss of Revenberge, her love, and Bro's love, and the realization that the best of the emotion transcended both desire and space, all her questions of her own value and the overwhelming need to break the old uncooperative and unquestioning pattern of the Methueyn Order, a pattern leading only to thoughtless, changeless failure.

She had long given up on ever Rising, hung from the sword, but now she fell with it to some new death, escape, or state of being.

The image of Nimrheal impaling her friend with its black spear, smashing his colossal chest with it, while the big man's hands burned from the rope passing so quickly through them came to Ave. There was no avoiding it. The demon had been right there, just one turn away from the top of the bell tower and the both of them. She expected at any moment that this act of violence would happen and her speedy passage from the sky to the earth would accelerate to a final, lethal velocity. She knew that this would be the end for both of them.

There was a commotion above, shadows moved quickly. A small sound was heard over the howling, growling knots of terrified skolves. The rope, the sword, and Ave all jumped wildly, the presage to a final release.

There. It has happened.

The fall accelerated. And abruptly came under control again, faster than before, but not in freefall. Ave craned her neck up to see what had happened. She saw something big, blocking the light. *Bro? Slumped on the edge?*

The reflective hard floor was coming fast now, and Val instinctively turned back to it. The volatile mess of skolves had stopped their churning, were watching her rapid descent.

A cracking of thunder shook the Steel Castle. Below Ave, a black, threatening mass congealed. It emitted a sound like burning and evoked a reminiscence of screams.

Nimrheal!

The sword jumped again, and both it and Ave went into freefall, hurtling toward the ground and the ill-formed threat waiting there.

There was an explosion as Ave, riding the sword of the Methueyn Treaty, smashed to earth. She was flung from her perch, tried to roll onto the stone floor, flopped hard against the hilt of her sheathed sword, lost an instant of time to blackness and a flash of pain through her ribs, sprung to her feet, and drew her sword.

"Come on, you bastards!" she roared.

The skolves were crouched low, unmoving.

Nimrheal was gone.

Ave reeled, trying to regain her balance and her breath. The skolves did not move. The Methueyn Treaty had gouged a great wound in the polished stone floor of the church, cutting a into the thick flagstone a foot or more before toppling over. It lay flat on the floor now, thick rope coiled all around it.

She opened her mouth to speak again, then closed it and sheathed her sword. It took several minutes to untie the great sword of the Treaty and heave it up crossways over her shoulders. She walked out of the Steel Castle past the genuflecting skolves with the sword so balanced, saying nothing.

There were no words to be spoken.

~

"So you want our support and this is all you are going to tell us? At the last moment too?" *Really?* Val could barely believe it. Even though she had expected this.

"Halwyn Glace knows," said Yeyncie.

"In a cartographic sense," said Green. Meaning he could not simply teleport to the final destination point. He would have to meet the Methueyn Knights at coordinates he had already been to—ideally the closest point to the final destination—and then jump each line of sight the rest of the way while the knights ran, carrying the Methueyn Bridge.

"You don't want anyone knowing where you are taking it." Val said, not letting it go. *You're that scared of losing it.* "Aren't you afraid of dropping and breaking it?"

Yeyncie laughed. "The Bifrost cannot be broken, Katherine. Not even Michael, if he had his great sword back in his hands, could do it."

That I did not know. "May I examine it?" *It must be unlike anything else in the world.*

"Yes. Give me a moment."

Yeyncie walked out a side door, leaving Green and Val alone.

"Val ..." Green said, hesitating.

She stiffened, fearing more uncomfortable talk about love, even while knowing that she needed to handle the issue better. Even though a part of her wanted to talk about it, say the words, take the next, the necessary, step. Even as another part of her felt stuck, mute, terrified.

"Do you think we're big enough for this?" he said, surprising her. "I mean, the Methueyn Knights are down to just these last seven—okay, eight if you count Volsang, wherever he is—plus those squires they sent to help build the wall. The Renet is gone. Maybe Vercors is coming to help. Maybe not. But we are giving up half of what's left of Engevelen in the hope that we can pull this plan off." He looked down. "Courant is gone, Val. Everyone there is probably dead by now. We just left them."

He's crying. Val could not quite understand the tears at first. She was too task-oriented, too focused. She did not want to consider these feelings. Her priority had always been to move on to the next task, not dwell on what the last one meant.

To dwell on the past is to drown in it.

Val realized that no one had seen the destruction of Courant more thoroughly than Green as he moved the Elysians in and out, one step ahead of Skoll but with an eye on the consequences. He could not have missed seeing—and appreciating—the thousands we had left there to their fate.

So what do I do?

In the heat of the operation, with Green freezing from the cost of teleporting so many times, Val had unhesitatingly hugged him, but she felt frozen now, unable to reach out, unable to speak of her feelings. She knew it was up to her now to take the initiative and cross the distance between them, but all she said was, "We did what we had to do, Halwyn. Without you, none of us could have gotten out of there. Farrah would not have been retrieved and nothing would have been decided. You have given us a chance. So yes, I think we're big enough. I think *you're* big enough. For whatever this is."

Even to Val, this felt banal and inadequate, but Green had stopped crying. Now he met her eyes and held them.

No. Not again. Beating back an internal resistance she did not understand, Val stepped across herself and added, "You're big enough for *me*, Halwyn."

It was little enough, but she felt a tremendous release from saying even that much, almost as if she had jumped off a cliff. She gazed at him, in free fall, loose for one moment from her crushing fears for her country, from her own reticence to speak about feelings, from her continuing inability to break free of her stultifying hide-bound pedantry.

Green' eyes widened. "Val—"

"Here we are!" Sir Michael announced in his usual stentorian tone as he and Yeyncie marched through the door, Yeyncie with a bread loaf-sized crystal in her arms.

"Elysium!" Val exclaimed. She felt the crystal's power even before she opened herself to the empyreal sky. Achieving the sky felt effortless so close to the Bridge. "It's a hole." It was a hole to . . . somewhere . . . She could see the lines of power running virtually unimpeded through the crystal. Whenever Val had opened herself, she could see the connection that the Methueyn Knights, and to a lesser extent the Deladieyr Knights, had with some source of power. They called their source Elysium, but Val had no idea what that really was. And some Knights, she had observed, had a stronger connection than others, but she had no idea why.

But the Methueyn Bridge was something else entirely. If the Knights had a thread-like connection to heaven, the Bifrost was a wide-open door. To . . . somewhere.

What would Huygens have said if he had seen this?

The Bifrost also had a *weight* in the sky, as if all of reality bent toward it, leaning in. "No wonder Nehring Ardgour tried to steal it," she breathed. "What a wizard might do with this in her hands is unimaginable."

Green had moved next to her. He held a hand up as if to shade his eyes from a tremendous light. "And Ardgour is either still trying to steal it, or he is going to do something with it to close off Skoll and Hati's access to *their* power."

"Or both," said Michael. "According to the Vymyty wizard."

"And that is why the location must be kept a secret," said Yeyncie. "If we fail, you Elysians will have to retrieve the Bridge. If we succeed, it may have to stay where it ends up for some time, perhaps months, perhaps years. *Secretly.* There are others besides Ardgour who would like to possess it."

"All that may be true," Val said. "But keeping this a secret, even from our allies, seems like a mistake waiting to happen." She was still unable to let go of the absurdity of the plan. *And I've left too much unsaid already.* "That cannot work forever. Why not just say?"

"You know why," said Yeyncie.

Green stared at Val eyes. His eyes smoldered. "All the important words have already been said."

CHAPTER 25

THE LOST AND THE FOUND

"That sounds bad," said Barbara. "Should we try going around?"

It did sound bad, even if they had expected there would be fighting in Villiers. They were still more than a half mile south of the walls, but they had been hearing the sound of fighting for five minutes or more. It had started as something on the very edge of perception, like a slowly rising wind or as if they were hearing the world with their heads under water. Was it some ghostly re-imagining of the terrifying escape from Courant? Distance diluted the content of it, made it seem illusory. But with every step, the sounds sharpened and became more real. The moment came all too quickly when Dav knew exactly what he was hearing: the howling of skolves, the attenuated screams of massed arrows in flight, the shouts of soldiers.

"But from which direction?" Dav asked.

There may be no safe choice. Anywhere.

Except to turn back and abandon the mission, which was not a question for him or Barbara. Dav had become more and more convinced that Marianne and Darcelle and the rest of their eight had abandoned them back in Argenteul. Bysshe still maintained that they must have been swept up by some other officer, but Dav remembered how tight and nervous they had all become, even after the immediate danger had passed. The flight from Courant may have brought him and Barbara Bysshe together, but it had terrified the others.

They found the nearest officer and volunteered. Volunteered to go anywhere other than with me.

Dav's left hand twitched.

"What did you do back in Charney?" Barbara asked. "You were starting to tell me."

She still wanted the whole story of Charney, of how he had rescued Major Peridot and escaped the ruined city—was owed it, really—just as she was owed the story of his left hand, its strange effect on Skoll, and his botched officers' test. But the unexplained disappearance of their eight had distracted from the telling.

"Well?" she prompted.

"We stayed out of it as long as we could," Dav said. *Because once we were in it, there was no getting out.* "We watched from a vantage point."

"Like that hill?" Barbara said, pointing to the northeast.

"A lot like that." Dav squinted. "But that one looks like it has a small castle up top. You're the captain, captain. Lead on."

They left the broad trading route they had been following and headed toward the hill, very quickly intersecting another roadway that wound up the slope. It was in good condition with numerous recent wagon tracks and other signs of use. A crumbling low stone wall seemed to encircle the plateau near the top of the long rise.

"When are you going to tell me everything, Lieutenant?" Bysshe asked him, marching quickly. "You could have told me at just about any time on the way here."

Dav did not glance at his left hand, did not tempt it to some new betrayal. "Yes," he said.

"Yes?"

"Yes, I could have . . ." Dav trailed off, taking a better look at the stone wall ahead near the summit of the big hill. It was old and not very high, but piles of smaller rocks suggested someone had been working on it recently. "There will be a right time for that story."

She glanced at him with hooded eyes. "Try not to miss it when it comes."

"Hold it right there, potlickers!" shouted a man in a grossly constricted voice. He sounded like he was gargling pebbles.

"Don't you move now," came another voice.

Both Dav and Barbara froze. *This doesn't sound military. At all.*

The second voice continued, "You better not be more deserters coming up here to hide."

"Or come to steal our muffins!" warbled the first speaker.

"What are you talking about? Muffins?" said the second speaker.

"That's what they're baking this afternoon."

"Oh. With butter?"

"Yes, with butter, of course with butter. Now go check these potlickers, Louis!"

"You check 'em!"

"It's your turn, sleeveen."

"Do you want to go again?"

"Go where?"

"Fight, idiot!"

"Again?"

"We're coming up from the south," said Barbara, interrupting this bizarre chatter. "And we aren't after anything but a view down the north side."

"What for?" asked Louis.

"Because we have to travel north."

"North of Villiers?" said cricket voice. "Well come on, then."

Barbara and Dav cautiously approached a gap in the wall, and two old men poked their heads around it. They were both stooped and short, and one of them almost tripped as he stepped out of the shadows.

"I'm Louis," he said, showing a mouth more full of gums than teeth.

"Doog," said the one with the voice like a frog. "We saw you coming, you know." He pointed a thumb back over his shoulder at the castle maybe a hundred yards farther up the hill. "Saw you from the house."

"Come on, Fenris!" called Louis after Barbara and Dav had introduced themselves and shook hands with the old men. Seconds later, a small dog—a puppy—ran from out of the brambles on the house side of the wall and enthusiastically sniffed at Dav and Barbara. Dav petted the dog, bemused, trying to understand what world they had just walked into.

"Come on, you two," said Louis. "We don't got all day, ya know."

This appeared to be ironic. Louis walked slowly and was given to stumbling, possibly due to a drop foot. Dav looked down the wall and noticed another old man, then two old women in bright, floral dresses sitting on chairs behind the wall. One of the ladies had an umbrella propped up against the sun.

Lovely. But weird.

There might have been others farther down the wall, slumped in chairs, or snoozing at their posts, but Dav had trouble imagining what the point was. They were spaced too far apart to be effective as anything but scouts. *What do they think they . . . ?* Then he spotted several loaded crossbows on the top of the wall, though none of the strange geriatric guards were in a position to see anything, let alone shoot.

"We're watching!" announced Doog, noticing Dav's roving eyes. "For when it's time."

"Time?" Dav asked, careful with his tone.

"*Our* time. Time to save all them soldiers down there," answered Louis.

"Villiers was reported as evacuated," said Barbara.

"Ha!" croaked Doog.

"They abandoned us," exclaimed Louis.

"No. Really? I cannot imagine," sputtered Barbara.

"Not old yet, are you, captain?" Doog said knowingly.

"That is an appalling dereliction of duty," declared Barbara, summoning some indignation. "Who was in charge here? I will report them—"

Dav stopped her with a sharp look and a hand on her arm. "Well, we're glad you're here."

"Damned right you are," said Doog. "Come on now, we have someone you need to meet. Then we'll take you around to the breakfast patio. You can watch the battle from there."

As they ambled so very slowly across the plateau, they passed an area of small grass-covered mounds. The mounds were only five or six feet long and about a foot or two high. A few of the mounds were fresher, with patchy, immature grass. *What?*

Dav looked ahead and answered his own question. They were graves. An open one lay just ahead, freshly dug, black dirt and rocks in a ring around it. He could even smell the freshness of it, reminding him of earthworms.

No markings.

Doog's hand went onto Louis's shoulder as they passed the small, open pit.

Dav saw Barbara staring at the open grave and traded a look with her. Neither of them spoke.

The "house," as Doog and Louis called it, was strongly built and looked more like a small castle than an enormous manor house. Dav looked up and caught the edge of some strange structure on the roof. He followed its shadow down into the yard. *That can only be a water reservoir.* The shadow played across four wagons, which must have just arrived, for the horses were still hitched and large sacks were being unloaded.

Participating in this labor were a number of men and women in buttoned white jackets. And four chainmail-armored soldiers in foreign livery.

"These here are Vercors Rangers," said Doog.

Louis crossed his arms with some self-satisfaction and added, "They've just been to the north."

Barbara's eyes widened. "Gentlemen," she said, "I think we could use your help."

~

"So you want to cross north," said Doog lounging in his chair like some shrunken king. The two strange old men had made their introductions to the Vercors Rangers and the staff of the house and guided them all with exaggerated munificence to the patio. And the muffins. "Through *that*," he pointed past the edge of the patio, down the hill, to the north walls of Villiers and the furious battle being fought there, "to go find some magical weapon to slay some new devil?"

"Because some wizard said you should?" said Louis, sitting beside him, gumming down a muffin. "Did she have a pointy hat?"

No, but some would say she had a sharp eye.

Louis was not done yet. "What, were you both born yesterday? Whaddya think, Reyn, are these two outa their potlickin' minds?"

Reyn said nothing. Sitting at their ease on the raised patio of the house on the hill, eating fresh-baked muffins, the story did sound unlikely. Except that Dav had *seen* it through Farrah's eyes. He had seen the destruction of his entire country, his people, everything and everyone he knew, and north was the only direction he had been given that might help.

There is something familiar here. Have I seen this place? From above? Dav scanned the view down to the town proper, then brought his gaze back to the low wall encircling the house. *I have seen this!*

"We have little choice in the matter," said Barbara. "Lieutenant, help me here."

Dav remembered Farrah's eyes, the hill, an old man with a giant sword. "We actually have *no* choice," he breathed. "No choice at all."

Barbara frowned at him, expecting more. When her stern look produced nothing further, she turned back to Reyn. "That is . . . correct. But from what mister, uh, Doog and Louis have said about you, we could use your help. Our eight was . . . lost on the way. Will you guide us?"

Reyn was not saying much. He was outside the command structure of Engevelen, and Dav could only guess what strange set of circumstances had led to him unloading sacks of flour at a home for old people. The sergeant had listened silently, expressionlessly, to Barbara and Dav, and whatever he thought of their story was a mystery to everyone but himself. The quiet man touched his well-trimmed goatee and stared off into the distance.

"We were practically *in* Chamberry, Sergeant," said Dylan, the ranger with the dubious-looking blackened teeth and black ring marks on his face.

"We should help, Reyn," said Aron, who also appeared to have had a hard time of it. His movements were stiff, and his voice was the barest whisper. Bound ribs and shallow breaths will do that. "What else are we going to do once the wagons are unloaded?"

Dav stood up and walked to the edge of the patio. He placed his hands on the low stone wall there. *I remember . . . singing.* He turned back to face the house and the strange collection of old people and soldiers that had assembled there. "This is the place, Captain," he said to Barbara. "In the Heraldry. The final battle happens right here."

"Are you sure?" she said. "I-I didn't see the end."

"It's here. Right here." He pointed at the flagstone floor of the patio. "*Here*. Not down there."

"This fight," warbled Doog, "is it a big one?"

Dav remembered the uncountable bodies, the endless rubble, Skoll and Hati, and hesitated. *Did I see* them*? See them dead?* He could not be sure. He had not known them when he had seen through Farrah's eyes, so he would not have noted the two old men among all the others. Finally, he said, "I didn't see everything that happened, but it is terrible."

Instead of a groan at this awful prediction, or any sign of anger or denial, Doog and Louis both started laughing and clapping their hands. This performance went on for some time while the others gaped, unsure how to react.

Finally, Reyn shook his head at the two old men and stood up. "Let's go Aron, Dylan, Tudor." He turned his attention to Dav and Barbara. "The rest of my eight are down there." He pointed at the battle. "It's past time to gather them up."

Barbara stood and straightened her tunic with a professional air. "Thank you for believing us, Sergeant."

"I don't know what I *believe*," Reyn said, still looking down the hill. The sounds of the fighting drifted up on stray winds. Streaks of arrow shot and bolts blurred an arc degree of sky. A gray smudge of skolves pressed up against the distant walls. "But something has to change."

Doog and Louis and a big man in a dirty white orderly's jacket—Roland—walked them to the north edge of the plateau.

"Keep an eye out for one of ours," said Roland. "His name is Mick. Send him back up here if you can."

"Mick's fine," snapped Doog, scowling at Roland. "But when you see him, tell him we are all set."

"We will, uh, do that," said Barbara confused but trying to be polite.

When they passed through the wall, Roland, Doog, and Louis stopped. Dav paused with them after everyone took their leave. It felt like there was something he had failed to fully appreciate. Dav decided to plumb the mystery by saying, "I am sorry I told you that the fight may be coming up here to you on the house."

"What? Don't be sorry. That news is . . . a relief," said Louis. He rubbed his hip, then his knee. "I really didn't want to have to *walk* to any final battles."

Dav stared at him, not sure whether he should laugh. Roland was staring too.

"You don't get it, do you?" said Doog. "Neither of you."

Roland just stared back, mute, but Dav sighed and said, "I would like to."

Doog's smile reflected the sunlight. "We can make a difference."

"One last time," said Louis.

"First time for you," quipped Doog.

Louis visibly stopped himself from firing back at his friend and returned to Dav. "You can't know what it is like."

"What *what* is like?"

"To be ignored. Considered useless or broken." He looked back at the house and nearly fell. "To have no hope of better days or more generous opinions."

Doog shuffled over to his friend and put an arm around his shoulders, "To be put away and forgotten."

Dav thought about his secret and the reaction that had followed his strange written test results. He thought that maybe he did understand.

~

VILLIERS WAS LESS DAMAGED than Dav had expected. There were plenty of ruined buildings and rubble-strewn streets, but the damage was scattered and random seeming—a pattern indicating the presence of either Skoll or Hati at one time—but for a city on the front lines, it was remarkably well organized. Numerous side streets were barricaded and manned by small groups of soldiers. Various eights moved about in the back streets, carrying equipment to and from small, well-distributed depots. A few such groups had passed by, transporting equipment up the hill, as Dav and Barbara were descending it.

The neatness and good order did not extend to what Dav and Barbara heard as they neared the other side of the city. The sounds of battle grew louder and sharper with each step they took toward the north wall. The sounds grew stranger too. At one point, Dav was sure he heard a shout of, "Handsaw! Handsaw! Handsaw!" which made no rational sense on a battlefront.

"Was that *scofflaw*?" Barbara asked as Sergeant Reyn procured a new sword and sheathe from a tent, explaining that he had loaned his to the missing old man, Mick.

"What is an old man doing down here, anyway?" she asked as Reyn belted the sheathe. "They should never have let him down here, whoever he is."

The howling cries of skolves answered her, followed by a series of shrieking arrow storms. Reyn said nothing. He merely turned and marched on.

As they proceeded through Villiers, Dav became aware of a stench like rotting meat. He could not see it, but as the awful smell intensified, he saw that they were walking into a wall of smoke, each step taking them deeper in and closer to the source of the wretched odor.

"Outlaw! Handsaw! Scofflaw!" came the shouts again, much louder now, carried by hundreds of voices on a tide of sound in between howls and the gusts from massed arrow fire.

"What *is* that?" Barbara said.

"I think I can hazard a guess," said Reyn in a laconic tone. "Quiet now," he added looking at Dafydd and Aron, both of whom seemed about to say something. "The wall is just around the corner, and we don't know what we are going to see."

They rounded a high barricade of rubble and saw the wall and the north gate directly ahead. The top of the wall was lined with soldiers standing on the narrow ledge, some with pikes, or spears, others with crossbows or longbows. Here the shouts coalesced into some greater sense, if not greater order.

"Shoot on command, dammit!" said a heavyset man in chain. "Now: load. Aim. Shoot." A gust of projectiles flew. The gates bulged. The crossbar cracked, and a tangle of men and women pushed desperately against it, trying to hold it closed. Pikemen and spearmen thrust downward over the wall, cursing, screaming, one or two falling back, clutching at a face, arm, or throat, choking on blood or pain or fear. Or all three.

A skolve abruptly appeared atop the wall, sweeping soldiers off with a long-handled hammer. Two more joined it.

"Grandpa! Help!" someone screamed. A woman or a young man.

A soldier in plate armor jumped up from the ledge and ran along the wall, leaping over pikes and crossbows, bringing her sword to bear on the skolves. The enormous sledgehammer swept her off too. She flew in a jumble out of sight, onto the north side of the wall and presumably into the massed ranks of skolves there.

"Grandpa!"

By common, unspoken consent, no one in Dav and Barbara's group moved. The situation was too chaotic to know what should be done. They watched in horrid, shocked fascination.

"Grandpa! Grandpa! Grandpa!" came the chant.

Grandpa? The call made no sense to Dav.

Until a huge figure charged suddenly out of the mass of soldiers manning the gates, moving faster than a man should, his long white hair streaming behind him. *Grandpa* wore a chainmail overcoat that was not belted down properly, and the metal fluttered and chimed as he ran. He wielded a massive, five-foot-long blade like a spear, and his footfalls sounded strangely loud. Other soldiers scrambled out of his way like they would avoid a charging horse. He sped past Dav and then abruptly turned, leaping improbably onto the ledge and then the wall, straight into the knot of skolves, and began laying furiously about him with the two-handed sword.

A shock of memory buckled Dav's knees. *I know him!* It was the old man from Farrah Harbinger's heraldic vision.

"Dav!" Barbara shouted.

But Dav was already halfway to the wall. He had not decided to move, had not even known he was moving, until he found himself closing in on the old man—grandpa.

A heavy bolt shot like a half-seen bird in flight over grandpa's shoulder and split the forehead of the hammer-bearing skolve. The old man kicked it in the chest, sending it howling off the wall. Another skolve hit him ferociously in the shoulder with its rusty sword. There was a sharp, loud, metallic impact, an explosion of chain links, and grandpa staggered back, windmilling, one arm coming off the hilt of his sword, barely managing to keep his footing on the wall.

The beast seemed confused. Its blow should have sliced the old man's arm off, not just sent him reeling. And then it did something Dav had never seen a skolve do. It hesitated. It reconsidered. And in that instant of wariness, Grandpa regained his balance, shook his head clear, and returned a lightning-fast, two-handed stroke that whistled the air before cutting through the skolve's long jaw, detonating a line of long teeth into a yellow explosion that just preceded the blade embedding itself in the back of the creature's ugly, elongate skull.

The last skolve had been impaled by three pikemen and thrust backward off the wall before it could come to the aid of its fellow, so the old man shook his sword free of the other skolve's twitching body and kicked the carcass off the wall. Then, to Dav's astonishment, he followed the dead skolves. He leapt off the wall and disappeared out of sight on the other side.

Raise up my shield, sun's light will warm!
Raise up my maul, my scroll and pen!

The old words reverberated in Dav's mind, and he felt his left hand coming up, his eyelids fluttering. A fit was starting.

No!

He made a fist of the offending hand, biting down on the moment, and opened both eyes wide, needing to see what happened next in this present moment rather than what might occur in some remote future. Breaking out of the fit felt like bending a strong green sapling, but Dav pushed through and found himself rushing up the steps of the wall. Instinct told him that he *had* to see what was happening on the other side. He shouldered his way through a group of gaping soldiers to see grandpa standing overtop the plate-armored knight who had been knocked off the wall a few seconds before. They were surrounded by a seething mass of skolves.

"Load!" roared the thickly built, chain mail-clad man that Dav had seen earlier. He was now standing just ten paces down the wall. "Aim! Loose!"

A high-pitched scream of bolts shot from close range into the skolves.

"Archers, draw! Aim! Loose! Crossbows, quick now, load! Aim! Loose! Keep firing! Archers, draw! Aim! Loose!"

Volley after volley of arrows and bolts shot into the mass of skolves, each timed release sounding like the gust of an unimaginably powerful and vengeful wind. Some of the missiles missed, a few failed to penetrate the tough hides of the large, stringy animals, but some bit deep, and every hit from such a close distance clearly hurt. Skolves staggered under the heavy fire, a few collapsed with four or five arrows or bolts sticking into them.

Ignoring all the arrows in the air, the old man kept station over his fallen friend. As Dav watched, he swung his two-handed sword savagely at a skolve that lunged out of the pack toward him, hitting its raised axe handle once, twice, three times, until the weapon broke in half and the skolve staggered back.

"Grandpa! Grandpa! Grandpa!" shouted a group of spearmen.

"Come on, bastards!" roared Grandpa.

The skolves abruptly melted away. Arrow fire followed them, but as soon as they were forty yards away, the heavyset commander called out, "Let 'em go. Cease fire. Save your arrows."

"That's *him*," said Barbara from beside Dav. "From the Lady Harbinger's vision."

Grandpa was on one knee beside the plate-armored woman, talking gently to her. The gate had opened, and medics were trotting out with a stretcher.

"That's Mick, or so he claims," said Reyn, climbing onto the wall beside Dav and Barbara. "From the house on the hill."

"A remarkable man," said Barbara.

Reyn glanced toward her and nodded. "Heaven-sent, some would say."

"Though he'll be sent back to heaven soon if he keeps acting that way," said a woman in Vercors Ranger livery and a corporal's marks on her shoulder.

"Did you see the shot I made?" shouted a soldier from behind them, also dressed in Vercors Ranger livery. "Did you see, Reyn?" He was holding a remarkably heavy style of crossbow—an arbalest, Dav realized. "I got that one on the wall right between the eyes."

Reyn sighed. "Come along, Captain Bysshe and Lieutenant Davignon. That is private Eurion and Corporal Alwena. The rest of my eight will be nearby." He looked back to the tree line where the skolves had disappeared. "Now may be a good time to talk over your mission."

CHAPTER 26

OF THE ESSENCE

"We need to bear westward," said Corporal Alwena. She was the only Vercors Ranger besides Sergeant Reyn, Dav had learned, who lacked a nickname. "There's still too many coming from the east."

"Further west still?" asked Dav.

"Time is of the essence," added Barbara.

"Getting there *alive* is of the essence," retorted Alwena dryly. She had a shrewd look about her and was not in the least impressed by Barbara or Dav's higher rank.

"See the matting of the underbrush," said Dill earnestly. The forest looked like herds of cattle had recently moved through. The grasses were matted, smaller brush was crushed, and the bark had even been rubbed off trees. There was also a distinct odor. Of rotted meat. "A big group of skolves moved through here. Very recently." His blackened teeth somewhat detracted from the gravitas of his tone. He held up the thin broken limb of a sapling for Barbara to see and said, "This is freshly broken."

Dav looked up through the trees, trying to gauge the time. He knew it was a foolish gesture in a quest embarked on as much from blind faith and hope as from the horrors that Farrah's green eye had shown him. *I have no idea how much time we have.* Very little, he suspected.

"You can't get killed fast enough," whispered Alwena as she slipped by him, holding her heavy spear point up to the sky. She released the haft with one hand and pointed toward her head. "*Think* about it."

"West," said Reyn. "Take point, Eurion."

Eurion held his arbalest in both arms as he went by, following a game trail quite adroitly through the woods despite the weight he carried

"Trust us," said Dafydd from behind. "This is what we do."

Slow, quiet, and nimble seemed to be the Vercors Rangers' specialty. As goofy as they had been at the house on the hill and in Villiers proper, and as disreputable looking as Dill's face and Dafydd's head made the whole group look, it was difficult to argue with their seamless efficiency in the bush. Their movements were very different from Dav and Barbara's recent nighttime flight out of Courant. That had been a mad, terrifying rush from hugel mound to hugel mound, secretly guided by Dav's left-handed vision and punctuated by gruesome encounters with skolves. In contrast, the Vercors Rangers, minus only Aron, who had been left behind because of his injuries, were more like a group of comedic foxes twisting silently through the underbrush, sneaking up on the chickens.

It was morning, and the sun's light filtered gently through the pastureland trees. Dav experienced the pleasant delusion that they were in no danger at all, that the care and attention of the rangers would see them to Chamberry without incident.

It will seem safe right up until the moment that it isn't.

Eurion called a halt at the edge of the forest. They gathered close, still undercover, taking a knee, looking out upon the open terrain. "It's pasture and crop all the way to Guijaumet," he said pointing past the last bushes to the low amber wave of a mature barley crop.

Alwena had pulled out a map. "We are going to miss the hills this time. Too far west."

"Not much cover," said Dill.

"Wind from the north," whispered Dafydd.

"These two wanted fast, let's do fast," said Alwena.

"Skive and dive?" asked Dill, terms of art that Dav had never heard.

"Hmm," said Reyn.

"Run like one?" whispered Dafydd, continuing the rapid-fire patter.

Alwena shrugged and said, "Meh."

"Pack and stack?" suggested Dafydd.

Reyn shook his head unenthusiastically. Dav narrowed his eyes suspiciously at the taciturn sergeant, looking for a punchline.

"Scoot and shoot?" asked Eurion.

"With just one arbalest?" sneered Alwena, less sanguine. "And no enemy in sight?"

Reyn looked at his troops, stilling them. After a moment's silence he said, "Ok. Low and go."

"What do we need to know?" asked Barbara, unfazed. Dav suppressed his amazement at how the strict up-and-down captain was adapting to the unconventional soldiers from Vercors and their eccentricities. But then he remembered that she was the only one who had come through the hugel fields and not abandoned him or the mission. She had proved herself robust rather than brittle, with unexpected depths. He also knew that he still owed her a story, and a part of him wished that they could sit down for tea together outside Harbinger Hall in Courant and he could tell it to her. Despite the appeal of that fantasy, especially while crouched in the bushes with enemies about, he knew the time was still wrong.

"Don't run," said Alwena.

"One foot always on the ground," said Dill.

"But fast," said Dafydd.

"And mix up your cadence," added Eurion. "You aren't marching in sync. Keep it quiet in case there are ears to the ground."

"Ready?" said Reyn, looking everyone in the eyes in turn. "Okay, go then."

They shot out into the morning sunlight, one at a time, as fast and quietly as they could move with packs, weapons, and sturdy boots.

As Dav moved quickly across pastures, fields, and between abandoned towers and stone houses, he continued to wonder if the rangers were putting one over on him and Barbara with their rhyming maneuvers. If so, Reyn's stoic face had not given the joke away.

There was not much to laugh about as they passed silently through a silent, empty country. The consequence and meaning of what they were trying to do were inescapable. They were moving over the bones of what had once been civilized, productive land. Even if Dav did not understand what the One True Devil was, or the nature of the weapon he was searching for, its importance was reinforced by every empty house and castle they passed, every unharvested field, every untended garden gone to seed.

They were ghosts in an empty land, interacting with nothing and no one.

~

"So ... this weapon is underneath that tower?" said Alwena. "The one in the lake?"

Dav took a breath and said, "That is my understanding."

"That's not right," said Dill, showing a blackened tooth. "The lake has risen, *and* the tower fell down. We saw Hati do it when he smashed through here."

"Thought it was great fun," said Dafydd.

"It's flooded," said Barbara, unbelieving, her eyes wide in a rare, unguarded moment.

"It's not *that* flooded," said Eurion. He pointed toward the ruin. "Look, most of the rubble is above water."

"Let's just go down and take a look," said Dav. They were on the apron of a hill that rose to the east. Looking down on the ruined city of Chamberry, he could see that it had once been a beautiful architectural achievement, but also—worryingly—that it was getting late in the day.

Time is of the essence.

But Dav had no idea how much time he had, when the One True Devil would arrive, when Skoll and Hati would join the skolves and crush Villiers, or what would happen to everyone in the house on the hill.

This is a lot worse than Villiers. Chamberry had literally been levelled from the outside in. Villiers had taken damage, it had been sporadic, and someone—citizens, most likely, before they were evacuated—had cleaned up much of the rubble, but Chamberry was like an overcooked pie that had been hurled onto sharp rocks.

"Chamberry was at one time our capital," whispered Barbara when they paused to drink from their wineskins next to a pile of rubble that looked like some colossal mushroom stamped on by a giant, booted foot. "That was back before the first fall."

"It doesn't seem big enough," replied Dav.

"I guess that's why they moved it."

"Have you been here before?" he asked her.

Barbara looked around, saw that none of the rangers were watching, and touched the back of Dav's head for a long moment, then said, "I was too young to remember it well. But I have a dim recollection of the lake and the library. It was a beautiful place, I remember that much." She removed her hand and looked up at the darkening sky. "Come on, let's go before we lose the light."

A few blocks later, they found the engineered lake, now choked with large blocks of stone, the displaced pieces of a destroyed civilization. So much rubble had been hurled into the shallow water that it had risen over its banks and inundated the surrounding buildings.

"There's a high point over this way," reported Dill, leading them in a hook around the water.

Dav recognized the bones of the tall tower he had seen in Farrah Harbinger's Heraldry, scattered like the wax of a violently blown candle. "We have to get in there," he said. "Near its base."

Dill found a high, jumbled path through the mess of rock. It kept them above the water, but the going was rough and treacherous. “Watch your knights-damned ankles,” Alwena said sharply after she twisted hers.

Pieces of the tower were still intact. Other sections were broken open and filled with dark, dank water. Dave could not find any way to get inside what remained of the edifice. Then he remembered the system of redundant cisterns in Courant and the image of a twisted route through the old underground water reservoirs that he had seen reflected in Farrah’s eye.

Where would the middle of the square have been? In the opposite direction of the lake!

“What?” asked Barbara as Dav began to back up and turn around.

He motioned for her to follow him.

There!

He found a grate. It was rusted iron, the edge just visible among small rocks and broken timber.

“It’s here,” he said, flinging the detritus away.

Barbara’s expression was skeptical, but she helped dig the grate free. Moments later, the rangers gathered round, staring at the grate, now fully uncovered.

“Help me!” Dav shouted, jamming his fingers into it. Dafydd and Dill knocked their heads together in their haste to reach the spot, but even with the three of them crowding in and pulling, the grate would not move.

“Hit it with a rock,” said Eurion from the sidelines.

“Or both your heads,” said Alwena.

Dav found a head-sized rock and smashed it against the grate, then he and Dafydd and Dill tried again. It shifted. The old iron was blotched and corroded with rust, but it still weighed well over a hundred pounds. They heaved it noisily to the side.

A dark opening was revealed. The sheen of black water could be seen only a few feet below.

“And how is this watery tomb supposed to help us?” asked Alwena, shoving her way to the edge and peering down into the depths.

“It is a system of cisterns,” Dav explained. “In the style of the old cities of Engevelen. From before the aqueducts. Runoff would be collected in every city square and pumped to fountains and wells.”

“But they have a lake!” exclaimed Dill, arms raised in a dramatic show of perplexity.

Barbara looked over her shoulder at the water behind them. “This system was built before the creation of the lake.”

“This is the way,” said Dav. “Through the old waterworks.”

“That’s knights-damned crazy,” said Eurion.

“I’m not going in there,” said Dafydd.

“Me neither,” said Dill.

Reyn looked into the dark void. “No one is.”

Dav stood up, Barbara’s eyes following him. She was the perfect officer of Engevelen. Professional. Opaque. What they had shared in Argenteul was nowhere on display, except in how her eyes found his. He smiled fractionally at her, unbelted his sword, and pulled his tunic off, followed by his chainmail.

She said nothing, though her eyes did not leave him.

“Seriously?” said Alwena.

Dav undressed to his pants and sat down, astride the hole. He looked from person to person. Barbara’s expression was opaque, and Reyn’s face was also unreadable, but the rest of his team were shaking their heads.

“I never thanked you for coming,” Dav said, addressing the rangers. They had miraculously avoided the thousands of skolves north of Villiers, but he knew that the mission remained terrifically risky, indeed very likely suicidal. “Why did you decide to help us?”

“Morbid curiosity,” said Alwena, grinning.

“To keep clear of the wizards,” said Dill. “Look at my teeth. *They* did this.”

“Never mind your teeth. She peed on my face,” said Dafydd.

Barbara's face lost its normal professional detachment. "A wizard peed on you?"

"No!" Dafydd replied. He pointed at Alwena and said, "*She* did. But it was *because* of a wizard."

Alwena shrugged. "I do what I have to do."

Reyn shook his head, "Don't bother," he told Barbara, "It's a long story and well past its season."

Dav looked into the dark space below him, then back at his crew. "Well, thank you all, whatever your reasons. I *have* to try this."

Barbara's face was unreadable again. She said, "You won't be able to see anything down there. And you will very likely drown. How is that going to help any of us?" She gestured peremptorily. "Come on. Get your gear back on. I *order* you not to go in there."

"I have to."

"No."

Dav would never have detected the well of emotion behind that simple word had he not shared the experience of Courant with her.

This is the moment. Smiling at Barbara, Dav said, "I think the time has come for me to tell you the story of the Battle of Charney."

CHAPTER 27
ALONE

"No," said Val, "this area *must* be kept clear. If someone wanders aimlessly into this space when Green teleports back, they are going to be killed."

"No one here wanders aimlessly," croaked one of the old men. Doug or Doog or something. A dog stood between his legs, its long furry tail thumping back and forth against them.

"No, *you* farted," shouted another old man bafflingly as he tapped his way with a thick cane at a glacial pace right through the center of the cleared teleportation pad that Val and Green had set up on the patio of the house on the hill.

The commander of Villiers, Major Serres, had suggested this alternate teleportation location when Val and Green had arrived in the town proper, claiming it would not only be safer but an easy rally point if the town was lost. So far, it had been an exercise in frustration. Old men and women wandered about everywhere, underfoot, like slow-moving, slow-witted children, interrupting whatever arrangements Val tried to make with Brigitte Landry, the head of the place, and Roland, her chief attendant.

Before Val could respond to the "farting" comment, Brigitte gently grasped her arm. "Lady Katherine," she said with a calming smile and a soothing tone, "let us just step aside and allow Roland to block off the area."

Roland nodded at Brigitte, distracted. He was in the midst of being scolded by the Doog fellow, his dog, and another, very short old man who could not seem to stand still, mincing his feet again and again as if feeling for the ground.

Brigitte smiled as if everything was fine and walked Val to the wall at the edge of patio, where two elderly women with floral dresses sat at a small table One of the women's long white hair was so thin that Val could see more scalp than hair.

"Would you like a lovely cup of tea?" Brigitte asked. Val opened her mouth to say something very unlovely to this ridiculous invitation, then stopped herself. *My monster is here again.*

She could feel her frustration. The Methueyn Knights had left, running at racehorse speed toward the north. Green was juggling a dozen-too-many tasks, and she had just missed—by one day—a chance to intercept the mysterious Lieutenant Davignon Delatam. She knew where he was going, more or less, but could do nothing about it.

Everything is moving too quickly, and nothing is moving quickly enough. The lack of control was provoking every bad instinct in Val. She knew this. She had made a thorough study of her faults, but in the vice-like pressure of events, knowing them was not enough.

"Yes," she managed to say, holding off the monster. "A cup of tea might do very well."

"I'll be right back," said Brigitte.

"It's such a wonderful day, isn't it?" said one of the ladies at the table. The one with thicker hair.

"I suppose," Val said, frowning, irritated at the banality of the comment.

"And the monsters have stopped attacking too," said the other ancient lady. "Perhaps Mick will come back now. I do worry about him down there."

Val remembered the strangely familiar old soldier she had seen with

Major Serres. His name had been Mick. She had thought he was some old fixture of a sergeant. *They called him Grandpa.* "Grand—Mick lives *here*?"

"Oh yes," said the first lady. "I'm Lady Aurorette," she said. "Names are important."

Val introduced herself and learned that the other old woman was known simply as Carol.

Aurorette said quietly, "Mick isn't his name, you know."

And Grandpa probably isn't either.

"Oh?" Val managed.

"No," said Carol, "It's—"

"Here is your tea, Lady Valcourt," said Brigitte, holding out a fine glass teacup. As Val accepted it, she added, "Mick must remember his own name, ladies. We cannot do it for him."

He's a lunatic. Val restrained herself from speaking the thought. She had heard of the death of the mind before the body, though she knew that most people did not live long enough to suffer that nightmare. She had never seen it, until now. She felt sure that was what had happened to Mick. "He seemed . . . fine."

Brigitte took a sip from her glass mug. "Oh, he is considerably better now that everything else has become so much worse." She thrust her mug toward Doog, who was still arguing with Roland, or possibly trying to help him block off the teleportation area with tables. "All this has given everyone here a purpose."

"What purpose is that?" Val asked. Mick had looked physically strong, but none of the rest did. Far from it. She did not even want to imagine how badly it would go for them when the skolves reached the hill. Lambs to the slaughter.

"For me, it will be tea," said Lady Aurorette brightly. "They are going to move the wounded soldiers up here, and *I* am going to serve them tea." She lowered her voice and dimmed her smile. "Or water. Whatever I can give them that might help."

"Standing watch," said Carol, though she didn't look strong enough to stand anywhere for long.

Brigitte nodded, smiling beatifically. “It doesn’t matter *what* the purpose is. Everyone just has to choose one.”

Delusionally?

“I helped design this place,” said Brigitte. “A central location for the elderly. It seemed like a good idea at the time, but I have since realized that I overlooked something.”

At some point in this conversation, Val’s monster had relaxed. She was more perplexed now than frustrated. “What did you miss?”

“We moved our residents out of the concerns of the world. We isolated them. That was a mistake.”

“Sometimes there is no right answer,” said Lady Aurorette.

Val certainly had no answer to this. *I’ve made my own mistakes.*

“Brigitte,” Val said, curious now about the mentality of these strange old people, “this Heraldry of the Harbinger that I mentioned ...,” she began.

“Captain Bysshe and Lieutenant Davignon spoke of it when they were here.”

Val looked from her to Lady Aurorette and Carol. “It wasn’t a . . . pleasant vision by all accounts. I didn’t see it myself, but I have heard enough. A lot of people are going to die. A lot of people *here*.”

“That’s quite all right, Lady Valcourt,” said Aurorette. “Death is never far away here.”

Carol nodded, her thin hair plastered to a pasty, white skull. “At least we won’t be alone now. When we go to sleep.”

“I USED to count my crimes before going to sleep, you know,” Garragorah said to Halwyn Glace.

“Why?” he asked mildly. Halwyn was just the sort of person that Garragorah loved. They were so easy to fool.

“So I could feel punished without actually *being* punished.”

Marias looked out over the ruin of Aurillon. Judging by the stench of rotted meat and fresh scat everywhere, the skolves had not been gone long. *There are probably some nearby.*

"I created a narrative for myself. You must be aware that we all do this. Construct a story for ourselves about our lives. It's the only way, really, to feel good about one's life, one's choices, mischances, misfortunes, diseases, old age.

"Anything in our lives, good or bad, gets woven into the tapestry. It all happened for a reason, as they say. And that reason takes away, reduces, anyway, our culpability. It enables us to hide, rationalize, or minimize our faults, our selfishness and cowardice, in a story where we are the hero."

She winked at the young man. "Or in my case, perhaps that I was a victim, doing my best in appalling circumstances. I've told myself that a lot."

"Were you?" Green had the most liquid, non-judgmental eyes she had ever seen.

"Doing my best?" Garragorah laughed. "Oh, yes, I did my best, but you see, my best hasn't been very good. My best is not quite the worst. I never stuck a knife in anyone, not directly." That was not completely true, but as honest as Garragorah was being, there were still things she would not willingly admit. "But I knew that I was lying when I lied. I told myself that I had no choice, but that is never really true. I never killed anyone, but I probably helped kill tens of thousands."

"Really?"

"Certainly. Sow doubt here. Confusion there. Say it was all a mistake. Say that we meant to do better. And it was *easy*. People like to say they want to cooperate, but disrupting cooperation is child's play. The Methueyn Knights are like children. They're simple, and so they were easy to isolate. Engevelen was also a simple matter. Far too proud. They practically destroyed themselves before help started coming." She looked at Halwyn. "Before you and your Elysians arrived."

"I am not sure what we have accomplished," Halwyn said.

"Yet," said Garragorah pointedly. She walked toward the unhinged, broken doors of the church, resisting the urge to look back to see if Halwyn would follow her inside.

He was a nice man, and he did.

There was more skolve skat inside, of course, but also something unexpected. Great coils of thick rope lay unspooled on the polished stone floor, and nearby, directly below the bell tower, there was a great rent in the thick flagstone. A deep gouge had been cut into the rock, but by what Garragorah could not imagine.

Halwyn's mouth gaped open.

On an impulse, Garragorah asked, "Do you think that perhaps a Deladieyr Knight once Rose here? Perhaps I, too, could hang myself."

"Don't."

Garragorah considered Halwyn. He was tall and too lean, but he had a humanity in him, a kindness. *I wonder if I can seduce him.* She had used, and used up, as many others—men and women—as had suited her in earlier days. *No. He loves another.* She had seen it, and she was feeling too tired and defeated to try to overcome that fundamental barrier. She could no longer get away with merely counting her crimes. "Yes, well, I'm no angel after all, to hang here *or* to reach heaven."

Halwyn looked up to the dome of the bell tower. He squinted. "Is that a man up there?

"I'm not certain," said Garragorah. "If so, he's dead. As I will be soon."

"I'm sorry."

"I am sorry" were the three little words of weakness as far as Garragorah had always been concerned. They inevitably led to opportunity and a poor compromise from her opponents. This was the first time she had failed to pounce on them. And she worried that if she pressed him, he would abandon her. "At least I won't have to face Nehring Ardgour again."

She remembered his spirit in the dark room of her castle, somehow darker than the mere absence of light could ever be. And his voice. Inhuman.

"Is he truly so frightening?"

Garragorah smiled at Halwyn's naivety. "He is barely human at this point. Perhaps it is he who is this One True Devil your Harbinger warns us of."

"I don't think so," said Halwyn softly. "*He* may think so. You may think so, but none of us are the gods or monsters we sometimes like to believe we are."

This surprised Garragorah. *Is he speaking of me?* The empathy was unexpected, and the relief she felt shocked her. *I thought I didn't care at all. Look who's naive now.* Discomfited and comforted simultaneously, Garragorah changed the subject.

"Do you think it a strange punishment to leave me here in these particular ruins?" she asked in a gentler voice.

"I was supposed to take you farther north," Green said.

"Why didn't you?"

"I thought you should have at least a chance." He looked into her eyes and laughed ruefully. "Also, I haven't been to many places north of here. Not yet at least. Well, Lyle, but it doesn't have the . . . gravitas suitable for a . . . woman like yourself. I couldn't leave you there."

Garragorah noticed a slight shift in his stance. He was getting ready to leave. *Don't go!* "You never answered," she said, trying to hold him there with her only real talent. "About my punishment. To be taken out into the wilderness I helped create and left there. Alone."

He considered her for a dozen heartbeats. At last, he asked, almost like a child might, "Are you sorry for what you have done?"

The question caught Garragorah off guard. It almost confused her. "Ah, yes," she said at last. "Back to my internal narrative. My nightly penance." She searched for a better answer but could not find anything that would do. She knew that lying would not keep Halwyn with her—she had been too honest for that already, and now found herself not wanting to lie to the last person she would ever see—but without a narrative to weave, she was, she found, helpless. Recognizing the bare truth at last, she shrugged.

"I'm sorry that it did not work out better. All of it."

"Me too."

She felt a sudden emotion, a surprising one. “Thank you, Halwyn. For staying and talking with me.”

He nodded ever so slightly, more from his chest than his neck—it was almost a bow—and said, “I think it would be kinder to kill you than isolate you in this way.”

“Do you?”

His jaw tightened, he bent his knees and pushed his hands out from his hips as if moving some great weight. “Goodbye,” he said.

And disappeared.

Leaving.

Garragorah.

Alone.

A Methueyn Knight is always isolated as only the truly certain can be. They live—and die—in a chamber of their own creation, untouched and unthreatened by other thoughts or ideas. Yet never alone, for their one Idea is ever with them.

Ave smiled to herself, happy enough never to have found out what that certainty felt like, and sad beyond words that neither Bro nor Revenberge was there to speak her thoughts to. Her steps were heavy, and not simply from the five-hundred-pound sword that she carried across her shoulders. It was certainly heavy. And exceedingly hard and sharp. Only chain mail, toughened skin, and meticulous attention to how she held herself kept Ave from cutting off her own head.

Villiers was a long way to carry such a burden, but Ave was untroubled, happy even. Pain and suffering were the only catharsis she could imagine now. One friend, her lover, had died teaching her to embrace the value of her own decisions. The other had died teaching her that her questions were okay, and somehow from that doubt, to acquire a new faith in her own being. Ave did not enjoy the suffering because she hated herself. The mistrust and self-loathing that had hobbled her were gone, sublimated by those deaths and the lessons she had learned from them. But remembering her friends . . . that was good. And the weight helped.

She kept an eye out for skolves, or as much as someone carrying a twelve-foot sword could. Sneaking was not really in the game. Ave could only guess why the skolves in Aurillon had let her go with that oddly human genuflection.

Did they think that I'd killed Nimrheal? Or were they affected by the imagery of the falling sword?

Answers were unlikely to be provided, and so while Ave could hardly creep away quietly, she stepped as softly as she could with all the weight she was carrying. One step became ten, ten became a hundred, on and on into the tens of thousands

On a rocky stretch of pasture between two abandoned towers, she intercepted the trail of an enormous mob of skolves. Trampled grass and scat could have been mistaken for a herd of cattle, but skolves always left their unique, awful smell behind. It was like rotted, half-digested meat. But worse. The skolves also were heading east toward Villiers. She bore slightly south to avoid them, hoping that this would not lead her unknowingly into other groups of them.

She rested in the embrace of a wild bush for a few hours that night without fire or food. A rumbling passed by in the dark, moving north at tremendous speed. Ave wondered if it was one of the demons, beings that she now knew were of a prideful as well as brutish disposition. While they might be difficult to predict, she understood that their desire to dominate came from self-regard and that perhaps they needed to be seen to dominate to keep their hold on the skolves.

The memory of all those skolves on their knees before her returned again. *Yes. Skoll and Hati are desperate to keep their respect. And they lose control whenever they leave for too long.*

This would explain the start-stop nature of the war. The skolves had split into too many groups, and neither Skoll nor Hati could control all of them at any one time. They were an incredibly powerful weapon, but ill-disciplined, requiring a constant show of authority.

But more of them are heading to Villiers.

Lady Sylvie had also spoken of the One True Devil, a being infinitely worse than skolves, far more terrible than Skoll and Hati. She had said that two soldiers would find the weapon with which to overcome it and bring it to Villiers. That prophecy had persuaded Ave to go there. To face something new and worse. The masses of skolves that she and Bro had fought in Aurillon, and then the terrifying arrival of Nimrheal, had almost driven this new devil from her mind. It was, after all, only a story.

Walking once again with her sharp, steely burden, Ave crossed another broad swath of skolve tracks heading east. She wondered if all these thousands of skolves heading to Villiers made the Harbinger's Heraldry more likely to come to pass. She wondered if her going there also made it more likely. As she passed over yet another stretch of skolve-trampled grass, she began to believe it was possible that everything awful truly was heading to that one place.

If the decisive battle happens there, will it be luck or fate, or both, with the various parties riding the winds of chance yet making a collision inevitable? The word of the Harbinger sends the two soldiers to find the weapon. Their success forces the One True Devil into the light. The skolves massing there brings Skoll and Hati. A single word of direction magnifies chance into a decisive moment.

She had made her decision on that hope. A chance to make a difference, to step outside the long passive road of doing what had always been done. *That* old road had been a walk that led only toward oblivion. Going to Villiers could scarcely be riskier, but Ave knew that a fundamental change of direction was exigently required.

Come what may, I am on my way to fight the One True Devil. And whatever else may be there.

One foot in front of another, Ave crossed the abandoned country. Alone, except for the symbol she carried across her shoulders.

CHAPTER 28

THE BATTLE OF CHARNEY

"Missile superiority matters less if the missiles don't incapacitate the enemy," said Major Peridot. "But it still matters. Psychologically." She lowered her telescope and pointed between the close branches of the hide we had all crowded into. "Look at that dead ground. The skolves are massing there. I wonder if that's by chance or design?"

Her green eyes shone in the light. Peridot was the most humane of the senior commanders in the Renet, and I found that gleam in her eyes disconcerting. *She couldn't be this happy purely for the intellectual enjoyment of it, could she? No.*

My confusion warned me that I was misunderstanding something. We had taken two companies across the border to observe the skolves besiege the town. As you know, twenty years ago, Charney was part of Engevelen. Until Nehring Ardgour took it from us. But when Skoll, Hati, and the skolves turned on him, they attacked what they understood to be his cities first.

Peridot was young, barely older than me, tall, green-eyed, dark-skinned. Even in chain mail and harness she was obviously a woman, but as woman or soldier, it was her mind and deportment that stood out. Peridot was the perfect, upright officer of Engevelen. Professional. Cool. Graceful. Always in control, she did have one special quirk: she wanted to learn new things and apply them. Sending a team to observe the siege had been her idea. She had no doubt that we would eventually have to face the same threats, and soon. While there was still time, Peridot wanted us to learn how to fight the demons and the skolves both. Better, she said, to learn from other's mistakes than through our own. There was surely no arguing with that.

The bulk of her soldiers were hidden well away behind the hill we both stood on. Only a very few of us had been invited to observe the action from a thicket of brush on this high vantage point. Our orders were to avoid any contact with the skolves—we were there strictly as observers—so we stayed as hidden as we could. We suspected that the skolves were highly territorial and that they rarely, if ever, retreated.

Suddenly, Peridot seemed to come to a decision.

"Captains Camille and Armand, take everyone back to camp. Senior Sergeant Delatam, stay with me."

"Nothing going on here anyway," said Captain Armand brusquely, pushing his way through the brambles and out of sight.

Camille was not in such a hurry. She gave me that sideways look she always did when I was asked to attend on Peridot alone. If she suspected we were a couple, she was likely not alone. But of course we were not. Peridot trusted me, that is all. She was a true professional and never, ever, spoke of anything personal with me unless it pertained to our mission as soldiers. If something other than professional respect was going on, it was between the lines and a mystery to me.

"What do you think is going to happen, Dav?" she whispered as soon as Camille and the others were out of earshot.

I flipped open my telescope. Peridot wanted a real answer, not a guess. I held the device to my eye and pointed it from one high point, the tall and airy hill that I was on, to another high point, the sharp, rocky hill on which fortress perched. The town of Charney ascended the far side of the valley in between. Despite all the years of occupation by Nehring Ardgour, it was still every bit a city of old Engevelen, full of narrow, winding passages between fine old buildings and palaces, opening suddenly onto elegant squares. In the oldest parts of town, labyrinthine tunnels and arches connected the ancient, squat stone structures, while the newer parts were ringed with soaring aqueducts. Now the town was infested by at least a thousand skolves. A few of the townsfolk still hid inside some of the taller stone buildings. We had seen a few of them now and then sneak down out of their redoubts, probably to find water or scrounge for food, only to be slaughtered by roving skolves. Most of the people had fled up the steep slopes of old granite to the fortress when the skolves had first descended on the town. We estimated from the bodies lying about that more than half of them had been killed less than two hundred yards short of the gates of the keep.

Courage is an unknown quantity, I thought. It was something Peridot said to me often. And fleeing from skolves looked like a very bad idea. Fighting them was only marginally safer, but running away appeared to be nearly uniformly fatal.

They were difficult to kill with arrows or bolts and harder yet with most swords. Their skin was remarkably tough, *they* were tough, and the slowest skolve was much faster than anyone not Elysium-sent.

Skolves did, however, have weaknesses. They did not appear to be capable of reducing a well-held, fortified position. Skolves did not use siege weapons or ladders. They seemed to have no strategy other than relentless frontal attack regardless of the cost. Even a simple battering ram appeared to be beyond them.

And once they started attacking, they were very reluctant to stop. I had seen a group of them clamber and scratch at the gates of Charney's keep for hours, slowly accumulating arrows and bolts until they were finally dead. They evidently had some limited ability to learn, however. Over the course of the week we had seen them learn to stand outside missile range, to regroup there, and sometimes even to leave for no clear reason. We assumed they probably left to find food. They also seemed to have learned about dead ground, those spots in topographic lows where the soldiers on the wall could not see them, much less fire upon them. These basic adaptations appeared to be the full extent of their tactical flexibility.

"It's a stalemate," I said, folding up my telescope. "As long as the skolves cannot get in, and the soldiers don't leave, nothing is going to change."

"And ..." Peridot said, a question in the word.

I had been thinking about this. "No stalemate lasts. This one will end abruptly. The people in the keep will run low on supplies and will attempt a breakout, which will lead to their immediate annihilation. Or the skolves will up and leave. We don't know anything about their psychology. We don't even know if they are *capable* of quitting the field altogether with an enemy in front of them. Or Skoll or Hati will arrive. If what we have heard is true, either could easily punch a hole in the walls of the keep, and that will be the end of everyone inside."

"So, one way or another, everyone dies," Peridot said.

"Yes."

She turned and gazed into my eyes. "Most of the people in there were *our* people once." She paused but kept her eyes on me.

I did not reply, wondering where she was going, but patient enough to wait.

A long moment passed. Major Peridot stepped closer. I was glad that Captain Camille was not there to see this, but Peridot did not have a romantic assignation on her mind. She lowered her voice still further. "Let's discuss how we might rescue our people."

She had not been taking joy in watching the siege. She had been nurturing another mission.

~

We were close to our own supply lines, and Captain Armand needed to be kept busy, so Peridot sent him and the fourth company to bring the equipment we would need. The plan was more hers than mine. She was both smarter and better trained than me, but I was good at putting her ideas into practice, which is why, I believe, she confided in me.

Also, the full plan ludicrously exceeded her orders, and she trusted me to keep that to myself.

"Pikes tighter, Sergeant, or they are going to fold up," I said to Fleur. She was short, stout, and tough, her harness—over-shoulder vertical leather straps looped into her sword belt—had three extra knives, and when she looked at me, I added, "Imagine you are fighting something every bit as fierce as you are, but at least three times stronger and faster. These eights have to hold in mass, or they will be overwhelmed."

"Nothing's swarming my lads," she said, sure as suet that she was the toughest thing walking. I had seen too many tough corpses to agree with her, but I did not challenge her bravado. *It has a use.*

We had been experimenting with small-group formations all morning, keeping well to the rear. I had three eights under my command, two of them geared up with the heavy pikes, and one with a new model of heavier crossbow. *Another few weeks and we could actually be ready.*

The ground abruptly shook, causing one of Fleur's lads to stumble. And it kept shaking, hard. A roar tumbled down the hill and swept over us, deep and foreign to our ears, but registering on a primal level as a threat. *But what?*

Even as I wondered, I knew. Skoll or Hati, or both, had arrived. We didn't have another few weeks. It was already too late.

"Fleur, Teniel, Vasseur! Check equipment and bring your eights up behind the observation post. *Quietly.* And out of the line of sight." I ordered. "Wait for me there."

I rushed off ahead of them, trusting them to do what we had practiced. The main camp was already in chaos. Everyone looked as bewildered as terrified. A private was cursing loudly, having spilled hot beans on his lap. Runners were running, though I wasn't sure where to, and I saw another sergeant bark herself on the side of a supply wagon, her eyes wide. "Put the arrow back in your quiver until you have a target," I shouted to a young private who was half-drawn, head darting about jerkily.

He's going to shoot someone. "Everything is fine," I added confidently and with volume.

It wasn't.

"Form it up, lads and lasses!" I bellowed as I passed heads poking out of a tent. "Armor on, find your people, and stand ready for orders. This is what we *do*!"

All this while the ground continued shaking in fits and starts accompanied by more of the impossibly loud roaring sounds.

I wasn't alone in the effort to project an illusion of confidence. Captain Armand and his troops were away, but Captain Camille was trying to shout some starch into her startled troops. "Where's the major?" I asked her, stopping.

"Watching," she said. She frowned, eyes searching my face, and added, "We're withdrawing, right?"

Maybe.

Her question momentarily opened her mind to me and I could see she was wary, undoubtedly a little worried, more than a little scared. She suspected I knew something she did not, and was trying to extract some comfort from me. Being an officer of Engevelen, she would never just ask, though, and being a senior sergeant and trusted confidant of the major, I could not address unstated needs. I said, "I'm taking my three up as a contingency." I looked behind me and saw the pikes of Fleur's eight coming forward at quick time.

"Take a couple of runners in case this goes badly," she said, her face professionally opaque once more. Then she turned smartly away to project the illusion of confidence to her troops.

I saluted the back of her head and was off, marching as fast as I could without actually running. "You two with me," I said to the scouts standing by the fletcher's tent, looking like they didn't know which way to go. A young man and an older woman, both with big eyes standing out from lean faces. "Grab your gear. Quick now, and catch me up," I added. "Now!"

Like all the others, they were members of the Renet, Engevelen's elite corps, but no one is immune to fear. Something that could shake the earth from, it seemed, miles away *was* to be feared, though I wasn't about to admit that. Not if I wanted to get these soldiers in good trim.

Around a broad slope and up another I jogged. When the scouts caught up, I said, "Double time, on me close and neat," and began running up the hill in earnest. One soldier running rarely looks good, but three can boost confidence provided they stay in good order.

The ground kept speaking its abuse to us in fits and starts as we ran up the hill, but there was also a deep, low shouting from somewhere up ahead. I could not make out the words from among the sharper reports of what sounded like rocks colliding.

A scout came down the slope at a sprint, skidding when she saw me, and fell on her ass, sliding right to my feet. I spoke calmly as if she had not just dumped herself. "Report, private," I said, giving her a hand up.

"M-major P-peridot says to b-bring your three up, S-sergeant," she stammered.

"Very well," I said, smiling at having anticipated Peridot. "They shouldn't be too far below me. Are you to report back to her or are you on to someone else?"

"Captain Camille, Sergeant!"

"She's in the main camp, center. Off you go."

We rounded the top of the hill, hit the now widened game trail to the hide, and crowded in with the major. She did not react to our presence. She had her telescope pressed to her face, following the astounding development with complete seeming coolness. I pulled out my own and finally put images to the sounds we had been hearing and the tremors we had been feeling.

Eight Knights! I was gazing across the valley at what looked like a colossal man dressed in shining plate armor. It was Skoll, I learned later. Though it looked like a god, its actions left little doubt about what it really was. *A monster. A demon.* My first glimpse of the dreadful thing saw it hurtling through the thick stone walls of a Steel Castle as if they were made of paper. It smashed into the structure with an explosion as harsh and powerful as a thunderclap. After coming out one side, the demon turned and charged through the building in the other direction. Just prior to impact, a strange blue light coruscated around it.

I felt a sharp pain in my left hand.

No, I thought, making a fist, trying to close it off.

"What do you think, Sergeant?" Peridot asked in her best professional voice. The only sign that she was excited was that she had asked so soon. Skoll had a lot more to reveal.

The sinister pain in my hand receded.

The beast smashed through a palace—one we had a poor view of, as it was in the rats' nest of a maze that was the town's old quarter—then repeated the process again and again and again, ten times, then twenty, until every building in one of the town's finest squares had been tumbled into rubble, twisted metal, and broken oak. When the grim work was complete, the demon turned and charged up the hill toward the keep. Skolves lined up along its path as if to watch. They crouched low as it passed them, then stood up in its wake, but always faced toward it.

Skoll stopped about a hundred yards from the keep.

It's going to smash the gate now.

But it did not. It stood there, as if considering the fortress, watching soldiers and citizens line up on the wall. Only when the battlements were thick with onlookers did it act.

"Bow to me and live," it roared in a voice that carried clearly to our hill.

A moment passed, then another. Finally, one arrow arced out from the wall and hit Skoll. It bounced harmlessly off the demon.

"We need to act," Peridot said. "But how, Sergeant?"

As her eyes flicked toward me, I was hit by a convulsion. My left hand shot up, burning, swollen, clutching vainly at the air. My eyelids fluttered, and an unearthly garish light splashed across the inside of them. Then moving images, distorted, incoherent, began to form out of the shifting lights.

"You two, *get out!*" Peridot hissed at the messengers. I could no longer see her, only the confused images taking shape behind my eyes. They were the last words I heard before the violent images took me over.

Staccato pictures flashed by in a frenzy I could barely keep up with. I saw Charney so broken that it appeared to have been yanked into another world, but inside out. Somewhere inside the maze of broken things was Major Peridot. She was alone, lost amid dust and broken stone. Then I saw her surrounded by skolves. My perception was pulled sideways and twisted left, focusing on Skoll. Somewhere else. *Somewhen* else.

A new inversion came, colors and images twisting into new forms. The Renet, the entire force of thousands, lay ruined and broken in a city I did not recognize. Among all the bodies was one that made me cry out. "Peridot!" I shouted, nauseated, rejecting the image of her death like a sickening knot in my gut.

I heard a firm, gentle voice in my ear. "It's okay, Dav. Your courage is being tested, that is all." *Peridot. Still alive. Here, now.* She had often spoken of courage to me, always making the same cryptic point. "Courage has a definite quantity, but it is an *unknown* quantity."

Until we are tested. Then we know.

I opened my eyes, saw her face, felt her hands on my harness holding me upright. "Don't go down there," I whispered. "Don't go down there, ever."

Yes, Major Peridot knew my shame. I have a sinister hand. It is a thing both backward and evil. I have kept it secret. I have needed to, for in our tradition such a left hand is thought to come from hell. I would have chopped it off and burned it, except there was no point. As much as the power manifested in my hand, it lived, I knew, in my mind. And my soul. For in addition to twisting my written words, it also gave me visions, like some perverse form of Heraldry, I supposed. Peridot, astute, alert Major Peridot, was the only person to have ferreted out my secret. She had found it useful more than once.

This was the other reason she kept me close.

She did not intend to confront Skoll. There was no thinking of it, she promised me there in the thicket while I clutched her to me, crossing the professional line in my terror at having seen her dead and broken in my vision. Eventually, I recovered myself, and we stepped apart, back to our respective roles. She was the major again, and I her senior sergeant.

We watched Skoll for the rest of the day. After giving its ultimatum to the fortress and receiving only a feeble arrow shot as a response, it appeared to lose interest and lumbered back down the hill to resume its destruction of Charney, presumably as a demonstration of its power for the defenders of the fortress. Captain Camille joined us, looking suspicious at finding just us two in the thicket. We passed the remainder of the day counting the palaces and squares that Skoll obliterated.

"The demon truly is a siege weapon all on its own," said Camille. "Though what it wants, apart from sheer destruction, is beyond me."

Peridot and I both knew. Camille would know soon enough. Skoll's only interests were in force, dominance, and submission. To prove this, it continued smashing Charney, pulling down its fine buildings, destroying its art, and trashing its elegant infrastructure as if it wanted to unwrite the town's very history.

By nightfall, Charney no longer looked like a city at all. It was a bird with its feathers plucked and its guts pulled out. What had been on the inside was out and what was once outside was under piles of rubble scattered on pulverized cobblestones.

"That's twelve o'clock," Peridot said as the demon demanded the surrender of the people in the keep once more. "Set a watch, Lieutenant, with orders to call us up if something changes." She looked at me. "Otherwise stand down the troops for the night."

"SHE'S GONE, Dav. She just left."

The voice was Captain Camille's. She was squatting in the open fly of my tent.

The image of my major sprawled out dead in a field of rubble flashed across my eyelids. I was out of my blankets and on my feet in a fraction of a second, scrambling to pull on padded undershirt and pants, to find chain, belt, harness, and sword, all while throwing short, sharp questions at Camille, who was now the most senior officer left in camp.

Dawn may have arrived, but the sky was the pink of blood to my eyes. *So early. Why didn't she wait for me?*

Camille had explained that Peridot had risen early—very early—and had seen movement in the old town of Charney, in and around a twisted set of squares. It was not skolves, she was sure, but people trapped in some old palace, people who knew Skoll was about to destroy their hiding place. She took two of Camille's eights to bring them in.

And then she had ordered the entire force to mobilize for retreat.

I brushed past Camille, roared for a runner, and sent her to call up Fleur, Teniel, and Vasseur's eights.

That done, I turned back to Camille. "Is Armand back yet?"

"Yes."

"Did he bring in the rest of the pikes?"

Camille's eyes widened, but she nodded. "What should I do?"

This was a question I did not expect. *Courage is an unknown quantity.* I smiled at her, recognizing her vulnerability in this narrow moment, wanting to repay her precious trust. "Arm them all up the way we planned. Pikes in front, crossbows in the rear." I saw Fleur and the others jogging up slowly, heavy with their big weapons, looking like a herd of hedgehogs, if hedgehogs moved in herds. I pointed them up the slope, and Fleur led them that way, a smile of joy and havoc on her face.

"Where are you going?" Camille asked.

"To get our major," I replied, straightening my sword, turning to go. The jumbled layers of twisted imagery I had seen the previous day flashed through my mind. “I’ll be coming straight up the hill in two hours,” I added.

Camille would recover her courage. It was not as depleted as it had seemed. She, like Peridot, had always confided in me. I could see in Camille’s face that the captain in her was returning. But what she would choose to do next, I had not seen. If she followed her orders, she and both companies would be gone when, or if, I returned from Charney.

“Form on me, Fleur. Quiet now. Pikes, steady at the front, crossbows, load and raise.” I saw Fleur’s teeth reflect the pink light of morning and added, “Drop your water, drop your food. Hold those pikes tight.” I looked the soldiers over, made eye contact with each of them, nodded at each in turn, and then quick-timed them down the hill. It was as fast as we could hope to move, as encumbered as we needed to be.

The wind was light and in our faces, smelling faintly of skolve and rot. The stink grew steadily as we got closer to the city, and I knew it was building in the minds of the men and women who ran in silence behind me. I could hear only their breathing, the sound of their feet on the grass, and the occasional jangle of their chainmail.

If the skolves happen to look our way in the next ten minutes, it is over, I thought. We were exposed coming down the bare side of the hill, as open to detection as we would ever be. Once we hit the twisted mess of rock that had only a day before been a city, line of sight would become meaningless.

As much as I watched ahead, careful not to trip, and keep to the old goatherders’ path, I listened. Skoll had not started up again. The demon had ended its destructive rampage in the early evening, not because it needed rest, I guessed, but because it wanted to be *seen*.

We were approaching the outer edge of Charney now and rapidly losing our line of sight. I looked inside instead, trying to remember and sort out the sprays of images I had seen on my eyelids and make sense of the heavy feeling in my left hand. I bore left around the first smashed building. The stone walls had collapsed, and the timber roof had cracked, its back broken like a twig.

A howl split the still morning air. Ahead and to the left.

Another howl shook the sky. An instant later, the ground shook in a series of heavy, violent percussions.

It's Skoll.

I signaled a stop and faced my soldiers. Fleur's teeth still showed, but mostly I saw wide-open eyes and fear. "Stay close and tight," I said. I wanted them to feel their fellows on either side. They were less likely to break then. "Let's go!" I said.

We wound through rubble, around buildings, over heaping piles of stone in the narrow passageways between perilously leaning walls.

I heard the sound of iron on iron and then a scream. It was not far off. Another howl, also close. A group of howls. Distant pounding.

I signaled another stop and closed my eyes, remembering . . .

"Every other crossbow, place them here," I swept my arm out, and said "loaded." I could hear the soldiers breathing now. Fear had a sound as well as a look. And a smell. All were in evidence, and building. "Those without crossbows, you are the loaders. Unpack your loading rods. You will work in teams of two. Pair up now."

We had practiced this over and over. Teams of two had a better chance of sticking together even if terrified. And listening to the howls and the sounds of metal on metal, and feeling the ungentle shaking of the earth, I knew that terror was close.

I waited until everyone was paired, then led them through another narrow, rubble-choked, passage across a weirdly clean—almost polished-looking—square surrounded by wholly intact, three-story marble buildings. A woman's voice rose keening, close by. I sped up, waving at Fleur to keep her team on my heels, wound through another darkened pathway and out into another square and a scene of ongoing carnage.

Five pikemen faced a knot of snarling skolves. Two held up their pikes, desperately fending off skolve sword blows from all sides, but three pikes were already on the ground, broken, beside a female soldier, who lay bleeding garishly from her head, where she was missing a hand-sized patch of hair and skin. Two other pikemen were running away, without their pikes but thankfully not toward my eights. I did not call them to us—panic is infectious. But I needed to find Peridot. *There!*

Maybe sixty paces farther across the square was my major with another group of pikemen, the remains of the other eight she had taken with her, defending a group of civilians. Together, they looked like an open sack of wine, spread out across the square, leaking red.

A small child—a girl—was sprawled farthest away. One of her legs was missing. An old man rolled around on the stones near her, clutching his overflowing guts between the spread fingers of shaking hands, unable to scream from the pain. He could only manage this chuffing sound that I do not want to remember, but cannot forget. Two other women lay in wet pieces closer to Peridot's position.

"Hold pikes!" I heard her say as three skolves slammed into the six lancers she had left. I could only guess how her two eights had gotten separated, but she had another woman and two children with her behind the protective thicket of pikes.

A howl split the air once more, and a horde of skolves appeared from the far side of the square.

"Crossbows fire!" I called, pointing at the skolves with the sword I found suddenly in my right hand. As soon as I heard the bolts fly, I called the next orders. "Pikes, form up on the major. Crossbows, follow, then reload." Then I charged toward Peridot.

The skolves were quicker, much quicker. They had surrounded her position before I was halfway there. *Peridot!* I screamed inside as I saw her clipped on the forehead by what looked like a staff. She fell sideways, and I hurtled toward her, my left hand as hot as coals.

I stuck my sword in the thick skull of the first skolve I reached, an especially tall one who had just grasped Peridot's wrist in its grotesquely long paw. Whether it was about to drag her away or pull her arm off, I never found out. Neither did it. Halfway through an inch of bone, the blade would not come free as the skolve collapsed beside the major.

I sensed Fleur's pikemen stopping just behind and to the side of me as another mass of skolves hit their sharp end. I released my sword hilt and reached down to draw Peridot's senior officer's blade from her scabbard. It blazed in the morning light. It was Vercors steel, the rarest kind, embossed with an "E" on the hilt. E for Engevelen, Peridot always said with a laugh.

That sharp blade went clean through a rusty sickle that was whistling toward my face, sending the business end of it flying off into the cobbles to my right, then continued on its way to slice off six inches of skolve snout followed by a paw, as I brought the impossibly sharp sword around.

With my left hand.

The skolve spasmed violently, spraying gouts of blood and snot into my eyes. My vision changed then. Everything seemed to twist inside out. My left was my right, up was down, forward was backward, and my sword arm swung of its own volition. Or *I* struck mindlessly, I don't know, for I could never remember it correctly afterward, except that events seemed to exist outside of time.

Blood flew, skolve parts filled the air as if thrown from an impossibly fast meat grinder, and in the next blink I found myself fifteen yards away from the pikes, surrounded by skolves and skolve pieces.

"Sergeant!" I heard Fleur shout. "That's got them! Let's go."

Coming back to myself, I turned and looked at her. She was grinning fiercely. Fleur and the pikes had stopped their own pile of skolves. The second eight—Teniel's—had swung at an angle to refuse envelopment by the tall, lean animals and had protected the heavy crossbows. The ground still shook, and the howls seemed to be coming from all around the city.

"Reload crossbows," I shouted, rejoining my crew. I sheathed Peridot's sword. It was loose in my scabbard, being narrower than my own had been, and heaved the unconscious Peridot over my shoulder. "We're leaving."

Of the eleven lancers we had found, only four were still on their feet and all but two of the rest were dead. I ordered them to pick up their wounded and come with us.

One of the little girls Peridot had sheltered was still alive. The other child had gone. I could not see her or the woman, but I knew that I did not want to find what was left of either. They were dead, lost somewhere in the lost time at the end of all battles. The mathematics of violence are such that all are losers, though looking at Peridot's dead pikemen, it was clear that some lose more than others.

Fleur abandoned her pike and picked up the girl, who might have been eight years old, and I led us backward out of the blood-slick square.

Halfway through the narrow passageway, my left hand abruptly throbbed. I hated that hand, but I knew to stop immediately and let it speak. I had a memory of skolves ahead. It felt imprinted on the back of my eyelids. "Turn around," I hissed between the howls of skolves, just louder than the shaking of the earth, and led my terrified soldiers back to the square and across it in the direction that the two routed lancers had gone.

I marched as fast as I could with the major over my shoulder, looking for another way out. A dark shadow and a broken storefront sign almost hid it, but I found another unblocked corridor leading the way we needed to go. We plunged from it into an even narrower passageway, this one with a single crumbling brick archway two stories in the air, connecting two narrowly separated palaces. On we went, through the ruined and choked passages of history, trying to escape the city, the skolves, and the demon.

We emerged from the dark into a new square, this one piled with heaps of rock and thick with dust that hung like a mist in the atmosphere, having found some macabre deadpoint. I carried Peridot to the center, where a twisted, mangled signpost still stood. It was a city map on a metal plaque, but the post had been tied into a knot as if it were rope, and the plaque was crumpled like paper.

"I can't read a thing from *that*," huffed Fleur, who had come up to stand beside me, the girl still in her arms, face hidden by her own long hair and the sergeant's shoulder. I looked at Fleur.

Still fierce.

Even carrying the little girl, Fleur was still herself. Unblemished by fear. A flash of memory told me where we needed to be. "Come on," I called and turned away from the sign.

"Not much farther," I said, leading them through another ruined square, directing their formations, encouraging their discipline. "Stay tight, Vasseur," I ordered, when her eight fell a couple of paces behind. That was not much, but I remembered what Peridot had taught me about fear, and knew that I needed to talk to the soldiers as much as I could, exert my authority and my faith in them as often as possible. Skoll was close, the skolves were closer, but we carried a greater enemy than either, right within us in each of our chests: our own fear. Peridot had always said that our training and our connection to each other was all that we had to fight fear with. Pikes worked against a strong, disorganized enemy. The heavy crossbows, well aimed, could take down a skolve. But better than this was the effect that well-drilled, comradely crossbow teams and formations of pikemen had on each other. Working so closely together stiffened morale.

Another pandemonium of howls and thunderous footsteps shattered the air, ratcheting up the tension.

I cannot let them feel alone.

"Put me down," whispered Peridot.

Her voice set my body and my soul on fire. *Thank the knights*, I thought, and unconsciously held her tighter. "Wait one moment," I said to her, *sotto voce*. "Here!" I roared. "Line them up here! Crossbows to the rear."

We were at the far end of another narrow space between palaces. "Step to it!" I shouted. Fleur put the girl down beside me, and I lowered Peridot to her feet and held her steady. Howls sounded close, and closing. An instant later, an ugly, roiling mass of skolves loped into view and thundered down the corridor toward our pikes.

"Loose!" shouted Fleur. The little girl curled up, huddling behind her.

"What is the situation, Senior Sergeant?" asked Peridot in a voice of calm despite struggling for balance even with my help.

"We are almost out of the city," I said. "Heavy contact. Defensible position."

"Load!" came the voice of the fierce, diminutive Sergeant Fleur.

"Hold steady, sons and daughters of Engevelen!" I shouted. To my immense relief, I saw now that there were only perhaps nine skolves in the pack. It was a manageable number. Our pikes were thick across the passageway, and in that narrow space the intemperate violence of the skolves was working against them. The ones in the back pushed the foremost hard into the long, sharp steel wall we offered them.

"We cannot stay here," said Peridot. "More will come."

A skolve on the left side of the narrow front pushed a pike inward and scrambled along the wall, gaining the inside of our line quicker than thought. Its long claws ripped into the face of a pikeman.

Fleur hit the skolve in the chest even as the pikeman shrieked and dropped his weapon to clutch at the shreds of skin and scraped-off bone hanging from his grotesquely spasming face. Fleur's sword barely penetrated the huge beast's leathery gray hide. My next memory is of the hilt of Peridot's sword in my throbbing left hand and the blade splitting the skolve's head vertically as easily as a nut.

Blood sprayed both Fleur and me, stinging my eyes.

I pulled the blade loose and shook it, flinging heavy knots of red blood onto the collapsing skolve. Then I turned to give the sword back to its owner.

"Keep it for now," Peridot said. "Where do we need to be?"

"Pikes—thrust!" shouted Fleur. A breath later. "Crossbows—loose!" Another breath. "Pikes. Thrust!"

That was it for the skolves. They were all down. A few of them were thrashing about as pikemen continued thrusting sharp tips into tough hide. Thrust, thrust, and thrust enough, and even skolves will die in cruel narrow spaces against superior numbers.

"Lead us out, Senior Sergeant," said Peridot, loud enough for everyone to hear.

"Gather that wounded man!" I said, "and follow me smartly."

It wasn't far. I had given myself fully over to my devil's hand and its staccato visions, taking us in an unfaltering, though winding, path around flattened, shattered, or pulverized palaces and storefronts. Even so, fleeing Charney was a nightmare. The pikeman had lost an eye and was babbling piteously to someone. I don't know if it was to his wife or his mother or his sister, but in his lonely pain he wanted comfort from her.

We were just on the right side of effectiveness, having to deal with wounded and the little girl. And no one except me had any real idea of where we were. We emerged from the city abruptly, shooting out onto the wild barley and grass on the edge of the city.

The shaking of the ground had been increasing in violence and pitch. Peridot stumbled from the quaking earth, and I steadied her. My hand flared, and I stopped, knowing it was too late to run farther.

"Halt!" shouted Peridot, trusting me, understanding.

I turned and saw Skoll step free of Charney, stamping its hate and need to dominate into the unoffending soil.

"Pikes, form up!" shouted Fleur.

Peridot's eyes were on me. I felt her regard, warm on my face, and smiled.

Raising her sword in my right hand, I stepped around the pikes and walked toward the demon.

Skolves were emerging from Charney too. They formed a ragged line behind Skoll. Ten yards in front of the pikes, I stopped, sword held aloft.

More skolves joined the line. They waited.

I felt a new shaking of the earth. It came from behind me this time. I turned to see a neat, organized line of soldiers form and march steadily toward us. Camille had brought up both companies in a direct violation of her orders.

The sun blazed off the end of their pikes.

"Raise up my horn, to heavens warn!" I roared, quoting a line from the old poem. A horn blared out in answer from Camille's still approaching line.

The skolves outnumbered us three to one. Skoll alone could kill us all. A city of fractured rock told this truth.

I stepped forward, closing with the demon, my back to Fleur, Peridot, and the other soldiers.

Skoll stomped its way toward me, then stopped perhaps thirty yards distant.

"Kneel before me—"

My left hand came up, and a blinding light filled my eyes.

The ground heaved and kept heaving. I stumbled and opened my eyes. Skoll was running, but not toward me and Peridot and our soldiers. It was running away from us, smashing through the masses of skolves who had been standing silent watch.

~

"And then what happened?" asked Dill, tongue against his blackened front tooth.

"How did you escape the skolves?" asked Dafydd.

"The skolves retreated, didn't they?" said Reyn thoughtfully.

Captain Bysshe was staring at Dav. She said, "We called it a great victory." She shook her head. "But they left because Skoll ran away. Scared by your hand." Her voice trailed to a whisper. "Just like in Courant."

"You're a wizard," spat Eurion. "You tricked us into bringing you here."

Alwena reached down and grabbed Dav's hand, gave it a rough squeeze, and dropped it. "Feels like any other hand to me."

"I don't know *what* it was," said Dav. "But Charney was *not* a 'great victory.' It was misinterpreted no matter what I said or Major Peridot said."

"She protected the secret of your hand," said Bysshe wonderingly.

Dav nodded. "Maybe if we had told them about it, they would have known better."

"No one would have believed it," said Reyn flatly.

Dav ignored that. "They thought because we routed Skoll and the skolves there that we could do it anywhere." He looked down into the dark waters below his feet. "And now the Renet is gone. And my friends are lost with them."

Peridot! She was always on his mind. Still alive. Somehow. Dav felt like he was drowning—more surely even than if he were trapped under the dark surface below his feet. His relationship with Peridot had always been a professional one on the outside, but finally telling the story of Charney had forced him to face the deeper truth. *It was more. It was always more.*

"*Are* you the one last devil?" asked Tudor, his voice shaky. The question jolted Dav out of his morbid reverie.

"One *True* Devil!" corrected Dill. "Haven't you been listening at all?"

Alwena gave the two privates a withering scowl before turning a surprisingly sympathetic expression toward Dav. "You don't know what happened or why, do you? Or what you are."

"No."

"What was written in your book that day in Courant?" Barbara asked. "I saw you hide it."

Dav still had the book. It was tucked into the surcoat he wore over his chainmail. He swung out of the opening and dug in his clothing for it. "Here," he said, handing his last secret to the captain. *There is no point hiding this anymore.*

He was still ashamed, but he had made his decision.

Barbara opened the leather bindings and flipped hastily through it, searching for the last entry. Dafydd and Dill shuffled over to look. "I can't read this," she said at last.

Dill pointed, excited. "It's backward! It says . . ." he mouthed the words slowly to himself before reading them aloud. "They all die. Leave them."

"Nice," snorted Alwena, peering at the strange backward scrawl. "Yup. No one would believe this crap. *Backward*." She looked at Dav pityingly. "I don't believe it. Ha. You write backward. So what? Something's wrong with your brain. There are others like you in the world, you know. Lots of them, probably."

"No officers, though." said Reyn thoughtfully.

"Yes, fine, no officers. But—" Alwena pointed at the hole, "you go in there, you'll find out you aren't so special. You can't scare off the darkness. You'll just drown."

"He's going," declared Barbara Bysshe.

"Why?" retorted Alwena. "Because he feels guilty about his major?"

"He loved her," said Tudor.

"Yup," said Dill. "That's the point of the story."

"It's a *love* story," said Dafydd.

Dav found himself looking into Barbara's blue eyes. There was a little red in them now. She was tired, and he could only guess how his story had affected her. But her voice was clear when she said, "But that wasn't the point of the story, was it?"

"No," said Dav.

Barbara did not break eye contact. "Why did Major Peridot attempt to rescue those townspeople?"

It had never made sense to Dav. He had asked her afterward, but she had not answered. He knew why now. He smiled at Barbara. "Sometimes you just have to do the right thing. Even when it makes no sense." He thought for a moment and added, "*Especially* when it makes no sense. That is when your courage becomes a known quantity."

CHAPTER 29
LIKE NOTHING BEFORE

Like eggs in a pan, like flour in a gravy, like pudding stirred at heat, they all abruptly change from thin to thick. Their heart is like the stirring whip. Like is to like is to like, and thus we go from what we know to what we thought we didn't know.

Val broke through. The five skolves on the wall spasmed violently, their blood congealing with the instantaneous thermal change she had initiated. They dropped in every direction, two backward off the other side of the wall, one forward—vomiting uncontrollably as it died—onto a soldier who shrieked as the thing brushed against her, the other two sprawling on top of the rough stone.

In her systematic way, Val had experimented with stepping up the temperature five degrees at a time and, after many trials, had found the most efficient innovation for killing the animals. Now she could do it with little thought or effort. Internal Acutist wizardry was effective because there was no way for any mammal's thermal regulation to keep up. Nothing and no one needed to be set on fire. No need for flashes of light or explosions and no risk of dangerous collateral effects such as those that Christopher Carlyle had carelessly inflicted on Sergeant Reyne's Vercors Rangers. The killing temperature for skolves was not even particularly high. There was nothing extravagant about what Val did.

Feeling barely a chill, Val considered the notion of tripling the effect of the process and killing three times as many skolves with each go. *Like is to like is to like.*

A little pedantically, she would have liked the skolves to gain the wall in greater numbers just to test the limits, if any, of her process. It should be easier, she reflected, to create the analogous effect at a larger scale than to devise anything new. She reckoned she had already killed more than a hundred skolves using this method, though never more than the five at once that she had just dispatched. Of course, a large number of skolves gaining the wall would be terrifying for the soldiers. Some of them might even be killed.

She looked away from the two dead skolves and considered Mick—or Grandpa as they affectionally called him—as he strode the thin, hard line of stone, flickering like a Deladieyr Knight in the empyreal sky.

Who is he?

There was something familiar about him.

Someone had found Grandpa a big two-handed sword, and he ferociously laid into any skolve that attempted to join him up there from the other side. But there were more and more skolves every hour, and Grandpa could only be in one place at a time.

As can I.

Chris and Rebecca were doing their best farther down the wall, but Calvaine Chesshyre and slow-talking Samantha Westerberg had refused to join in the defense so far. They claimed they had to save their strength for Green's return and the vital role of supporting the Methueyn Knights against Nehring Ardgour. Val had not forgotten Samantha's suspicious story of becoming separated from her escort of Knights of Armadale in Courant. And later seeing one of those knights, alone on a street in the city.

Her thoughts were shattered by a wildly spinning sledgehammer that flew from the other side of the wall and smashed brutally into the chest of a medic standing less than five feet from her. The man was flung into the air and then into the dirt, a ten-pound hammerhead where his heart should have been. It happened in an instant, faster than even a wizard could have responded. Suddenly, she understood a little better Calvaine and Samantha's reluctance to expose themselves.

A tumbleweed of movement on the wall caught her eyes. One, two, then four skolves flowed up, swinging rusty weapons—a pitchfork, two swords, and an iron pry bar—scattering the spearman standing nearby before the men, or Val, had time to react.

One of the retreating spearmen, she saw, had fallen and twisted his leg into an obtuse angle that no whole bone could imitate, but before the skolves could finish him off, Val divided four by five and achieved the breakdown. The skolves died messily in helpless, agonizing howls.

Trembling more from fear now than hypothermia, Val quickly climbed the nearest stairs and reached the ledge, then peered, very cautiously, over the side.

Into a sea of skolves.

Enough of them to drown the low wall protecting Villiers.

Val felt her vision narrowing. She looked to the right, just in time to see one of Christopher's porcelain dolls—this one dressed in an elegant courtier's suit—cartwheel into the seething mass of gray, stinking bodies and explode in a burst of blinding light and raging flames, swiftly followed by a wash of snow. A hail of sticks, spears, and rocks were returned over the wall by the skolves nearby. The ones not yelping, burned, or rolling on fire.

We need to retreat to the house on the hill. Right now.

"Val!" It was Green's voice, high-pitched, urgent, terrified. Val felt the shadow of something coming rapidly toward her from the left just before she was yanked roughly off the ledge by a big female spearman. An angular, foot-wide rock arced through the space that Val's head had so recently occupied. It came down fifty yards farther on, bouncing heavily on the cobbles. Chips of rock and cobble flew into the air with each impact.

Eight Knights! How are we going to retreat from this? Is it already too late?

Val spotted Green calling and waving to her from the end of a nearby street, but even as she ran to stop him before he entered the killing radius of the wall, she imagined what would happen when the soldiers started retreating. There was too little reserve left, and the hill would take too long for an armored soldier to climb.

"Val," Green said, still shouting, as she stopped an arm's length away, shocked at his appearance. His face was ashen, and he was trembling violently. Val was aghast. She had seen him looking distressed too often over the last few weeks and, she reflected, had done little to relieve him. But now he looked far more than just distressed. *He is burnt out, almost finished.*

Yet Halwyn Glace, she realized, was the tactical key to a retreat rather than a rout and a massacre. Val had little choice but to use him. Even if each time she did so—and each time she failed to address his feelings—she felt worse. But somehow the time had never seemed right—and *she* was never in the right frame of mind—to talk about feelings. A part of her, a suppressed part, wondered how he felt right now and how being the last person to speak with Marias Garragorah had left him feeling, but another part of her, the "sensible" part, still ruled. "Did the knights get there?" she demanded. *There wherever the machine is.*

Green hesitated, looking both hurt and perplexed, and Samantha Westerberg—appearing from nowhere, perhaps from hiding behind a tent or a stack of supplies, but certainly not from the wall and the fighting—interrupted. "Did Nehring Ardgour try to steal the Methueyn Bridge?"

"N-no," said Halwyn. "It's worse than that. M-much worse."

~

I WAS OPERATING with line-of-sight teleportation after we met at the Renet's old observation hill just south of Charney. The Methueyn

Knights were fast—faster than I could have imagined. After each jump, I hardly had to wait for them to catch up. In the course of the day, we traveled over one hundred and fif—I'm not supposed to say how far—and found Sir Volsang's body impaled on a black spear just a few miles from Ardgour's site. It looked like Nimrheal must have murdered him just a day or two before.

"Volsang is gone," said Yeyncie Green.

"He will come again," said Sir Leylah, who for some reason scared me the most. *Hands that heal, hands that kill.*

"Across the Bridge," finished Sir Darday'l.

In grief, only the three female knights spoke. They tell me that gender does not matter for the Methueyn Knights, male or female, but I don't know. Like me, the men said nothing. Even though I was appalled, I kept my mouth shut. It was beyond my understanding. And what was I going to say other than, "At least take that spear out of his ass!" I can barely speak the words to you now. I said nothing, for I know I'm ignorant, small, an unlikely player in momentous events like these.

In any case, there was no time for reflection or ceremony. A colossal black cloud was spinning ominously on the edge of the horizon. The umbral light and the sounds it made told us that something more colossal than Volsang's murder was transpiring.

Nimrheal had been here. And was perhaps, still close.

We hurried along, or rather the knights charged faster than thought, it seemed, while I teleported to each distant horizon, across bridges, and finally to . . . the meeting place. Two Vymyty wizards met us at Ar—at a castle not far from our final destination. They were old colleagues of Taratoraff, and in no better shape than him. Lean and beaten looking, but wearing incongruously clean pants, tunic, and capes. They met him with a strange silence.

"You escaped," said the older wizard, a woman named Varvara. She was carrying a leather satchel and had long, straight white hair and a deeply lined face. She spoke neither coldly nor warmly, but with a strange finality.

"Yes," said Taratoraff. He hesitatingly approached her, put his two hands lightly on her shoulders, and bowed his head until his forehead touched hers.

The younger wizard, Vsevolod —a mere boy except for his shockingly old, weary eyes— said, "We are all that is left. Us and you."

"Yes," said Taratoraff once more, still standing with his hands resting so gently on Varvara's shoulders.

Abruptly, she stepped free of him and said, "Let us show you what is left to be done." Wordlessly, they led us to a balcony high on the castle wall.

"There it is," said Vsevolod. "See through the spray? The torus." He pointed at a massive, barely visible structure that seemed to float in the air. Around this engineering marvel swirled the ugly purple and black storm cloud. "There is a tower at its heart. That is where our master awaits you." He meant Nehring Ardgour.

"Why waste our time with this?" said Sir Michael angrily. Finding Sir Volsang so violated had not cooled his disposition. I understood why that gratuitous humiliation had enraged him, but it still bothered me that he spoke his anger here, not there where his brother-in-arms had been found.

Varvara replied, "Because there are things you need to know before going farther."

"Speak quickly then. Skoll and Hati are close behind us," said Yeyncie Green.

"They are not," replied Vsevolod.

Varvara gestured toward the storm. "They crossed over the east bridge early this morning. Now they await you just outside the torus."

Sir Darday'l was visibly excited by this news. "Why didn't they attack you?"

She turned to face her fellow knights. "Why aren't they attacking *us* now? Surely they know we are here with the Bifrost." Her dusky face and curious eyes turned to me.

"We have a wizard with us, a *teleporter*," she exclaimed. "And we know now that Skoll and Hati hate the wizards most of all."

Varvara sighed. "They do hate wizards. But they felt our lord Nehring Ardgour's machine come alive, ready for its great workings, missing only the thing you call the Methueyn Bridge. When it spun up last night, it sang a threat to them that they cannot ignore." Her eyes hardened as she added, "But do not feel left out. Should you approach any closer, they will surely attack you and attempt to take for themselves that which you have brought."

"Are you saying we should not approach?" asked Sir Michael. "Because we *are* going to finish this now. *Here*." He took a belligerent step toward Varvara, but Darday'l's hand locked around his bicep.

"We haven't heard it yet," she said. "The true bad news."

The remark struck me as darkly humorous, but a smile must have been beyond the capacity of Vsevolod's boyish face and ancient eyes. He did manage a nod as he replied to Darday'l.

"Yes. The *true* bad news," he intoned. "There is a central tower within the torus. Nehring Ardgour and the machine wait on its highest floor for one of you to bring your bridge."

"Why don't Skoll and Hati simply attack him?" asked Darday'l.

"They cannot get into the tower. The machine," Vsevolod's arms gestured faintly, "has a power of its own, and it strikes the demons hard when they approach. It is a lightning, only not from the sky but from the torus itself. The closer they come, the harder they are lashed. They fear it."

Yeyncie Green smiled then. "This isn't bad news at all. Ardgour is waiting there for one of us, arrogant, thinking himself safe. So we simply charge in, protecting the carrier of the Bifrost, and see it done."

Varvara laughed bitterly. "That is exactly what you must do, but still we haven't told you the *bad* news." She rubbed a hand on her tunic and stared in a kind of horror at the sweat stain she left there. "The machine is also deadly to people, just not as dramatically as for Skoll and Hati. Our lord had one problem yet to solve when he climbed the tower last night. He solved it, we think, for Nimrheal came for him."

"But Nimrheal has not left," said Darday'l, eyes widening. "Because Nehring Ardgour was already dead."

For a long moment, no one spoke.

"That's bullshit!" roared Michael.

"So now you see," said Varvara as if Michael had not spoken. "Nimrheal will not leave until he kills at least one person. Skoll and Hati do not count, and so it has not attacked them. And Nimrheal will not leave the area where the offending discovery was made."

"It flickers here and there, seen and unseen. Like death, waiting," added Vsevolod.

Yeyncie Green whirled to Taratoraff and said, "Is this true? Or does Ardgour wait, playing one final trick on us?"

"It must be a trick!" shouted Michael. "Ardgour can't be dead. He's just trying to cheat us of justice."

If an empty burlap sack had lips, it would have spoken with more life than Taratoraff. "It is no trick," he said emotionlessly. "But your task is unchanged. You came to stop demons, did you not?" He turned his thin neck to gaze upon the great structure. "Skoll, Hati, and Nimrheal await you."

Michael put a hand on his sword hilt. "So we fight all three of them. Fine!"

"I'll do it," said Sir Sendeyl. "In and out, quick as that." He snapped his fingers.

Varvara looked at him pityingly. "If only it could be so. Whoever takes the Methueyn Bridge up the tower must stay for some time. There is a process to be completed." She produced from her satchel a sickeningly thick stack of papers. "Our lord had a problem to solve when he last climbed the tower, but he left instructions for the rest in case he did not return."

~

"So Nehring Ardgour died a hero?" snorted Christopher Carlyle, laughing even as, not a hundred paces away, soldiers fought to desperately hold a low wall against a sea of skolves.

"I think that's called irony," said Rebecca.

"Who would have thought" asked Samantha Westerberg, dragging each word out and gesturing dramatically, "that we would all get along in the end?"

Well I never thought so. Val doubted that Ardgour would ever be viewed as a hero. *He reaped what he sewed.* Val did not speak those thoughts. Other suspicions had formed.

He can't be dead.

Nehring Ardgour had been the bogeyman for a generation in Engevelen—in the world. He had defeated or tricked all comers: the Shining Knight nearly killed, Volsang, Nimrheal, and the other Methueyn Knights evaded.

How can he be dead? Just like that?

Killed by his own apparatus?

Gone with no more drama than that?

Still disbelieving, she asked, "Did anyone actually see his body?" It was better to doubt the news than to believe the reality. The most powerful man in history was dead. What could the rest of them do?

"No." Green shook his head. "But we are certain he's gone. Nimrheal is still there. Waiting."

"Nimrheal." Val remembered Taratoraff's stories. Nimrheal never left until it had killed someone. "Interesting." *Approaching the tower is a certain death sentence for at least one person.*

"I wonder what Marias would have thought?" Green mused.

"You're on a first-name basis with Ardgour's chief henchwoman?" sneered Rebecca, ignoring the monumental news that Nehring Ardgour was somehow dead.

But no one saw it happen. No one really knows.

"And you care what she thinks?" asked Chris. "She is a mass murderer, man! You need to harden up, Green."

History is going by, a history of all the best . . . and the worst, and it is getting little notice.

Samantha shook her head theatrically. "We should not make light of it." But she was not speaking of Ardgour. "Leaving someone to die, even a person as horrible as Garragorah, could only have been a wrenching task."

"But he called her *Marias*," insisted Rebecca gleefully. "When did they get so close?"

"Enough," said Val before more foolishness could ensue, still reeling from the news of Ardgour' s death but irritated also that Green was being teased.

And making fun of Mariah Garragorah's punishment seemed crass too. That Samantha Westerberg was doing so—who seemed to have so little trouble leaving others behind—made it worse. Especially when she pretended to have sympathy. *Samantha really is the worst of them.* Val fought to control her irritation and keep to the point. "I take it that the Methueyns are ready for their assault now, and they want us to join them."

"Yes," said Green, steadier now. Perhaps telling the story and handing responsibility to Val had helped him. "They wait. Impatiently, from what I have seen."

"Then we must go," Val said. She looked back at the wall, where the sounds of battle had only intensified, and saw Grandpa spun about by the ferocious blow of a sledgehammer to his temple. He stumbled and was pulled back off the wall by Major Serres. It was a blow that would instantly have killed anyone not heaven-touched, but even so, the old man was down, shaking his head, seemingly unable to stand. In his wake, skolves now filled the ledge. A few were already leaping down on the near side.

They need to pull back while they can. To the house on the hill.

"We can't go yet," Val said. *They should have retreated days ago.*

The Methueyn Knights can manage a little longer without us. What difference can we make compared to them anyway? But here, here perhaps we matter.

She raised her voice. "We must help execute a retreat. All of us but you, Green. Go tell them we will come as soon as we can. Keep them in place for at least an hour. Then come back and get us, but not here. At the house on the hill."

CHAPTER 30
A NAME

"Your hand isn't evil, Dav," said Barbara Bysshe, looking down on Dav. "It saved us in Courant. And it saved Major Peridot in Charney."

Her face was framed in light.

Dav smiled from his position in the cool, dark water, trying to commit her backlit face to memory before swimming away from the light into the shadows of the old cistern network of Chamberry. She had not wanted him to commit so utterly to what now seemed a suicidal exercise. Even after hearing his story of the Battle of Charney, no one thought that swimming through a dark, subterranean water-works was likely to succeed in achieving anything but Dav's death. But it was a time for left-handed decisions. The One True Devil was near, and if there truly was a weapon to fight it with, he needed to give the sinister hand free reign.

In truth, it felt easier to lower himself into a lightless warren and embrace the probability of drowning alone than it was to let what it was inside him loose. Dav had hidden it for too long, had feared what words it might speak through writing and, worse, what actions it might take, had only willingly allowed it agency in the most exigent of circumstances: at Charney to rescue his major, the only person who had ever known his secret up until then, and in the escape from Courant. Barbara took that as proof that, whatever his hand was, it was good, but Dav had spent a lifetime fearing it and could not so easily accept the evidence at face value.

Consumed with these thoughts and carried on slow, strange currents, he drifted farther away from the light. Instinct directed him also, and by the subtlest of movements, he adjusted his course as he moved below the ruined city.

If, in the end, I prove a coward or my hand proves truly sinister, let them not hear me drown.

Letting it free was in many ways akin to accepting his own death. Hiding its strangeness in school had been the most difficult. Whenever he could, Dav wrote with his right hand. He could do it with effort, but if he lost concentration even for a moment, the quill would find its way leftward and what he wrote would be sinister or backward. The Renet Officer's written test had only been the most recent embarrassment. Maps drawn backward or inverted, objects out of spatial position, orders the opposite of what they should have been and what Dav had meant them to be.

No defense could be given for it, no explanation. Engevelen was a nation built on tradition and ancient pride. Its people believed in a right way of doing things. The Renet was its most prestigious military institution and, if anything, carried this rigidity even further. Dav had known better than to attempt to explain what had happened. Major Peridot had kept his secret as well as she could, but she could not protect him from himself.

Dav had never expressed his misgivings to anyone other than Peridot. Even now, with Barbara Bysshe, he could hardly admit his fear of letting go. She knew his secret, or at least all of it that Dav could explain, but hearing his doubts would only have made his attempt to find the weapon more difficult. If Barbara knew how terrified he was, she would have fought harder to prevent him from the attempt.

Is it only something wrong with my mind? Is it merely something different and not wrong at all? Or am I cursed with evil? Is it a sinister gift, waiting its time, waiting for this very moment to be unleashed? What if I am *this One True Devil?*

His predicament reminded him of something that Peridot had said to him once. "When facing desperate choices, we must take desperate gambles." *Am I making a desperate gamble now?*

Peridot had always believed in him. Barbara believed in him. But Peridot was gone. The Renet was gone. Dav had seen a terrible future in Farrah Harbinger's green eye. The only choices left were awful ones.

And yet.

Barbara *had* been correct. Escape from Courant would have been impossible without Dav's hand—without its special power to sense the future and frighten a demon away. The same had been true in Charney. Without his left hand, without its gift, no one would have come away alive. The great Farrah Harbinger had also trusted Dav.

She knew.

She knew his secret and had made use of it. She had invited him under the leather hood with her. She had treated him like a . . . colleague, almost an equal. At this, a wholly new idea occurred to Dav.

Am I some kind of failed wizard? My left hand doing by instinct what they *do on purpose? Acting like a Methueyn Knight at other times?*

He could not know. Farrah had not said. But of all the people in the world, she had invited him to join her, to see unprotected what she saw.

She knew.

In her most extreme hour, that canny lady had trusted him.

It is time I trusted myself.

Treading water in the dark, he closed his eyes.

Whatever I am, strange wizard, secret knight, let it be so.

Images flashed brighter than the sun in darkness. An epileptic shaking seized him, then as quickly subsided into stillness. Dav floated gently away.

"TOSS THE DOLL, CHRISTOPHER!" Val shouted. A stream of soldiers ran laboriously from the city toward the house on the hill, like pegs in a board, forming a dotted line from the present to the future, leaving those still on the wall to hold back the horde of skolves until that line disappeared.

Val did not see it, but she felt the doll's head come off in the empyreal sky an instant before a blast of thermally volatile air buffeted her. Ear-splitting howls and whines followed, then a stench that made a horrific, even more acrid complement to the smell of rotting meat, the odor of skolves burning.

I hope I never get used to this.

"Pull them back, Major," Val shouted to Serres, who stood in plate armor beside her. "We're running low on dolls."

Serres's beak-like helm turned toward her and paused. It was only for a moment, but the silence seemed incongruously stretched in the thick of battle, when the air was filled with screams and howls, not to mention the deadly hail of rocks, spears, and hammers flying from the far side of the wall and the screaming sheets of arrows and bolts flying back the other way. "Do you have enough for a last heavy barrage?"

They had discussed this earlier. Val nodded.

Serres turned toward the heavyset man beside her and spoke in the metallic tones produced by her helm. "Let's pull everyone back, Havard. Do it now, and stay out of the way of the Elysians. They're going to turn the skolves into a brilliant burst of sunshine."

Moments later, the final retreat was called by brass horn. The remaining soldiers sprinted away from the wall, carrying only the weapons they had in hand, flowing past Val toward the barricades set up on every street. The horn blower came into sight, a slim young woman, also backing rapidly away as she finished the haunting melody of withdrawal. Even as the final notes faded away, Val heard Rebecca's deadly rhyme roll out upon the air.

"For all that you have ruined and those you have tormented

For all the hopes you have erased and all the lives you have ended

And even for the horror you will surely wreak on the morrow
I return to you a thousand-fold the price of all our sorrow."

The last ringing note was followed by a blinding sheet of lightning that in a single blink of the eye illuminated the entire length of the wall. A great cracking sound followed, loud enough to shake the ground.

Rebecca had always been the deadliest of them all, even if she was the least reliable.

"I'll never rhyme again," muttered private Aron, standing beside Val. As the only Vercors Ranger left in Villiers when she arrived, he was acting as her personal guard. "Uh, can we go now?" His eyes were big as they rolled toward her.

"Yes, we had best," said Val, turning away from the wall. The scientist in her wanted to see the effect of Rebecca's performance, but she stopped herself. *Curiosity can kill the Acutist as well as the cat.*

Major Serres and Sergeant Havard trotted by with the last group of soldiers. Rebecca followed, walking stiffly, arms pinned to her side for warmth, smiling evilly. Christopher was beside her, his bag of dolls nearly empty now. Only Grandpa was left. He stood on the wall, alone for a moment—a silhouette of old age and implacable strength—then turned and walked calmly toward Val and the first barricade.

She felt two hands on her lower back. Aron was pushing her into motion, like a child pushing his mother, except he was larger by far than her. She had taken less than ten steps when she heard new howls from the direction of the wall.

She ran.

Samantha Westerberg waited at the first barricade, standing beside a waist-high barrel of liquid. *Kerosene.* Sweat beaded along the edges of her receding hairline, and for once she had no long drawn-out comment to make. Val passed her without pausing, knowing that Samantha was going to speak this time in the elemental language of fire.

"Come on, Mick!" shouted Havard, not far ahead, keeping pace with Major Serres.

Val looked past them to the retreating soldiers, hidden partially by the turns of streets and the truncated lines of sight created by the barricades. Beyond them, she saw that the other line of soldiers—the line of those already ascending the hill—was as long and slow-moving as before. *We need more time.*

The howls of skolves rising from the north did not speak well for her hopes. She turned back to face Samantha and shouted, "Wait as long as you can, Sam!" Ahead she noticed Aron flagging, one arm hugging his ribs.

He saw her looking at him and cracked a wincing smile. "I'm fine. Besides," he gestured with his head over his shoulder, "if I really get too short of breath, Grandpa can always carry me again."

Val whirled to see Mick right behind them. At that instant, Samantha's elemental working exploded in a flash of white fire.

Acting on some instinct, the old man tried to shield both Val and Aron from the heat blast with his body. Not even a man as big as Mick could shield two others, but he tried, flinging his arms wide as if to hug them. Even so, the wave of heat was painful, and the blast of icy cold air that followed scarcely less so. Rings of condensation shot in strange patterns past them in the air like waves in the ocean.

Westerberg jogged by a few moments later. Val did not look back to see the bodies of the immolated skolves. She did not turn until they passed through the next street's rubble-strewn choke point and she was certain she would not see them, but the smell followed them, not caring about lines of sight or right angles.

More skolves followed them too, always more as the long retreat went on. At the next main barricade, Calvaine Chesshyre used his strange incomprehensible incantations to widen the gap. At the one after that, Rebecca spent another pair of her rhyming couplets.

And so it continued until at last they found themselves close to the edge of the city, only a street away from the last barricade and the beginning of the hill. Here Chris waited with his last, and largest, doll. Behind them, yet another horde of skolves suddenly appeared and charged down the street faster than racehorses, more numerous than cattle.

Like is to like is to like. There are so many. Val struggled to calculate the closest multiple of five for the number of skolves in the horde. She had always needed to do things correctly, in their time, with planning and in order. The quirks of living people had always been a challenge, but Green's incalculable feelings—which she knew were not subject to such order—could not be dealt with out of turn.

Val knew she was limited like this. She had identified her issues time and again and tried to overcome them. But now she was being borne down upon by skolves innumerable, and her deep instinct was to count them. It was a limiting instinct, just as her literalism and need for measure and precision usually were.

They were coming fast, running faster than their stench, almost faster than their own howling sound, their long teeth and longer claws flashing. They were a chaotic, powerful mass.

I must act, not calculate. I must . . . guess.

Exigence overcame calculation. Val initiated her guess, achieved the greater breakdown, and unleashed her thermal wizardry on everything she could see.

The front edge of the skolves collapsed like a house of cards.

Aron threw up, for some reason trying to hold the vomit back with his hands. Percussive, thermally volatile waves of air whipped the stench of his vomit away and brought in the stench of the dying skolves.

"There's more coming," said Mick, shoving Aron into motion. He drew his two-handed sword.

Val's feet felt like heavy blocks of ice. She could barely move them, and a strange lethargy took hold of her, but a puke-wet hand pushed her on, and she lost sight of Mick.

As they reached the last barrier, howls rose behind them once more. The ground shook with what was coming. Nothing seemed to matter to the skolves. No amount of wizardry, no amount of death stopped them. *How are we going to make it to the top of the hill? And how can its low wall possibly stop them?*

"Throw the last doll, Chris," she cried as her numb legs carried her past him. It was a big one, white-skinned and garishly painted with red and black highlights around its lips and eyes like obscene makeup.

Chris smiled, but he was also shivering from his exertions, and when he broke the doll's neck and threw the pieces, its head went straight toward Mick, who was standing on the skolves' side of the barricade. "Dammit!" Chris shouted.

No!

Mick could surely not survive the error wave from that head. It would be a hundred times worse than the one that Sergeant Reyn's eight had gotten in the way of. The only consolation was that the old man had been about to be engulfed by hundreds of skolves anyway. And that the whole retreat was ending in failure. Everyone on the hill would die regardless of how many skolves the last doll killed.

~

Dav opened his eyes on total darkness, but he did not fret. He no longer needed his eyes. Before this, he had never given his left hand its full freedom, even in extreme duress. Now, having made the choice to accept whatever this sinister power truly was, he seemed to have freed not just his hand but his spirit. He was seeing a very different world, though not with his eyes. It was as if the essential nature of the things around him was directly accessible, unmediated by the senses, revealed through an instinctive apprehension of the true underlying *substance* of things. *I am experiencing the meaning and form of the world.*

Dav did not know what this new form of vision was, but his memories of Farrah Harbinger's Heraldry and his own staccato glimpses came together with a new idea, crystalline in its clarity, of where he needed to be and how to get there.

Taking a deep breath, Dav dived down to the bottom of the cistern, found the narrow passage that he knew lay open there, and swam, as relaxed and easy as if it hardly mattered how far it was to the next cistern and the next breath of air. He knew that anxiety would not help him get there any faster.

Dav had always been at his best when compelled to take command, and in the deep dark waters lying under a ruined city, command was essential. He could not fight the water any more than he could fight himself.

And so, trusting his place in the world, he slipped effortlessly on his way from cistern to cistern.

The last of the eight cisterns he passed through was almost entirely dry, but it proved the most challenging to pass through. The long, narrow passage to the next section of the underground system was heavily choked with rubble. Pulling himself over a block of kiln-hardened pottery stone, Dav found himself at the base of a set of stairs going up.

I'm in a higher part of the city now. Perhaps under one of the few intact buildings.

He ascended the stairs, emerging in a square room, formed from perfectly cut stone. There was, for the first time since he had lost sight of Barbara Bysshe's face, light. It came from another narrow, twisting set of stairs that appeared to lead up to the surface, but Dav did not follow those steps. Before him lay a stone tomb. This, he knew, is what he had braved the dark waters for.

I could have simply entered from whatever door is above. There was no physical reason to swim through the underground waterworks.

Then he looked at his left hand and knew why matters had fallen out as they had. He set that realization aside for the moment—there were other priorities—and turned his attention back to the tomb and the task that awaited him.

Dav examined the surface of the monument. There was writing there. He tried to read it in the dim light even as his fingers traced the etching. A date. More than half a millennium in the past.

Before the first fall of Engevelen.

Dav groped around the tomb, fingers tracing the cold, heavy lid. He placed two hands on it and pushed. It would not move.

He tried again, this time using a large chunk of hardened pottery from the cisterns as a lever. It broke on the third try, but it had ruptured the seal on the lid. Pushing against the broken seal with all his strength, he was able to slide the lid slowly aside with a great grating sound and a final crash as it fell three feet to the hard stone floor.

A thick burlap sack surrounded the bulky contents. Panting from excitement as much as from the effort of removing the lid, Dav used a sharp piece of the broken pottery to cut through the material.

He found himself gazing down, transfixed, at the weapon that Farrah Harbinger and his sinister hand had sent him, by circuitous and dangerous paths, to find.

And collapsed onto his buttocks on the hard stone floor.

What?

He recoiled from the answer that had been waiting so long to be received.

How?

Why have we rushed across skolve-and-demon-infested lands for this? Why now?

No. Oh no.

Weeping, Dav finally understood what the One True Devil was. And what its coming meant.

~

"Endy."

The Shining Knight reined in his horse at the sound of his long-unheard name. Veronica Brice, riding beside him, also reined in. She was dressed in the same shining armor as he, its thousand and more perfect, tiny, interlocking pieces of cold-forged metal glinting in the light. Veronica was one of the few people alive who knew the Shining Knight by his true name, but the voice in his head had not been hers.

For too long he had been an object of fear or love depending on where you stood, known only as "the Shining Knight." Everyone, except for Veronica and a few others, had thought him dead. He might as well have been, for Ardgour had so burned, so ruined him, that he had felt more dead than alive. He still was far from healed. Injured to the very edge of death, then left disfigured, hardly human, Endy had never felt more like a thing.

And now this voice in his head had come to remind him that he was still a person. It was glorious in a way, but also terrible, for it could only mean one thing.

Behind them, a double column of riders stopped, followed by hundreds of foot soldiers. Further back, wagons of food and supplies pulled by horses and oxen also slowed to a stop.

"What is it?" the duchess asked.

"I heard my name," the Shining Knight said. "It is the end."

Veronica put boots to her horse and said, "Then we had best hurry."

MILES UNDER BURDEN, Ave walked, still undeterred. The twelve-foot shining etched metal of the Methueyn Treaty reflected the merciless sun. She carried the punishing symbol for Bro, and for Revenberge, whom she had loved. She carried it for the other Deladieyr and Methueyn Knights, for an entire order that had been ground down to one hair away from nothing over the last two years.

Twice she had come across packs of skolves, reeking and feral. Twice they had made grotesque bows to her and moved onward, heading, it seemed, toward Villiers.

Were they in Aurillon? If not, what do they see that affects them so? What do they want?

She had never been able to stop herself from questioning things, but it had taken her a very long time to accept that this was who she was.

"Aveline."

With the word came a feeling of power. Ave straightened and began to walk more easily. The immense weight of the sword seemed to disappear. She did not know at first what hearing her name meant, but for the first time she was able to break into a jog with five hundred pounds of steel resting crossways on her shoulders.

Many steps into this new state, Ave's questioning mind realized what hearing her name meant. Comprehension had come so slowly only because the sound was not a thing she ever expected to experience. It was a thing both great and awful at once.

But I never Rose! How can this be?

Hearing her name surely meant something else.

Darday'l—the last Darday'l but me—has died.

She made herself breath as deeply as she could., She knew her time was up. *All* of time was up. *I must get to Villiers now if I am to be of any help.*

~

MICK CAUGHT the doll's creepy, life-like head with one hand and hurled it into the avalanche of skolves racing toward him. The world exploded in frost and fire. He staggered, simultaneously burned and frozen. His feet slipped from under him on suddenly icy cobbles, and he kept his balance only by using the two-handed sword like a crutch, one hand gripping the bare blade. Near the hilt, the steel was still sharp, but a day of slicing through armor and leathery skolve hides had blunted and nicked the edges, aging the sword like time had aged him and his friends at the house on the hill.

Secure on his feet again, Mick remembered that they still had not buried Sir Valence. *My friend.* He had sworn to bury Valence properly, with a service. For once, one of them would not be put into the ground in secret as if dying was a crime and a person's life had meant nothing. He had made Brigitte and Roland promise that Valence would not be moved from the basement to the earth until he returned from town.

How far?

He turned away from the hideous pile of burning skolves to look past the last barricade at the boundary of the town and then up the hillside. Too many soldiers were still climbing the long slope. The young female wizard—*Val?*—was only a little way above him. He could see that her eyes were wide with shock and fear. Private Aron was not far above her. He was clearly hyperventilating, finding the climb hard going after all the fighting at the wall.

No one will be remembered if we don't survive this day.

He ran toward Val even as the howls of more skolves rose behind him. "Faster, Lady Valcourt," he said as he caught up with her.

"It's too late," she said, looking back. "Get behind me, I'll make them pay the price."

"No," he said. Nothing in him would allow that, but he felt a sudden and powerful wave of love for Val and her courage.

Skolves poured out of the town like gray water from a sewer, except they flowed uphill.

His chainmail hung loose on him. It had been thrown over him by Havard only a few hours ago, but like the sword, it had aged out of usefulness. The skolves were coming on fast, implacable, innumerable, unstoppable, but he shrugged out of the damaged armor. He would face them bare armed and with the blunted two-handed sword his only defense. He lifted the weapon high above his head.

They flowed up the hill like a flock of geese in flight with a single leader at the front of the V. Mick widened his stance and struck the lead skolve thunderously, his blunted sword caving in its chest and flinging it back into its brethren. Inertia left a stream of saliva hanging in the air for a long second after its mouth and body had shot away.

Mick kept swinging, backing up slowly, not letting anything past him. Two skolves tried to outflank him, one swerving left and the other right at exactly the same moment. One of them would surely get by

Val!

He knew she was there, just behind him and to the left, doing he knew not what, but dropping clumps of skolves in their tracks. He could feel the breath of her workings on him. She was acting on skolves farther away to keep from accidently killing him, Mick knew, but one of these two was going to get its jaws around her and kill her in an instant.

Releasing the sword with his left hand, he struck right with it and thrust his left arm out, directly in front of the open jaws of the skolve bearing down on Val.

"Maréchal."

What? It had been years since Mick had heard that name or, having heard it, remembered its significance. It was connected to other words too. Mighty words, words of tremendous significance.

A song.

He looked down. The skolve's jaw was moving slowly, as if in honey, closing slowly around his forearm. Then its long white teeth exploded off his arm as if he was made of steel instead of flesh.

"Who are you?" asked Val, eyes wider than ever.

Shaking the skolve away as if flicking a burr off his sleeve, Mick replied in a vast and powerful voice.

"I am Heydron."

Lifting a suddenly weightless sword, he entered a timeless state. He did not remember any single action, any swinging of the blade, any turning of his body, any sound he made, any breaths he took. But he did know that he mowed through the skolves like a machine, cutting them down like wheat, scattering them like kernels in a thrasher.

But Val followed his movements. She saw him hurl the hilt at the face of another skolve when his sword finally shattered, saw him find a sledgehammer and whirl that until the metal head flew off and disappeared down the hillside. She saw him seize an unusually tall skolve by the ankles and swing the beast as a weapon. She saw Heydron smash skolves with his fists, with iron bars taken from them, with anything he could get his hands on, all to protect her, the other soldiers, and his friends in the house on the hill.

He only stopped when the remaining skolves bowed low to him and slunk away.

COULD THE WORST BE OVER?

It did not seem likely, but in the aftermath of the retreat and Mick's miraculous victory, Val felt a ray of hope. They had found something to awe the skolves. And it was not powerful acts of wizardry but the heroics of one old man.

Perhaps we can hold this house now with all of us together here.

Samantha Westerberg, Christopher, Rebecca, and Calvaine had all made it back alive. Chris even had a new bag of dolls—his reserve bag, he told her—at the ready.

And hundreds of soldiers, perhaps a thousand or more, had made it to the house on the hill. If she had not been so exhausted, Val might have already counted them. And probably categorized them by rank into the bargain.

No, it is not exhaustion. The details don't matter.

They had miraculously stopped the skolves when Val had been certain this was no longer possible. Looking down the hill, she could see them still thick on the ground all through the city. Twenty thousand of them or more milled about. But they were not coming up the hill. Mick—or Heydron—had seen to that. Val did not ask herself how the old man could have merged with the angel Heydron without the Bifrost, but she *had* finally remembered him. He had been Heydron. Before. She had seen him once when she had been a little girl. Perhaps that explained it. But he had been thought long dead, lost in the north somewhere.

I need to ask Brigitte Landry about this. She seems to know something more about his provenance.

It was a good problem to have, a small, mysterious detail about a great person. Val suddenly found herself laughing through her tears of relief.

I cannot wait to see Green. I will tell him this story. And that the worst is over. I will tell him that I love him.

As if summoned by the thought, there was a short, percussive, popping sound, and Green appeared on the breakfast patio teleportation pad. A ring of condensation marked a wet circle on the flagstones under him.

"They wouldn't wait, Val," Green exclaimed, eyes bulging, "it has all gone left-handed."

CHAPTER 31
LAST WORDS

The entire contingent of Elysian wizards popped into existence inside a dimly lit stone room. An incredible explosion of snowflakes floated through the air—tiny crystals of chaos from Green's tremendous act of teleportation. The shadows of the flakes flowed gracefully down the walls in softly shifting patterns.

"T-that was o-odd," said Green.

"What?" asked Val, then noticed he was shivering. "Are you okay?"

Green smiled at her—at her concern, Val realized—and said, "T-there was just a s-strange ..." he hesitated, "*resistance* at the t-tail end of the t-teleportation. I almost c-couldn't push through."

"Perhaps it was your good taste at war with your choices," Rebecca sneered. "This place is more than a little dank."

"Why did you pick a dungeon as your platform?" asked Chris.

"For s-safety," Green replied, still shaking from thermodynamic shock. "T-Taratoraff suggested it. In c-case things went really badly and the d-demons attacked." He seemed to think of something new and added, "A-and if they g-go well, too."

Val, at war between her sense of urgency and her concern for Green, began rubbing his arms with her hands. When she moved to his chest, Samantha Westerberg raised an eyebrow and drawled, “We may all be starting to get along a little too well.”

“He’s really cold,” Val protested, stepping back from Green.

“Not anymore,” purred Rebecca.

“Thanks Val,” Green whispered, smiling for a vanishingly brief moment before his face turned miserable again. He raised his voice and addressed the room. “I should explain a few things before we go out there. The Methueyn Knights gave up on waiting. I couldn’t stop them. They simply decided to . . . go.”

“But why?” asked Chris, clutching a doll to his chest.

“You know why,” spat Rebecca. “We’re a mere footnote to the *mighty* order of Methueyn Knights. We hardly figure. They decided they didn’t need us.”

“No,” Green said. “Well, maybe. I don’t know.” Blowing out a breath, he said, “Nimrheal really was there though. Skoll and Hati. too” He walked across the room to the door. “And one by one, the Methueyn Knights fell.”

“No,” said Chris. “They fell? They died?”

“I don’t believe it,” declared Sam.

They’ve been dying for two years now. Why are we so surprised? But Val was shaking now, too.

Green ignored Chris. “I-I couldn’t even teleport all the way there to help. The machine, it interferes. So I came to get you.”

The door sprung open just as Green reached for the heavy iron handle. Taratoraff, looking like a demented, big-eyed scarecrow, sprang through and used his entire, emaciated body to push it shut again.

“They’re coming!” he exclaimed.

“Who?” asked Val.

“See?” said Chris. “Everything is fine.”

But Chris was misreading Taratoraff’s face. The old wizard was terrified. “Skoll and Hati!” he said impatiently. “She *did* it! Sir Leylah completed the procedure, and the machine repulsed the demons. They can’t go anywhere near it now.” Taratoraff’s hands, which usually moved dramatically when he spoke, only shook now. And worse than Green's had been shaking a few moments earlier, though not from cold.

Samantha's eyes narrowed. "But if the Bifrost has been ... uh ... properly placed in this great working, why are Skoll and Hati still a problem?"

"Yah," said Chris and Rebecca, together.

"And why cannot the remaining Methueyn Knights deal with them?" asked Calvaine Chesshyre.

A massive impact sounded from the castle above. The walls, solid as they were, shook with it. "They're here," said Taratoraff, whispering for some reason, his eyes darting in his shrunken, lined face.

Val grabbed him by his tunic and shook him. "Where are the rest of the knights?"

He looked at her aghast, as if she were an idiot, and said, "They are dead. All of them. Like we will be if we don't leave here now."

All of them? Oh, dear knights.

Ardgour. The Methueyn Order. All gone. No one left.

Except us.

"What about Leylah?" Chris asked, eyes on the door. "Y-you said she'd turned the . . . thing on."

Another impact sounded. Closer this time. Taratoraff looked from Christopher to Val to Green. "Leylah did not emerge from the tower. Nimrheal is gone, and now the demons come for us."

"How can they all be dead?" shrieked Chris, still stuck on that awful news, clutching at his doll's head.

"But why are they coming here?" asked Rebecca. "I thought they were supposed to die when the thing did what the thing does."

"Did you not listen?" The old wizard seemed to shrink in on himself. "They are weaker now, yes, much weaker. But so are we. They can be killed, maybe, but not by us. We need to get away from here." The walls shook, and a roar like ten lions ten inches away assaulted the air. "They can't get the Bridge now, and with Nehring gone and the Bridge out of reach, they must know they are trapped in this world forever. They will want to reassert their dominance." He swallowed. "And kill wizards."

"But who are we?" said Chris, distraught, streaming snot and tears onto his doll. "We aren't Deladieyrs or Methueyns! *We're nothing.*"

With a sharp smack, Rebecca slapped his wet face.

Another great roar shook the room. Then a great pounding sounded. Steps, coming closer.

Samantha Westerberg was wild-eyed too, but she was not crying. "Whatever we are," she said, sticking to her slow drawl despite the panic in her voice, "we need to get out of here."

"Yes," Val said. Her analytic mind wanted to understand what had happened before deciding what should be done.

But there was only one thing to do. *Get out of here. And fast.*

"Green, it's time to go."

"Come in close," he said, gesturing urgently. When everyone had gathered tightly around him, Green pushed his hands from his hips. And stopped. "I can't!" he said. "There is some strange resistance. It's not twice as hard, it's ten times harder."

The heavy iron door was suddenly struck a savage blow. It dented sharply at the center and fell halfway off its hinges.

Val wrapped her arms around Green and buried her head in his chest. "You have to, Halwyn," she said.

"YYYYaaaaaaaahhhhhhhhRRRRrrrgggGGG!" Green screamed, squatting as deeply as he could, with Val holding him tight for balance, and pushed his palms away from his hips harder than he had ever pushed before.

And with an explosive detonation, they disappeared.

"THEY'RE BACK, MICK," warbled Doog. "If I can still call you that. Mick."

Mick smiled at his friend. Another friend, Fenris the puppy, was curled up in his arms. He remembered rescuing the young dog from under that collapsed house. It was the oldest memory he could clearly recall. The oldest recent memory, anyway, for there were others—far older ones—behind a long blank abyss.

I have been unwell.

"Course you can call him Mick," said Louis. He thrust his chin pugnaciously. "That's his name, ain't it? Mick. Well, let's go, old man."

"Better hurry," said Doog.

There was something in his tone that told Mick to move quickly. He patted Louis on the shoulder as he passed, careful not to buckle his bad knees. Passing out of his old rooms and into the hallway, he saw a soldier on a cot, his forearm torn open, skin flapping, thick. *If only Leylah were here.* Her healing hands would have a lot to do. But just as instinct made him march faster and faster through the house, passing more and more of the injured, the mangled, men and women who might or might not recover, he knew that Leylah was not coming.

He could not feel Heydron any longer, and he was sure it was not because he was again unwell.

Something has happened to make the angel move on.

Soldiers snapped to attention as he passed, even some of those lying injured on cots tried to salute him. He passed through the doors to the breakfast patio, stepped through and stopped in his tracks.

"G-g-g-green! G-g-g-get u-u-p!"

The tortured words were coming from a blue-lipped, violently shivering Katherine Valcourt, desperately rubbing her hands on the stiff, supine form of the teleporter, Halwyn Glace. The other wizards were there too, looking about them dazedly: Calvaine who spoke to heavens in words only he and the angels understood, Rebecca who spoke truth through rhymes, Christopher the doll-throwing maniac, and Samantha, who worked with more elemental powers. A lean and shrunken old man was also with them, though he was on his side, his chest still.

"Get them blankets!" Mick roared, jumping forward to put his arms around Val, to rub the warmth into her that she was losing to Green.

"G-get u-up, G-Green," she cried. "G-get up, H-Halwyn G-Glace. R-rise a-again, like a-all the other times. R-rise up, my l-love, g-get up Green. I l-love you, I love you, I *love* you. G-get u-up."

Halwyn was so badly frozen that his skin shone bone-white. A piece of his hair broke off when Val touched it. Doog passed Mick a blanket. He wrapped Val in it and stayed with her until she collapsed.

"So you think they're coming, Sir Heydron? Skoll and Hati?" Serres was looking at Mick for some kind of certainty. It was a thing Mick could not give her, though he wished he could, for he remembered Serres from before the blank abyss in his memory. But sentiment could not produce certainty. He had never seen either demon, just what one of them—Hati, he now knew—had done on its previous visit to Villiers.

"I have no idea," he replied. "But Lady Katherine thinks perhaps." When she had cried herself down and warmed up, she had explained what she had learned. The demons would likely go to wherever the skolves were. And they were, by some strange twist of fate, all at Villiers now. Or so many of them that it did not matter if it was not quite all of them.

"Well, I hope they come," declared Louis.

"I can't believe Ardgour's gone," croaked Doog. "And the knights."

"Fuck Ardgour!" Louis shot back. Serres, Mick, and Doog looked at him, and Louis added, "We have our own Methueyn Knight, better than all the others."

Doog looked at him incredulously. "Yes, but—"

"Let's get this over with," Louis barked, dismissing Doog with a grumpy wave of his hand, "once and for all. Right here." He thrust his bony chest out, "We don't want to have to chase all over creation to send their asses back to hell."

"Yah," said Doog with a slow smile but a good deal less bravado. "This *is* what we've been hoping for. Let them come."

"Oh, they're coming," said a new voice. They turned to see a tall, grimy woman in badly damaged chain mail. "They'll have to, if half of what I've heard is true." She was footsore, covered from head to toe in dirt and ruined chain, but Mick could feel the strength in her, and he knew her for a fellow.

They brought her water and fresh bread, carefully wiped the dirt from her face in the old Engevelen fashion, and heard her story. Escuyer Aveline, she said she was. She had carried the enormous metal sword of the Methueyn Treaty with her. As she freshened up and ate, Mick, Doog, Serres, and Louis told her what had been happening in Villiers, and the tragic news from the Elysian wizards.

"I see," was all that Aveline said, but the tears welled in her eyes when she heard that all the Methueyn Knights were dead.

"You don't seem surprised," ventured Doog.

The look she gave Doog made him freeze. "This has been happening for two years now. Seven—eight?—Knights gone? We've lost hundreds more than that, though not together at the same time." She turned to Mick with such a look of suffering that he almost reached out to her. "Since you disappeared, just before the war started."

"You knew me?" he asked, shocked. *Back when I was Heydron.*

"I saw you once," she said, her face deeply lined despite her youth. "The greatest Heydron of all. A Methueyn Knight for over fifty years, a Heydron for all that time when Heydrons never last, and then you just disappeared. Two others died before Yeyncie came, and now everyone remembers her, because she was the best of those, and she outlasted so many of the others. But none of them were half what you were. Not even Yeyncie, as incredible as she was. Where did you go?"

They were all staring at him now. Aveline. Serres. Doog and Louis.

Mick tried to remember when it had happened, and why, but he could not. There was a dim feeling of not being needed . . . and then nothing. *I was always best when there was someone to protect.* "I don't know exactly," he said. "I'm not what I used to be."

"Well," Aveline said. "Whatever we are, we are all that's left. The last, worst hope."

Louis spat, "We're all that's needed."

"Last best, you mean," said Doog.

"Finally you said something right," Louis turned to Aveline. "Now show us this Treaty. I've never seen the thing."

They followed her outside to see the great symbol of the Methueyn order.

When she showed it to Mick, stuck where she had thrust it sideways into the outer stone wall of the house, he had said, "You are Sir Aveline now."

Her eyes were bright under their layer of exhausted redness. "But I never Rose." She placed a hand on the long, heavy hilt stuck sideways in the air and said, "I never hung off *that*."

Mick laughed. "In the ceremony of Rising, a Deladieyr need only carry the Treaty's weight for a few moments. You, sir, carried it from Aurillon. I think you did enough."

She stared at the shining metal and the words graven into its impossibly hard metal. "I thought I heard a voice in my head, Maréchal. It said my name."

"That was the voice of your angel," said Mick. "Before Nehring Ardgour's machine was turned on."

"Why are you so sure the demons are coming?" asked Serres, clearly less interested in strange machines than who or what would attack next.

Aveline's eyes slid toward the major. "Because they are bullies. Because all the skolves are here. Because Sir Maréchal here showed himself to be formidable and the skolves bowed to him. Because Skoll and Hati have no imagination and nowhere else to go."

"But when?" asked Serres. "Tomorrow? The next day?"

"Maybe tomorrow, but I suspect sooner. I don't know where they will be coming from, not exactly, but there is a radius of probability," said Katherine Valcourt, returning from inside, still trembling from some residual chill. "Perhaps before nightfall."

Serres took a deep breath, picked up her steel helmet, and placed it on her head. "Let's get everyone ready then, shall we?"

~

Like a metal door that could not be broken, like a weight that would not be pushed, like the inevitability of thermodynamic shock, the evidence is inescapable. Like is to like is to like, and thus we go from what we know to what we thought we didn't know.

Val frowned at the cup, the bucket, and the barrel in front of her. Nothing she tried was working correctly. No water had frozen, none had boiled. Pushing through had become terribly, unaccountably hard.

Why is this unlike anything else before? What has changed?

Halwyn Glace was dead. That was different. The hard fact of it felt like ice in Val's stomach. When she thought about it, about him, his love, his frosted eyes, she struggled to breathe. She did not know, in those moments, how to go on, or if she even could.

Her chest tightened again, and she could not draw air. Then her mind instinctively escaped to the technical problem, hiding from her feelings in forests of problems and calculations as it had always done. But this time, Val really needed the protection. The blow felt mortal. She needed to step aside from it by asking questions of the world instead of looking inside at her pain.

There was no way that door should have held up after even a single blow from a demon that can blast its way through entire stone buildings as if they were paper. And no way that Green should have been so affected by so few acts of teleportation.

Something has changed. Something drastic.

Val's eyes found the water vessels again. *We may be only moments away from battle. I need to figure this out.*

~

Val found Chris, Rebecca, Calvaine, and Samantha keeping watch from the breakfast patio—Green's last teleportation pad. The memory stabbed at her.

"There's something wrong with my manipulations," she said.

"They are harder to work than before, and my losses are excessive. All my calibrations are off. Widely."

They all looked at her. *Pityingly?* It was difficult to know. They were not really friends. Val had never thought of them as such. Only Halwyn. And they had made pathetic, ungovernable subordinates. "*Katherine*," Samantha drawled slowly, "you have been dealt an awful blow. We *all* have, but for you it is the hardest. That's all. You aren't yourself."

"No," Val said. "That's not it. I can be objective. I performed tests. There is evidence that something has been altered. I believe it has to do with Ardgour's machine."

Chris pulled out a doll and turned it toward Val. It had bright red tears painted down her face. "Give it up Val," he said, moving the doll's head as if it was talking. "My pretties didn't sign up for your Acutist fussing."

"Will you just listen for once!" Val shouted. "The Methueyn Knights have died somewhere—we don't even know where the place is—and sacrificed not only themselves, but their most sacred object, to stop Skoll and Hati. Such a sacrifice may be affecting *us*, too."

Samantha shook her head. This time there was definitely pity in her eyes. "It is *you* that is affected, Valcourt. And by something personal. We aren't demons. Whatever they did, it doesn't affect us."

"It didn't even work," said Chris's doll. "Skoll and Hati are still here."

"But—"

"Just stop," said Samantha. "Take a rest. Sit this one out."

"I can't stand all this negative talk!" shouted Rebecca, stamping one foot.

Eight Knights, it's like talking to children! Val's monster growled. She took a slow, deep breath, struggling to calm herself. "Test one of your dolls, Chris. Sacrifice a little one and see. I think Huygens has changed."

The doll's head turned away from Val. "I don't believe in any Huygens, and this is my last bag."

Val looked at Rebecca, but the rhymer only shook her head. "No, Val. I'm upset too, believe it or not. I don't think I can make any new rhymes in this state. I have to keep all I have safe."

Val looked to Calvaine and Samantha.

"The angels only hear my prayers once," said Calvaine. Samantha looked away, apparently done.

"Listen!" Val cried. "This could kill you."

No one was listening. Trying one more time, she said, in a calmer voice. "Just think about what I said, please."

~

"I HEAR SINGING ON THE WIND," said the Shining Knight. They had felt the vibrations from the north, heard distant shouts, but now this singing from up ahead, somewhere high, confounded them. He could not make out the words, but the melody was haunting.

"It's coming from the hill," said Veronica Brice.

The Shining Knight adjusted his lance, a weapon of the same liquid sheen and dazzling brightness as his armor. He had forged it himself, with a great letter "E" engraved on its guard. "We must go there *now*," he said urgently.

Veronica nodded and turned in her saddle. She shouted to the rider behind her, "Fayne! We're taking the horse up the slope at a gallop. Drop the wagons and bring the foot soldiers as fast as you can!"

~

THE APPROACH of Skoll and Hati was never slow or subtle. The ground shook for miles with their steps. And they seemed to want it to. Surprise was not in their tactical arsenal.

The heavier the step, the closer the connection to heaven. Or to hell.

Mick remembered that now. Just as he remembered, so many years ago, a young lady who had wanted to train as an escuyer of the Deladieyr order. *Serres.* He had befriended her even though she had no weight in the sky. And now she stood beside him, a mature woman, weightier in soul than ever.

Now. Now she could have been one of us.

But she was better than that, he realized. She did not need to be part of any religious order, she did not need to marry an Idea. Major Serres was her own woman.

There was a great crashing in the city below, rumbling the ground and sending a piercing roar into the air. The sun was nearing the horizon. The future was coming into definition, lit by its red rays.

Skoll and Hati strode forward to the edge of the city and the foot of the hill, a tide of skolves behind them, more even than before. The two demons did not wear the shining armor that Mick had been told to expect. Perhaps their battle with the Methueyns had taken a toll, after all. They were garbed in simple tunics, as far as Mick could tell at the distance he was squinting at them from. They carried gigantic swords, though. One of them, Skoll, Mick guessed, carried the fallen Michael's great sword. They stood taller even than the skolves, but perhaps they were weaker now than the titans that had fought and killed his brothers and sisters of the order—Katherine Valcourt had said they should be. Whatever the case, these two demons just looked to Mick like big, very angry men.

He had fought plenty of those in his day.

Mick stepped out in front of the wall. Serres and Sir Aveline came with him. He knew that Katherine Valcourt and her wizards waited behind the wall, biding their time, still recovering from the traumatic loss of Halwyn Glace. Doog, Louis, Lady Aurorette, Carol, Brigitte Landry, and even Roland also waited there, armed with crossbows. A thousand and more soldiers stood with them.

Please let me protect them. He tightened his grip on the big sword Serres had found for him.

I will bring all that I am to the fight.

Smiling, Mick realized that this was exactly what everyone was bringing.

"Kneel before us. Now. Kneel and be spared."

The words were a hurricane blast of sound, percussive and barbarous. Mick looked at Serres. "This reminds me of some *important* words."

"Oh?" Serres said, her voice reverberating in her helm. "Can you remember what they were?" she asked in a calm voice. Somehow, she was able to speak normally even with the two goliaths standing so near.

"It was a song," Mick said. "We sang it once. Together. When you left the order."

Metal-gauntleted hands reached for the helm. Removed it.

"I remember," she said, her voice clear and natural now.

Mick began to sing, as loudly as the power in him would allow:

And did these thoughts in time gone by
Dwell in our people's thoughts and hearts?
And were the dreams of each angel
In Engevelen's temples carved?

Serres's voice joined his almost from the first word, and by the second line, more voices had joined in. Brigitte Landry's high, lovely voice he could pick out easily. By the third line, Mick could hear Doog's croak and Louis's rasping burr. By the end of the first stanza, the entire wall had joined. As one, they continued singing.

And did the empyreal sky
Break through and its secrets reveal?
And was Engevelen built here
Against the will of Nimrheal?

Raise up my shield, sun's light will warm!
Raise up my maul, my scroll and pen!
Raise up my horn, to heavens warn!
Raise up the Bridge to Elysium!

I will not end my holy fight
Nor shall I stop paying the cost
Till we rebuild Engevelen
And regain all that we have lost.

Brutish men had no vocabulary with which to deny words of such beauty, and Skoll and Hati, for all their power, were little more than brutes. All they could do, when the song ended and a thousand cheers went up from the house on the hill, was to roar with mute fury and charge.

The first blow from Skoll sheared Mick's sword in half. He threw what was left into the demon's face. It bounced off with a loud *clong!* as the demon hurled Mick backward against the wall.

Skoll raised Michael's great blade high and swung down at the stunned old man.

Another, stronger blade, Aveline's, caught Skoll's at an angle and, though it could not stop the blade's descent, deflected it away from the old man's head an instant before that head would have been split in two. "It *is* much weaker than before!" Aveline shouted.

In response, Skoll kicked her in the chest, slamming her, too, against the wall and shattering her chainmail in a shower of red-lit rings,

Thirty yards to the right, a hail of bolts hit Hati just before the demon reached the wall. It roared, perhaps in pain, perhaps only in anger, and smashed itself into the stone, making a great dent in the ancient masonry.

I MUST ADJUST. Modify or die.

Val calculated that Mick and Aveline, even without her help, could survive Skoll's onslaught and prevent the demon from entering the house for several minutes at best. Hati, on the other hand, would be through the wall of the house any second now. The skolves were sure to follow.

Ten times? Let's suppose the cost is *ten times what it was.*

Val had not solved the problem in the hours of waiting for Skoll and Hati. She had posited that it was now twice as difficult to break through. It had proved more than that. Then she had gone with four times. That had not worked either.

If it is harder than ten times, we are doomed anyway.

Few wizards would be capable of doing anything safely if Huygens had changed more than that. Val hated guessing. It went against all her training and everything she stood for, but time had run out. It had to be now, or it would be never. She had to abandon her little analytic monster and trust her intuition.

Val took a deep breath and initiated the process, multiplied to the power of ten, to burn Hati from the inside out.

"Raoyayyyyhhhh!" screamed the demon as it froze in place.

At the same instant, Val went limp and collapsed backward off the wall into the strong arms of Aron, who had once more decided to act as her personal guard.

"You're cold as death!" he exclaimed, breath steaming in the suddenly frigid air.

"Is *it* dead?" Val gasped. As if answering her, the wall shook with another devastating impact.

No. Something in the demon resists manipulation. That was more than just Huygens.

Oh. They are like Knights.

She had heard how exceedingly difficult it was to kill a Methueyn Knight with wizardly manipulation. *We suspected this.* Cursing her own stupidity, Val scrambled to her feet just as the wall exploded beside her and Hati stepped through.

~

Major Serres' sword bounced off Skoll's back with a metallic clang. Distracted, the demon turned from Mick to crush the plate-armored woman.

No!

Mick was on his feet in an instant. His hands flew up and around Skoll's sword arm. His feet slid across the hard ground as the demon pulled him along like a puppy. It seemed to smile as it overpowered him, and with Mick hanging off its arm, raised its sword to obliterate Serres.

No!

Images of the young warrior as he had once seen her, walking away from the Methueyn Order, flashed through Mick's mind.

Mick stopped sliding. His feet dug into the earth.

Skoll stopped, frowned, looked confused. And did not see the ferocious blow from Aveline coming.

"Yerhah!" it screamed as her blade bit into its hip bone. But the demon kept its feet, and pivoting sharply, it knocked Aveline once more against the wall and pulled the sword out of its hip.

Blood spattered onto the ground.

"Die, demon!" came a shout from somewhere behind as a foot-and-a-half tall porcelain doll—absent its head—landed at Skoll's feet.

Nothing happened.

Skoll stared at the headless figurine for a moment, then casually crushed it with one foot.

"No! That can't be!" came the voice. It was Chris's, Mick realized as he found his feet. He braced himself just as Skoll, shaking the ground horrifically, turned and charged into him, smashing them both into the crumbling wall and just missing Aveline, who was still recovering from her own impact with the ancient stones. On his right, Mick saw with horror that Hati had broken through the wall completely and was heading to the house, dozens of skolves already hard on the demon's heels.

Blows landed from the left and the right. Mick shimmied up, using the wall for balance, and was hit again. The wall gave way behind him, and he stumbled backward four, five steps before hitting the ground. Skoll slowly turned and retrieved its great sword, *Michael's* sword.

"Step on this, fucker!" Chris shouted as another, larger doll cartwheeled through the air toward Skoll. The demon stopped the doll's flight with its free hand, contemptuously, then looked shocked when the porcelain figurine exploded in a searing white flash. The explosion knocked Skoll off its feet and set its tunic on fire, and with an earth-shaking crash, the demon fell to the ground and began to slide down the hill.

As Mick pulled Aveline upright, he saw that Skoll had recovered from the doll and was once more stamping its way toward them. Behind him, Mick glimpsed soldiers running from the wall as more skolves poured through it. Chaotic missile fire flew from every angle.

He looked around desperately and found a discarded blade. Aveline hastily retrieved hers from the ground and stood beside him, watching the demon approaching again, more enraged than ever.

A cold rime shivered the air. A flash of lightning cut across the deepening twilight.

"We have to get between the skolves and the house," Mick said, pulling Aveline into motion. He almost stepped on the stiff, supine form of Christopher Carlyle, the doll-throwing wizard. He was frozen as permanently as Halwyn Glace had been.

~

"YOUR GIBBERISH GUY JUST DIED," said Aron, crouching beside Val.

"What?" she said, trying to get her bearings. Skolves had come through the wall in a ferocious mass. She had seen Louis shaken apart by one of the beasts in the first moments of the breach. Doog, improbably, had shot that skolve through the eye with his crossbow from a pace away, but Val had not seen what happened next. She and Aron had been too busy by then running toward the house.

"The wizard who talks nonsense. He just spoke his last blather burning up a handful of skolves. Frozen stiff as ice."

Walking obliviously through the carnage, somehow missed or ignored by skolve and demon alike, was an old man with a cane, muttering as he went. He walked slowly, almost haltingly, but as if surrounded by a halo, as if his utter obliviousness prevented anything from touching him.

What in Elysium?

"What should we do?" Aron was saying, pulling Val away from the improbable sight.

Val looked to her left and saw that Mick and Sir Aveline were still on their feet, fighting Skoll but looking beleaguered. They had been driven three quarters of the way back to the house. "Why don't you get inside, Aron." Val said.

"To hide with the dog and the wounded?" he said. When Val looked at him, he smiled sheepishly. "What would be the point?"

"Okay. Watch my back, then." She put Aron out of her mind and tried to focus on Hati. *Perhaps I can kill it with another try at an even greater breakdown.*

She knew she would not survive this.

It was almost fully dark now and hard to see in the amber backlight from the house, but Hati was difficult to miss as it charged, roaring, across the patchy ground toward Val.

For Green. Val prepared what she was certain would be her last act.

A fully armored knight on horseback appeared as if out of nowhere. He seemed to flow rather than gallop across the hilltop, lance extended, light from the house glinting off its tip. The knight's armor blazed with more than reflected light from the house. In a thunderous collision, lance, rider, and horse piled into Hati.

"It's the Shining Knight!" roared Aron. "The Shining Knight is here!"

Val glanced in the direction the knight had come from and saw a column of lancers following in support, led by another rider very similarly armored. It was a woman. *Veronica Brice?*

A garbled rhyme was carried to Val's ears over the sound of hooves. Lightning struck somewhere near the wall.

Is it really the Shining Knight? Can we yet win?

She ran toward Hati, determined to help the Shining Knight if he was still alive. Against a still heightened resistance, she opened herself to the empyreal sky. Hati's connection to a bright singularity of power was much weaker than before. But there was another connection too, something beyond that of Hati and of Mick and Aveline as well. The Shining Knight!

She watched him struggling to free his left leg, which was trapped under his fallen horse, while Hati stared in horror at the end of the lance sticking out of its abdomen. With a scream of pain and rage, the demon yanked the lance from its body and threw it to the ground.

Gouts of blood followed. Hati staggered.

"Get up!" shouted Aron. "Get up, get up, get up!"

The Shining Knight had finally pushed the horse off his leg. He got to his feet only to receive a ferocious kick from Hati. In the empyreal sky, Val saw hundreds of the tiny squares in his armor move to absorb the blow. Even so, he was knocked into the air, landing with a groan and skidding to a halt at Val's feet.

Hati charged toward them. Aron helped the knight to his feet as a song rose in the air.

"For hell's most vile and evilest being
Receive in kind the edge of forked lightning."

The voice was Rebecca's, and her verse was followed almost instantly by a dazzling flare of light and the deafening crack of lightning.

Val opened her eyes to see a smoldering line of grass and at its center—but untouched— the figure of Hati. The demon's sword was still in its hand, and it appeared to be trying to decide where to charge next. Aron was on the ground, spasming, knocked down by the lightning. The demon's eyes passed over him and the knight, paused on Val for a moment, then spun somewhere to her right, where she saw Rebecca crouched inside a circle of frost. Before Hati could make up its mind who to finish off first, the Shining Knight charged again, on foot now, swinging his sword in a blurring arc.

Hati caught the blow with its sword and struck back. The Shining Knight stepped nimbly to one side, timing the demon's swing perfectly, and hit it in the throat with the hilt of his sword, then—almost as if he had seen it coming an instant before—leaned back to dodge a sweeping strike to his helm from Hati's free hand.

He did not quite make it.

The sound of the impact was like a cast iron frying pan hitting a pumpkin. The Shining Knight's head did not explode like a pumpkin would have, but he spun crazily like a pumpkin might have done, and only managed to raise his sword in guard by lifting it as he spun to catch Hati's follow-up.

Val could not tell if this fortuitous block was luck or something more miraculous. Neither, it seemed, could Hati. The demon paused, astonished, then roared and attacked again in a frenzy, forcing the Shining Knight to back desperately away, his sword blurring in the air as he somehow managed to catch and redirect each incessant, savage stroke from Hati.

Trying to minimize the danger from hypothermia, Val attempted a series of smaller, focused thermal attacks on the demon. Instead of targeting its whole body, she zeroed in on its sword arm. ***"Yerhah!"*** it roared each time, but did not drop its blade or even slow the flurry of blows aimed at the retreating knight.

On Val's third attack, however, Hati seemed to lose patience with her persistence. It abruptly disengaged from the Shining Knight and charged at her, only just failing to stamp on Aron on the way. He still lay writhing on the ground.

With a shriek, Val tried to dive left, but she was spun sideways by something hard, catching a brief glimpse on her way down of a wave of skolves savaging the Vercors cavalry. She hit the ground in a flash of pain, but her training kicked in and she rolled to her feet again, not sure what had just happened. She saw the Shining Knight leap up from the ground where he had evidently been sprawled as well—a result of the same mysterious collision, she gathered. He stepped between her and Hati.

~

Sir Aveline's sword was knocked wide by a savage stroke from Skoll. Arms outstretched and off balance, she could only watch as Skoll snapped her leg in two with a vicious kick. The limb dangled as if only attached to her by her clothes and her chainmail. The demon laughed then. It was a laugh from hell, its brutish timbre ringing in the darkness like some unearthly thunder. Aveline collapsed against the wall of the house, helpless.

Mick struggled to his feet, slowly, painfully, using the wall for support. He groped in the dark until his hand found something. Something hard and heavy. A blade. An enormous blade. He followed it where it lay at an angle from the house until he found the hilt.

The Methueyn Treaty!

With both hands, Mick pulled twelve feet of steel into the air. A blade made of promises and hope. He should never have been able to balance something so heavy, but there was Aveline lying in the dirt, unable to rise. Serres, too, was somewhere in the dark, perhaps badly hurt, needing urgent help. His friends . . . they all needed his help. He lifted the enormous sword and walked toward Skoll, singing.

"Raise up my shield, sun's light will warm!
Raise up my maul, my scroll and pen!
Raise up my horn, to heavens warn!
Raise up the Bridge to Elysium!"

As he finished the glorious verse, Mick spun laterally and swept the sword in a wide arc. When it struck Skoll's blade, the demon's guard collapsed, and it was swept off its feet. Grunting, Skoll sprang up again in a great cacophony of sound and raised Michael's sword once more.

Wielding a twelve-foot blade in combat can only be done one way —by ferocious, lateral swipes, predictable, brutal, unsubtle. If Skoll had been anything but a stupid bully, if stepping back or stepping aside had been in its repertoire, it could have avoided Mick's next massive stroke easily. But it was capable only of brute force, not strategy. Mick struck again, almost getting past Michael's sword this time and knocking the demon heavily to the earth. Then Mick let Skoll rise to its feet so he could hit it just as hard once more time. But this time, when Skoll fell, Mick struck again before it could get up—not as hard as before because the length of the blade now worked against his motion, but hard enough. And then again and again. Skoll could barely raise its own blade now and began crying piteously, crawling away. Mick kicked it in its enormous butt.

Somehow, Skoll struggled to its feet once more and faced Mick, holding Michael's sword, now heavily battered and nicked, in front of it. Mick saw that the skolves had paused their ferocious attack and gathered in a silent mass, watching, awaiting the duel.

Mick spun, striking Skoll once more. Michael's sword sheared in two, and the Treaty bit deep into the demon's ribs. Skoll dropped the hilt, turned, and fled into the darkness.

Do I give chase?

Mick looked around him. The skolves stared at him. Awed. Hati was still there, fighting Val and a man in strange, reflective armor. *If I leave now, what will happen?*

The skolves will kill everyone. All my friends.

"Hati!" Mick shouted.

He ran toward the other demon, locked in furious combat with two wizards and that strange shining knight.

~

"You were right, Valcourt," Val imagined Rebecca saying, for the rhyming wizard had evidently made her own adjustments and survived the night. But Rebecca said no such thing. She was mourning Christopher and she had no grace left in her.

Even though the battle, when all was said and done, had been relatively short, only Val, Rebecca, and Samantha Westerberg—whom Val suspected had done precisely nothing— had survived of the Elysians.

A similar proportion of the other defenders had also been killed or horrifically mangled. Few injuries from skolves were ever minor.

But the skolves had unaccountably slunk away before finishing *everyone* off. After Mick had made Skoll take to its heels and then joined in a similar beating of Hati—aided by the incredible Shining Knight as well as Val and Rebecca—the skolves had simply melted away into the dark. Some of them had groveled to Mick before departing. Even so, victory was not complete. Skoll and Hati had escaped. Though some had shouted that the demons should be followed and hunted down, few took the idea seriously. Mick could not chase them for fear of what the skolves might do if he left. Aveline's leg was shattered, and the Shining Knight did not think that any tactics they could employ off the hill would be effective. Not as they were. They had won, but the dead had not been counted, many of the injured still lay on the grass in need of care, and the world away from the house on the hill was large, dark, and full of skolves.

And the Shining Knight was apparently leaving.

"Have I not done what I promised?" he was saying to Veronica Brice. His words sounded hollow from his helm. Though overmatched alone, he had fought unlike anyone Val had ever seen besides Mick, and his incredible armor had absorbed every ferocious blow from Hati, though not without those blows taking a toll. He was limping badly, and his voice was like the sound of rocks grinding against each other. Val remembered how burned he was under all that reflective gear.

"You did," she replied.

Is the Duchess of Vercors crying?

"Then I will go. I will return to my farm."

The duchess moved slightly, as if aborting the urge to hug him. "Goodbye, Endy," she said.

CHAPTER 32
THE ONE TRUE DEVIL

Where are the skolves?

As before, they had swung west again on their return south to avoid skolves and had seen only their tracks and the ruin of their passage. The evening before, they had huddled in the dark listening to the distant sounds of battle, the attenuated sounds of breaking rock, ringing metal, and screams. It was so far away that Private Tudor had suggested it might all be their imagination, but Alwena had said, "Shut it, Turd."

Everyone knew that people were dying, probably helplessly, certainly horribly, somewhere in the dark.

"Let's head farther west," Reyn had said the next morning. "Just in case."

"I'm for that," said Alwena. "We can't get there dead fast *enough*." She looked at Dav and muttered, "And besides, this thing needs to get to where it's going much more than it needs to get there in a hurry."

They were laden down, each of them, with a piece of the weapon that Farrah Harbinger had charged them to retrieve. The thing that could be used against the One True Devil, an evil far more powerful than anything they had faced so far. Worse than Skoll and Hati. Worse even than Nimrheal.

"I still don't understand it," said private Dylan.

No one answered him, not even Dafydd. Dill had said the same thing a hundred times at least. And Dav did not enjoy explaining it. The truth was too painful.

"It's okay," said Barbara. Her smile was brave. When he had emerged from the ruins a few hundred yards from where he had entered, and where she still waited, Barbara had been elated. She had been certain he had drowned alone and for nothing.

Whether it was for nothing or not remained to be seen.

The trudged on, fearful of some sudden avalanche of skolves or the shaking thunder of Skoll or Hati, but nothing came near them except a herd of cattle, abandoned, placid-eyed, wondering. Perhaps they were looking for people, for their farmer. They did not yet know that people in these lands were an anachronism.

As they approached Villiers, they could see whisps of black smoke from the town, but from a distance at least, the house on the hill seemed intact. Not much farther, they smelled putrid burned meat. They decided to keep south and defer tacking east until they were in line with the hill.

"I don't hear anything," said Tudor, lying on his stomach in the late-season barley while Alwena, Reyn, Dav, and Barbara scanned the horizon through telescopes.

"That doesn't mean much," said Alwena, still peering through her glass. "You said you couldn't hear anything last night either."

"What's with all the fresh tracks?" Eurion asked, huddled over his arbalest. There was fresh horse dung leading toward Villiers, and the road had been recently marched upon by several companies of foot, horse, and heavily laden wagons.

"Another mystery," said Barbara.

"My tooth just came out," Dylan said.

"And what does that mean?" asked Dafydd.

"It's good luck."

Alwena collapsed her field glass and sneered at him. "Well, isn't that just chasing rainbows? I'll give you an important hint about life, Dill. Losing a tooth is never good luck.

"You're mean."

"You're welcome," she snorted. Still looking through her field glass, she said, wonderingly, "There are people on the hill. *Lots* of them."

"A strange amount of Vercors livery," said Reyn.

"Now *that*," said Alwena, "is a rainbow. Let's go see who's alive today."

Dav traded a look with Barbara. They had both become accustomed to the mannerisms of the Vercors Rangers, even if they still seemed strange to soldiers brought up in the more formal discipline of Engevelen.

I bet Major Peridot would have known what to do with them.

HALFWAY UP THE HILL, they were passed by a company of somber-looking Engevelen soldiers. Captain Bysshe spoke quietly to their captain. "They won," she said simply, then explained that the company had been tasked with checking the road south to Argenteul. Thousands of skolves were still massed in Villiers and to the north, but were thought not to be a factor, at least for the moment.

"LOOK WHO'S BACK," said Doog, sitting in a rickety chair in the shade of the south gate, Fenris by his side. "Got that weapon you were looking for?" Before anyone could answer, he stood up, sending his chair sideways into the dirt, and said, "Because we kicked the other two bastards right the hell out of here! You got more devils, just send them."

But for all that bluster, his eyes were red, and his friend Louis was nowhere to be seen. When no one answered, he waved a weary hand and said, "Well, come on then. They're all waiting for you." Over his shoulder, he added, “Saw you a while ago creeping your way ‘round the hill.”

The plateau was crowded with soldiers and wagons, a big contingent from Vercors included. There was also row upon row of diggings for graves, many still being deepened. The passage between the graves and the living was narrow, and not even the irascible Vercors Rangers had much to say as they passed between. The only sound was of shovels working dirt.

Broken spears and shattered arrows lay everywhere. There were long conic burn shapes orienting away from the house, and in a few places huge grooves had been gouged into the ground.

They were taken through the house, which was filled with the injured on cots, in the hallways, or on the floor, and then led out to the breakfast patio where the current command group awaited them. This included an Elysian wizard named Katherine Valcourt—whom the Rangers stayed well clear of—as well as Major Serres, a Deladieyr Knight with a splinted leg named Sir Aveline, Mick, and Veronica Brice, the Duchess of Vercors. The rangers bowed to her.

They laid the weapon out across two long tables. No one said anything at first. No one jumped up. Mick stared at it, glassy-eyed. A full minute passed before Veronica Brice traced her hands over one of its pieces. Serres and Val followed, as if touching made a difference to understanding.

“I don’t get how this is any kind of weapon,” said Val flipping through the pages of the first of the oversized, foot-thick tomes.

“That’s what I keep saying!” exclaimed Private Dylan from his place along the low wall overlooking Villiers. He was undeterred by the grand company at the table, except for Val. He had been staring at her, but apparently surprised himself by agreeing with her.

“It is . . . unexpected,” said Sir Aveline.

“I *did* think it would be more . . . pointy,” said Dafydd.

“Imagine,” said Eurion. “The urgency of it . . . and all for *that* . . . confuses me too.”

Doog stood at the head of the table, smirking, not impressed or put off by the company at all. He shared that attitude with the Vercors Rangers. "I think what he's saying is that everyone is feeling a bit let down by this so-called weapon."

Dav understood the confusion. He said patiently, "Read a sentence."

"From where? Which book?"

There were so many.

"The one in front of you," Barbara said gently.

Val flipped open the heavy leather binding, skimmed, stopped midway through, and read, "The mother of the Mayor of Cambrain, a Lady Perlkis, would bake fresh bread for the meetings, which took place at three o'clock every Senday. Tea was always served with the bread, which was buttered or presented with clotted cream. Meetings would end only when the teapot was empty and the last slice of bread was eaten." Val looked up, brows arched. "What *is* this?"

"Memory," said Dav. "These are Engevelen's Books of Memory, kept in a sealed vault from before the country first fell."

"So what?" asked Doog, shoving himself into a chair beside Veronica Brice.

Dav had not even flipped through most of the books, but he answered as best he could. "Inventions. I saw some of those documents. Customs, like Lady Valcourt just read out. Little pieces of people's lives mostly."

Barbara's eyes met his. "Personal histories," she added.

"Why is that important?" asked Private Aron.

"Why is anything?" countered Alwena.

Doog reached out and tentatively touched the leather edges of the book that Veronica had been examining. "We should write down what happened here yesterday. And who was lost."

"We should," said Serres.

Tears slowly tracked down Sir Aveline's face. "I never want to forget my friends."

"It is a terrible thing," said Mick, his face unreadable, "to forget."

Val sat back, still, contemplating the books and the people grouped around them. A moment later, she pushed herself away from the table. "This is a message from the past."

"And it says *remember this*," said Barbara.

"No," croaked Doog. "Remember *us*."

Major Serres was staring at Mick with great watery eyes, but she said nothing.

Dav squeezed his left hand and placed it on the table. "And now you know what the One True Devil is. It is forgetting." He looked around the table, making eye contact with each person. "Forgetting who we are, losing, no, erasing, our past—good or bad."

"Cultural entropy," said Veronica Brice, speaking for the first time. "But also a preservation of the long struggle for progress." She looked over her shoulder as if seeking the eyes of someone else, but no one was there.

Val's face was marked by goose bumps. She said wonderingly, "And Farrah thinks this is more important than anything else, this saving of memory?"

"She does, and it *is*," said Dav.

"But why the big rush?" asked Dafydd. "Why not just pick this up later?"

"You won't want to hear this," said Dav. "But Farrah was looking far into the future when she decided this needed to be done now."

"He's a wizard, too, you know," said Dylan.

"Just be quiet, Dill," said Sergeant Reyne.

"How far into the future?" asked Val.

"I don't know," said Dav, "but I think a long time, more than decades. Hundreds of years." He gestured at the books. "If we hadn't retrieved this now, we never would."

Serres slapped a gauntleted hand down on the table. "What would stop us?"

"The skolves," Dav said. "Think about it. They are scared now. Scared of *him*," he said gesturing at Mick. "But for how long? And Skoll and Hati are still out there."

“We should hunt them down and kill them,” declared Veronica Brice.

“Who is *we*?” asked Aveline. “I would like to, but my leg . . . and I have to ensure that the Deladieyr Order survives, that the wall gets built before the skolves come back. There is no one left to scour,” she gestured north, “all that.”

“So we are giving up?” The awkward question came from the Duchess of Vercors.

Dav hated being the bearer of awful predictions, but there was no one else to do it. “You won an unlikely victory yesterday. Take it and go build your wall. Take these books—this piece of time and history—and remember Engevelen well. For she will not rise again for a very long time. Long enough that we would have forgotten what Engevelen was, and could be again, without these books.”

There was a long silence as everyone digested this. Dav thought about Farrah’s Heraldry

The skolves will not stay cowed forever. Probably not even for long. Skoll and Hati will not be hunted down. Not for years. Not for centuries.

Alwena, leaning against the patio wall with the other rangers, left the weightier questions behind, as most people do. She said, “I get the people part, but are you really doing this because you want to rebuild your country someday just the way it was? That seems a little—”

“Boring,” said Dafydd from his place farther away along the wall.

“Remember that old man in Aurillon?” asked Tudor. “The one who told us how to march ‘properly’ down an *Engevelen* road? Might be you’re all too rigid, you know.” He jumped when he felt Veronica’s glare and added in a smaller voice, “Just saying.”

“I still don’t get it,” said Dylan.

“I think I understand,” said Val. She looked at Mick. “It’s like the song you sang.”

“Hmm?” the old man said, confused.

Serres put an arm around his shoulders. “The song we sang together.”

"Endy and I heard it from south of the hill," said Veronica wonderingly.

"It was beautiful," breathed Val. "We don't need to be slaves to what was, but we likely won't do any better if we can't remember who we were, what we cared about, how we acted, or whom we loved."

EPILOGUE. THE BEST MEMORY

The old man looked down on the headstone. *This is a grave. But whose?* There was a name there. It read, “Sir Valence, Knight of Engevelen.” Something told him the man had been important, that the memory of him still was, that remembering was important, but the message was foggy, heavy, dissipating as quickly as it formed.

And it was far from the only grave.

There were other mounds, too—all around—and other headstones. Many of them were fresh. Just beside Sir Valence’s headstone was another. “Louis Lac, fighter to the end,” it read. An uncomfortable heat rose to the old man’s face. *Louis! My friend!* He suddenly remembered Valence, too, buried at last and honored properly.

But the struggle to remember brought an awareness that was hard to face. *Damn, I’m starting to forget again.*

It brought a fear to a fearless heart. Mick did not want to become purposeless again.

“Mick, we have to go now.”

He knew that voice—Doog. Mick turned slowly, hiding his consternation as best he could and faced the short, bow-legged man.

A small, heavily furred dog stood between Doog’s feet. *Fenris.* A puppy. When he crouched, Fenris came to him, tail wagging unconditionally.

Mick's hands ruffled Fenris as he looked past his old friend toward a large house. It was more of a castle really, surrounded by a low stone wall. A line of wagons waited there, more than Mick could easily count, and men in armor too. Lots of them. Maybe a hundred. More.

They were looking his way. Some were saluting.

A large man with a larger forehead stood halfway between the soldiers and Mick. It was Roland, whom Mick had beaten the last time the fog had taken him. It was an awful memory, one he wished was false. Roland did not deserve to be beaten. It was clear that he had fought against the skolves. His filthy uniform, crusted in blood and grime, buttoned right to his neck told of that. *I'm sorry, Roland.*

"Mick," said the bow-legged man. "It isn't safe here anymore. The skolves, they left—they're afraid of you. But we don't know for how long. We have to go south. They are building a great wall there. We will be safe." He crouched with a slow deliberateness and put a hand on Fenris. "We need to save Fenris."

"Oh." That made sense to Mick. Memories of the battle were already fading from his mind, but he knew what a skolve was. And Fenris was just a puppy. He should be loved and cared for. "Let's go then."

They walked slowly toward the wagons, the man in the high-buttoned coat, and the soldiers.

Mick stumbled, righted himself, and saw that he had caught his foot on a thick, heavy stick. It was smooth and uniform, with one rounded end and one rough. Perhaps it was an old shovel handle broken in two. An idea flickered across his mind.

There is time yet for one more thing. It was sunny. The day was fair.

He picked up the stick. "Fenris!" he said, waving the two-foot length at the instantly excited dog. "Do you want this?" He waved it again before throwing the stick in a lazy, spinning arc through the air.

Fenris gave one puppyish bark, bunched his muscles, and sprang in pursuit of the stick.

Mick laughed in joy. Then he said to Doog, who was watching sadly, "Now there's something to always remember."

"He's fading," said Val sadly.

Sir Aveline hobbled on her walking stick, struggling to turn around and look at the young wizard. Val was genuinely upset. She had reason to be. Maréchal was a great man. He had been lost and found again.

"Yes," Ave said. "And quickly." She considered the house on the hill and wondered how he had found his way there.

As if reading her mind, Val said, "What kind of magic put him right where he needed to be? In a house for the discarded old. The only house not abandoned in the evacuation. And what kind of magic brought him back to such strength at exactly the right time?

"Purpose," Ave breathed. "He found his purpose again. All these people did. There is magic enough in that."

Val's eyes were red. They had never been clear from what Ave had seen, but the young wizard's mind was sharp enough. Val asked, "And what will *our* purpose be?"

Get these people somewhere safe. Build the great wall while we can, while the skolves retain their fear of Maréchal? Find, someday, what has been lost? Quest for the Methueyn Bridge, left in a machine no one alive understands, in a place no one knows? How long will all this take? Will it truly be hundreds of years as Davignon suggested?

Ave had only questions, but she had learned somewhere along the way that questions were good.

ACKNOWLEDGMENTS

Last Worst Hopes was inspired by real people, but it is a work of fiction. Nevertheless good fiction, which I hope this is, always carries a core of truth even if the main goal is only to entertain. Thank you to all the people in my life who have inspired me. We are all imperfect, and it might seem sometimes that we fall short of being heroes. But I have yet to meet anyone who did not have something special about them, some intrinsic property that, on the right day, might give hope.

Certain literary and technical works inspired elements of this story. William Blake's "And did those feet in ancient time," which many know as "Jerusalem" was playing through my mind when Mick sang in the final battle. The Shining Knight could have written Daniel Kahneman's 2011 book, *Thinking, Fast and Slow*. Homage was made to Ronald Fisher's famous eight-cup tea experiment for statistical significance from the 1935 book, *Design of Experiments.* And finally, S. L. A Marshall's 1947 *Men Against Fire* informed my conception of Major Peridot and Dav as they prepared to fight a horde of skolves.

Thank you to my test readers. I cannot express how much your suggestions have meant to me, except by using some of them. You made this book better, and you did it by donating your time and creativity, those things so precious.

About the Author

Born with only one working lung, and having had the last rites read to him as he lay dying of an influenza-related viral pneumonia, 25-year-old geophysicist Lee Hunt experienced several near-death dreams. The power of communication and the need to both understand and be understood was at the heart of each. He had already found that nothing was more important than being able to cross the distance between people.

Lee's interests are eclectic. He is an Ironman Triathlete, hiker, traveler, and an enthusiastic sport rock climber. Lee also continues to work as a geophysicist on Carbon Capture and Sequestration projects, and is a writer for BIG-Media.ca.

The dream of understanding and being understood has never left his mind, and Lee continues that quest in his works of fiction through metaphor. His works include *The Dynamicist Trilogy*, *Last Worst Hopes* and *Bed of Rose and Thorns*.